The DARKNESS Within

SCARS AND STRIPES TRILOGY TWO

RAQUEL RILEY

The POW-MIA Prayer

Almighty God, the author of peace,
Whose boundless love reaches
beyond out limited vision,
And who holds all thy children
In tender compassion and concern,
We pray for those men and women
Listed as "Missing in Action".

Give especially to their families and loved ones
The assurance that none are even
missing in thy sight,
But held forever in the safety of thy love.

So we would pray that the day will come
When peace will always prevail.
So that no more loved ones need ever again
Be listed as MISSING IN ACTION.

By the love that undergirds our lives,
And by thy grace that gives us
courage and strength
We raise this prayer.

AMEN.

Copyright © 2024 by Raquel Riley

www.raquelriley.com

All rights reserved.

No part of this book may be used, reproduced, or transmitted in any form or by any electronic or mechanical means, including information storage and retrieval systems, without written permission from the author, except for the use of brief quotations in a book review.

This is a work of fiction. Names, characters, places, and incidents either are the product of the author's imagination or are used fictitiously. Any resemblance to actual persons, living or dead, businesses, companies, events, or locales is entirely coincidental. The use of any real company and/or product names is for literary effect only. All products and brand names are registered trademarks of their respective holders/companies.

This book contains sexually explicit material which is only suitable for mature audiences.

Cover design by Raquel Riley

Editing by Clocktower Editing

Proofreading by Laurie Cappolino

For Nash,
I hated telling your story,
Hated that you suffered so much,
That you're still suffering.
But I'm forever grateful you found your unit.
Just remember...take it one day at a time.

For Brewer,
Thank God for you.
Not just for the people you help, but for saving Nash.
You showed him how to live step-by-step.
You taught him how to love day-by-day.
You inspired him to dream big.
I owe you everything.

CONTENT WARNING_

This book deals with heavy sensitive topics like mental health and depression, low self-esteem, survivor's guilt, PTSD, addiction, and healing after loss.

On-page death of side characters, vulgar language, disfigurement and amputation, anger, and self-hatred.

Alcohol and pill abuse.

FOREWORD_

I spent hours researching for this book, but I'm no expert on military life and law. There may be inconsistencies mentioned.

Mention of military bases with retired names, like Ft. Bragg, are referred to as such as this story takes place during the Obama administration before the names were changed. Ft. Bragg is now Ft. Liberty, and the FOB or Forward Operating Base in Iraq, Camp Baharia, is now defunct.

Careful research and sensitivity screening was done for survivors of war and survivors of trauma, and recovering addicts. Any derogatory words mentioned by the main character are his own feelings about himself, not others, due to his grief process.

I chose to refer to Post Traumatic Stress Disorder as PTS, dropping the D purposely to change the stigma surrounding the word disorder to encourage more vets to seek help. This is a widespread movement that I sincerely hope catches on.

Some parts of this book may be hard to read, but it only makes the hard-earned HEA that much sweeter.

Please read with an open heart and heed the trigger warnings. I hope Nash and Brewer hold a special place in your heart like they do mine.

With Love,

Raquel Riley

Chapter 7
NASH
Landstuhl, Germany

It amazes me how long I can stare at a tree, as if I've never seen one before. The giant oak standing sentinel outside my window captures my attention for hours. How the dappled light filters through the branches, casting shadows on the linoleum floor of my room, or the endless variations of color; greens and yellows in every shade of the spectrum. The breeze ripples the leaves like confetti blowing in the wind.

If I close my eyes, I can imagine the thick roots beneath the dirt, the way they spread far and wide like greedy fingers, how they dig down deep in the earth anchoring the sturdy trunk above, searching for nutrients to soak up so it can thrive.

Underground.

Beneath the dirt.

Those words always trigger terrifying memories. Not everything thrives underground. Not everything finds an anchor in the soil. The darkest parts of the Earth, underneath the ground where the light doesn't reach, depleted me of everything I need to thrive. The darkness almost took my life, and at that point, I was ready to give it up gladly for a moment of peace.

I can smell it, the earthy, dank soil, the heavy stale air. The pungent, rusty smell of blood. The acidic ammonia scent of urine. The scents invade my mind and my nostrils until I can experience them with every one of my senses. I can taste them. I can feel them. So much so that they become a part of me.

They'll always be a part of me.

"Sergeant Sommers."

They're whispering again, plotting, searching for me.

"Sergeant Sommers."

If I keep my eyes closed, maybe I can hide. Buy myself a few precious moments.

"Sergeant Sommers."

The voices are louder, which means they're coming closer. Pressing myself down into the mattress, I try to become as small as possible, to make my body flat beneath the blanket. Maybe they won't see me. Maybe this time I'll be spared.

"Sergeant Sommers. I have your medicine. Can you sit up for me, please?"

The past collides with the present in terrifying clarity. "Don't fucking touch me!" I snatch my arm from her grip, swallowing down the thick, bitter taste of fear coating the back of my throat.

"Sergeant—"

"Don't fucking touch me! Back up."

I failed again. To be invincible. To be invisible. Actually, I'm completely invisible, although everyone can see me. They don't *really* see me, though. They see the shell of the man I used to be. They see the consequence of my captivity. But they don't see *me*. They don't see Nashville Sommers.

"Take cover! Everyone get down!"

Gunshots echo through my living room, men shouting orders, the grinding of chunks of rubble from the desecrated buildings crunching into dust beneath the tracks of the tank. The explosion from the tank's cannon is so loud, it might as well be happening in real life instead of through my TV screen.

"Nashville, what in the world are you watching?" my mother shouts from the kitchen.

"A movie, Mom."

"Saving Private Ryan was the one decent thing we were able to pull out of this whole God awful, shitty mess."

"Language, Nashville!" she admonishes.

"It's not me, it's the show, Mom."

"Shut that off and go outside and play. My show is about to come on."

Reluctantly, I shut the TV off, and when I turn back, my father is standing there with a stern look. "You know better, son. Your mother isn't keen on war movies."

"Yes, Sir."

"So why do you keep watching them?"

"Because I'm gonna be a soldier someday when I grow up, Sir."

It's rare when I make my father laugh or smile. To see it on his face now fills me with pride.

"Well, don't let your mother hear you say that. Now run along outside and play. Be back for dinner and don't be late."

"Yes, Sir."

"Sir... Sergeant. Can you sit up for me?"

When I open my eyes, it's not my father I'm staring at, but the nurse. "Just... Stand back. Please," I beg in a panicked voice.

"I'm just going to set these right here on the table until you're ready to take them yourself," she says in a patient voice, backing away slowly like she's confronting a frightened animal.

I guess I am. Even from across the room, her presence feels suffocating, like she's crowding me out of my safe space, and I know she won't leave until she watches me swallow these pills. It's all they do, shove pills down my throat. But no one talks to me. I sit in this bed, rotting away, day in and day out, with the exception of physical therapy. They deliver my meals in silence. And when I have an episode, they come in and tie me to the bed and shoot me up with drugs until I become as silent and distant as they are. Grabbing the pills off the table, I shove them down my throat and swallow them dry. The soft soles of her shoes whisper across the linoleum as she sees herself out.

In this hospital, things work on a reward system. If I want to be rewarded with solitude, I have to take the drugs. If I take the drugs, I'm rewarded with another kind of solitude, from the dark shadows that haunt me. When I'm high, I disappear. I become so invisible they can't find me. Like hiding in the darkest corner.

A dark corner in my mind so isolated that I can't smell the blood and the urine.

So isolated that I can't hear the echo of shouting in Pashto.

So isolated that I can't tell if it's dark or light, if I'm above ground or below it.

The green and golden leaves begin to blur until all I can see is a muddy shadow that dances across the floor, creeping closer to my bed. If I don't run, the roots are going to wrap around my limbs and drag me below the ground, into the darkness. But I can't run. I can't move at all because my legs feel so heavy from the drugs, like dead tree limbs. It flows through my veins like a hazy cloud, turning my blood thick as molasses, until it reaches my head, where it drops a heavy blanket over my consciousness, and I can feel myself fading away. My heartbeat slows to a crawl and my eyes become heavy, my field of vision becoming narrower with each blink.

I never know how much time has passed when I open my eyes again after blacking out. Could be a day, a week, or just a handful of hours. Not that it really matters—the passing of time no longer holds any importance. I have nowhere to go, nothing to be late for, and no one is coming to see me. I have no reason to measure time.

Time is for people who have a life. They worry that they are wasting it. I'm not worried about wasting time. I'm not worried about anything.

A knock on the door brings my head up, and I open my eyes to see my physical therapist standing in the doorway. He looks hesitant to approach, and I wish he would just go away. I have little respect for the man. He's terrible at his job. He has no spine, no patience, and he does nothing to motivate me. Am I supposed to be excited about physical therapy? It fucking hurts. Every step I take on my broken left leg is excruciatingly painful.

"Sergeant Sommers, it's time for therapy. Are you interested in participating today?"

"No." My reply sounds as flat as paper.

"Okay then, have a good day, Sir."

It's that easy to get rid of him. If only it were that easy to get rid of everyone. Sometime later, my nurse comes in to check my vitals. She doesn't speak to me. She comes back with a tray of food, again, not speaking to me. All the while, I stare out the window at the giant oak, watching as it changes colors in the waning sunlight. The golds and the greens become darker as day turns to night.

The sound of a dog barking echoes in the hallway, and suddenly, I'm transported to another place and time as my hold on reality slips away. The last thing I see is red. Nothing but red as the smell of blood comes back to me.

Day 1 in captivity

. . .

Our mission was simple: sweep the building, confiscate any weapons we found, and clear the fuck out. The tiny village on the outskirts of Kandahar didn't seem like much of a threat. Intel hadn't alerted us to the fact that the place was hot. The team split, with Gutierrez and I taking the bottom floor. We cleared three rooms before crossing a large, woven rug that covered a trapdoor in the floor. As soon as we fell through the hole, insurgents pounced on us, securing our mouths and hands with thick tape. I could feel my heart pounding in my throat, like I had swallowed it, and tasted bitter fear as I heard gunfire through my comms.

My team was under fire, and I had no way to assist them or alert them. Gutierrez screamed behind his tape, and I kicked until they tied my feet together as well. Adrenaline coursed through my veins, sharpening my senses, and giving me a tremendous surge of strength. My fight or flight mode kicked in, making me feel practically delirious with rage that I couldn't unleash on my captors.

I knew in that moment I was fucked. We both were. They hadn't captured us just to turn around and set us free. The trap we'd just fallen into might as well have been the gateway to hell, and I was just another hostage. A prisoner of war. At least, if I were lucky. Otherwise, I was just going to end up dead in a matter of minutes or hours.

I could hear my team shouting through my headset and knew that at least one of them had been shot. In minutes, the gunfire became sporadic until it ceased altogether. Either my team had fled, or they were all dead.

Taliban soldiers shouted through my comms and in my face,

and I knew others were getting closer, converging on Gutierrez and me.

Shit was about to get real.

They dragged our resistant bodies through dark tunnels over dirt-packed floors until we reached a short, dead-end hallway. Like an alcove cut into the hard-packed earth. With our backs against the wall, and our wrists and ankles tied, we were pretty useless, unable to do anything but curse behind our gags. They shouted at us in Pashto, and I couldn't understand a fucking word. They shoved guns in our faces. They kicked us in the ribs. And when they finished 'welcoming us', they left behind one armed guard and two dogs. The dogs sat still as statues, snarling, and drooling, and I knew without a doubt, if I so much as moved one muscle, they would tear my limbs from my body and dine on my bloody flesh.

I didn't know how much time passed while we sat there. It could have been hours or days. My stomach growled with hunger. My body was covered with cold sweat. And when I couldn't hold it in any longer, I whimpered behind my gag as I pissed myself, choking on a sob as warm urine coated my thighs and ass, soaking into the packed dirt floor beneath me. And all the while, the crazed dogs barked, and barked, and barked.

The smell of urine assaults my nose as my agitation mounts. My fingers tighten in my hair, grabbing fistfuls and pulling the strands loose from my scalp as I scream. The barking echoes inside my head, building to a deafening roar, drowning out everything else. Drowning out reality and rationalization, and the four walls of my hospital room. Behind my closed lids, all I can see are dirt walls. The machines hooked to my chest beep maniacally as my heart rate spikes, and my blood pressure becomes so unstable that my head feels dizzy.

The guards are back. They rush into my room, poking their guns in my face.

But they aren't guards, and they aren't guns. They're nurses with sharp needles, piercing my flushed skin, and the light-headed feeling becomes so strong that I feel detached from my body, floating above the bed as I watch them subdue me into an incoherent Haloperidol haze.

Five...four...three...

As I count down the seconds before I lose consciousness, I can smell the stale breath and rotting teeth of the dogs, hot and thick in my face, choking me.

———

Coming to after being sedated is a bitch. My head aches, the slightest movement sends a sharp pain throbbing through my temporal lobe. My vision feels off and everything appears blurry. My mouth is dry, and my throat burns, like maybe I was screaming, but I can't remember a damn thing. Even my arm hurts. My biceps are sore, probably where they jabbed me with the needle harder than they needed to, most likely a punishment for ripping out my IV.

I remember the blood, which is partly what triggered me. But glancing down at my gown, I can't find a trace of it, nor is it staining my sheets. They must have cleaned me up while I slept. A knot of emotion thickens my throat, and I have to fight back the tears that rush to my eyes.

I feel so fucking desolate, so hopeless. I was so out of it that I wasn't even aware they were touching me. They had to have undressed me and washed me to put a fresh gown on. They rolled my body so they could change the sheets beneath me while I slept on them, and I never even stirred. I've lost all consent and autonomy over my body.

Over my entire life.

As a patient, I'm entitled to certain rights, but as a patient displaying signs of mental illness, I seem to have been stripped of every one of them. I'm nothing more than a puppet dancing on their strings. The thought of being touched while unconscious fills me with so much fear and anxiety that I almost can't breathe. The machines beep loudly as my heart rate spikes into the danger zone. I can feel the signs of a panic attack coming on, and if I don't get control of myself quickly, they'll sedate me again.

They'll touch me again while I'm unconscious.

Every time they put me under, I feel like I'm losing another piece of my soul.

Sucking a deep breath into my lungs, I hold it in my chest, trying to slow my breathing, slow my heart rate, slow my racing thoughts and my rising panic. I focus on the oak. The way the leaves dance in the wind. The little black bird perched on the lowest branch. I release the breath. One... Two... Three... And suck another one into my lungs. I hold it for the count of three and release it again. My heart rate slows. The beeping stops. But the tears I was holding back rush forth, dripping down my cheeks in wet trails. Tears of frustration and impotence. Tears of loneliness and isolation. Tears of self-pity and shame. My heart and my head are a *Rubik's cube* of emotions, and I can't vent a single one of them without fear of losing control and losing my tether on reality. I hoard them inside of me until I'm so stuffed that they leak from my eyes against my will.

The doctor comes in, and I swipe away my tears with the hem of my blanket.

"Sergeant, how are you feeling?"

All I can manage is a halfhearted shrug. I don't trust my voice after crying.

"Well, I bring good news that hopefully will help you feel better. You're being discharged."

His heavy German accent sounds so foreign after hearing nothing but Pashto for weeks. "To where?" My voice croaks like a bullfrog.

"Stateside. The Army arranged for transport. They'll be here sometime tomorrow to pick you up. I'm transferring your records to Walter Reed Medical Center."

Walter Reed. I'm done. I know I'm done and that my career is over. My glory days are behind me. What does that mean for the rest of my life? What does my future look like now that I'm nothing but a head case?

"W-will I be sedated during transport?" The fear of being unconscious for hours as I cross continents is terrifying enough to make my heart stop beating.

"Not as long as you can remain calm. There will be a medical professional on board to administer meds, should you need them. But if you lose control, they'll have to sedate you."

I swallow down my panic and nod my head. What else can I do? I really don't have a say in the matter. All I can do is my best to remain calm. Having to remain vigilant about my surroundings every second to avoid being triggered is exhausting. And it's terrifying, always afraid of what someone might say, afraid that my memories will betray me because I'm not in control.

I am powerless. Ruled by everything and everyone.

A victim of my circumstances and my surroundings.

The doctor shuffles the papers and reaches for a pen from his coat pocket. "Just state your name and ID for me before I give you these papers to sign."

He checks the plastic ID bracelet on my wrist. It's standard practice to identify the patient before administering any kind of service. After weeks in the hospital, I know this, but I'm on edge, I'm afraid, and therefore, I'm vulnerable. His simple request makes the pain in my head spike, and all the light fades from the room, and the memories pull me back down into the darkness below the ground.

Day 4 in captivity

Hunger gnawed at my empty stomach. My mouth felt so dry, it might as well have been glued shut. We'd only been given a piece of flatbread to appease our bellies and a few sips of dirty water. I don't want to know where it came from. I didn't have much choice. If the parasites didn't kill me, dehydration would have. Everything hurt. My shoulders ached from being tied behind my back. My head throbbed from being beaten repeatedly, and I'd be surprised if my jaw wasn't broken. I was bloody and dirty and sweaty and fucking miserable.

Exhaustion had weakened my body along with the hunger and the dehydration and the constant fear. The crashes of adrenaline had depleted my energy. The dogs barked night and day, it never ended. Soldiers yelled, always yelling, shouting orders in a state of confusion. They sounded angry, but who knew? It could just be the way they spoke. We had a new guard. He was younger than the others, with dark skin and eyes, and his head was covered in a red cloth. I believed his gun was Russian, which didn't surprise me.

"Will they come back for us?"

Gutierrez leaned against my shoulder. He was probably too exhausted to sit up straight any longer. He didn't even sound like the same man he was four days ago. His voice sounded haunted and weak. Broken.

"Of course they will," I rallied, trying to give him hope.

Did I believe that? I didn't know. Maybe. If they did come back for us, what would they find? What would be left of us by then?

The conversation earned me a kick of the guard's boot into my hip, and I grunted in pain.

"Name!" he shouted. "Intel! Intel!"

I could barely make out what he was asking me, let alone figure out why he was asking it. What did he care what my fucking name was? Did he think he was going to recognize me? Like we'd met in a past life? Why did it matter who I was?

I refused to give in, remaining silent as he continued to shout in my face, but it only earned me another vicious kick.

"Intel!" The command was followed by a stream of Pashto that sounded completely incoherent to me.

My silence was pissing him off more, so he turned on Gutierrez, kicking and shouting at him to give up intel. Frustrated beyond all reason, Gutierrez mustered the last bit of his strength to scream, a long, loud wail of desperation and frustration. The guard knocked him in the head with the butt of his rifle hard enough to knock Gutierrez out.

My entire body stiffened with panic as he turned his attention back to me, shouting in my face, sticking the muzzle of his gun against my lips.

"Intel! Name!"

When I remained silent, he shoved the muzzle into my mouth, chipping my bottom tooth. The cold metal tasted metallic, and I could taste the bitter astringent tang of gunpowder. I pushed at the barrel with my tongue, but I wasn't strong enough to spit it out.

He continued to shout, sweating and angry, as I remained silent. I shook like a leaf, sweating, and about to piss myself again, but I'd be goddamned if I'd let him see my fear. He cocked the gun, sliding a bullet into the chamber, and I knew the rest of my life would be measured in minutes or seconds. My heart beat so fast and loud there was no way he couldn't hear it. I really had nothing left to lose by speaking. Remaining silent was no longer an option. If he squeezed his finger the tiniest millimeter, he'd blow my head clear off my shoulders, and it would splatter onto Gutierrez.

"Intel!" he shouted one last time, jamming the barrel so far down my throat I gagged.

Tears streamed down my cheeks, and I hated myself for showing them to him. My words sounded garbled around the muzzle, and he finally pulled it free of my mouth.

"Sergeant Nashville Aidan Sommers. United States Army. 89-6717-4613."

Of course, he didn't understand what I was saying, which was why I couldn't understand why he'd even asked, but he continued to shout over and over.

"Name! Intel!"

"Sergeant Nashville Aidan Sommers. United States Army. 89-6717-4613."

His booted foot destroyed my ribs.

"Sergeant Nashville Aidan Sommers. United States Army. 89-6717-4613."

The barrel of his gun made dents or fractures in my skull.

"Sergeant Nashville Aidan Sommers. United States Army. 89-6717-4613."

The more I recited my name, rank, and ID number, the more detached I felt, calmer, falling into a trance as I repeated the words and numbers over and over.

"Sergeant Nashville Aidan Sommers. United States Army. 89-6717-4613."

And then he switched things up. The guards were trained by the Taliban to excel in interrogation tactics, a.k.a. torture. He pointed the gun at Gutierrez, and my body went cold. He knew I didn't care about my own life, but I cared about my brother. He was going to leverage Gutierrez's life against me for information.

Instead of threatening me to see if I complied, he acted impulsively, squeezing the trigger before I could agree to his terms. The gunshot echoed through the tunnel, deafening me until my ears rang. Pieces of leather and bone splattered in every direction. He blew the top of Gutierrez's boot clean off. His blood soaked into the dirt floor, and his scream was unlike anything I'd ever heard before.

Louder than the dogs' barking.
Louder than the guards' shouting.
Louder than the ringing in my ears.
All I could hear was his pain.

"Sergeant Nashville Aidan Sommers. United States Army. 89-6717-4613."

The words came out broken, an anguished sob, as I fell apart and cried, revealing my pain to him finally. I didn't care if he saw it. I didn't care if he knew how desperate and hopeless I felt. I had nothing left worth losing, not even my life.

"Sergeant Nashville Aidan Sommers. United States Army. 89-6717-4613."

The doctor chuckles. "Your birthdate would have sufficed."

Shaking off the memories, I sign my name on the dotted line and hand him back his pen.

"I'll just process this, and you'll be all set to go. I wish you the best of luck in your recovery, Sergeant. Thank you for your service," he says before leaving.

Thank you for your service.

There are no five words I hate more. He doesn't give a fuck

about my service. Or my sacrifice. He doesn't give two shits that I'll spend the rest of my life, every single miserable fucking day of it, haunted by my twenty-two days in hell. It's just lip service. A formality. It's fucking bullshit.

Even before my captivity, I hated those words. I remember back at Bragg, before my first deployment, I heard it everywhere I went. At the barbershop, at the dry cleaners, the alterations shop. They said it as casually as one would remark on the weather. Drop a tip in their jar, "Thank you for your service." Swipe your credit card, "Thank you for your service." I felt like a fraud because I hadn't really served, I hadn't really sacrificed anything for my country at that point.

I thought those words should be reserved for men and women who wasted away in this desert, who *served*, who *sacrificed*. But now that I'm one of those soldiers, those words just feel hollow.

Dark shadows dance across the walls. Another day coming to an end. Another day I didn't participate. Another day wasted in this hospital bed, struggling to survive. I stare out the window at the dark shadow of the giant oak. Will my hospital room at Walter Reed have a tree outside the window? Will it even have a window?

Chapter 2

NASH

Walter Reed Medical Center, Bethesda, MD

BEING AT WALTER REED SUCKS WORSE THAN THE HOSPITAL in Germany. People actually talk to me here. They try to involve themselves in my recovery. They pretend like they care. It's exhausting, and I resent having to deal with them.

The window has no view. Just the side of a brick wall of the next building six feet away. Instead, I stare at the guard standing watch at my door. He stands there for hours, with his hands clasped behind his back, shifting his weight from one foot to the other. When he leaves, another one replaces him. Everyone here knows who I am, even if they don't know me. My story was all over the news, people tying yellow ribbons around tree trunks and lighting candles, praying for my safe return. Reporters crowded the halls, vying for an interview until the

MP's sent them packing. Military police limit the hospital staff allowed in and out of my room. They limit the amount of visitors I can have, not that anyone has tried to visit me.

After I was admitted to Walter Reed, I spoke with my parents on the phone. My mother broke down in tears. My father didn't say much other than that he was grateful for my safe return. Neither of them made plans to come and visit me. Not yet, at least. Maybe when I return home to Bragg. Arizona is a lot closer to North Carolina than Maryland.

When I left home after graduating high school to join the Army, my parents were less than thrilled. They didn't even show up at my graduation from Boot Camp. In the eight years I've been enlisted, they've visited twice, and I went home once.

To say things are strained between us is an understatement. But when your only child comes home alive instead of in a wooden box, like Gutierrez did, wouldn't you put your bitter disappointment in his career choice aside and just go see him? Just hold him in your arms and thank God?

Apparently not.

The debriefing committee took two weeks to interview me. More like interrogate me. Five different branches of the Army asked me to repeat my trauma five different times. They treated me like a witness on the stand, trying to poke holes in my story, as if I made the whole thing up. I've never felt angrier in my life than I have these past sixteen days. Fuck the Brass. Fuck the Army. My military career and accomplishments used to define me. It was my whole life. Something I was proud of. Now I feel nothing but resentment and shame that I had prioritized my life around an institution that fed me nothing but lies.

Brotherhood. Honor. Leave no man behind. The fucking Soldier's Creed.

I am an American Soldier.
    I am a Warrior and a member of a team.
    I serve the people of the United States and live the Army Values.
    I will always place the mission first.
    I will never accept defeat.
    I will never quit.
    I will never leave a fallen comrade.
    I am disciplined, physically and mentally tough, trained and proficient in my warrior tasks and drills.
    I always maintain my arms, my equipment and myself.
    I am an expert, and I am a professional.
    I stand ready to deploy, engage, and destroy the enemies of the United States of America in close combat.
    I am a guardian of freedom and the American way of life.
    I am an American Soldier.

I was a member of a team that left me behind. I placed the mission first, at risk to my own life and that of my team. For twenty-two days, I suffered and never accepted defeat. I never quit, and I never left my fallen comrade, even when his body lay next to me rotting. I was a guardian of freedom, and the American way of life, and now I have nothing to show for my sacrifice. No life. No freedom, not from the memories that haunt me.

Unfit for active duty, I'm being medically retired, sent out to pasture.

I gave, and I gave, and I gave, and the Army gave me nothing in return. They no longer have any use for me.

"Time for your meds, Sergeant," the nurse says, pushing past the guard.

Of course it is. It's always time for meds. I take meds for everything. To stabilize my mood and fight depression, to control my blood pressure and anxiety, and vitamin supplements because I'm deficient in almost everything. That's what having no appetite does to you. Then there's the meds to control my acid reflux, hypertension, and the migraines. Added to that pharmaceutical cocktail are sleeping pills and mild sedatives.

She hands me a small paper cup of meds, and another one filled with water. I down them in one gulp, fighting my gag reflex as they stick in the back of my throat.

"Would you like to go sit outside for a while? The weather is beautiful."

This is something they avoided at the hospital in Germany. Human contact with me. Do I want to go sit outside in the fresh air? Of course I do. Nothing feels better after being shoved underground for nearly a month than being above it, outside in the fresh air, unconfined. Free. But there are too many stimulants, too many variables. Anything could trigger me and I'll spend the rest of the day knocked out. I've already lost too many days of my life as a prisoner, I don't want to lose any more. I hate being afraid of everything, afraid to live my life.

When I was being held against my will, I swore to myself, if I could just get free, I would live my life to the fullest. I would never waste another day. Yet all I've done since I made that vow is waste every single day God has granted me. Would Gutierrez waste his life if he were still alive? Would he hide inside of a hospital room isolating himself from the world? Maybe he would. I'll never know what he would choose. I just do the best I can.

A familiar and unwelcome weight settles over my chest, and I have to breathe deeper to get a full breath. It's the depression, the anxiety. A constant companion. *Fuck*. It wasn't the Army's fault I got left behind. It wasn't my team's fault they made it out without me. It's easy to blame everyone else, but the reality is that it was just fate. It was just the hand I was dealt. Mostly, I'm angry at what I've lost. I'm angry that I allowed myself to become so disillusioned, believing I was fighting for something that now means nothing to me.

When Gutierrez was bleeding out a slow death, I bargained to God, to Satan, to anyone who would listen to just spare him, to just let him see the light of day one more time. I swore that I would do anything, give anything, for that freedom, to give him that opportunity. That's when I realized the ideals I believed in when I signed my name on my first contract had changed drastically over the years. I was now fighting for the man beside me, for *his* life and *his* freedom.

Keeping Gutierrez alive is my mission, and I will always place it first.

I will never accept defeat.

I will never quit.

I will never leave a fallen comrade.

I stand ready to deploy, engage, and destroy Gutierrez's enemies in close combat.

I am a guardian of his freedom and his life.

I am an American Soldier.

No matter who it might be—Gutierrez, Martinez, Simpson, Whittemore—I would stand ready to defend every one of them in the same way. Theirs are the lives I'm fighting for. It's their faces flashing through my mind every time I swallow the muzzle of a gun. I'm just fighting to survive, to get us both out of here. Everything else—freedom, the right to vote, the right to bear arms, all of the amendments of our constitution that we defend—that's someone else's fight, not mine.

If I'm being honest with myself, the Army doesn't owe me anything beyond what they've given me; a healthy settlement, medical retirement, a promotion, and a handful of medals.

Everything else, like what I'm supposed to do from here on out, that's my problem, not theirs. If I wasn't so drugged all the time, maybe I could give my future some consideration, but the fog clouding in my mind is growing heavier, so are my eyelids, and for now, it's just easier to close them and take a break from reality.

I must have slept through the night because when I open my eyes, bright light filters through my window. The nurse pushes past the guard, balancing my breakfast tray in her hands, along with a cup of meds. The breakfast of champions.

"Good morning, Sergeant. Is there anything else I can get you?" she asks as she arranges the meal on my tray table.

"I'm good," I croak, reaching for the cup of pills first. I've become so dependent on them I can't function without them, much less eat a meal or take a shower.

"You're scheduled for an x-ray on your leg today and physical therapy. But first, you eat."

Sounds wonderful.

I may be scheduled for an x-ray and therapy, but the only thing I'm realistically going to do today is sit in this goddamn bed and count the bricks in the wall across the breezeway through my window. My appetite is nonexistent, a side effect of stress, and also a couple of the medications I take, but I nibble at my toast. I've learned from experience that the nausea I feel from taking meds on an empty stomach is worse than forcing myself to eat. As I chew, I study the guard's back, my eyes tracing the digital camo pattern of his jacket. He shifts his weight, and my gaze drops to the gun holstered at his hip. The bread becomes sawdust in my mouth, and I spit it out onto my tray, fighting a wave of nausea as bitter bile tries to climb up the back of my throat.

Sometimes, when something triggers my memories, I lose touch with reality completely, not able to see or hear or feel anything in the present. Sometimes, the past and the present collide, as if I'm viewing my current surroundings through a sheet of vellum colored with the past, aware that I have a foot in both worlds at once. And sometimes, like right now, the memories are just that, bad memories, a nightmare remembered while I'm fully in the present. I wish they were all like this, but unfortunately, my head isn't able to pick and choose the way it processes trauma.

His gun looks like it tastes cold. A taste I'll never forget.

Day 7 of captivity

"I can't feel my foot anymore. The lower half of my leg is numb."

Gutierrez sounded too weak and tired to be upset. Maybe he'd given up and just accepted his fate.

I could smell his body rotting. The stench overpowered the urine and the feces, now dried and hard. His skin was flushed and hot and he was covered in sweat. Sepsis. If he didn't get out of there soon, he'd die from the infection.

"Are they going to come for us?" he whispered in a small voice.

"You bet. They're just figuring out how. But they're coming. We've just got to hold on a little longer." I wasn't sure if I believed the words I promised, but what else could I say? We were fucked? We were going to die there and the dogs would eat our dead bodies? All I could do was give him hope. Even if it was false hope.

"Hey, remember a few weeks ago when they served spaghetti at chow hall?" Gutierrez didn't respond. "Do you remember? I sat with you. You were pissed because Whittemore stole your bottle of hooch and finished it off without you. Do you remember the spaghetti that night? It was fucking terrible," I recalled with a forced laugh.

His chest heaved. "I remember. It wasn't cooked all the way, and it stuck together like pasta nuggets."

"Yes! And the sauce was so watered down it looked like Kool-Aid." *His shoulders shook with silent laughter before his body was racked with a deep, wet cough.*

"If you could eat anything right now, what would it be?" *he asked, clearing his throat. He spit a green-tinted loogie on the dirt floor.*

"I don't know, maybe Chinese food. There's this all-you-can-eat buffet back home outside base. They serve the best crab Rangoon you ever tasted."

"I know the place. Wok Choy. It's your favorite."

"What about you? What are you gonna eat when we get back home?"

He blew out a deep sigh. "My mother's paella. She puts these fat shrimp and scallops in it, and seasons it just right. You've never tasted anything so good in your life."

"Hell, that sounds fucking delicious."

"We're gonna get back home, right?" *His voice broke on a sob. The tortured sound gripped my heart, squeezing like a vice.*

"Yeah, G, we're going to get back home," *I lied through my teeth.*

A guard, accompanied by two dogs, hurried over, speaking in dire tones with the guard currently watching us. Then he grabbed me under the shoulders and began to drag me away. Desperately, I reached out for Gutierrez, clutching onto him like a life preserver. Angry, the guard grabbed fistfuls of our hair, knocking our heads together twice, which made my skull ring like a bell.

Momentarily dazed, my hold on Gutierrez slackened enough for the guard to drag me away.

"Nash!"

"It's okay, G, hold on man. I'll come back." *His anguished sob followed me down the tunnel, and I called out,* "You hear me? I'm coming back. Hold on!"

They dragged me to a room even darker than the tunnel I had called home for the last week. Two guards manhandled me into a large plastic crate filled with freezing cold water. My heart and breath seized as every nerve ending in my body tensed from the icy bath. Was he going to drown me? Waterboard me for intel? Or was he simply cleaning the urine and feces off me?

The filthy fatigues clung to my body like a second skin, and I held my breath as he pushed my head below the surface of the water. It was a mindfuck for my senses; the dark room, the freezing cold water, and not knowing what was coming next. The whole experience was completely disorienting and terrifying, and all I could do was hold on, hold my breath, and hope that I survived.

Are they doing the same thing to Gutierrez right now?

What if they don't reunite us? What if they keep us apart?

What if they kill him?

I just don't want him to die alone. I fucking promised him I would come back. I promised him his mother's paella.

They allowed my head to surface before I ran out of breath, and just as quickly, they pushed me back under, with my lungs only half full of air. The tightening in my chest grew heavier, the primal urge to breathe, to feel my lungs expand with air, was overwhelming. I could feel a pulse behind my eyes, the pressure in my head growing to be too much, until they finally let up and allowed me to breathe. I sucked deep breaths into my lungs, my chest burning with the effort, and tried to brace my knees against the bottom of the crate, to leverage my body and keep my head above water. The guards grabbed my arms and hauled me from the bath, my clothes dripping wet on the dirt floor, making a muddy puddle. They tied me to a chair and shoved a piece of flatbread in my mouth with their dirty fingers. I was desperate to spit, but reluctant to let go of the food. So far, they hadn't poisoned the water or the bread, and as much as I hated to accept anything from them, I knew that the food was vital to my existence.

They taunted me as I chewed, poking me in the ribs with the butts of their rifles, kicking my legs, laughing at me like I was the brunt of their joke. I would burn every one of these motherfuckers to the ground, rip their bodies apart with my bare hands, and piss on their fucking bloody remains if I had half the chance.

Fuck them. Fuck their joke.

More voices sounded outside the room, echoing down the hallway, and then three more faces appeared in the doorway, dressed in muslin robes covered with camouflage jackets. They surrounded me, speaking to each other in a language I couldn't understand, and then their filthy hands grabbed my arms and my legs, and they carried me down the hall. They deposited me in a small dark room with barbed wire fencing serving as the door. Two armed guards stood on the other side of the razor wire. My body hit the ground and rolled, the dirt floor sticking to my wet clothes, making me filthy again in a matter of seconds. I lay still, waiting for my eyes to adjust to the darkness before I tried to move.

"Is that you?" he whispered. "Nash?"

Gutierrez. "It's me. Are you okay?"

"They bathed me."

"Is that what you would call it? More like fucking waterboarding. How's your foot?"

"I can't feel it anymore," he sobbed, giving into tears. "My leg feels hot, like I'm being stuck with hot pokers, but I can't feel my foot anymore."

"Maybe it's better that way. The pain would only weaken you. We have to stay strong. Until they come for us."

"Are they really coming?"

I slithered over the dirt floor in the darkness until my fingers connected with his leg, and I pulled myself up his body to sit beside him. His clothes were as cold and wet as mine, and he shook despite the heat in his leg, most likely fever from the sepsis.

"Yeah, G. They're coming. Just hold on."

Chapter 3

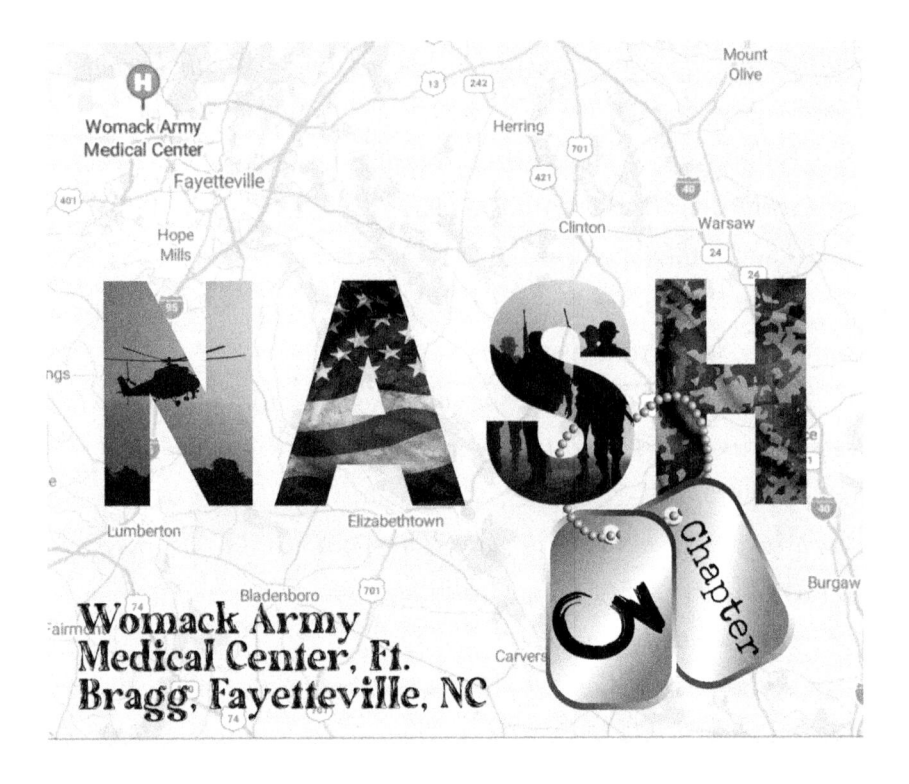

Womack Army Medical Center, Ft. Bragg, Fayetteville, NC

I've dreamed of returning home for weeks, like a single obsessive thought. Returning to the United States, back to Fort Bragg. But being a patient at Womack Army Medical Center? No, I didn't dream about this shit. Also, the staff here are a lot less professional than at Walter Reed.

"The guy across the hall says he can smell you all the way from over there," my nurse Liza remarks as she pushes into the room with her rolling med cart.

I wonder if she purposely tries to bang it on every surface between the door and my bed, or if it's just coincidence. A deaf person could hear her coming from a mile away.

"The guy across the hall has two options. He can shut the

fucking door or go fuck himself." My sweet smile belies the acid in my words.

Liza chuckles. I've learned nothing phases her. "Your dinner should be here shortly. In the meantime, you can start with this delicious amuse-bouche I've prepared for you," she says with a flourish of her wrist as she presents me with a paper cup. When I just stare, she adds, "I could crush it and sprinkle it over applesauce for you, or pudding."

With a glare that could burn holes through her, I swipe the paper cup off the tray table and down them in one gulp, fighting my gag reflex when they stick in my throat.

"You don't have to be a badass," she adds, placing another cup on my table. I chase the cocktail with water. "If you're going to shower, do it before these meds kick in."

We're interrupted by the delivery of my dinner tray from food services. It's less appetizing than the cup of pills or the promised applesauce and pudding. Spaghetti, and the red sauce is watered down, a clear pink liquid forming around the edge of the plate in a puddle. The guy in the kitchen must be the cousin of the guy who cooked for us on base. My stomach turns and then knots, and I can feel the pills coming back up. Pasta nuggets and watered down sauce. I swallow down bile and push the plate away without interest.

"You have to eat, Sergeant. You can't keep taking pills on an empty stomach. You're losing weight."

"I can't eat that," I croak.

With a tired sigh, she shuts and locks her med cart and pushes to her feet. "I'm about to go on my dinner break and I'm ordering Chinese takeout." Her face softens as she leans on the rail of my bed. "Can I order you something?"

I'm not just triggered by the bad memories, I'm triggered by the good ones as well, the ones that bring tears to my eyes and make my throat close up.

"Do they have crab Rangoon? There's a place down the street that makes the best crab Rangoon." I hate how broken my voice sounds, how close my emotions are to the surface, plain for her to see.

"Wok Choy?"

"That's the one," I rasp, losing my battle with my tears.

"I'll make you a deal. If you get up and take a shower, I'll go and order dinner. My treat."

Her kindness is my undoing. The tears fall unbidden, fat wet drops on my blanket. Liza risks touching me, something no one has done in weeks. She slides her small soft hand around my shoulder and squeezes me to her slender body, smelling sweet with perfume. It's such a jarring contrast to the men who roughly handled me, who tortured me mercilessly, that I don't even mind. It's a comfort.

"Have you eaten anything besides hospital food?" I shake my head, and she sighs again. "I hope you have an appetite because I'm going to order a lot of food," she teases with a smile.

When I get out of the shower, Liza is gone and so is her med cart. Padding back to the bed, I climb under the covers wearing a clean pair of worn gray sweats with the Army logo. The remote sits on the bedside table, and although it weighs no more than a couple of ounces, it weighs on me like a brick. I haven't watched TV since... I'm not even sure how long it's been. In the desert, I watched a couple of movies in the rec room, but TV? It's been more than a year.

When I came back to the States, the nurses at Walter Reed confiscated my remote control, warning me about being exposed to things that would trigger me. They were right. My name was all over the TV; pictures of me were in the headlines every day.

'POW returns home minus one.'

'Sergeant Sommers, real life American hero.'

What I wouldn't give to laugh at a sitcom or lose myself in a movie. To fall asleep to a documentary. But the likelihood that it would trigger a relapse is very high. I'm afraid to even try.

A surge of anger flashes through my body, heating my blood. I'm so sick and fucking tired of being afraid. What was the point of surviving if I'm afraid to live? I don't want to just merely exist each day, struggling to while away the hours before the sun sets and the drugs steal my consciousness. I owe Gutierrez more than this. I owe it to *myself*.

When Liza returns, she's carrying two brown paper bags, and I can smell the mouthwatering aroma from across the room. She places them on my tray table, and instead of dropping my meal off and leaving me to eat in solitude, Liza pulls the plastic chair in the corner close to my bed so she can share the table with me. The close proximity causes a small wave of panic. Is she going to make conversation with me? Probe me for information and details about my captivity?

It's been so long since I've carried on a normal conversation like this with someone, and I want it. I want the mundane ritual of sharing a meal with someone again, as much as it scares me.

"Crab Rangoon for you, potstickers for me," she says, pulling cardboard containers from the bag.

It's still warm from the deep fryer, and when I pop it in my mouth, I can taste the grease and the creamy cheese. The crunchy wonton wrapper breaks apart on my tongue, filling my mouth with tantalizing flavors that I dreamed of on the darkest nights, when my stomach turned itself inside out with hunger. My eyes fill with unshed tears, but I'm so lost in the rapture of the taste, in the experience of the texture, that I don't even care if she sees me cry over Chinese takeout.

It's more than that, more than how delicious it tastes, it's a dream realized. I dreamed of this, and I survived, and now I'm being rewarded. Nothing can diminish the pleasure of this moment, of this meal, except maybe knowing that Gutierrez never got his mama's paella. But before I can dwell on that, Liza breaks the silence.

"Is it everything you dreamed of and more? Sometimes, the memory doesn't live up to the reality."

"No," I rasp, clearing my throat. "It's even better than I remembered."

She hands me a tissue from the bedside table, and I blow my nose noisily. I'm a fucking mess, but to her credit, she doesn't say a word.

"You better eat up and get a good rest tonight because tomorrow you start therapy with Riggs." She laughs when I roll my eyes. "I've read your chart. I know you haven't participated in more than ten minutes of physical therapy since you were first hospitalized, but Riggs won't put up with that."

"He can't make me," I say, sounding like a toddler.

Liza's brow hitches like she doubts me. "I wouldn't be so sure. Riggs has ways." She finishes with an evil cackle, rubbing her hands together. It's the first time I laugh today.

"Why are you so against therapy? It would improve your limp greatly."

"Is it gonna fix my head?" I snap, feeling like an ass when her smile falls.

"I'm sorry. I didn't mean to imply it would fix everything. But when you're older and arthritis sets in, that limp is going to hurt a lot worse."

"I'm sorry."

Liza chews her last bite of egg roll and licks the grease from her fingers, nodding. "I can't imagine what you've been through, or what you're still going through, but there's no point in cutting off your nose to spite your face, Sergeant. Take the therapy, get better, walk easier, and you can deal with the rest another day."

"So, this Riggs guy, what's he like, the second coming of Christ?"

Liza laughs and wipes her hands on a napkin. "I haven't had a patient as charming as you since..." A fond smile touches her pink lips. "Since Wardell."

"Nice guy?"

"The best. Like you." She collects her trash and drops it in the can. "Are you still hungry?"

"No, this was more food than I've eaten in weeks." Liza smiles and pushes her chair back to the corner.

"Maybe tomorrow we can order burgers and fries."

I groan like a glutton, imagining the taste of the greasy broiled meat and salty fried potatoes. "Liza?" She turns at the door. "Thank you," I say softly.

Thank you for treating me like a person, like I'm human.

Liza wasn't kidding. *Fuck Riggs.*

The remnants of last night's sedatives are still trickling through my blood, and Liza won't give me another dose until I finish therapy. I'm short-tempered and tired, and his clipboard and pen-clicking are pissing me the fuck off.

"Good, give me another ten reps."

I'll give you a fat fucking lip in a minute.

He's immune to my glaring and cursing, just plowing through the workout with a bright and determined smile.

I fucking hate him.

"Ten…nine…eight… get your knee higher… seven… six… five. Don't forget to breathe."

I wonder if kicking him would suffice for my last five reps.

"You're doing great, Sergeant."

I let my leg drop heavily, making the weights clang. "Were you a drill sergeant before this?"

"No, Army nurse," he says with a smirk.

"That explains a lot."

"I could point out that if you'd been doing therapy all along, it wouldn't be this hard right now, but I won't."

He's still fucking smirking. "How gracious of you," I mumble with a sour face.

There's a woman across the gym with one leg lifting more weight than me, and she doesn't even appear to be winded. I power through another set of reps, the muscles in my thigh burning like fire. The bone aches—that's what I hate about therapy, the pain deep down in my bones. My shattered femur is crying out for mercy.

"It gets easier, Sergeant. Don't give up before the magic happens."

"I'll keep that in mind."

For the remaining two weeks I'm at Womack, Riggs works me over just about every day, and by the time I'm discharged, I'm able to add twenty-five pounds of weight to my workout.

"So, what are your plans after this," Liza asks.

"Even with the Brass fast tracking my discharge, I've still got a couple weeks left on base. I've got a townhouse here I used to share with—" *Gutierrez.* "I'll need to look for somewhere new to live for now."

"My friend has an apartment off-base. She's staying with her boyfriend, so I can ask if she'd sublet to you temporarily."

"That'd be great." Like hell I could go back home without G. His family had no doubt been by to collect his things, but I'd still feel his ghost everywhere. That would be more than I could take.

"Well, don't be a stranger, Sergeant. When you get hungry for takeout, stop by and see me," she offers.

My best and only friend is an Army nurse. Of all the unlikely odds, what could be more absurd? But Liza is one of a kind, and I'm grateful for her friendship. Her confident, no-nonsense attitude and sunny smile make everything feel more manageable—less dire. She puts things in perspective, reminding me there's a whole world happening outside my head, a world I need to be a part of.

Riggs stops by one last time. He drops a glossy brochure on my tray table.

"What's this?" I ask, picking it up. "BALLS?"

"Beyond The Army: Legion Of Love Soldiers."

"Sounds like a group of Mormon Vets. No, thanks."

Riggs chuckles. "Figured you say something dumb like that. Just do me a favor, smartass. When you're feeling at your lowest, come see me there. I'll be waiting for you."

I nod, but deep down, I know it's highly fucking unlikely I'll ever see Riggs again.

NASH

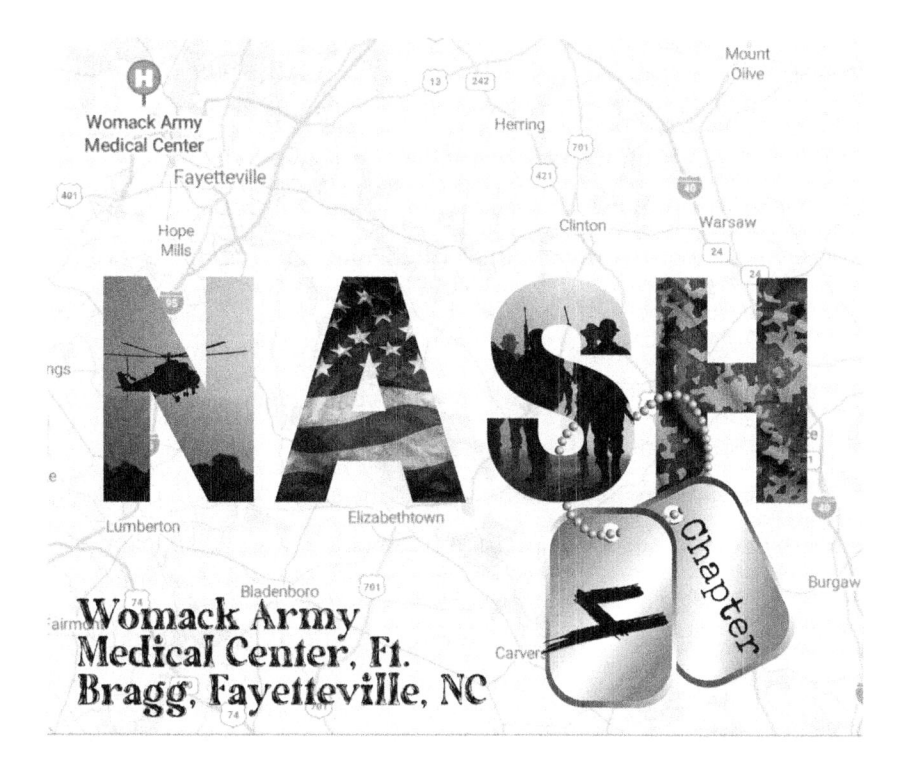

Chapter 4

Womack Army Medical Center, Ft. Bragg, Fayetteville, NC

Returning to active duty without my unit feels like having a limb cut off. I've never lost one, but I imagine this is what the phantom pains feel like—the tingling numbness where a part of you is missing that's always been there. There's only one other face I recognize in my rear detachment unit, Colonel Berdorf. He blew out his knee and was sent home before me, while I was in captivity. He knows what I've been through, which is probably why he makes wide circles around me. Everyone else is new.

They offered me an apartment on base, but I declined, more than happy with my current accommodations. I felt like I needed to get as far away from the base as possible, far enough that the memory of Gutierrez wouldn't haunt me at night. Apparently, my new apartment isn't far enough away because I see him every night in my dreams.

Mind-numbing busy work wastes the minutes and hours in my day—taking inventory of supplies, maintaining and cleaning the vehicles in the motor pool, scoring my unit on PT tests and physical evals, signing leave slips, and coordinating overseas phone calls for the unit to call family back home. This mundane shit is all I'm capable of anymore.

The inventory is soul sucking, and it's endless. It's fucking endless. As soon as I complete one checklist, there's another one to be filled out, and another. The words on the page become blurred, and I close my eyes, feeling lightheaded and detached. Empty.

The pills are the only thing getting me through the day anymore. I rely on them like a crutch, like a vital organ in my body, designed to perform basic and necessary functions in order for me to live. I can't exist without them.

My commanding officer, Warrant Officer Chief Burgess, has his eye on me. He's probably a decent guy, but I'm always pissing him off for one reason or another. Because that's what I am now, a fucking disappointment. A goddamn headache.

"Sommers, you were late again today." He drops a stack of papers on my desk, and I have to fight to keep my eyes from rolling back in my head. "Look, you've got one foot out the door, so I'm not gonna write you up, but if you're late tomorrow, your consequence is going to make this paperwork look like a fucking wet dream."

He looks into my eyes, like he can see right through me, and I have to look away. It's an eerie feeling that makes my skin crawl. Does he realize my pupils are dilated and that my eyes are red? Can he tell how distant I feel?

"Put that shit away," he says, pointing to the stack of paperwork in front of me. "I've got something better for you to do."

Thank God.

Burgess places a sheet in front of me. All I see are phone numbers, and I have to blink several times to bring my eyesight into focus. "What's this?"

"The Military Welfare and Recreation agenda. I can't think of anyone more suited to the position than you," he lies, clapping me on the shoulder.

That's fucking bullshit. It's payback for being late and high. He can't bust me for it and request a drug test because they're prescription pills, but he can make my life hell by putting me in charge of planning the MWR functions. The committee that plans get-togethers and social functions for the families of the deployed soldiers is the last thing I'm suited for. I'm not a fucking social director or an event planner. I'm a soldier, and lately, not even a good one.

"Sir, you realize I'm easily triggered, don't you?" I'm not above using my diagnosis to get out of this nightmare. I'm desperate, and I can't think of anything more triggering, more *traumatic*, than fielding phone calls from military wives all day.

His wicked smile makes me wary. "I'll grab you a box of tissues. In the meantime, get to work. You've got a lot of phone calls to make."

Sixteen phone calls later, and I have the potluck dinner somewhat planned for the following weekend. The key is to delegate the responsibilities to the experts, a.k.a. the wives. Whittemore's wife volunteered to organize the menu and find out who is bringing what. All I have to do is get my unit to set up tables and chairs and purchase the paper products.

At five p.m., I clock out and head for home. *Home,* I scoff, what a joke. Have I ever had a home? When I was growing up, the house I lived in belonged to my parents. It never felt like a home. Just a house. Since then, I've lived in many residences, but none of them ever felt like a home. The closest I ever came to feeling at home with anyone was when I lived with Gutierrez. We invited friends over for barbecues on the weekends. We played drinking games at our dining room table. We cooked together in the kitchen.

I haven't taken anything from our place with me. Just a mattress on the floor. No TV, gaming console, couch, or kitchen table. It hurts too much to look at them. But I know, no matter how far away from the base I relocate, his memories will always haunt me, because they're not in the possessions we shared, they're in my head. They're in my heart. And I can't run from his memory.

When I'm stopped at the red light, I reach for two more pills from my prescription bottle and swallow them dry. With each passing mile, his memory begins to fade to the dark corners of my conscience, replaced with thoughts of potluck dinners and inventory, and what I'll have to eat when I get home.

Nothing. Because I'll be passed out by then.

No shower. No dinner. I can barely keep my eyes open as I unbutton the jacket of my BDUs and strip out of my pants. I crash face-first onto the mattress, catching a whiff of old sweat on my dirty sheets. Maybe I'll wash them tomorrow. Or maybe I'll...

Moonlight peeks through the window, illuminating a white stripe down the middle of my bed. I have no idea what time it is, sometime during the night. How long have I slept? My head feels heavy. Rolling over, I rub the blur from my eyes, my back connecting with a solid body. I need water. My mouth feels like it's glued shut. With my bad leg, it's hard to stand because the mattress is so low to the ground, and because I'm so tired, it's easier to just crawl. So I crawl, across the floor of my little bedroom, down the short hall into my living room, into the kitchen, where I use the counter to pull myself up.

There's no bottled water in the fridge. There's nothing in the fridge. Grabbing a plastic cup from the counter, I fill it with water from the sink, downing it so quickly it dribbles down my chin. I just need another handful of pills so I can go back to bed. Rifling through my ruck, my hand closes around the cold metal handle of my shovel instead of the pill bottle.

Gutierrez's ditch digger. Why do I have it? Because some asshole borrowed mine and never gave it back. Now I'm the asshole who borrowed his and never gave it back. Grabbing it from the bag, my back slides down the wall until I'm flat on my ass, and my chest squeezes tight with emotions I wish I could feel if not for the pills. My thumb rubs across the worn cord wrapped around my index finger, a constant reminder of what I lost.

Gutierrez's boot lace.

Instead of the tears I wish I could shed for him, I feel nothing but anger, and a sadness so heavy it crushes me under its weight. A flash of heat moves through my body, igniting my temper. A maelstrom of emotions and memories flood my head and my heart, causing a tornado of anger so thick it chokes me.

"Why?" I scream into the darkness.

My voice echoes off the empty walls.

"I hate this shit! I hate myself! I just want to stop feeling. I just want it all to stop."

Squeezing the handle of the shovel, I hurl it at the wall with all my strength. The pointed tip embeds deep into the drywall with a satisfying clunk. Not satisfying enough to close the gaping hole in my chest, but satisfying enough that the destruction I caused resonates within my soul.

With my anger depleted, I just feel empty. Tired. I never make it back to my bed. Just lay down on the floor and let my eyes drift shut.

I'm late again for work. Not that I give two shits. The most pressing thing on my agenda today is to inventory our gear and get a headcount for the amount of tables and chairs I need. Something a monkey could do with its eyes closed.

As I lock my apartment door, my neighbor exits at the same time.

"Morning," he greets, clutching a travel cup of coffee. I can see steam rising through the hole in the lid, and I'm envious that I didn't think to bring my coffee maker from my old place.

"Morning," I mumble, my voice full of gravel.

It's not until I glance up that I receive a shock to my system, more potent than caffeine. My neighbor is huge—a big, burly man stacked with muscle and scarred over most of his body. Half of his face is covered in burns. Fresh ones from the looks of it because they're swollen and red.

"Rough night?"

"Excuse me?"

"Last night, it sounded like you were having a rough time."

"The fuck?" Oh God, the shovel. Did it actually go all the way through the wall into his apartment? "Yeah, I was. The remote control slipped out of my hand and hit the wall," I improvise.

"I see," he chuckles, stroking his dark goatee. "That's happened to me a few times."

He's wearing a faded khaki Army pride shirt, and it hits me. This man is not much different than me. He served. He suffered. And from the sound of it, he knows I'm suffering, too.

"So listen, if you need help fixing that wall, just knock on my door. I've got tools, and together, we can knock it out." When I just stare blankly, he adds, "You know, so you don't lose your deposit? By the way, I'm Armando Cahill, but you can call me Mandy."

He sticks out his hand, and I realize he's waiting for me to introduce myself. "Nash Sommers. Thanks for the offer."

As I head toward the parking lot, Mandy follows, and I know he's assessing my gait. There's no hiding my glaringly obvious limp. "You headed to base?" It's an easy guess considering I'm dressed in my BDUs, the same dirty ones I wore yesterday.

"Yeah, just biding my time in the Rear D until my retirement comes through."

"Been there, done that," he chuckles. "When I come over to fix your wall, you can tell me all about it." He opens his car door and ducks inside, calling out, "Have a good day, Sergeant," before shutting the door.

Huh, an encounter that actually went pleasantly. That's fucking rare.

―――――

Thank God it's Saturday and I don't have to be at work. In fact, it's almost two in the afternoon and I'm still in bed. I'm awake, been awake for hours, but just lying here in the dark, sedated, hiding from the world. My phone beeps with a message, and I'm reluctant to check it because I don't want to answer to anyone or put clothes on. The screen lights up, flashing too bright for my sensitive eyes, and I have to squint as I read the message.

Liza:

> I'm in the neighborhood and figured I would drop by and say hello. See you soon.

Fuck me. I definitely have to put clothes on. Sitting up, my head spins and my stomach gurgles, reminding me that I skipped dinner last night. Rolling to my knees, I struggle to stand, reaching for my jeans. There's a gray T-shirt on the floor, crumpled in a ball, and I shake out the wrinkles and sniff it. Sour, but it'll do. In a groggy haze, I shuffle to the bathroom to take a piss and brush my teeth, and it hits me in a moment of clarity.

Liza is coming over!

I don't have a stitch of fucking furniture in this apartment. No food in the fridge. No plates or forks to eat it with anyways. I have nothing. And I'm not high enough to endure her concerned wrath. My foggy brain struggles to come up with a solution as I stare at my reflection in the mirror. I have no time for a shower, or to shave my two-day beard growth. I only have time for one thing. Grabbing the phone again, I reply to Liza.

> Apartment 17A

As fast as my leg will allow, I rush next door and bang on Mandy's door loud enough to shake it from its hinges. He answers the door holding a hammer, a lazy grin stretching across his scruffy lips.

"Ready to fix that hole in the wall?"

"Actually, I need you to do me a huge favor." It takes balls to ask for a favor from a guy you don't know. And I'm too high to care if I have any or not.

"Sure, what do you need?"

"I need to borrow your apartment." The confusion on his face is priceless.

"Borrow my apartment? How does that work exactly?"

This sounded better in my head. "Like, you go stand in my apartment and I pretend this one is mine." Mandy laughs like I'm playing a joke on him. I might as well be for how outlandish my request sounds.

"Oh, you're serious," he realizes when I don't laugh with him. "For how long?"

"An hour?" Just when I think he's about to slam the door in my face, he crosses his arms over his wide chest, his lips spreading into a slow smile.

"Okay, deal, but you owe me a favor."

"Anything. Anything you want, it's yours."

"I'll remember you said that. There's a pot of coffee on. Drink it. You look like you need it."

Mandy grabs his tool bag and strolls next door, still holding the hammer. Awkwardly, I walk into his space, not knowing what to do with myself, or where to sit, and hesitant to touch his things. It's not my home. By the grace of God, he went along with this scam, probably because he's a good guy. A better one than I am.

Who isn't?

An hour later, Liza pulls out of the parking lot, and I shut the front door and breathe a sigh of relief. Either she didn't notice I was high, or she chose not to say anything. She did, however, point out I've lost too much weight, and that I look like shit. I feel completely exhausted, both mentally and physically, by the time I open the door to my apartment.

"You borrowed my apartment to entertain some chick?"

Mandy sits upon the countertop in my kitchen, with his arms crossed over his wide chest.

"No, it's not like that," I say with a tired sigh, raking my hand through my hair. "Liza's just a friend. What were you doing, spying on us?"

Mandy scoffs. "Please, I saw her leave. You have no curtains on these fucking windows. In fact, you have nothing in this entire apartment! What the hell is going on here? What kind of weird shit are you up to?"

I just don't have the energy to sort this out right now. But one thought makes my heart beat faster. "You didn't go into the bedroom, did you?"

He jumps off the counter, looking wary. "Dude, that's it. I'm getting the fuck out of here."

"Wait, Mandy."

"Talk to me in the hallway." I follow him out the door, and he turns to me, handing me the shovel. "Here, you left this in your wall."

"Thank you. For fixing it, and for switching with me, and for just being... Understanding."

"Understanding? I don't understand any of this. What I

understand is that you're going through a hard time and you could use a friend, and I hope that's me. But don't forget, you owe me a favor. In the meantime, if you need anything, toilet paper, food, Wi-Fi, just knock on my door."

He's gone, leaving me standing here staring at his closed door, and I shuffle back inside in a daze, dropping the shovel on the counter and grabbing the bottle of pills. The rest of my Saturday is spent in bed, in and out of consciousness.

BALLS
Black Mountain, NC

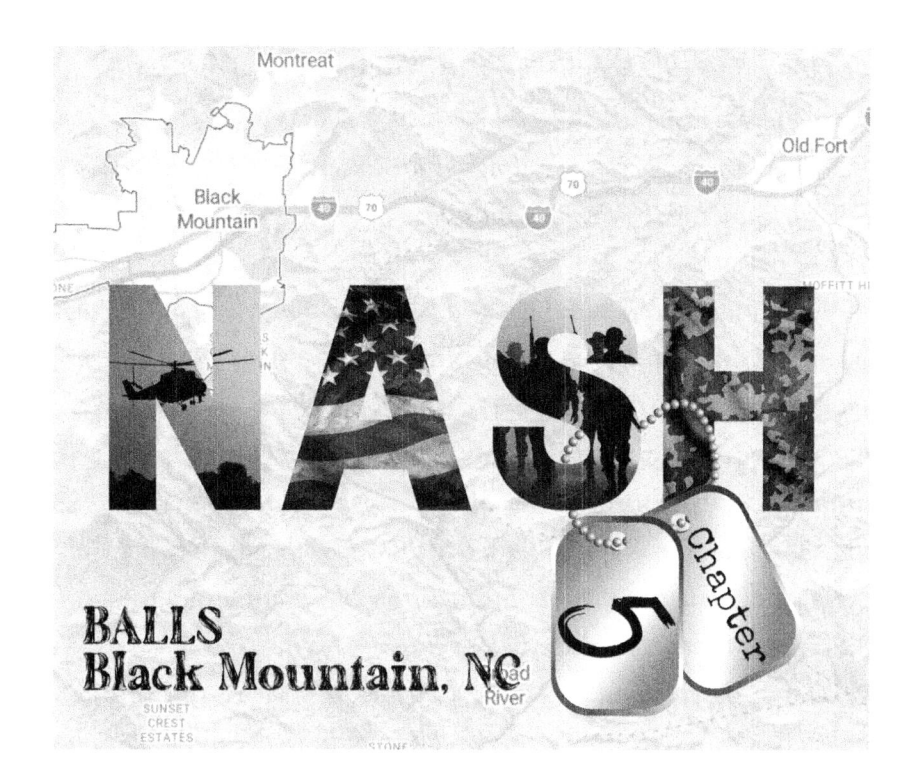

DAY 10 OF CAPTIVITY

The smell of his rotting flesh was enough to turn my stomach, if there were anything of it left to turn, but it was empty from hunger. We spent most of our time sitting side-by-side in silence, sometimes lying down, or just leaning against each other. Sometimes, we talked. In the silence, I could hear the scurrying of tiny feet, the high-pitched squeak of rats or mice. God only knew what else was down here with us. Scorpions? Most likely.

Gutierrez whimpered constantly. I wasn't even sure if he was aware he was doing it. Sometimes, he reached for my hand in the darkness, just needing something solid and warm to hold on to. Other times, he beat his head against the packed dirt wall, and I had to hold him still.

Raised voices echoed down the hall, and my entire body tensed, knowing they were coming for us.

What now?

One guard held a lantern and the other a bowl. I had no idea what was in it, but I knew I wanted it more than I wanted my next breath. Wordlessly, they grabbed the back of Gutierrez's head, holding him up while shoving the bowl against his lips. He drank greedily, spilling most of it down his chin, and then they did the same to me, grabbing a fistful of my hair as they held my head back, pouring the rest of the bitter broth down my throat. I barely had time to swallow before choking on it.

Then they pulled us to our feet and pushed us out into the hallway. Gutierrez wailed, and I could only imagine the pain he was in, having to walk on his ruined foot. I'd bet it wasn't numb any longer, unless the fire was shooting up his leg.

The guards led us to a room lit up by battery-powered lamps. There were two chairs positioned in the middle, and I knew they had our names on them.

They pushed us down onto the chairs and stood across from us, holding a camera aimed right at our faces. A guard I hadn't seen before handed me a piece of paper.

"Read. Read."

Scanning the words written in a crude hand, I was able to piece together the gist of the message, even if it wasn't too clear.

Name
Rank

Ask help
Go home

They wanted us to beg for help, to beg for the Army to come rescue us and take us home. It was a trap. I doubted very much they were bargaining for our lives. The United States didn't negotiate with terrorists.

A sick feeling washed over me, threatening to make the broth come back up. We were at a crossroads, our time becoming shorter by the second. If I didn't read the words on the paper, they would kill me. But if I read the words, they'd kill me, anyway. Either way, I was a dead man.

"Read. Read!"

"Don't say anything, G. They'll kill us either way, but don't give them the satisfaction."

He was barely conscious, most likely checked out from the pain, and was only able to nod his head as it rolled on his slack shoulders.

Seething and panicked, the guard pulled out a knife from his belt and held it to my throat. The cold metal kissed my skin, burning as the sharp blade cut through the surface layers.

"Read!"

When I remained silent, he pressed harder, and I could feel the warm, wet rush of blood flow down my neck, soaking into the collar of my T-shirt. The blinking red light on the camera turned green. The bastard was recording this shit. No doubt he would play it for the people in charge of deciding my fate.

He spit in my face and then moved on to Gutierrez, holding

the knife against the side of his head. Gutierrez was barely able to respond to the threat.

"Read," he shouted at me.

Swallowing past the lump of fear in my throat, I remained stoic and silent, knowing I held Gutierrez's life in my hands. But really, it wasn't up to me at all. I knew deep down they were going to kill us both, whether I read the statement or not. I refused to give in, to give them what they wanted. I would not be weak in my last moments.

The sound of the knife slicing through his skin curdled the broth in my stomach, and I regurgitated it over my lap. The pain of losing his ear was enough to rouse him from his subdued state, and he screamed in agony as blood dripped down into his shirt. Hot tears blurred my vision, but I refused to let them fall, not while these fucking bastards were filming me.

"Read! Read!"

Go fuck yourself and die.

I spit a wad of saliva onto the dirt floor by his boots. The guard standing next to the cameraman unholstered the gun at his hip, strode forward, and shot me in the thigh. At first, all I could feel was the heat of the bullet piercing my skin, like being sliced open with a hot knife. I felt the spray of warm blood bathe my face, could taste the copper tang on my tongue. Seconds later, the real pain set in. Adrenaline coursed through my blood, making it as thick as my fear, and my heart rate beat triple time. Gutierrez continued to scream, his eyes closed, head lolled back, but it was drowned out by the sound of my own blood whooshing in my ears.

He'd hit the bone. It must have shattered because there was

no way in hell a simple gunshot wound could hurt that badly. Bleeding from my neck and my leg, I could feel myself becoming weak, lightheaded, only keeping my wits about me from the adrenaline and the fear.

"Read!

"Go fuck yourself."

He slammed the butt of his gun against the side of my head, knocking it back in a flash of blinding pain.

"Go. Fuck. Yourself."

Then he slammed the butt of his gun against Gutierrez's head, knocking him blessedly unconscious.

"Go fuck yourself."

The guard spit in my face and hauled me to my feet. The fire in my leg and the throbbing in my head was enough to rob me of my vision long before he dragged me all the way back to my dark cell.

Knock, knock.

Knock, knock, knock.

The pounding goes on and on relentlessly as my head throbs, and I can feel my heartbeat like a pulse behind my eyes.

The longer I try to shut it out, the louder the pounding becomes until I can't ignore it any longer. Reaching out blindly in the dark, I search frantically until my hand connects with something solid, and I breathe a sigh of relief as my fingers twist in the worn cotton t-shirt. Crawling to my knees, I manage to stand on shaky legs, desperately searching for the offending sound.

Knock, knock.

Jesus fucking Christ. It's coming from the front door. Someone is about to beat it down. Throwing it open hard enough that it slams against the wall and bounces back, I glare at my visitor. "What in the ever-loving-fuck?" I croak.

"Morning," Mandy chirps. "Or should I say afternoon? It's almost three."

Fuck. I rub the grit from my eyes.

"What about it? Was I late for something?"

"Actually, we're about to be. I came to collect on that favor you owe me."

Oh, hell no! "Mandy, I'm not feeling my best right now. Maybe another time?"

He steps past me, shouldering his way into my empty apartment. "Nah, now is as good a time as any. Go get dressed. Maybe shower first. I can smell you from next door. And brush your teeth."

"Mandy," I snap, "I don't feel up for going anywhere."

"You don't look like it either, but I'm not taking no for an answer. A deal is a deal. Now get dressed."

With a tired sigh, I shuffle down the hallway. "Where are we going?"

"I'll tell you when we get there."

Bastard.

The parking lot of the enormous white stucco building is nearly full. The large sign out front says BALLS- NC Mountain Region Branch.

A feeling of déjà vu nails me in my throbbing head as I try to recall where I've heard that name before.

A pleasant floaty feeling insulates my brain, like it's submerged in the sea, sloshing back-and-forth on gentle waves. The sensation lulls me into a state of deep serenity, and I struggle to keep my eyes open.

"Come on," Mandy says, clapping me on the back. "Let's get you inside. Margaret Anne will load you up with some coffee. You look like you need about six cups."

Moving on autopilot, I follow his lead, inside the building, through the pristine lobby, where an older woman greets us with a pleasant smile.

"Sergeant Cahill! How lovely to see you. Who did you bring?"

The fact that he was a sergeant dimly registers through the fog clouding my head.

"This is Sergeant Sommers. I'm hoping to recruit him," he says with an evil cackle. "He looks like he could use some coffee, doesn't he? Nobody makes it better than you," he gushes.

"Oh, you're too kind," she beams, brushing him off with a wave of her manicured hand.

I just stand there, aware that I haven't spoken a word yet, feeling ridiculously foolish and useless, as Margaret Anne fetches my cup of coffee. She hands it to me with a bright smile, and I close my eyes as I take my first sip, breathing in the fresh aroma of roasted beans. Pure nirvana. It's potent enough to snap my eyes open.

"Can we get a ball sack?" Mandy asks.

Margaret Anne laughs. "Sergeant, you know that's not what it's called." She hands me a black nylon drawstring bag filled with God knows what. "Here, take a flyer as well. It lists our services offered."

She hands me the flyer, but the words just blur together on the paper into a black smudge. I can't read for shit after taking my pills, and I definitely took some because that was the only way I was leaving the house.

"Come on, I'll show you around."

"What is this place?"

"This is the gymnasium where they play basketball," he explains, ignoring my question. "Down here is the cafeteria. They serve free hot meals every day, and across the hall are occupational therapy rooms. Let me show you the gym."

"Mandy," I hiss, tugging on his arm, "I don't like being blindsided. Tell me why we're here."

"This place, BALLS, helps vets after the Army is done with them. Things like physical therapy, employment, education, and therapy."

"So why am I here? And why are you here?"

"Because sometimes, we can all use a little help, including you. *Especially you*," he mumbles under his breath as he turns toward the double doors. Mandy leads me into the gym, and I have to admit, it's pretty impressive.

"This is the physical therapy room. State of the art equipment and certified physical therapists on staff every day, free of charge." Mandy surveys the room and spots someone he knows, waving to them as he shouts, "Hey, Riggs, are you coming?"

"Yeah, let me wrap this up and I'll be right there."

The name Riggs has my head turning sharply, and that's

when I remember where I've heard of this place before. "Riggs? What are you doing here?" His smile is instantaneous.

"Sergeant Sommers, I wondered when you would come to see me. I'm glad you finally made it."

"I'm not here for you."

The smile falls from his face. "Here with Mandy?"

Mandy chuffs. "He owed me a favor and I'm collecting."

"Clever, Cahill. I like the way you operate."

Mandy chuckles. "Don't be late."

"I'm right behind you," Riggs calls.

I follow him out in a hurry, feeling like I'm standing in a pressure cooker under Riggs's scrutiny. "Where are we going now?"

"I'll tell you when we get there," he says, just like he did earlier when he was trying to get me into the car.

Armando Cahill is a manipulative son of a bitch, and you can't even blame him for it because his heart is in the right place.

I follow him down a long corridor, a right turn, and another long hallway before we get to some classrooms. There are already men inside, big, scarred men, some missing legs, all of them covered in tatts, seated in a circle.

"What's this?" The fine hairs on the back of my neck stand at attention. Something doesn't feel right.

"Support group. Welcome to the Bitches with Stitches."

Jesus Christ, I walked right into this like a rat chasing a chunk of cheese. "Support groups aren't my thing."

"Well, whatever you're currently doing isn't working out for you too well, so sit down," Mandy says without a trace of empathy.

I don't really have a choice because he drove me here, so it's either sit in here, or sit out in the lobby with Margaret Anne. Taking a seat between Mandy and a guy covered with tattoos with one leg, I keep my head down and my mouth shut. Maybe no one will notice if I doze off.

An annoying clacking sound pries my eyes open out of curiosity and mild annoyance. *Knitting needles?*

"Did I forget to mention we knit? It's therapeutic," Mandy explains.

He must be full of shit. These guys look like a lot of things, but not one of them looks like a knitter. But sure enough, each one of them is knitting something. A guy with flaming red hair and hot pink yarn is knitting what looks like... "Is that a pistol?"

The man looks up with a smile. "It's a gun cozy. Keeps the dust off of Beretta."

Is that what he named it? He named his Beretta, *Beretta*? Maybe he's here because he has a head injury in addition to his missing leg. There's another man to my left, next to the guy with one leg and tatts, who seems to be knitting... "Is that a butt plug?"

"See," he says to the man between us, elbowing his ribs. "I told you that's what it looks like. It's a tree for our Christmas village," he explains.

The man seated between us is laughing too hard to comment, and so is Mandy, but silently, behind his hand. And if all of this isn't enough to make me run for the hills, what happens next has me pushing to my feet.

"All right, gentlemen, quiet down. Let's get started. We have a special guest today, a newcomer that I want to introduce you to." Riggs locks his eyes with mine, and my throat closes.

I can't swallow.

I can't breathe.

Panic claws at the walls of my chest, squeezing my heart until it beats too fast and hard, and I race for the door.

Mandy is hot on my heels, tugging at my arm. "Nash, hold up."

"No, this is too much."

"Hey, you don't have to talk. We just want to introduce ourselves to you. Make you feel welcome."

I have to take two deep breaths before I can speak, swallowing hard past the lump in my throat. "I don't want to feel welcome. I want to go home."

Can he hear the desperation in my voice? Doesn't he know I'm scared shitless? "This is absurd. Men who knit? Get the fuck out."

"You owe me a favor, and I brought you here, so you might as well sit the fuck down and listen."

"That's how he got me here," the man who was sitting beside me says. "Brandt cashed in a favor, and by the end of the hour, I realized it wasn't so bad. Mind you, I'm not completely convinced yet, and I've been coming for months," he teases with a twist of his lips.

Ignoring him, I plead my case to Mandy. "I don't want to talk about my feelings, and I don't want to listen to them talk about theirs. I don't give a rat's ass. Why can't we just leave?"

"Because you need help, and this is help." Mandy speaking

calmly in the face of my anger only makes me feel more frustrated.

"Are you fucking kidding me? Do you know the shit I've seen? Do you think sharing my feelings and knitting a fucking scarf is going to make me forget that I held my best friend's dead, rotting body in my arms for seven fucking days while rats ate pieces of him?"

The look on Mandy's face transforms from pissed off to horrified, and I want to bite my fucking tongue off for letting those words past my lips.

"Jesus Christ, Nash. I didn't..."

"I know, you didn't know. How could you? This isn't the kind of therapy I need."

Instantly, he's pissed again. "You don't know what you need! You think you have all the answers, but you don't. That's why you look like a goddamn mess. That's why you live in an empty shell of an apartment that resembles a crack house. In fact, I've probably been in nicer crack houses. At least they were furnished. Until you have a better idea of how to help yourself, this is the best idea we've got. Sit the fuck down and shut up and listen for the next sixty minutes, and then I'll take you home."

Fuck.

Fuck him.

Fuck this.

Fuck me.

Reluctantly, I follow him back to our seats and chance a look at Riggs. He's looking at me patiently, with understanding and a touch of sympathy. But I can tell it's not pity. Not with

Riggs. He doesn't pity anyone. Why do I feel like crying? My throat is swelling again, and my chest feels heavy. All the shit I haven't dealt with that I bury deep down is floating up to the surface, in danger of leaking from my eyes. I've been surrounded by these people for ten minutes and already my guards are trying to come down, probably screaming out for help like I'm holding my soul hostage, trapped in my nightmare against its will.

I'm no better than my captors.

I'm holding myself hostage, torturing myself.

I don't want to keep suffering, but I don't know another way out, and the thought of sharing everything I've been through with anyone sickens my stomach and scares me to my core. It's easier to just stuff it down deep and numb myself with pills and alcohol than it is to face the truth of my trauma.

They treated their dogs better than they did us. My best friend, one of the best guys I've ever known, died a horrible death without honor, like he was lower than a rat.

No, he had honor. He fought, and he held on as long as he could. They blew his fucking foot off and still he held on. They cut his fucking ear off. They starved him and beat him, and he held on until his body gave out on him. He died with honor, like a warrior, fighting for his life and his freedom, and I'll honor his death and his life until my last breath.

With my mind stuck somewhere in the past, I didn't notice they'd started the meeting until Brandt stands and walks over to me. He hands me a folded up piece of paper from his back pocket. A sheet with a bunch of phone numbers that blur together.

"This is the Bitches with Stitches phone tree. Anytime you need to talk to someone, reach out and call one of us. Start at the top of the list and work your way down." Then he glances at the list, reading off the names in his head, and his face scrunches. "Actually, McCormick might not answer if he's on a date. But you can call me. I'll always answer."

"Fuck it," the big redhead complains. "Carly dumped me. I guess I can answer the damn phone."

"Thank you, Aguilar," Riggs says. "Let's open up the meeting, starting with McCormick. Tell us what happened."

"I don't know, man. I thought things were going fine. She said I wasn't putting her first, and that our relationship wasn't a priority."

Riggs keeps the tone of his voice neutral. "And did you? Did you make her a priority?"

"Not really," he sighs. "I mean, I didn't always answer her calls, but she wanted to get together like every night! Ain't nobody got time for that bullshit. She didn't understand that I wanted to go ride with the guys, or that I was working on a knitting project. She expected me to take her out every night, and when we stayed home, all she wanted to do was talk."

The pills dull my filter, making it hard not to laugh when it's inappropriate. My snicker draws many eyes, and then everyone's laughing.

"I take it she didn't want to talk about knitting and motorcycles?" Riggs asks.

"We really didn't have that much in common," he admits, dragging his stubby fingers through his short hair.

"You fed her the boiled hotdogs, didn't you," demands the guy seated beside him.

"Dude, you've got to stop riding my ass about the hotdogs. They're not as bad as you make them out to be."

Riggs interrupts the man's exaggerated retching. "I'm glad that you put yourself out there and gave it a shot, but maybe it isn't fair to your partner if you're not one hundred percent ready to give your all."

The man, McCormick, looks stunned. "My *partner*? Shit, my partner is right here beside me." The men fist bump.

"That explains so much," says the man at the end of the row with a mohawk.

"I think you have your answer, McCormick. Stiles? How was your week?"

"Well, I'm still employed. So I've got that going for me." He high-fives McCormick.

Riggs intervenes again, like a preschool teacher trying to make a bunch of toddlers cooperate. "That must have either taken great improvement and dedication on your part, or luck."

"Or luck." The man with the mohawk snickers.

"Keep up the good work," Riggs praises. "Anything else you want to comment on?"

"No, I'm feeling pretty good this week. I'll take my win and pass the baton. Jax?"

It's finally the man with the modified mohawk's turn to speak. "Still struggling with my anger, but I'm doing better than I was last week. I guess it comes and goes. Some days are better than others, some days are worse. I'm alright today. Not great, but I'm alright. I guess I feel grateful I have a place to come to, and people that I can trust with my feelings."

Riggs nods. "It's something that a lot of people don't have. I'm glad you realize it's a gift. Hang in there. As for me, I'm starting to settle into my old routine now that I'm back from deployment. It always takes me a while to shift things in my head. I still feel a bit distracted and distant, closed off from my surroundings. Like a part of me is still over there with my patient. I can't get him off my mind for some reason. Anyway, I'm adjusting, and I think it would do me good to join you all for lunch today after the meeting."

The crowd claps for him, and one thing he said resonates through the hazy fog in my head. He asked for help. I know how much courage it takes to ask for help. For some reason, I always feel like it would make me weak, but I don't think Riggs is weak at all. He just sounds brave and strong to me.

Why do I hold myself to a different standard than I do others?

Why am I always at the bottom of the stick?

I wish I could give myself the same leniency I give others, but I always feel like I'm playing by a different set of rules.

The man who handed me the phone tree is next.

"I had a tough week. Suffered a blow to my peace of mind. The doc said I've lost more of my hearing, which sucks because I've only got one good ear that works. I'm worried I'll continue to lose my hearing until I've got nothing left, and I'm living in a silent world. That scares the shit out of me. I know there's worse things I could lose, obviously, but haven't I fucking given enough? Haven't I lost enough?"

The man seated between us grabs his hand, lacing their fingers together in a show of strength and support. "You're never gonna live in a silent world, Reaper. You'll always be able to hear my voice. Always."

Brandt loses his struggle with his tears, and they slide down his scruffy cheeks. "I know. I could never forget the sound of your voice. Whatever, we'll figure it out," he sniffles, swiping at his eyes and nose. "I'll learn sign language if I have to. Or start wearing that damn hearing aid the doctor tried to give me. It's not the end of the world."

"It may not be the end of the world," Riggs agrees, "but it's the end of something you're holding onto with both hands that you don't want to let go of, and I completely understand that. Of course, you're scared, and it's okay to be angry, but no matter what happens, you're never going to live in a silent world where you are alone, not as long as we're all still living in it with you."

"Fuck, Riggs, cut that shit out," he says, swiping his eyes again. Even with my feelings numbed, their exchange tightens my chest.

His partner?—Boyfriend?—speaks next. "Yeah, so I haven't really focused much on myself this week because I've been worried about Brandt. I'm not really worried that he'll lose his hearing because it doesn't matter to me either way. I know he'll be fine. Just another bump we've got to roll over. I'm just worried that he'll get down and lose hope, and that I won't be strong enough to carry him through it like he does for me on my darkest days." He gives a self-deprecating laugh. "Yeah, so somehow I've managed to make this all about me instead of Brandt. Because I'm a selfish bastard."

"No, you're not," Brandt insists, taking his hand again. "We're in this together, forever." He brushes his thumb over the ring covering Brandt's finger. "Three legs. I won't let you fall."

"I know you won't. We're a tripod."

I don't know what all that shit means, but it's clearly affecting both of them as they wipe fresh tears from their eyes.

"Mandy? Would you like to go next?" Riggs asks.

He breathes out a heavy sigh, resting his hands on his knees, and leans forward. "It's been a tough week. Brewer keeps telling me to be of service, to get out of my own head, out of my own way, and focus on others. That's the best way I can help myself, and I believe he knows what he's talking about, but all week I've been trying to be of service, to help others, and all it's doing is opening the door for my demons to come back and haunt me, and I'm fucking exhausted and scared and, yeah," he sighs again, "I've had enough."

Is he talking about me? Is my bullshit making his life harder? When he looks sideways at me and swallows guiltily, I know he's talking about me, and I feel his guilt and a good dose of my own flood the hole in my chest where my heart used to be.

Do I have to ruin everything I touch? Everyone I come in contact with, do I make their lives worse?

"I'm not gonna give up. I have faith in Brewer and in myself. I'm stronger than my demons. I'm stronger than my insecurities. I'm going to push through and come out the other side feeling better, and I'll let you know when I get there."

"You're not alone, man," the guys remind him. "We're here for you, Mandy."

Mandy lays his hand on my knee and squeezes, and I feel all

eyes in the room drawn to me as the pressure in my chest tightens. It's my turn, and I really don't want to say a fucking word.

"Sommers? If you have something you'd like to share with the group, now is your chance. If you'd rather not speak this time, that's fine, too. I just want you to know I'm really glad you're here. I've been saving you that seat for a long time, and it fills my heart with joy to see you finally sitting in it. That seat is always going to have your name on it. You're always going to have a place in the circle, so I hope you keep coming back."

"Thanks, Riggs." My voice barely sounds intelligible. "I think I'll pass this week."

And with that, they continue until the meeting comes to an end. Mandy lays his hand on my shoulder. "Come on, your sixty minutes are up. Let's get you home, *Cinderella*, before you turn into a pumpkin."

I follow him out the door and into the hall, almost running into his back when he stops short.

"Hey, Brewer."

"Cahill, I'm so glad I ran into you. I haven't heard from you since our session last week. It was a pretty heavy one and I've been worried about you."

"I'm hanging in there. This is Sergeant Sommers. I dragged him with me to the meeting today."

Stepping around Mandy, I stick my hand out automatically to shake the man's hand, and, as my eyes follow, traveling up his torso to his face, I get stuck. Completely fucking stuck.

My tongue grows thick and dry in my mouth, making me stumble over my words like I have a stutter. "I'm N-Nash. Nashville S-Sommers. Um, Nashville Aiden Sommers, Sergeant Nas—"

He interrupts me with a chuckle, his smile genuine and beautiful. "I get it. Sergeant Nashville Aiden Sommers, but you go by Nash." The twinkle in his amaretto-colored eyes makes them shine. "I'm Brewer Marx. It's my pleasure to meet you, Sergeant."

"Do you go here?"

"You could say that. I'm a therapist here. I specialize in addiction and trauma, and I run the addiction support group next door to the one you were just in."

"A-Addiction support group?" Of course there has to be a flaw somewhere.

"Yep, anytime you want to come join us, you're welcome. Even if you just want to sit in the very back with your head down, and just listen. And if you ever want to talk, one-on-one, my door is always open."

I realize I'm still holding onto the man's hand when he tries to retrieve it. I brush my thumb over his knuckles before letting him go. His skin is soft and warm and free of a ring, and the last thing I want to do is let go of him.

"One-on-one? I'll keep that in mind."

"Come on, Casanova. Let's get going," Mandy urges, tugging on my sleeve.

Yet my feet remain rooted in place. The longer I stare into his eyes, the more the gold flecks in his irises resemble shining stars.

Jesus fuck, I must really be high.

Mandy tugs harder, and I stumble after him, calling out over my shoulder as I steal one last glance, "Good to meet you, Brewer."

"What the fuck was that?" Mandy hisses in my ear.

"What?" I ask, truly confused.

"You and him making eyes at each other. You suddenly forgetting how to speak."

Oh, that. "We weren't making eyes at each other." I won't mention the way his glisten.

"Yeah, you were. Look, this isn't about liking guys, I couldn't give two fucks. This is about Brewer. That guy has been through some shit, and it took him a long time to get it together and come out the other side. He's in a good place, and you're not. Your head is a fucking mess, and your life is a shit show right now, and neither of you needs that kind of distraction."

"Chill the fuck out, Mandy. All I did was introduce myself. You're the one that dragged my ass here against my will."

"You're right, I did. Because I care. Which is why I don't wanna see you get in over your head with a guy like Brewer. Or any guy, for that matter. Right now, you just need to focus on yourself."

"Yes, sir," I sneer with a mock salute. "Trust me, I'm not thinking with my dick. It probably doesn't even work thanks to all these pills and stress."

But my imagination works fine. And I can't help but think I'll be imagining Brewer for days to come.

BREWER

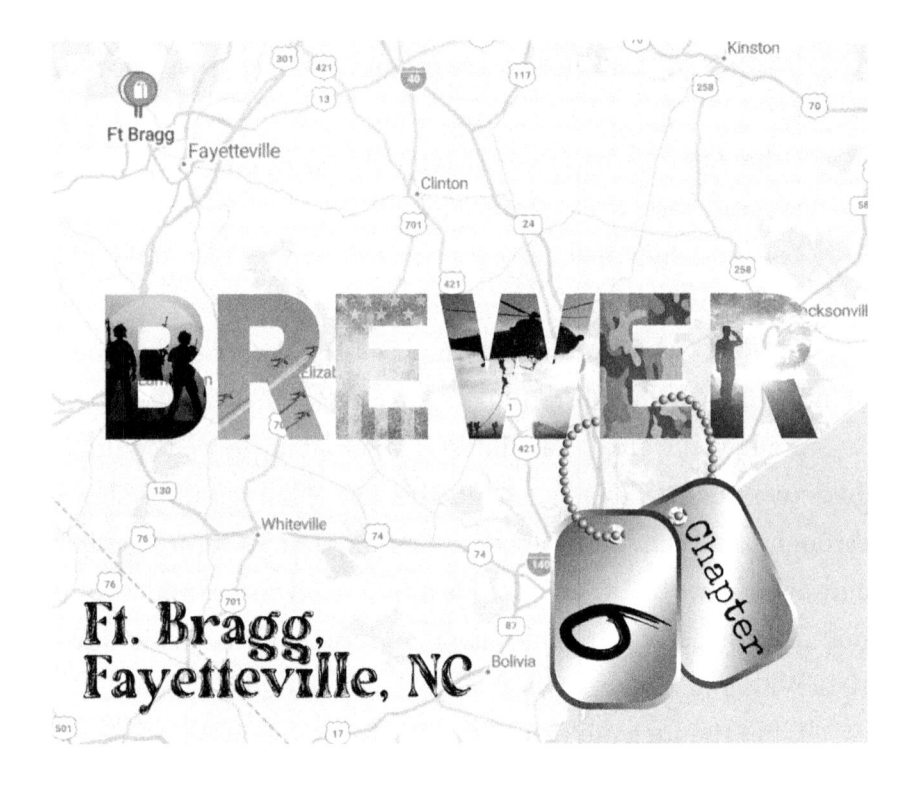

Ft. Bragg, Fayetteville, NC

Chapter 6

"Take a seat, and I'll get you a drink."

Attending these functions isn't high on my list of entertaining ways to spend my weekend, but when a patient asks for help, I can't say no.

She squeezes my hand, her gold wedding ring glinting under the fluorescent lights. "Thank you, Brewer."

Then again, I knew Nash would be here.

Yesterday, when the gorgeous *G.I. Joe* look-alike introduced himself to me, I knew who he was right away. But I wasn't prepared for the awareness between us, the way his eyes stuck to mine, or how his hand became sweaty in my grip. He brushed his thumb across my knuckles, like he was caressing my skin. It felt intimate. If I close my eyes, I can still feel the heat of his touch.

Unfortunately, I can also see the way his eyes looked, unfocused and glassy, with dilated pupils. Most likely his clammy hand was a side effect of the pills he'd taken, and not the spark between us that I probably imagined.

As I stand in line at the buffet table, my eyes make a circuit of the room, trying to pick him out in the crowd. Bypassing the fruit and cheese platters and a bowl of something I can't identify, I load the paper plate with fried chicken and pasta salad, and as I make my way back to the table, I spot him. Nash isn't among the crowd, he's sitting alone in the corner. Either he's resting his eyes, trying to find a moment of peace among the noise, or he's passed out.

With years of experience under my belt, both professional and personal, I can spot an addict a mile away, and without a doubt, Sergeant Nashville Aiden Sommers is an addict.

Not that that surprises me. Considering all that he's suffered through, I can understand him looking for an outlet to cope with his pain. The mind can only endure so much before it turns on itself or shuts down. Nash had found a way to shut it down before it turned on him, but abusing that crutch was a slippery slope to addiction, and Nash is sliding headfirst in that direction, if he's not already at the bottom of the hill.

Sliding the plate in front of my companion, I take the seat next to her as she looks over the food I chose.

"It all looks delicious, Brewer. I can't thank you enough for joining me today. I don't know if I would have had the courage to do this alone."

"I would never have asked you to do this alone."

My eyes stray to the solitary man in the corner, the man doing it alone. This day is just as tough for him as it is for my patient, yet nobody is holding his hand, or propping him up, lending him their strength.

God, he's so fucking strong and brave and incredible.

He probably doesn't see any of that, but he has to be to even sit here.

"Excuse me for a moment," I say to my patient before pushing to my feet.

As I'm crossing the room, a child approaches him, a little boy no more than seven or eight years old. So far, he's the only person here brave enough to approach Nash, not that I blame these people for not knowing what to say to him. His presence is a reminder of the risk their spouses are exposed to every day. Quickening my steps, I get close enough to overhear their conversation. Nash looks panicked and confused.

"Do you know my daddy, sir? He dresses just like you do. Do you work with him?"

"I don't know. W-Who's your daddy?"

"John. John Whittemore."

Nash's face can't hide the stark pain he feels. It's written all over his face so clearly that even I can feel it standing six feet away.

"Yeah," he croaks, his voice barely there. "I know your daddy. I worked with him."

"Can you tell my daddy I said hello?"

"I'll try. Your daddy is a brave man. A good man. Don't ever forget that."

He's about two seconds away from breaking down. It's in his unsteady voice and watery eyes, and his gaze finds me over the boy's shoulder, begging me, pleading for an interruption, for a life preserver.

"Let's go find your mom," I offer, laying my hand on the boy's shoulder.

"She's in line getting food. I'll go get her," the boy says, running off before I can follow.

"Brewer," he breathes, "you're here." I take the seat next to him, turning my body towards his. "I mean, why are you here? What are you doing here?"

Biting back my smile, I realize this is the second time he's become tongue tied around me. It's becoming a habit. "I was invited by one of my patients. This is a hard day for her, and she didn't want to face it alone."

My words barely register on him. Instead, all of his attention is focused on my face, on my eyes and my mouth, despite the distracting noise and chatter echoing off the cinderblock walls of the battalion's basement. His awareness and his scrutiny sends a jolt straight to my nuts. Like a lighthouse shining its beacon through the dark fog, my words penetrate his brain slowly. Recognition dawns in his icy blue eyes.

"Who is your patient?" He's realizing that it must be someone he works with. Nash follows my gaze to the woman sitting at the table, now surrounded by family members from the unit, but my gaze returns to him, waiting for his reaction.

"Violet Gutierrez."

A choked desperate sound crawls out of his throat, and he squeezes his eyes closed, like he's trying to block out painful images. And then, at the worst possible time, someone's service dog begins to bark, the sound echoing like a shrill alarm throughout the basement. Nash grabs his head, his large frame rocking back-and-forth as he tries in vain to block the sound. My heart beats in triple time as he begins to growl—there's really no other way to describe the sound coming from his mouth—and I realize he's losing it. He's about to fall apart in front of all these people.

Leaning in close so my voice is in his ear, I ask with gentle urgency, "Nash, listen to my voice. Can I touch you?"

I almost miss that he's nodding his head with the way his body is rocking and shaking.

"Nash, you're not alone. I'm here with you. Right here," I reassure, squeezing one hand as I wrap my other arm around his shoulder. To anyone else, it looks like a simple embrace, a friendly hug. His skin has a natural musk that I breathe into my lungs, and I immediately want to take another hit of him.

"Take a deep breath, Nash. Stay with me right here in the present. In the here, and the now, in the battalion headquarters basement. Take a deep breath and hold it in your lungs. Feel them burn as they stretch. Ten... Nine..." I count back the numbers slowly, giving him time to get a hold of himself. "Eight... Seven... breathe out slowly. Open your eyes, Nash. Look at me. Look into my eyes."

His baby blues snap open and lock onto me and everything around us, the noise, the hustle and bustle, fades into the background as we become the only two people in the room. He looks panicked, desperate, a fine sheen of sweat breaking out over his brow. "Take another deep breath and hold it in your lungs."

When I see his chest expand and his shoulders rise, I begin to count. "Six... Five... Feel your heartbeat slow down with my counting. Four... breathe out one more breath, Nash. Breathe with me. Good, hold it. Three... Two... One..."

I squeeze his shoulder and his hand as he blows out a rush of warm air against my cheek. The sour stench of alcohol teases my nose, a familiar and unwelcome scent. "Slow, steady breaths." His throat works furiously as he stares at my face. "Slow and steady." I pass my hand over his chest, and I can feel his heart beating through his T-shirt, trying to claw its way through his ribs. "Slow and steady, Nash. Breathe with me." He nods. "You're safe. I've got you, you're not alone." He nods again, his thumb rubbing over the worn and dirty cord wrapped around his finger.

"What is she doing here?"

"She's going through a hard time. Not only did she lose her son, but she also lost her husband. Sitting home alone isn't doing her any good, so I suggested she come and be surrounded by people who knew him. People who can offer her support."

"Her husband? He died?"

"Shortly after losing their son, Alfred's heart gave out from the heartbreak and the stress. He was a patient of mine, healing from his own war wounds. Violet sought me out for counsel and help after she lost him."

"She lost both of them?" He seems to be stuck on that fact.

"She did."

His gaze constantly darts back-and-forth between Violet and me. I can still feel his rapid heartbeat beneath my palm, and I worry that he's taking in too much information too quickly. My goal is to keep him calm, but there's really no way to do that while having this conversation.

"Is she—Is she okay?"

"Not yet. She's suffering and struggling, like you. But she will be because she's not afraid to ask for help." Nash catches the meaning behind my pointed look. Worry doesn't begin to describe how I feel about him right now. His world must be spinning in circles in his head, making him dizzy and disoriented with panic and confusion.

"Did you know who I was when we met yesterday?"

I take a deep breath into my lungs before I can answer. "Yes, as soon as you told me your name, I recognized you."

"But you didn't say anything."

Trust is imperative in any relationship, whether it's a friendship, a working relationship, or a doctor-patient relationship, and no matter what kind of relationship Nash and I develop, I want it to begin with the truth. I want him to trust me.

"I didn't because I didn't know how to bring it up." Nash looks away first, his gaze settling on that string wrapped around his finger. "Nash? It doesn't matter if I recognized you or not. It doesn't matter if I know your story before you tell it to me. I was honored and pleased to meet you, and I hope that someday you'll tell me your story in your own words. I hope that someday we can be friends."

It feels like minutes pass instead of just seconds before he lifts his eyes to mine. "I thought we already are."

"We are," I breathe in a whisper. "You can trust me."

"How did you do that? How did you pull me out of it like that?"

"I've learned tools for coping with PTS. If you come and see me one-on-one in my office, I can teach you how to do it."

"Can I meet with her?"

A heavy breath passes my lips. "Not today. I think she's been through enough today, and so have you. This isn't the time or the place." Somewhere behind me, a baby cries, a cell phone rings, and someone drops a dish and everyone claps, further proving my point. "Someday, when you're both ready, we'll sit down together in a quiet place, and I'll mediate."

"Does she even want to meet with me? Has she asked about me?" His heartbeat has slowed to a normal rhythm, and I drop my hand from his chest, instantly missing the warmth from his body.

"She has," I admit, "but I think Violet is afraid of learning what she doesn't yet know. I think she's also afraid of bringing you more pain. I don't think you have the tools yet that you need in order to cope with that kind of pain, which is why I really want you to come and see me."

When Nash nods, I add, "I'd really like to take you home, but first I'd like to get you something to eat."

"I'm not really hungry."

"I know. I knew you'd say that. But you can't take those pills you're taking on an empty stomach. They'll cause an ulcer, eventually. Let me get you a plate."

"Don't leave," he pleads, grabbing my hands.

"Okay, then why don't you come with me and help me pick out what you like?"

I can tell it's the last thing he wants to do, but he doesn't argue, and he lets me pull him to his feet. The buffet line is full, and a couple of kids dart past us, playing a game of chase, crashing into Nash's bad leg. His knee buckles, and he almost loses his balance until I catch him in my arms.

"Can we just leave? I've gotta get out of here."

"Yeah, just let me take care of Violet."

His expression transforms from physical pain to emotional, as if he's forgotten about her in the ten seconds it took us to stand in line. His head is truly a mess.

Nash doesn't wait around. I catch up with him in the parking lot, limping along at a snail's pace. He follows me to my car.

"In the morning, Mandy can drive you to work, and you can take your car home."

"I'm off tomorrow. It can wait until Monday." Whatever that string is tied around his finger, it holds all of his attention. "Is Mrs. G going to be okay?"

"Yes. One of the wives is taking her home shortly. She'll be fine."

Nash stares absently out the window. "I'm worried about her. She must be in so much pain."

What about your pain? "I think she feels the same way about you, Nash."

Everything about Nash brings out the worst of my caretaking tendencies and my savior complex. I've talked many patients through their flashbacks, but I've never hugged any of them, never felt that stirring in my gut that I felt today when his eyes dropped to my lips. I've never breathed in someone's scent and wanted more.

Nashville Sommers is dangerous for me.

If I'm not careful, he could be at the bottom of my next bottle. I know better than to think I can save anyone. I can't. I'm powerless over other people. They have to save themselves. All I can do is plant the seed and be there when they hit rock bottom.

He needs to eat, and he needs to rest.

Making a quick detour, I drive through a fast food restaurant and order a strawberry shake and a large fry.

"Here," I shove the shake at him, "try that."

His first sip is hesitant, but he quickly finishes off the entire shake before starting on the hot, greasy fries.

"God, that's good. How did you know?"

A knowing smile twists my lips. "I've been where you are, Nash. It's hard to process food when your stomach is torn up from pills and alcohol and stress. The shake is the perfect thing. But the fries? Alcohol makes you crave salty foods."

He wipes his greasy fingers on his cargo pants. "You said we're friends, and I want to be, I do, but we're on unequal footing, and the difference between us is too large. I'm a fucking mess and you can see every single one of my flaws. You don't want to be my friend. You just want to save me."

"Isn't that what friends do? Save your ass when your head is buried too far inside of it to save yourself?"

"Are you saying my head is buried up my ass?" A hint of a smile teases his lips. It's the first time he's actually looked at me this entire drive.

"Do I really have to say it for you?"

When I pull into the parking lot, Nash hesitates. "You don't have to come in. I'm a big boy, Brewer."

"Cut the sarcasm. I'm just going to help you inside. I'm not staying."

I remember wanting to push everyone away, to keep everyone at arm's length so I could hide all of my dirty secrets under the rug. He doesn't have to hide his secrets from me. I already know what they are.

I wasn't prepared for what I saw when he opened the door. There wasn't a fucking thing in his apartment. Not a chair or a rug or a picture. No couch, no TV, nothing. I expected a neglected mess, unfolded laundry, and unwashed dishes in the sink. I wasn't expecting… Nothing.

"I love what you've done with the place."

"Your personality isn't your best quality," he returns snidely, dropping his keys on the empty counter.

"Mind if I use your bathroom?"

"Go right ahead," he offers, pointing down the hall.

After I relieve myself and wash my hands, I peek inside his medicine cabinet and find the only cabinet likely stocked in this entire apartment. A cocktail of prescription drugs lines every shelf. I recognize most of the labels. Anti-anxiety, antidepressants, blood pressure, heartburn and nausea, migraines, sedatives, muscle relaxers, supplements, erectile dysfunction, and stool softeners. He's a fucking mess. Most of these manage side effects from other meds, and all of them are directly related to his trauma. If he hadn't been in captivity, he wouldn't need any of these meds.

It's a fucking tragedy and a shame.

But it doesn't excuse his behavior. He's abusing these drugs, and he's abusing his body.

When I emerge from the bathroom, Nash looks worse for wear. He's holding onto the counter like it's the only thing keeping him upright. Next to his hand is a prescription bottle.

"I think I need to go lie down," he mumbles, sounding barely coherent.

Jesus Christ, how many did he swallow?

He lets go of the counter and stumbles, and I rush to steady him. "I don't need your help," he gripes, pushing me away. "This is why I moved out here, to get away from everyone."

"It's called a geographical cure, and it's bullshit. You can move five hundred times, but no matter where you go, there you are. You're still stuck with yourself, and *you're* the problem, not the people around you trying to help you."

"You've got all the answers, don't you, Brewer? Do you know how to fix my fucking head?"

His nasty tone doesn't intimidate me one bit. It just tells me how much he's hurting that he's lashing out at me. "There is no fixing your head, only learning how to live with it. You can keep running, and running, and running, keep hiding, but the shit you're running and hiding from is always going to chase you, and it's always going to find you because it lives inside your head. You can't escape from it. That's why you need to learn how to live with it." As we move down the hall, he balances by throwing a hand against the wall. "Let me help you, Nash. Let me in."

"In my head?" He laughs sarcastically. "Not a fucking chance. Trust me, that's not a place you want to be."

"Please, Nash. Trust in me. Let me into your darkest nightmare. Let me sit beside you and hold your hand so you're not alone."

"You're really trying for that martyrdom, aren't you? You can't save everyone, Brewer."

Usually, I have all the patience in the world when it comes to my patients and recovering addicts, but Nash isn't recovering, he's just pissing me the fuck off. Can't he see what he's doing to himself and to others? How can he be so utterly blind?

My patience snaps, and I push him against the wall, getting right up in his face. "Look at you, it's killing you."

"It's not the drugs that are killing me, it's everything I love, it's killing me from within, slowly, day-by-day."

No! He's not getting off the hook with his poor-me bullshit. "You're a selfish bastard! When you destroy yourself, you're not your only victim. Every action has a consequence. The guy next door? The one with the huge heart who keeps showing up for you? He's got his own shit to deal with. You're not the only man who's gone to war and come back broken. There's a whole goddamn club of us and you can join anytime you fucking like. Membership is free. If something happens to you? Mandy will not be okay. The last thing he needs is another death on his conscience, a death he's not responsible for. But you can bet he'll feel like he is. And I'm not gonna let you do it to him. Nor to me. Or anyone else who cares about you."

Leaning back, I let go of him, but I'm not backing off. "I'm taking your pills and giving them to Mandy."

"You can't fucking do that!"

"I'd like to see you try and stop me. If you need to take a sedative or a pain killer, go next-door and see your new med tech. He's going to make sure you've eaten properly first, and he's only going to give you the prescribed dose. If you want to keep running and hiding, you'll have to figure out another way to do it."

He doesn't try to stop me as I make my grand exit, snatching up the pills from the counter and stomping out the door, slamming it shut behind me.

NASH

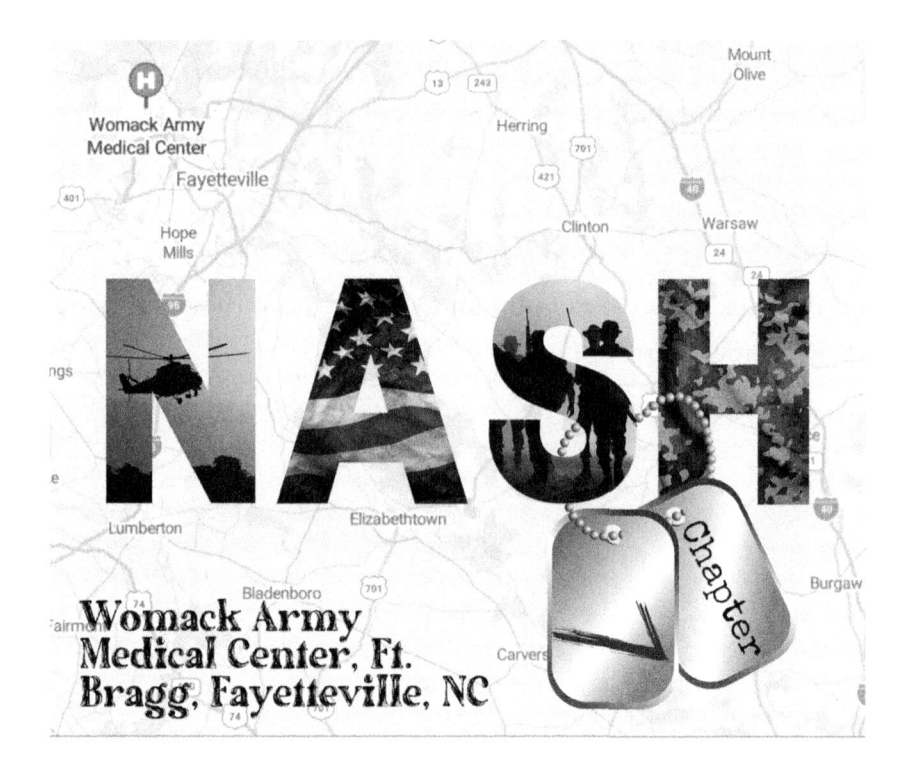

Chapter 7

Womack Army Medical Center, Ft. Bragg, Fayetteville, NC

Shortly after he slams my front door shut, I crash face first into bed. Fuck him. Fuck all the people he says I'm supposed to carefully consider before I hurt myself. I never asked any of them to care about me.

"He's gone," I murmur, reaching out for the solid presence of the body next to me. "It's just us now." Thanks to the black out curtains over my windows, I can't see a damn thing but a shadowy lump. "I've got you."

My fingers rub over the worn cotton T-shirt in a self-soothing gesture as my eyelids become heavy and drift closed. I don't even have the strength to fight the drowsiness, nor do I want to. I just want to float away until I become part of the shadows, hiding in the corners of my bedroom. The old familiar melody falls from my lips, like an unconscious thought, humming myself to sleep.

"The sun will come out tomorrow."

Day 15 of captivity

Collapsed in a heap and clinging to each other for solace, my fingers scratched soothingly over his dry scalp.

"When I die, don't let them take me from you. I don't want to leave you alone, and I don't want them to have me," Gutierrez rasped. His breathing sounded labored, his skin flushed with cold sweat.

"You're not gonna die. We're gonna get out of here and get you the help you need."

Either he doesn't hear me or he doesn't want to. "Promise me," he pleads desperately. "Promise me you won't let them have me."

"I promise, G. I've got you. I won't let go."

His body shook constantly, like he was cold, and I tugged him closer, sharing the warmth of my body. For some reason, my mind was stuck on a song I learned in my childhood, from the movie Annie. I began to hum until I hit the chorus, whispering the words softly in his ear. "The sun will come out tomorrow. You can bet that tomorrow there will be sunshine."

My words blocked out the screeching and scurrying rats, the barking dogs, and the shouting terrorists. It blocked out everything until there was just Gutierrez and me.

His harsh breaths evened out, and when he finally closed his eyes, he never opened them again. His body couldn't fight any longer against the sepsis that ravaged him. I felt some small solace in the fact that amidst this nightmarish hell, his final moments were spent dreaming of warmth and sunshine, of hope and healing.

I held onto him for what seemed like days but was probably only one. The silence was deafening. I could hear the rats coming closer, becoming braver. Their squeaking sounded like nails, sliding across a chalkboard, setting my teeth on edge. They nibbled at his gangrenous foot, and when the guards came, not even checking to see if he was alive or dead, they dumped buckets of icy water over our disgusting bodies, washing away the piss and feces, and the sweat and the dirt, leaving us in a cold muddy puddle of filth. It took the rest of my strength to drag him a few feet over to a patch of dry dirt.

Over and over, I rocked his body, cradling him to me, running my fingers through his dirty, wet hair, continuing to hum, holding onto him tightly, never letting go. When his body grew cold and stiff in my arms, I finally gave in to the tears I'd been storing inside of me for days. My body was wracked with anguished sobs, violent and ugly and broken.

One-by-one, I kicked the rats away from him as they tried to steal pieces of his rotting corpse, and I prayed, and I prayed, and I prayed some more, to whatever God was still listening, that we be saved before our captors dragged his body away from me and desecrated it beyond recognition.

. . .

For two days and two nights, I stay in bed tossing and turning in a cold sweat, caught in a never-ending nightmare. My body is wracked with chills and pain, and my head throbs. I can't even consider keeping food down with the nausea that grips my stomach in knots. I piss myself, just like in my nightmare, just like I did back when they held me beneath the ground. Behind my eyelids, I relive that dark hell. That giant old oak tree outside my hospital window in Germany comes back to me, its roots digging deep into the earth to wrap around my body and entomb me six feet below the ground, in a dirt coffin made of terror.

It's the pounding on the door that finally wakes me. I think the sound is coming from inside of my head, until they break the fucking thing down, knocking it off its hinges.

"Jesus Christ," Mandy wails just before I lose consciousness again.

My world stays dark, clips of my life playing like a movie in my head. Clips of every failure, every folly, every time I fucked up, ingrained in my memory forever, playing on an endless loop so that I never forget.

When I finally open my eyes, I'm rewarded with a light so bright it's painful.

Great, they thought of new ways to torture me.

"I'm back in hell," I croak, straining to bring the room into focus.

"Nah, just the hospital." *I know that voice. It belongs to...* "You know, if you missed me that bad, you could've just come to see me, you didn't have to go and get yourself admitted."

Liza.

Even though my vision is still blurry, I can make out the monitors next to my bed, and the tall square shape of Liza's rolling med cart.

"Tilt your head back, Sergeant." Without warning, she drips cold liquid in my eyes, and I squeeze them tightly shut, making the eyedrops roll down my cheeks. Next, she smears petroleum jelly on my dry cracked lips before wrapping a blood pressure cuff around my arm. The damn thing squeezes the blood from my limb, causing it to go numb with tingles.

"Everything looks good. Despite your best efforts to take yourself out of the game."

Take myself out of what game? I wasn't trying to kill myself. I was just trying to... Not exist. Doesn't she understand the difference?

"I've given you several different meds through your IV. Would you like a run down?"

"I don't care what you pump in me."

"Well, maybe you should, Sergeant. Maybe you should start taking better care of yourself, so I don't have to do it for you. And by the way, my friend says that the front door is coming out of your security deposit."

And the punches keep on coming.

"You have a visitor, so I'll leave you two alone. I'll be back shortly with your dinner. In case you're wondering what's on the menu, you're on a liquid diet."

Why can't she just knock me unconscious again?

Before she leaves, I call out, "Hey, what happened to me?"

"You're detoxing. Most likely you had a couple of episodes, and it raised your blood pressure through the roof. You came to a couple of times, but you were hallucinating. Something about tree roots and rats," she shrugs.

Before I can even wonder who my visitor is, his large body fills the doorframe, sucking all of the energy out of the room. The look on his face reminds me of dark storm clouds and thunder.

"We need to talk," Brewer demands in a no-nonsense tone. He closes the door behind Liza and takes a seat next to my bed.

The pain in my head doubles, pounding at my skull like a jackhammer. "I didn't take any more meds after you left. I didn't OD. I swear it."

The frown on his face softens somewhat. "I know you didn't. This is what withdrawals feel like. That isn't what I want to talk to you about."

I can feel it coming, that sense that he's about to turn my world upside down.

"I found something."

While he searches for the right words, my heart beats a mile a minute, causing the alarms on my monitor to scream.

Did he go into my bedroom?

"You need to stay calm," he insists, scooting closer to my bedside.

How in the fuck can I stay calm when he's about to have me committed to the psych ward?

"Do you want to try that breathing thing again?"

"No, I just want you to fucking spit it out. What did you find? You had no fucking right to find anything because you shouldn't have been inside my bedroom." His dark gaze narrows and I realize I said the wrong word, quickly amending, "I mean inside of my home when you weren't invited in."

"Were the EMTs supposed to wait for an engraved invitation? You could have died. You could've had a stroke or a heart attack. You were this fucking close," he bites off, holding his thumb and forefinger together. "Mandy called me in a panic, not knowing what he should do. I warned you not to let your actions become his consequences. I will not let your death be put on his conscience. So yeah," he seethes, leaning forward, "I went into your bedroom, and you know exactly what I found."

I can't swallow, hell, I can barely breathe. My throat is closing, my tongue becoming thick in my dry mouth.

Brewer just shakes his head, at a loss for words. "What the fuck, Nash? What in the goddamn fuck? What were you doing with that thing?" he hisses.

Embarrassment and shame drown my voice.

"What were you doing?" he repeats.

Hot tears gather in my eyes. I've never hated myself more than I do at this moment. "Nothing! I was just trying to... He made me promise I wouldn't leave him... But they took him from me, when we were rescued, they took him from me and separated us, and I never saw him again. I just... I needed to..."

Brewer slips his hand in mine. "You needed to feel close to him. You needed the solace of thinking he was still with you."

Nodding, I swipe the tears from my cheeks with the hand he's not holding. "What did you do with him?"

"It was just a bunch of his clothes stuffed into his uniform. I washed everything and folded it and packed it away in a box. When you're ready, you can give it back to his mother."

My Gutierrez lump is gone. He's truly gone. And now I'm completely alone.

"You can't go back there, Nash. You can't live alone right now."

I know he's right, but I can't make sense of anything right now. My head feels overloaded, and I just can't think.

"I want you to come live with me. Just for a little while until your blood pressure lowers and you're feeling stronger and able to make better decisions."

Move in with him? Is he fucking kidding me? Move in with the man who's consumed my thoughts since the moment I met him? Sign me the fuck up.

"I like the sound of that," I say, squeezing his hand.

Brewer chuckles. "I'll remind you of that when you see where I live."

How could it be worse than my empty shell of an apartment?

"I'll wrap it up because you have other visitors, but I'll be back to get you tomorrow."

Other visitors? Brewer moves his chair back to the corner and my heart drops. I don't want to see him go. He has to be the only person I can say that about. "Hey, what about work? How much trouble am I in?"

"Your chain of command almost listed you as AWOL when you didn't report in. It's been taken care of. They know you're in the hospital." I breathe a sigh of relief, and he smiles. "They're doing everything they can to fast track your retirement."

"It doesn't feel like it."

"Trust me, they want you off their hands before you do something stupid enough to make things uncomfortable for them. Nobody wants to throw a POW in the brig. It doesn't look good. You're a national fucking hero."

Go fucking figure. Me, a national hero.

"Good night, Nash." His voice is soft, like a caress that soothes my neediness caused by his leaving.

Brewer pushes past my visitors, and they file in one-by-one, their large bodies swallowing up all the space in my tiny room, until it's bursting with Bitches.

Wardell slaps a plastic zip-locked bag in my lap. "We brought you boiled hotdogs. It's a gift from McCormick." All the Bitches laugh, except McCormick.

"I didn't make those!" His cheeks are almost as red as his hair. "I told you, it's not as weird as you make it out to be. Lots of people like their hotdogs boiled."

Stiles claps him on the back. "Settle down, carrot stick. Can't you take a joke?"

"No, but for real, we got you something you might actually use." West or Wardell, whatever he goes by, drops a canvas bag in my lap. The logo says Bitches with Stitches: healing hearts one stitch at a time. When I peek inside I find several skeins of yarn, different types of knitting needles, and some handwritten instructions which I'm definitely going to need. I mean, if these guys keep showing up and harassing me, I guess I'm going to have to learn how to knit.

McCormick grabs the hot dogs from my lap. "Shit, if no one else wants them, I'll eat them. If I don't have to buy myself dinner, I can afford to go drinking after this. You want to come?" he asks the big bearded bear next to him.

"You know I can't drink after nine on a work night."

"Anyway," Wardell continues, shaking his head. "We heard you were having a bad day, and that's what Bitches do. We show up for each other on the bad days."

I can't explain the heavy weight settling in my chest. I don't even fucking know these guys, so why do I care? "But I'm not a Bitch. I only came to one meeting. I wasn't even going to…"

"You weren't going to come back? Yeah, we figured, that's why we had to hunt you down. Trust me, you're coming back, even if we have to drag your damn ass kicking and screaming."

"But why? You don't even know me."

It's his partner, Brandt, or Aguilar, whatever, that answers.

"Yeah, we do. We know who you are, Nash. You're a soldier. You fought the same war we did. You bleed red, just like we do. You suffered and sacrificed for your country, just like we have. We know exactly who the fuck you are. You're a Bitch. And when a Bitch has a bad day, the Bitches show up and support him."

"Hell yeah," they all shout, including McCormick, who has his mouth stuffed full of hot dogs.

I notice Mandy and the guy with the mohawk, Jax, are the quiet ones in the bunch.

"I heard you weren't coming back home," Mandy says.

He actually sounds disappointed. The fuck if I know why because I've given him nothing but grief since he met me.

"I'm going to stay with a friend for a while."

"Well, I guess it's a good thing your apartment is empty and you don't own anything. Less shit to move."

Liza pushes her way into the packed room, elbowing the hulking vets aside like they're children. When she makes her way to my bedside, she freezes. "Wardell? How do you know Nash?"

"We run in the same circles," he says with a smirk.

"I should have known the two most stubborn men I've ever met are friends. Looks like Brandt is taking good care of you."

"Real good care," a couple of the guys chide.

"Yeah, he's been keeping a close eye on me lately," West teases, looking his partner up and down with intent.

One thing I have to say about these guys, I admire their sense of humor. Sure, they sit around and bitch once a week and get deep into their feelings, but the rest of the time? They keep things light, positive, and try to lift each other up. If I have no choice but to be around people, these guys are exactly what I need.

"Visiting hours are over, guys. Come back tomorrow. Nash needs his beauty sleep," Liza orders. When the last Bitch files out, she cleans up my half-eaten dinner tray. "At least I don't have to worry about you when you go home tomorrow. You've surrounded yourself with good friends, and I'm relieved you're in good hands. Those guys won't let you down."

Chapter 8

Black Mountain, NC

"What the hell is this place?"

To say Nash is less than thrilled with my living arrangements would be an understatement. Actually, saying it's an understatement would be understating it.

"This is my home." It's hard not to laugh. I played a dirty trick on him. His reaction could be a lot worse.

"You live here?"

"Actually, I own it."

Serenity House is my home in every sense of the word. The large two-story beige Craftsman with the covered porch and red door is also home to three other men.

"What is this place?"

"Serenity House is a halfway house for recovering addicts

and alcoholics. The three men that live here with me are also veterans."

"That's so quaint," he snaps. "Could you please take me back home?"

"You are home, Nash."

"No, to the apartment I was staying at."

"You're not going back there until—"

"I know," he breathes out in frustration, "until I can make better decisions."

"Until you're stronger." His heavy sigh sounds like defeat, and maybe acceptance. "Let me show you around."

Nash climbs out of the car, slamming the door behind him, and reaches into the backseat for his rucksack, slinging it over his shoulder. "What are the rules here?"

"Curfew is ten o'clock on weekdays, eleven on weekends. Everyone that lives here has to stay clean and sober. We also take turns with chores to keep the place clean and maintained. Everyone cooks for themselves and buys their own food unless we're having a family dinner."

"*Family* dinner?"

"Yes, like you have the Bitches? These men have each other. We are a family."

"Great, more bleeding hearts," he mumbles.

Chuffing, I shake my head. Nash is so full of shit. He has a bleeding heart as well, buried beneath all the emotional scars. Sooner or later, I'm going to help him realize that.

Nash follows me inside, where I show him around the first floor. "The dining room, living room, and kitchen are common spaces that we share. There's also a covered porch outback. Two bedrooms and a bathroom on this floor, and three bedrooms upstairs with a shared bathroom."

"Am I upstairs or downstairs?"

"With your injured leg still healing, it's a good thing you're downstairs. Tex, Nacho, and Miles bunk upstairs."

"So you share the downstairs with me?"

My pulse kicks. *Oh, Nash, that look in your eye gives you away. You're interested in me, and you're a danger to my recovery. And my peace of mind.*

"Actually, you're on your own. I live downstairs in the renovated basement. I have everything I need down there. A bathroom, a kitchen, a sitting area, and my own laundry."

I have to will myself not to laugh as the light dims from his gorgeous blue eyes.

"Let me make you something to eat. I've got your meds. Then we'll get you squared away in your room."

"Brewer?" he asks as I turn away. "You really think this place is going to work for me?"

"Just remember, it works if you work it. If you want to get better, you will. Just don't give up on yourself, and don't give up on the people trying to help you."

Nash scoffs and shakes his head. "You're a walking cliché."

"Maybe I am, but everything I'm telling you makes sense, and it's the truth. Maybe you should start paying attention."

In the kitchen, Nash casually leans against the counter as I move around, preparing a simple meal of minestrone soup and grilled cheese sandwiches. It's not much, but he's coming off of a liquid diet and I don't know how solid his stomach is yet.

"You don't have to be back to work until the day after tomorrow, which means as soon as you wake up tomorrow morning, you're mine."

"Excuse me?" He chokes, and I realize my words sounded mildly inappropriate.

"Your day belongs to me. You go where I go, no questions asked."

"I'm game."

Plating the sandwiches, we move to the table, taking seats across from each other. Nash picks at his food, which is all I expected. When I detoxed, I also had zero appetite. It was all I could do to crawl out of bed and exist. His attention is divided between sneaking covert glances at me and toying with that string tied around his thumb. It's always there, and I can't help but feel like it carries bad memories.

"What is that? Did that belong to him? Is it his bootlace or something?" Nash startles, his gaze falling on his thumb, and his expression tells me everything I need to know. "Hand it over."

"Not a chance."

He becomes guarded and stubborn. I have a feeling Nash can be the most stubborn man I know.

"I'm not asking, I'm telling you. Hand it over." His dark blond brows slash down like two angry lightning bolts. "I'll make you a trade. You can have this instead, and I'll keep that safe for you."

Reaching into my back pocket, I pull out my own special keepsake, something I always carry with me. It isn't something I ever thought I would let go of, but offering it to Nash feels...so right.

"What's this?" He flips it over, reading the logo on the plastic poker chip.

"A white chip. It means surrender. It's meant to be a reminder of your struggle. The poker chip symbolizes that when we use drugs and alcohol, we're gambling with our lives. Use it as a talisman, to remind you of the hope you have for your future, not the hell from your past, like that bootlace."

"Surrender?"

"Yes, surrender. You better get used to surrendering because every time life gets hard, you're going to have to surrender again and again. Every time you have a nightmare, or a flashback, every time you feel like running away, you'll have to surrender again."

Without saying a word, he pockets the chip in his jeans and finishes off his bowl of soup.

Well, that went better than I'd hoped. We'll see how tomorrow goes.

After clearing the table, I reach for the large plastic zip-sealed bag holding his meds and begin doling them out one by one according to the dosage on the labels.

"Here, now that you've eaten something, take these."

Nash swipes them from my hand and swallows the entire cocktail without even looking to see what I gave him, chasing it with a glass of water.

"Sorry, I forgot this one," I add, grabbing the little egg-shaped brown pill.

This time, maybe because the pill is by itself, he recognizes it, and he becomes angry, roughly grabbing it from my hand.

"I don't need you to dole them out to me like I'm a fucking child," he snaps, swallowing it dry.

Years ago, another lifetime ago, my first reaction would be anger, to become defensive and snap back, but after years of professional training, I've learned to bite back the first words that dangle from the tip of my tongue and practice patience. Putting myself in Nash's position, I try to see things from his perspective. He's embarrassed, maybe even ashamed of the fact that I'm aware of his erectile dysfunction. So many men place false importance on their virility, or what they think is a sign of their virility. It's a crock of shit.

"You know," I muse, taking a seat beside him, "you could have ended up with worse side effects than ED." Nash glares, shooting icy daggers from his pale blue eyes. "Instead of shooting you in the leg, they could have cut your dick off." It's hard to say it with a straight face, so damn hard. "If I were you, I'd be counting my blessings."

Suddenly, his face shifts, like the sun emerging from behind a dark cloud, and his expression brightens. Nash chuckles. "You're something else, Brewer."

"It's perfectly natural, you know that, don't you?"

"There's nothing natural about having a limp dick."

"There is if you've suffered a great trauma. Also, it's a side effect of your high blood pressure meds. If we can bring down your blood pressure, you might be able to stop taking them all together."

"Really?"

"I see you've spent a lot of time researching this."

He laughs again, and I feel like I've been given a gift. Nash has a beautiful smile—even white teeth, full peach lips surrounded by pale stubble, set in a square jaw. I always think of *G.I. Joe* when I look at him. His arresting looks make it hard for me to turn away.

"You can't take those with alcohol, so, if you're not ready to surrender completely, let me know and I will eliminate them from your regimen."

He doesn't answer, just nods his head. "I haven't been taking them. Haven't needed to. It's the last thing on my mind."

"You know, your physical therapist, Navarro Riggs, has a theory about that."

"About limp dicks? Let me guess, he channels the anger and self hatred, which is a side effect of limp dick, into getting his patients to workout harder?"

I can't not laugh at that. Nash has a very dry sense of humor, which he displays at the worst times. "Not exactly. His theory is that libido is a great motivator to recovery. Not everybody wants to get better for the right reasons—"

"But everybody wants to have sex," he finishes.

"Well, not everybody, I guess, but most people do, and to have it, they'll work twice as hard to improve."

The way he studies me makes my heart beat faster. My stomach warms the longer he stares. I know he's thinking about *me*, about having sex with me. My eyes widen, my nostrils flare, giving myself away. He knows he's affecting me, and he smirks, a roguish half grin that makes him look infinitely sexier.

"Yeah, I guess that makes sense. With the right person, sex can be a great motivator."

Take back control, Brewer. Don't give him the upper hand.

"Don't forget, tomorrow, you're mine." *Fuck, way to go, numb nuts. You're making a bad situation worse.*

His roguish smile turns a bit wicked, almost dangerous, and I quickly amend, "Goodnight, Nash." I'm almost out of the kitchen, almost to safety, before I turn back and add, "And no lump buddies in your bed. You need to sleep alone."

Oh my God, just stop fucking talking, you fucknut!

His chuckle follows me out of the room, my face heating with embarrassment.

"Rough night?"

I came in search of Nash this morning, and I found him in the kitchen, hunched over the coffee pot, like he was praying to it, watching the machine percolate drop by slow drop.

"I'm fine," he grumbles.

"You don't look fine."

"Then stop looking!"

The frustration in his voice tells me he's had a long night. A bad night. My heart squeezes painfully. He faced it all alone, without his lump buddy, without the drugs and the alcohol. Nights are the worst. That's when the shadows are the darkest, when the memories creep back in as you're losing consciousness, and your barriers are down. In your sleep, the nightmares hold you hostage.

I don't ever want Nash to feel like a hostage again, not for one more minute of his life.

He fills his mug and cradles it in his hands, like he's trying to leach the warmth from the ceramic into his body. Aromatic steam wafts into his face, and he breathes it in deep.

"It's gonna be a long day," he mutters.

He has no idea how long.

He's in pain. Nash's leg makes it difficult for him to push himself hard during therapy. I'd love to know the story behind his injury, but I don't think he's ready to share that yet. His face is etched into deep lines, the hurt visible in his expression.

"Give me ten more reps," Riggs demands, counting aloud.

"I don't have ten more in me," Nash pants, sweating and breathless.

"Yes, you do, keep going. We're not quitting until we're finished."

"I said I don't," he seethes, spit flying from between his chapped lips.

"Seven... Six... You'll give me five more or we'll start over from the beginning. Five..."

Navarro Riggs has to be the most hated man in this building. He's also one of the most respected. He demands a lot from his patients, and he never lets them quit on themselves.

Nash drops his large frame into another squat, visibly struggling to straighten back up. His leg quivers, he grunts, and I'm convinced he's about to drop the weight bar he's holding across his back and shoulders.

"You can do it, Sergeant. Straighten up!"

I almost feel bad that I'm going to further torture him when he's finished here. *Almost.*

"One more, Sommers. If you hadn't quit on me at Womack, this might not hurt so bad now. Let's go, drop all the way down."

If Nash mortally injures Riggs, I'm going to have to testify that it was well deserved.

"Aagghh!" Nash straightens from his last lunge with a primal war cry of exhaustion and pain, throwing the weight bar down on the ground with a loud clunk. It bounces before rolling to a halt at Riggs' feet.

Riggs clicks his stopwatch. "Great. Now, was that so hard?"

An ill-timed snort escapes my lips as I try to cover my laugh, drawing Nash's glare.

"Are you here for moral support, or are you just gonna sit there and laugh at me?"

Riggs and I exchange a knowing look before I wipe the smirk from my face. "Moral support." Checking my watch, I add, "We've got ten more minutes."

"Until what?" Nash asks, using the hem of his T-shirt to wipe the sweat from his face.

"You're not allowed to ask questions, remember? Just follow my lead."

And ten minutes later, he does. Nash follows me down the long corridor to the classrooms where the support groups are held.

"These guys again?" he gripes.

"We're gonna try something new today."

"What group is this?" he asks, following me into the empty classroom next door to where the Bitches with Stitches meet.

"Step-by-step, a support group for recovering veterans."

"Recovering from what?"

"Don't ask me questions you already know the answers to. These are recovering addicts." Nash rolls his eyes. "Keep your feelings to yourself and treat these people with the respect they deserve."

"It's not that they don't deserve my respect, I just don't want to be here."

"No, you don't want to be one of them. You don't want to admit you have a problem, but I think it's pretty evident, don't you?"

Like a child throwing a tantrum, he crosses his arms over his chest and fixes his face with a petulant look. I would laugh if I weren't so annoyed with him.

Patience, Brewer. He's in denial, fighting what he knows to be true about himself. You were him once, and people showed you patience. You're here to give back what was so freely given to you.

Pulling a deep calming breath into my lungs, I take a seat as men and women begin to file in, filling up the empty chairs in the circle.

"I'm Brewer, and I'm a recovering addict. Welcome to Step-by-Step. I'd like to open the meeting with the serenity prayer before we begin sharing.

"God, grant me serenity to accept the things I cannot change, the courage to change the things I can, and the wisdom to know the difference."

One-by-one, they begin to share, checking in with their current mental state, reliving bad days from the past, and telling us how they're learning to cope now.

One woman shares, "My name is Denise, and I'm an addict. I've been having bad dreams lately, all the stuff I did, and even some stuff I didn't do come back to me every time I close my eyes. And when I'm awake, it's all I can think about. Especially the stuff I didn't do. Why is my brain torturing me with things I haven't done, like I'm paying for mistakes I never made? I'm beginning to obsess over it, and now, it's all I can think of. I don't want to live in a dark place each day, but I just can't get out of my head. I'm stuck in the past. Anyways, thanks for letting me share."

"Thanks for sharing, Denise. I hope you get with someone after the meeting before you go home. Don't take that with you. Would anyone else like to share?"

"My name is John and I'm an addict. When I was using, I fucked up my sinuses and my nose, now I can't breathe for shit. I've got to start wearing this CPAP machine at night. I guess I'm paying for the consequences of my addiction, and it fucking sucks. I don't know, I'm just kind of feeling miserable right now. Thanks for letting me share."

"Thanks for sharing, John. Sometimes our consequences are paid months and even years after we get clean. It doesn't always seem fair to continue to suffer after we've made a decision to turn our lives around, but it's reality. I would suggest making a gratitude list of things that ground you in the moment and remind you of all the benefits of your recovery."

And on and on it goes for a full hour until we close with the serenity prayer again. As we file out, we run into the Bitches who are entering the classroom next door.

"Hey, Sommers, you cheating on us, man?"

"No," he chuffs. "I'm being held against my will. Save me."

"Damn, once a POW, always a POW," Stiles teases. His joke falls flat. "What, too soon? Y'all need to lighten up, fuck."

Nash watches them leave, and I wonder what he's feeling, but even if I ask, I don't think he would tell me the truth.

"Come on, I'll buy you coffee."

"They have coffee here," he points out.

"Then I'll buy you lunch."

"Sure. I could eat," he shrugs.

Fifteen minutes later, I pull into the church lot and park the car.

Nash stiffens. "What's this?" He sounds panicked. "I don't need Jesus."

"That's debatable. But we're not here for Jesus. I brought you to an NA meeting."

"Narcotics Anonymous? I thought you said we were going to lunch."

"They have coffee and cookies inside, does that count?"

"Fuck this shit. Twice in one day? I'll walk home."

"On your bad leg? It's fifteen miles." He reaches for the door handle. "Wait, just come inside with me. We'll sit down in the back. You don't have to say a word. When it's finished, I'll take you to lunch."

I wish he could see how angry he looks. The only cause for this kind of anger is denial. Or fear.

"I don't have a drug problem like those people in the meeting."

"I know, you can quit whenever you want, can't you?"

"Fuck off. I don't take the drugs because I like them. I hate the way they make me feel. It's my head. I just need to escape my head."

Classic. "I hate to burst your bubble, Sergeant, but that's why every addict uses. You have a problem, and the first step to getting better is to admit that. With the overdose of drugs out of your system, you can begin to heal. You even have an appetite today, for the first time."

He slumps back against the headrest and sighs. "If you take away the pills, it will all come rushing back. It's the only thing that's keeping me numb, Brewer. I *need* them."

"It's not. You have support. You have *me*. All you have to do is walk with me right through those double doors. Just put one foot in front of the other, and we'll take it one day at a time. Together."

Chancing his rejection, I hold my breath and offer him my hand. He stares at it for a full minute before taking it, squeezing back.

"I'm afraid, Brewer. I know you know that. You can see it, can't you? I hate this shit. Hate feeling so exposed and vulnerable. What if somebody in there recognizes me and asks me questions? What the fuck am I supposed to say?"

Finally, honesty from him, and now I'm choking up. When Nash lets me in, he lets me all the way in. He's so fucking brave, even if he's afraid, even if he can't see it. *I* can see it.

"You don't have to say anything. I doubt anyone is going to put you on the spot like that, but even if they do, you don't owe anyone anything. Just trust in me to handle it for you, okay? Can you trust in me?"

Swallowing, he nods. "I do trust you, even though I've only just met you."

"I trust you, too. The disease of addiction makes us manipulative liars, and I am not convinced you're making good choices for yourself right now, which is to be expected. But I trust in who you are at your core. I trust the kind of man that I know you are underneath all that hurt and trauma. You're a trustworthy man, Nashville Sommers, a *good* man, with a good heart. And even though I've just met you, I know I'm not wrong about that."

"How long does this shit last?"

"Sixty minutes," I say with a straight face, even though I'm smiling on the inside. He's handed me a small victory.

"You owe me lunch after this."

NASH

Ft. Bragg, Fayetteville, NC

Chapter 9

Fuck my life *and* my body. Everything hurts. Possibly even my hair.

"There has to be something in here," I mumble, rifling through the kitchen cupboards. With Brewer keeping a tight grip on my meds, I'm desperate enough to *borrow* some from others. In the third cabinet, I find a label I recognize and dump a handful into my palm. The patient, Miles Atlowe, hopefully won't notice I confiscated a few of his muscle relaxers. I wonder if he has any prescribed sedatives.

The wooden floorboards in the hall creak, and my heart skips a beat. I can feel his presence, feel the heat of his glare burning holes through my back, and I know without having to look that it's Brewer.

"You know, the drugs just make you look weak."

Fuck him and his holier-than-thou bullshit. A man can hurt. A man can be sore. "What the fuck did you say to me?" I slam the cabinet shut.

"I said what I said. I didn't stutter. You heard me loud and clear. If I said something that you don't like, maybe you should look closely at that." He crosses the kitchen, coming closer, close enough that I can smell his spicy body wash. His hair is damp, the short ends curling in disarray, like he just stepped out of the shower. "I'm not your enemy. You don't need *my* help. You do a fine job all on your own."

"What's that supposed to mean?"

"It means, you are your own worst enemy. Nobody can hate you more than you hate yourself. The drugs just make you forget that for a little while."

His conscience is the last voice I need to hear this morning. "I'm sore from working out yesterday and I've got to go back again today after work."

"And how many pills do you have in your hand?"

"I don't know." Sighing, I glance at the cocktail. I should have swallowed it as soon as I heard his footsteps creeping down the damn hall. "Probably too many." I hand him three, keeping one for myself, which I swallow dry. "Don't look at me like that, Brewer."

How does he do that thing with his eyes that makes me feel instant guilt? My mother used to do the same thing.

"I just want to be able to trust you. I don't want to keep worrying about you, Nash. I want you to want this for yourself as much as *I* want it for you."

Why can't he care a little less, from a distance? "I'm trying," I grit out.

"Try harder."

Ignoring him, I set up the coffee machine and search out a mug among the many cabinets. I'm going to need to make a grocery list because now that I'm taking less pills, I'm beginning to develop an appetite. The smell of roasted coffee permeates the kitchen, further provoking my hunger. Grabbing a blue mug that says, "some like it hot", I breathe in the fragrant steam as I fill my cup and turn to face a silent and waiting Brewer while I savor my first sip.

The pill I swallowed barely does the trick. If I'd taken the entire handful, like I wanted to, I'd already be feeling the effects —blurred vision, seeing double, a floaty head and loosening in my limbs, and the most coveted of side effects, the thoughts in my head would be farther out of reach, harder to grab onto and torture myself with.

Well, fuck. My shoulders sag with defeat. I've just admitted to myself I didn't take them to relieve soreness. Shit, Brewer's right. I'm a goddamn addict. I'm running from myself, running scared, afraid to slow down long enough to let my past catch up with me. Because I'm not strong enough to face it. Or at least, I wasn't, because I was alone, but now I'm not. Now, I have Brewer. I guess I'm also a Bitch, 'cause it seems like those guys are nagging me every time I turn around.

"Will you sponsor me?"

He hesitates, and his rejection stings. "I don't know if that's such a good idea."

"Please don't say no. I have no one else to ask. I want this,

Brewer. I want to stay clean, I really do. I just don't know who else to trust but you. You say you want me to talk about it and get honest, but I can't just do that with anyone. It has to be you."

"I wasn't going to tell you no, I just need you to know that I'm... I'm gay. I'm attracted to men." He swallows. "In the program, it isn't always recommended that men like me sponsor other men. Just like men and women shouldn't sponsor each other if they're straight."

He isn't telling me anything I don't already know, but I eye him with a raised brow, encouraging him to continue. Brewer's nervous, or at the very least, self-aware, and it's kind of amusing, and a bit of a relief to not always be the one in the hot-seat.

"You know," he continues, "because they could be attracted to each other."

"Are you saying you're attracted to me?"

"No," he blushes, "that's not what I'm saying. What I mean is—"

His scruffy cheeks turn rosy, the color creeping down his neck into his collared Polo shirt. "So you're *not* attracted to me?"

"I didn't say that either. I just mean that—"

"Relax, Brewer. I know what you mean." Closing the distance between us, I straighten his already straight collar, just so I can get in his space and smell his body wash again. Mixed with his own natural scent, it's addicting. "I'm also gay."

He looks stunned. "You are? I mean—you know—"

"No, what did you mean?"

"I thought maybe you were bisexual because I felt like you were flirting with me."

I'm enjoying this way too much. "No, I'm only interested in

men. My squad knew, and so did Gutierrez. We didn't talk about it much, but they ripped me sometimes. Have I really been flirting with you?" My eyes drop to his lips, and he smirks when he follows my gaze.

"Please," he laughs "you're a terrible flirt."

"I'm terrible at flirting? Or I'm a huge flirt?"

Brewer Marx is flustered and ruffled by my proximity and my wandering gaze, and for the first time in... fuck, how long has it been? Months? A year?... I'm interested. Actually interested, and not just guarding my real feelings and thoughts.

"Both. And yes, you're hopeless."

"I'll make you a deal. You help me stay clean, and I won't try to sleep with you." Brewer chokes, which makes my grin grow wider.

"Like I said, you're a terrible flirt. I don't even think you know when you're doing it."

"Trust me, I know what I'm doing. It's a crutch for me, just like the pills. A way for me to focus my attention outward instead of inward."

"Look, it's not just me. I don't think you should be sleeping with anyone right now. I just want you to put yourself first, and focus on your recovery. Block out all of the distractions."

Hmmm, with his quiet strength and confidence, and his rugged-everyday-joe-but-hot-enough-to-be-a-model looks, Brewer could most definitely become a distraction. "Brewer, you don't have to worry about me. My dick doesn't even work, remember? I'm not trying to have sex with anyone," I deflect.

"Good, keep your limp dick zipped up," he teases, gifting me with his gorgeous grin and twinkling almond eyes.

"You're the only person I know who can get away with calling my dick limp."

"Because I'm the only person who knows."

And the only person I trust. "Well, you and the doc." *Completely fucking humiliating.*

Great, now *I'm* blushing.

Brewer clears his throat. "You know, I can help you with that." My nostrils flare. His words hit me like a gut punch. "When you're ready, I mean." *I'm ready. Right fucking now.* "I've learned techniques to improve virility in ED without meds. Visualization and meditation, aromatherapy, and the use of certain herbs that increase blood flow."

How utterly unsexy and disappointing. I was hoping Brewer would employ the personal touch technique, and that the oral part of his guided meditation would be less instructive and more wet heat.

"I'll keep that in mind," I assure him.

A lanky brunet strolls into the kitchen, whistling and barefoot. "Hi, new guy, I'm Tex."

Smiling, I answer. "Hey, Tex, I'm Nash."

He addresses Brewer. "Hey, doll."

The smile falls from my face as it tightens. "He's not some bitch. Don't call him doll. His name is Brewer."

"Really?" Tex challenges, smiling like he's being pranked. My eyebrow hitches. I can say a lot without saying anything. It's my sergeant training.

He scoffs, turning to Brewer. "I'm sorry, Brewer. I didn't mean any disrespect." With one last glare at me, he walks out.

Brewer turns his wrath on me. "What?" I ask.

"The next time you get offended on my behalf, why don't you ask me first if *I'm* actually offended before you defend me?"

"But he called you..."

"Again, that's my decision to make, not yours."

"I'm sorry." What in the hell am I supposed to say? I suck at apologies.

"You will be if you don't make things right with him."

Brewer leaves through the door that leads downstairs into his apartment. Rinsing my mug out in the sink, I head to my bedroom to finish getting ready for work. As I pass through the living room, I see Tex sitting on the couch, and I pause beside it.

"Don't start with me right now." He doesn't even look at me as he continues flipping through the channels.

"I just want to say I'm sorry." He looks up, surprised. "It wasn't my place to intervene."

"You think?"

Fucking smartass. "I thought you were disrespecting him," I snap.

"You have no idea how much I respect him. He saved my life a time or two."

How like Brewer. "Yeah, he does that a lot."

"I'm from the south. I call everyone darling or doll."

My eyebrow climbs again, and I'm curious if he plans on calling me doll next. Tex laughs. "Not you, it doesn't fit. I'll have to think of something else that suits you better."

"Take your time, cowboy."

He offers me the remote. "Do you wanna watch TV? The newbie always gets control of the remote."

"I don't watch much TV, but thanks."

Tex brushes his long honey-colored bangs from his forehead. He looks like he can't fathom how anyone can live without TV, even for a day. "Like any?"

"It's not a good idea when you're easily triggered by just about everything."

Nodding, he adds, "Yeah, I guess you're right. Well, if you ever want to know what's happening in the world, just ask."

And just like that, I've made a friend. At least, I think I have?

———

"Welcome back, Sommers," Chief Burgess greets unenthusiastically. "You can start by hosing down the vehicles in the motorpool. They're covered in pollen. After that, your new recruits are due for PT evals."

Fuck me. Maybe if I cut my whole damn injured leg off, they'll let me go home. I could fake a heart attack or throw myself down a flight of stairs.

By the time I finish making the Humvees spotless, five hours have passed, but it feels like a lifetime. What the fuck am I doing with my life? On my way out of the military, a stellar career cut short, with no plans for the future, I'm just sitting here wasting away the hours, counting the days until I retire… and then what? What do I have waiting for me after this? So far, nothing but an endless round of support groups and twelve step programs. Physical and mental therapies. A long and lonely life —a solitary life—with nothing to warm my bed but bad memories.

There has to be more than this. I didn't fight to stay alive for this. I didn't suffer extreme agony just to throw away my future.

"Four more laps," I shout across the field, clocking my stopwatch as each recruit crosses the starting line.

"Sergeant," Peterson pants, sweating and melting all over his boots, "I don't think I can make it four more laps, sir." He looks green around the gills, and I think he might be right.

"Don't be a pussy, Peterson. Get out there and knock those laps out."

"But sir—"

"Are you a pussy, Peterson?"

"No, sir."

"Five more laps."

His face falls, but he wisely keeps his mouth shut, jogging off. I'll eat my hat if he makes it one more lap.

Halfway around the track, Peterson collapses, hands braced on his knees, hunched forward, and he vomits his lunch all over the pavement. When he's finished emptying his stomach, he walks the rest of the track, slowing even more as he reaches me.

"Peterson, you're a fucking embarrassment. Get off my track and go wash your boots."

"Yes, sir."

"And drink some fucking water."

Goddamn, I was held captive and tortured, and it was preferable to this bullshit. What scares me is that guys like him wouldn't last two days in the desert in captivity. How would he act if a terrorist blew his foot off or shot him in the leg?

I'm doing him a fucking favor.

After the track, the squad lines up in formation for push-ups and jumping jacks. With my leg, I can't even pretend to participate. Instead, I just stand here with my stopwatch and my clipboard, sweating my fucking balls off, while I pretend not to see them cheat every way they can.

Holy shit, I've become Riggs!

Chief Burgess sneaks up behind me. The only warning I have is when my recruits stop cutting corners and do actual push-ups.

"Looking good, Sommers. Before the end of day, you need to complete training for gas masks."

"Sir, I won't be able to handle that without a relapse." I'm talking about flashbacks, and he knows it. Burgess stares at me for a moment before he nods. "CPR then. And first aid tomorrow."

"Yes, Sir."

"Oh, and Sommers? It's been a pleasure serving with you."

"Sir?" Is he telling me to read between the lines? I can't even see the bold print.

"Your request came through. They're letting you use your accrued leave time to ride out the remainder of your contract until your retirement goes through. Tomorrow is your last day."

"Yes, Sir," I mumble, feeling dazed.

Tomorrow is my last day as a soldier.

My last day in the United States Army.

My last day with a career and a purpose.

What the fuck am I after tomorrow?

BREWER

Serenity House
Black Mountain, NC

Chapter 10

He's struggling, and it's killing me not to interfere, to jump in with both hands and make everything easier for him. But I would only be hurting him. Nash has to want this badly enough to figure it out on his own. Yesterday he joined me at another NA meeting after working out with Riggs. And today, he went to the Bitches with Stitches group.

He's limping badly, worse than before, and I know the physical therapy is kicking his ass, but if he just keeps with it, he'll become stronger, he'll hurt less. Nash is in that stage where he's accepted his surrender to alcohol and pills, but he's looking for loopholes, trying to beat the system. He's searching for anything and everything to fill the void. It's my job to steer him back on track when he veers off course, to gently remind him of his goals, or not so gently if need be.

When I caught him stealing drugs in the kitchen the day before yesterday, I was beyond angry. But then I realized after taking a step back that I wasn't angry, I was hurt and disappointed, because I want this so badly for him. I want Nash to give me reasons to believe in him.

Needless to say, we won't be keeping prescriptions in the common areas of the house any longer. We never should have. It was poor judgment on my part, and it won't happen again. On the other hand, Nash isn't sleeping. The dark bags under his eyes are growing darker every day. He's struggling without the sedatives, but I refuse to give in. He's going to have to find a way to overcome it without pills.

Water trickles softly over slate rocks, filling the pond below the waterfall and making gentle waves ripple over the glassy surface. The sound is soothing, filling me with peace and serenity. I've invested a lot of time and money into transforming my backyard into a spot ideal for meditation and relaxation, not only for my benefit, but for the guys that live here at Serenity House. Everyone needs a spot to get away, where they can calm their mind and focus their energy. A place where they can remember what's most important to them.

Blowing out a calming breath of fresh air, my shoulders sag with release as I unburden myself. For the last twelve years, I've remained clean and sober every day, but I still have one addiction I struggle with more than any other—getting lost in other people's problems. I just want to help so badly, but sometimes, I use it as a crutch, to not have to focus on myself, to not put myself first. Lately, I've been so involved with Violet and Nash that I haven't taken care of *me*, my most important patient.

Tonight is all about me. A cup of coffee with my favorite coconut creamer. A banana nut muffin with chocolate hazelnut spread. After reading a passage from the NA textbook on letting go and letting God, I did an audio-guided meditation, reminding myself of my priorities and goals for the week.

Get a haircut.

Update my gratitude journal.

Make an appointment to get my yearly physical exam.

Try out the new Indian restaurant that opened down the street.

All little things, but taking time to put myself first is huge. It's how I remember not to get lost in others' problems. It's how I put my recovery first. It's how I remember to enjoy the little things, all the best things, about being clean and alive. Remaining grateful and living day-to-day is the key to my recovery. It's how I've stayed clean for over a decade.

After I get the chaos in Nash's head sorted, these are the small but crucial life lessons I want to teach him.

I want to show him there is still pleasure in living. His head will never be completely healed, no matter how much therapy he endures, no matter which meds he takes. The nightmares will always linger, in sleep and in his waking hours. His past will always haunt him. But my goal is to help him cope with his memories and his fears so that they don't overshadow the joy in his life. He has a long way to go before he's ready to stop and smell the daisies, but I have faith that he'll get there if he wants it badly enough.

The bones in my back crack as I unfold from my seated position and push to my feet. Christ, I'm getting old. Whoever said thirty-five is the new twenty never served in the military. Next to the glass door that leads to the sunroom is a door that leads down to my basement apartment. My private entrance. The muffin and coffee are enough to fill me for now, so I skip the kitchen and head straight for the shower, stripping off my clothes as I go.

Rolling my neck on my shoulders, I moan out loud from the pleasure of the hot water washing away the remnants of my day. After a bit of backyard *me* time, it's the perfect way to unwind. Gripping the bar of soap in my hand, it skates across my body, down my sparsely-haired chest, over my flat stomach, to the nest of dark curls around the base of my cock. Once they're sudsy, my fingers comb through the curls, spreading the soap onto my shaft, where I grip it loosely, stroking back and forth, pulling the skin of my uncut cock back so I can clean around the sensitive head.

Thick long fingers with nails bitten down to the quick. Torn cuticles and red knuckles. Pale dry skin rough with callouses. Hands that belong to a man who hasn't taken care of himself.

Do not touch your cock and think about Nash's hands!

This is why I have no business sponsoring him. But he needs help desperately, and there's no one else he trusts but me. I'd hate to think I'm just telling myself that as an excuse to get closer to him, but it might just be the truth. Yes, my motives for wanting to help Nash are pure, but underneath that layer of selflessness, I can't deny that I'm attracted to him, that I feel a pull toward him.

If I can just shelve that desire, I might be able to give him the help that he needs.

As I crawl into bed, clean and damp, wearing only a pair of black briefs, I close my eyes and can't help that my thoughts drift to him once again. Is he sleeping? Will he find any peace tonight? Or will the dark circles under his eyes be darker in the morning?

It feels like I'm barely asleep for more than an hour when my phone rings. Reaching blindly for it on my nightstand, I grab it and answer, my voice barely audible.

"Hello?"

"I can't sleep."

"Nash?" My eyes open wide, and I raise up on my elbow. He sounds wide awake, unlike me. "What's wrong?"

"I'm tired, Brewer. So fucking tired," he sighs. "But every time I try to close my eyes, I see him. I can smell him."

"Tell me. What do you smell? What do you see?"

"I can't," he whispers, like he's afraid to speak louder. "I can't drag you into my nightmare."

"You can, Nash. I won't let you suffer through it alone. Take me with you."

"It's so fucking dark. And lonely." His voice cracks, pinching my heart. "It smells terrible. It smells like dirt, and the air is musty and stale. Thick and hot. I smell terrible, like the worst BO, and Gutierrez, he smells..." Nash makes a choking sound, and then he sobs. "He's rotting, Brewer."

I swallow my gasp, my stomach roiling with nausea. What in the hell did he endure? How did he ever survive that hell for twenty-two days?

"His foot is gangrenous. They shot it off, and it's rotting. He's cold and hot in my arms, shivering, and we both know his fever is from the sepsis."

"I'm here, Nash. You're not alone this time. I'm here with you."

"I'm losing him, and I don't want to lose him. He's my best friend, and I don't want to lose him. I don't want to be alone. I'm scared, Brewer."

His voice sounds haunted, remote, and I want to reach through the phone and pull him through it, so that he's lying beside me, and I can touch him. So that he knows he's safe. That he's not alone.

"He's dying, and I can't save him. With every labored breath, he's slipping away from me." The sound of his breath caresses my ear. "All I can do is listen helplessly as he dies in my arms."

"Do you remember the last thing he said to you?"

"He made me promise not to let them take his dead body. And then…and then nothing. I was singing to him, and he closed his eyes and never opened them again."

Hot tears cloud my vision and drip onto the screen of my phone. How does he even wake up every morning and face another day? How do any of us?

"What were you singing?" My voice is barely a whisper, and he answers in the same tone.

"The sun will come out tomorrow."

"Nash." My voice breaks, and he knows I'm falling apart because his pain has sliced through my heart. He can hear it breaking for him.

"I'm so tired, Brewer. I just want to fall asleep and forget for a little while."

Without a second thought, I climb out of bed, pull on a pair of old sweatpants, and make my way upstairs, past the living room, and down the hall, stopping at the third door on the left. I let myself into his room on silent feet, crossing the dark room to his bedside.

"Brewer?" He hangs up the phone.

"Scoot over." He doesn't hesitate to move aside and make room for me. "I'll keep watch while you get some rest."

I should say something about boundaries, make it clear that I'm only here for his peace of mind, remind him that I'm only his sponsor and that we won't be crossing any lines beyond that, but when Nash cuddles into my side, winding his arm around my chest, I don't say a word. And when he breathes a deep sigh of relief, like it's his first easy breath in God knows how long, I keep silent.

Just for tonight, I'll be his pillow, his lump buddy—I'll be whatever he needs.

When I begin to hum the words to his song, I can't stop my fingers from carding through his silky, blond hair. His breath slows, evening out to a soft, warm puff across my bare chest.

I will slay each and every one of your dragons, Nashville Aiden Sommers.

I will chase all of the ghosts from the dark corners of your nightmares, until the sun is shining down on you, warm and bright, and safe.

I will be your light in the darkness, your hand to hold when you get lost and can't find your way.

Warm sunlight streams through his bedroom window, casting a golden glow over his pale skin. I'm dying to touch him, to see if it feels as warm as the sun makes it look, but I know better. He isn't mine to touch. I've also seen it tanned and healthy in the pictures Violet has shown me with her son, standing side-by-side with his best friend Nash. Maybe I can encourage him to sit outside today and soak up some vitamin D.

He stirs, his breath ghosting over my nipple, and it stiffens into a hard peak. Fighting back my groan, I sneak from the bed like a thief, stealing out of his room without making a sound. There is no way I can wake up next to a shirtless and sleepy Nash and still convince either of us things are platonic.

I'm just not that good of a liar.

Heading back to my room, I try to avoid all the known creaky floorboards so I don't make a sound. The last thing I need is one of my roommates catching me sneaking out of Nash's bedroom, first thing in the morning, with no shirt on. I grab one from my bedroom and then climb back up the stairs to the kitchen to start the coffee.

Grabbing my favorite mug from the cabinet, the one that says, 'fake it till you make it', I fill it with the steaming brew, and as always, I breathe in deeply before taking my first sip. Something about that first taste just resets my system and makes everything right in my soul. Leaning against the counter, I gaze out into the backyard, watching the squirrels and birds play among the flowers and trees.

This is my favorite time of day, when everything feels possible, and the world is bathed in a beautiful soft dew. The hours of the day ahead stretch out before me with endless opportunities to be productive.

"Morning, doll," Tex chirps, striding into the kitchen barefoot.

He has on a purple silk robe over plaid flannel pajama pants, no shirt. I never fail to smile when I see the evidence of his colorful personality on display. Tex is a happy, quirky, soulful man, who never appears to let his struggles get him down.

"I mean, Brewer," he amends, stopping short.

"Don't do that. Don't second-guess yourself. You've always called me doll, and it's not flirtatious or belittling. It's just who you are. I always want you to be yourself around me."

"Well, in that case, might I add that you look *very* well rested. Must have been some sweet dreams."

Actually, I can't recall ever having slept better. I don't even remember dreaming. Trying not to let my smile give me away, I answer with a straight face, "Must have been all that meditation before bed."

The kitchen fills up quickly. Every morning, it becomes the central hub of our home. Nacho and Miles begin cooking, and soon, Nash shuffles in, looking worse for wear, and a lot less rested than I feel.

Tex whistles. "Damn, 'pardner, rough night? You could use some eye cream and an IV drip of caffeine."

"'Pardner?" he repeats, but he lacks Tex's charming accent.

Tex covers his grin by taking a sip of coffee. "No? I'll keep working on it."

Burning with questions, I'm dying to ask him how he slept. If there's any lingering awkwardness between us? Did I cross a line? But I can't ask any of those things in front of our roommates. Can they feel the thread of invisible tension connecting me and Nash? I feel like it's so tangible it's unmistakable, the newfound intimacy, the way I feel closer to him now, connected in a way I didn't yesterday.

"So, this is Nash. Nash, these are the guys, Nacho and Miles," Tex explains.

Nacho, with his bronzed skin and dark hair, claps Nash on the back on his way to the pantry. "Welcome, man."

Miles is more reserved, brooding behind a shock of dark hair hanging over his eyes. He wears it that way to cover his scar. No words from Miles, but he dips his head in acknowledgment.

Nash's eyes find mine, and he looks hesitant. I give him an encouraging nod, and he turns back to Miles.

"I owe you an apology. I took some of your pills. If you need them, I have the same prescription, and Brewer can replace them for you."

"Thanks for telling me." For a huge, hulking man, Miles is a quiet guy. His size deceives most people into thinking he's a loud, in your face, alpha male ex-soldier with something to prove, but the man behind the stereotype couldn't be further from that.

Nash pours himself a cup of coffee and takes a seat at the table, slumped over with his head resting on his arms.

"He doesn't look so good," Tex observes.

"We've both been there before. I'll keep an eye on him."

"God, that shit makes me grateful to be clean."

"You and me both, Tex."

Without ever touching his coffee, Nash lifts his head and mumbles, "I think I need to go lay down again."

He shuffles out of the kitchen in a daze, looking ghostly pale, and a bit green.

"Well, that's the last we'll see of him today," Tex surmises.

Nash sleeps for most of the day, and I hover anxiously as he stirs restlessly, shaking and sweating and talking nonsensically.

It's killing me not to climb into bed with him and hold him, to cradle his body in my arms and sing that song to him that brings him so much comfort. Twice today, I've heard him mumble the words in his sleep.

With a cool, damp cloth, I wipe the sweat from his face, neck and chest, marveling at the man in my care. The man so clearly suffering.

I have so many questions for you.

What was the one thought or idea you clung to that gave you hope?

How did you put the pain in your leg from your mind so you didn't go crazy?

How can you be so brave and so strong and yet doubt that you can handle what comes next?

Detoxing from drugs and alcohol is a fucking mess that I wouldn't wish on anyone, but Nash is going to get through it, with my help, and the help from the people around him, and he's going to come out the other side much stronger and more resilient.

I'm going to help him believe in himself again.

"Don't... Don't leave me alone," he mumbles, sounding agitated. *Who are you talking to? Gutierrez? Someone from your past?*

"Don't go, Brewer. Don't leave me."

He's talking to me. He doesn't even know that I'm here, he's been asleep all day. But maybe, somehow, he feels me. He senses that I'm here with him, and that he's not alone.

"Don't..."

Softly, I slide my hand in his, and he squeezes back.

"I'm right here. I'm not leaving you alone."

Nash settles and doesn't stir again until the sky turns dark outside his window.

**Serenity House
Black Mountain, NC**

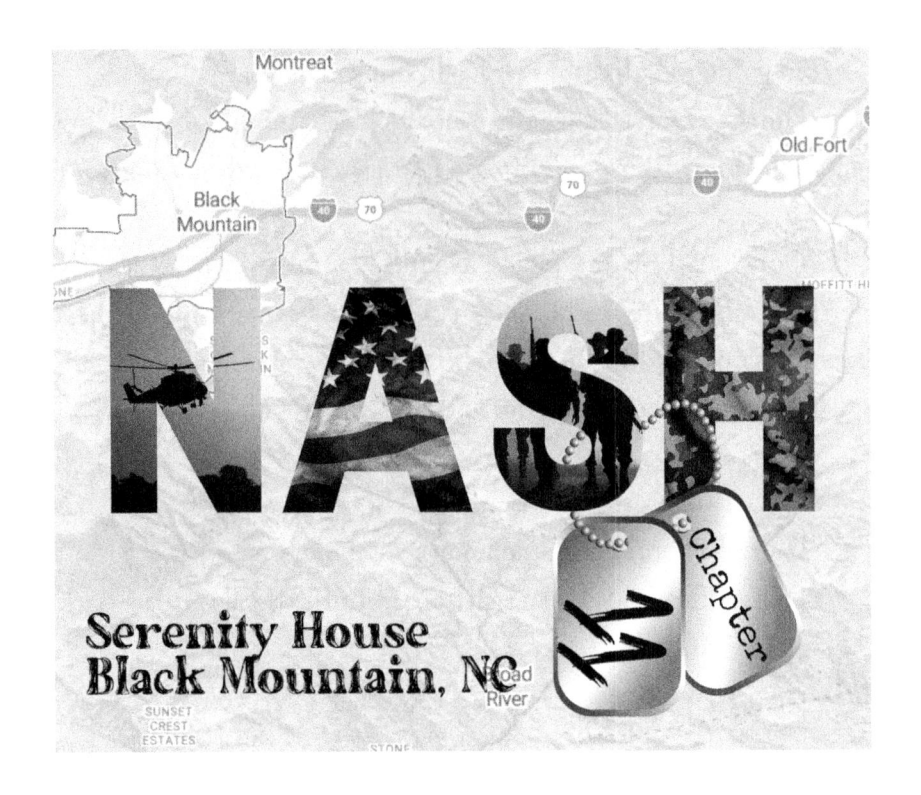

Chapter 11 — NASH

Day 22 of captivity

The pain in my leg had lessened to a dull ache, with moments of blinding agony when I tried to move. The tissue around the bullet was probably dying, festering. Maybe I would lose the entire leg. Assuming I made it out of here.

Gutierrez had become squishy. I didn't know how else to describe the fluids that seeped from his body. He was rotting. Not even the rats were all that keen on him anymore.

And still, I held onto him.

Still sang to him.

Still made promises to his lifeless corpse I didn't know if I could keep.

It kept me sane. From the loneliness, and the hunger, and the pain, and the fear. Pretending like he was still alive kept me sane.

"I can't wait to taste your mama's paella, but only if you try my crab Rangoon. I've taken you there before, but you didn't want any. You wanted egg rolls instead. You never had any sense. How can I even trust that your mama's paella is any good?"

I'd seen the movie Castaway. *I watched Tom Hanks befriend a volleyball out of loneliness and sheer desperation. I laughed, along with the rest of the world, at the absurdity of it, and now, I was laughing at myself because I was no better. Gutierrez had become my* Wilson. *I didn't give a fuck how insane it made me, or what others might think when they discovered us. All I knew was that I'd die before I let them separate us.*

Maybe he could hear me? Maybe his soul hovered, haunting our dark cell, haunting me for letting him slip away?

I'd gladly let him haunt me for the rest of my life if it meant I could hear his voice or see his face again.

The guard and dog that stood watch outside our barbwire cell took off in a hurry.

Something was happening.

Shouting. So much shouting. And barking.

I cowered with my head between my knees, trying to block the sound.

The hall filled with dust and smoke. It crept past the barbwire, burning my eyes and filling my mouth, choking the breath from my lungs. My body shook with deep wracking coughs as I spit the dirt from my mouth and lungs.

"I've got you, G. No matter what's happening, I've got you."

The shouting got farther away, the sound replaced with a whirring. A sound I recognized clearly. Helicopter blades. The buzzing was unmistakable, although I had to be hallucinating. I was sure I was hallucinating. And then the dogs were back, the barking I'd heard nonstop for three weeks, the barking that rang inside my head, even when it wasn't real.

"Sergeant! Sergeant Nashville Sommers!"

A cold, wet nose rubbed across my cheek, and then the barking in my face, the hot breath of the animal, so real and lifelike that I couldn't be dreaming. My heart rate spiked, adrenaline coursing through my veins so quickly it made my empty stomach feel nauseous. I grabbed onto Gutierrez even tighter. Whoever they were, if they were taking me away, they would be taking him as well.

I suffered excruciating pain as they dragged me, carried me, ripped me away from the only thing that was giving me life. Gutierrez.

"No! Take me back! Bring me back! G!"

They ignored my desperate pleas for mercy, moving quickly through the dark halls, the smoke choking me until they covered my face with a mask.

"G!" My breath fogged up the face shield, obscuring my vision.

Gunshots and barking dogs, soldiers yelling in English and in Pashto, the buzzing of the helicopter blades. I became dizzy from the sounds crowding in on my consciousness until I squeezed my eyes closed and tried to block it all out.

One thought was stuck in my head, repeating on a constant loop.

The dog hadn't eaten me, and the soldiers hadn't hurt me. They were American, speaking English.

American soldiers.

They were here to rescue us.

"G!" We're going home. They're taking us home.

We emerged from the dark tunnels into blinding daylight. Blinding in a way only the desert can blind, the relentless heat of the sun bleaching everything beige and white. The bright light burned my eyes, searing my fucking retinas until my eyes watered and my vision went dark again.

My leg throbbed almost unbearably as they jostled me onto the bird. Someone, maybe a medic, slipped a needle in my arm, IV fluids to hydrate me. Although it was scary as fuck not to be able to see, to hear so much chaos happening around me, I knew that whatever happened now was better than being below ground.

I also didn't care what they were doing to my leg, only one thing mattered. "G!"

Someone lifted the mask from my face. "He's coming now, Sergeant!" he shouted above the roar of the blades.

I could barely see, but I could hear as they slid a stretcher beside me onto the bird. The longer I stared, the more he came into focus.

A lump covered in a white sheet.

My best friend.

Blindly, I reached out for him, slipping beneath the sheet to find his cold, damp, stiff hand. "We're going home, G." Tears *streamed from my useless eyes. My throat closed with dust and emotions I couldn't swallow. "We're going home, just like I promised."*

Whatever they gave me through the IV knocked me out for the rest of the flight. When we landed, and I came to again, he was gone.

My hand was empty.

I can feel him before I can see him, and when I peel my crusty eyelids apart, his hand is in mine.

Brewer's hand.

"Welcome back, sleepyhead. How do you feel?"

"Like shit," I croak.

He chuckles. The sound warms me, making me feel not so shitty. Brewer gives me hope. No matter how bottom-of-the-barrel I feel, no matter how bad things are, he makes me feel like it's going to be okay, eventually, because *he's* okay, and because I trust he won't quit on me.

"You've been knocked out for most of the day."

The sky outside my window is dark.

Did he watch over me the whole fucking day?

"I had an appointment with Riggs." And I promised to make another one of his dreaded NA meetings.

"I called him. Those workouts and meetings are to make sure you put yourself first and take good care of yourself, and today, you did, in a different way. You needed rest. Abusing those psyche drugs did a number on your body and mind, and kicking them is taking a toll on you."

"I'm a sweaty mess." I'm not sure which smells worse, my body or my mouth.

"Go take a shower while I change your sheets. When you come back to bed, I'll have soup waiting for you."

"Brewer, you don't—"

"Go, Nash. Move your ass."

Damn. Is his no-nonsense don't-fuck-with-me-tone supposed to be such a turn-on? Fuck Viagra.

The hot shower feels like religion, like the most satisfying thing I've ever felt. Just standing still, I let the water beat down on my stiff shoulders and back, heating through my skin and loosening the tightness in my muscles. Eventually, I pick up the soap and wash my body. My smooth chest, dotted with a scattering of dark freckles, my pale brown nipples, now tiny and hard. Down my flat stomach, much less toned than it used to be. My thighs, once thick and muscled, the left one now disfigured with thick scar tissue and a divot. It's slightly thinner than my right leg, but I'm getting stronger, slowly, thanks to Riggs. Saving my flaccid cock for last, I soap the short blond curls around the thick base, rub my sudsy hand down my soft shaft, pulling back the foreskin to wash the uncut head, and I swallow back my self-loathing. It used to be a given that I'd jack it in the shower. Now? It repulses me.

It's fucking useless, a lot like me.

Crawling back into the bed now covered with fresh sheets, wearing clean soft sweatpants, my head hits the pillow and I close my eyes, waiting for Brewer to return. He comes back carrying a bowl of steaming soup and a glass of cold water. My mouth waters. My throat burns for a taste.

"Eat slowly," Brewer advises, placing the glass on my nightstand.

"You think I'll feel better tomorrow?" I ask between mouthfuls.

"A little. It's a process, Nash. It helps that you're still taking the meds in smaller doses instead of quitting cold turkey. But the alcohol is a different story," he adds, staring pointedly at my shaking hand.

When I finish my last bite, he takes the bowl and gets to his feet. "Get some rest, Nash. We'll worry about tomorrow, tomorrow."

"Brewer, will you come back?" He hesitates to answer, and I prod, "Please. I'm scared of my head, of where it'll take me, and I don't want to be alone."

"I'll be right back," he acquiesces softly.

My fear and anxiety settle. *He's coming back.*

I scoot over to make room for him, and he returns shortly, climbing beneath the covers. The heat from his big, solid body warms me to my soul. Breathing in his clean, fresh scent, I take a deep, easy breath, my first one today. Fuck, I just want to graft myself to his side, to cozy up to him, and fall asleep with his scent in my nose, but instead, I'm worried about crossing lines and pushing him away, so I hold still and keep to myself.

"Thank you." My voice still doesn't sound solid.

"For what? Soup?"

"For everything. I couldn't do this without you."

"Yes, you can, Nash. You have no idea what you can do on your own. You're..."

"I'm what?"

He clears his throat. "You inspire me. Your strength and determination."

Bullshit. "Brewer, I can't even get out of bed. I'm a fucking mess. I didn't even ask for help when I needed it most. You and Mandy made me do it."

He chuckles. "We can't make you do anything. Nobody can. Addiction is a disease, it ravages your mind, like a rash. It takes control of your willpower, steals your reasoning and compassion, and turns you into a heartless, hollow husk. That's why, when an addict hits rock bottom, they call it 'a moment of clarity'. The fog lifts long enough, whether for a minute, an hour, or a day, but long enough for us to get a glimpse of what we've done to ourselves. We see what we've become. It's at that moment that some addicts take their lives, and others are able to ask for help."

"What was your moment of clarity?"

Brewer scoffs. "You don't want to hear that sad shit. You have enough of your own to deal with."

"Please? I'm tired of feeling like the only one who suffers. Tell me?"

He sighs, deep and loud, and settles deeper into his pillow.

"I spent eighteen months at FOB Volturno. They called it Dreamland." He snorts.

I've read about Camp Baharia, stationed right outside Fallujah, Iraq. That place was no joke.

"We were the first deployment. Responsible for getting the base up and running. We had our hands full. Mind you, this was way back in '03, when all this shit started. The desert was a fucking mess. They didn't know the sheriffs were moving into town, and they were pissed," he recalls with a smirk.

"They tested us constantly, firing on us randomly, lighting up the sky above us, just to see what we'd do. We were en route from a village back to the FOB, exhausted from kicking down doors and following up leads, collecting intel for some missions the higher ups were planning. About halfway back, we fell under heavy fire. Completely surrounded out of nowhere."

A lump forms in my throat. It's about to get bad, for Brewer. I almost don't want to hear it. I move my head to his stomach, my cheek pressing against his warm, bare skin. He's so lost in his story he doesn't seem to notice.

"Everything was connected underground by tunnels, but we didn't know that yet." *Underground tunnels.* A shiver runs through me. "Anyway, my buddy and I returned fire. He was yelling something to me, but I couldn't hear him over the gunfire. He was telling me to retreat. That one second that he took his eyes off the fight to focus on me cost him his life. One minute I was staring at him, listening to him shout at me, and the next, he took a bullet through his head. Right through the side of his face."

His voice is in my ear, but he sounds far away, lost in another decade. Absently, he runs his fingers through my short hair, scratching softly at my scalp, and I close my eyes and just listen, absorbing his words and his pain.

"You can't imagine what that looks like. I froze. I was wearing his fucking face, covered in his blood. My buddy, the guy I trained with, the guy I bunked with, his brains were on my fucking face. In my goddamn mouth. He was just...gone. There one minute and gone the next." His voice cracks and Brewer swallows so loud I can hear it. "At least he died instantly. He didn't suffer."

"But you did." *Still are.*

"I've been suffering every day since."

A fat tear rolls down my cheek, dripping onto his stomach.

"Anyway, my brain stopped working after that. And just like with him, a second lost was all it took to change my life forever." His body tenses beneath me. "I took a bullet in my shoulder. It hit my artery, and I began to bleed out. Thank God, the guy closest to me was a medic. I could feel myself slipping away, getting weaker, my vision becoming darker, and he reached into the wound and pinched my artery closed with his fingers. Can you imagine? The pain brought me back. I threw up all over myself," he recalls with a humorless laugh.

My stomach roils, and I have to fight back a wave of nausea.

"He held my life in his hands for eighteen long minutes until air support came and cleared out the scene. On the chopper, my heart stopped beating from the loss of blood, and they gave me an emergency transfusion and brought me back. But at the hospital, they lost me again."

Thank fuck he's still alive. I can't imagine a world where he doesn't exist. Without him, maybe I wouldn't exist either.

"They brought me back again. But I was done after that. I kept getting lost inside my head, losing time." *Sounds familiar.* "My short-term memory was shit. I would freeze up and have panic attacks, and I was no good to anyone like that. I was broken. Damaged goods. I finished out my contract stateside. In the meantime, I put my G.I. Bill to good use and went back to school to receive my certification as a licensed therapist and addiction counselor. As you can imagine, it cost me a lot to get up and function every day like nothing was wrong."

I can imagine.

"I relied heavily on pills to get me through school, to help with my focus and my memory and the panic attacks. The anxiety was crippling most days. It's a wonder I even made it through. After I was discharged, I continued with school and received my bachelor's degree in social work and mental health."

He's so fucking strong. I couldn't have done it.

"I was such a joke. A living, breathing oxymoron. There I was, high as a fucking kite during my residency, counseling others on the dangers of addiction. Most days I could barely fucking stand myself, could barely stand to look in the mirror."

I still can't.

"That was when I hit rock bottom. It was the anniversary of my buddy's death, and I took his wife and two little girls to visit his grave. I was sort of Uncle Brewer, guardian of his family. That was the hardest part for me, seeing this beautiful family grieve for him, an honorable, responsible, wonderful man, and yet here I was, still alive, a worthless piece of shit. The unfairness of it all just made me so fucking angry and bitter. Angry at God, angry at fate, angry at myself."

I know that anger well. It fuels my veins, makes my heart pump, and gives me the energy to crawl out of bed every day.

"But my moment of clarity was when they walked back to the car and left me standing there alone, with just me and Eric. His wife thought I was some sort of hero or some bullshit, but

Eric knew better. He could see me for what I really was. He was watching me from heaven, or wherever the fuck he ended up, and he could see every fucked up deed and sin I committed. He saw me for the fraud I was. I was in the middle of a long tirade of apologies and self-recrimination, making empty promises of how I would do better when I spotted a man slumped against a headstone. Maybe he was a homeless vet or something, he sure looked like it, and I caught myself getting angry at him, like a self-righteous prick. How dare he desecrate someone's grave, their honor, and their sacrifice, by sleeping there, making a home there, with his dirty, unwashed body and his bad choices. He held a paper bag in his hand, and I knew there was alcohol in it. I fumed with anger. I was so fucking full of shit." He laughed. "I had no right to judge him. Maybe he knew the person buried there beneath him. Maybe he felt responsible for putting them there."

His voice breaks on a sob, and fresh tears fall from my eyes.

"I realized I was him. I was certainly no better than him, except my clothes were cleaner, and I had a decent haircut. There I was, looking after the family of the man who died for me, high out of my fucking mind. If I could have taken my life right there in that moment, I would have. Instead, I dropped to my ass in the dirt and swore to Eric and God and myself that I would do better. That I would get clean. And that I would use my degree and my experience to help others. I owed it to Eric and his family to make something of the life I was spared, to live the life he would have that he no longer could. That day, that was both my weakest and my strongest moment."

I owe that to Gutierrez.

"After that, I found BALLS, started to attend meetings there and NA meetings, got a sponsor, and began working the twelve steps, and when I celebrated two years clean, they offered me a job. Can you imagine? Me, an addict, a fuck-up." He laughs without humor. "Been clean ever since."

I've never felt more grateful for this man than right fucking now. Brewer knows what I've been through, he feels what I feel, and he knows my pain and anger and the guilt that gnaws at me daily until I'm completely empty inside.

He continues to stroke through my hair, his voice soft and low. "One day, you're gonna be able to say the same thing. Maybe your story will help inspire someone to hit their knees and find their moment of clarity, and all your suffering won't feel so worthless and futile."

If it brought me to Brewer, it wasn't worthless or futile for even one second.

Chapter 12

Serenity House
Black Mountain, NC

"This coffee tastes like shit," he grumbles.

Don't. Laugh.

"We're not here for the coffee," I remind him in a whisper.

"It sure as shit ain't the ambience, either."

I can't help that my shoulders shake with silent laughter. There's no hiding it. He's right, the dimly lit basement beneath the church isn't what I would describe as warm, or cozy, and certainly not inviting and inspiring.

What I love about Nash is that he can be the most compassionate and sympathetic man one moment, and then turn completely sour the next. It's his misery talking. He has no idea how to sit still within his own skin and just listen.

For the next forty-five minutes, Nash grumbles, shifts,

fidgets, and basically just does his best to drive me out of my mind. But when they call for a celebration of clean time, for addicts to come forward and claim the poker chips that denote how many days, months, or years they've been clean and sober, Nash becomes as still as a statue.

The meeting moderator asks, "Is there anyone who would like to pick up a white chip and surrender?"

"What am I supposed to do?" he whispers, sounding panicked.

"Surrender, Nash."

"But I already have a white chip that you gave me."

"Can you have too many?"

"Fuck," he mumbles under his breath, pushing to his feet.

I know he's nervous, scared, full of fear, but this is something he's got to do for himself. I can't surrender for him.

They close the meeting with everyone joined together in a circle as they recite the serenity prayer, and I can feel Nash beside me, stiff as a board from having to touch the man beside him. It's not because he doesn't like to be touched, it's because he's afraid that any sort of stimulus might trigger him. How exhausting it must feel to be on guard every single day, afraid to experience life because the experience might ruin you.

Sliding my arm around his shoulders, I squeeze him to me a little tighter, hoping to absorb some of his fear.

"God, grant us serenity to accept the things we cannot change, courage to change the things we can, and the wisdom to know the difference. Keep coming back, it works if you work it, so work it, you're worth it."

As I feared, we're bombarded with well-wishers, which

always happens when someone picks up a white chip. Then again, as much as it might unsettle him to be the center of so much attention, Nash needs to know that he's supported. He needs to know he's not in this fight alone.

"Welcome, brother. I'm Alex. Here's my number if you need someone to reach out to. Hit me up, we can catch a meeting together sometime."

He dodges several hugs by sticking his hand out to shake.

"Welcome, man, we're glad to have you join our family. If you ever want to grab coffee after the meeting and talk, I've got two good ears that work."

Nash just nods like he's in a daze, deflecting the well wishes instead of absorbing them. He's overwhelmed, and I need to get him out of here before things turn bad.

"Thanks, guys, we'll keep that in mind."

"Good to see you, Brewer."

"You, too, Alex."

"You know those guys?" he whispers as we head to the car.

"I've been coming to this meeting almost every week for twelve years straight. I've made some friends along the way. It wouldn't hurt you to make a few as well."

"I don't need friends. I've got you. What was all that bullshit at the end? 'It works if you work it, so work it, you're worth it'?"

"Everyone needs a reminder."

We climb into the car, and Nash buckles his seatbelt, blowing out a tired sigh. "I don't know, you really think all of this kumbaya circle jerk bullshit really works?"

Choking back a laugh, I try to look serious. "I know for a

fact it works. That's how I stayed clean this long. But like anything, it only works if you work it. If you don't want it, nobody can do it for you. Would you like to go for coffee? We can continue this discussion."

He rubs at his chest, his face pinching. "Not really. My stomach is off, and I'm battling heartburn so strong I feel like it's going to melt a crater in my chest."

"Then I'll take you home, and we'll get you some meds and something to settle your stomach."

We pass two miles in silence before Nash blurts, "What was all that bullshit about taking an inventory?"

"That man was talking about the twelve steps of recovery. They're the same no matter what twelve-step program you're in, no matter what you're recovering from."

"And what are they? Levels of achievement I have to unlock?"

"No, smart-ass, it's not a video game, more like written exercises you do with your sponsor. They're designed to help you with self-awareness and reflection. You've got to get honest about how you ended up here so you don't repeat history."

"Aha, and what's the first step?" He sounds so skeptical.

"Surrendering."

"Well, I did that tonight when I picked up that white chip, so what's the second step?"

Laughing, I shake my head. "It's not that simple. You have to surrender again and again. You don't rush through the steps or you'll miss something. Sometimes, it can take up to a whole year to finish them."

"A year?! Come on, Brewer."

"Think of it like pulling back a curtain, revealing more of the truth little-by-little. Some steps are harder than others and take longer to complete, but the first step is the most important. Trust me, you want to nail this one."

"So how do I know when I've nailed it?"

"I'll let you know. That's my job as your sponsor."

"When can we start?"

"Whenever you're ready. We go at your pace."

"I'm ready right now."

Hilarious. "Tomorrow is soon enough. Right now, the only thing you're ready for is food, meds, and bed."

His eyes find mine on the last word. *Bed.*

Is he going to ask me to stay with him again?

Am I strong enough to refuse him?

"Brewer?"

"Just...don't. Let's just go home."

Maybe I need a new mattress? New sheets? A white noise machine?

I haven't had trouble sleeping in the last seven years, besides the occasional nightmare. Why tonight?

Because you're waiting for him to text you, to ask.

A soft, mewling sound catches my attention. Sitting up, I look around in the dark, trying to find the source. It stops, but then starts again when my head hits the pillow. *Christ! What now?* My gaze is drawn to the door, the one that leads to the backyard. *Is someone out there?*

Padding barefoot to the door, I crack it open, expecting to

see Miles or Nacho smoking cigs, or Tex on the phone with a beau, but I see nothing. The sound comes again, and I look down. There, beneath the boxwood hedge, is a pair of small glowing green eyes. Bending to scoop it up, I cradle the tiny black hairball in my palm and shut the door.

I swear it isn't much bigger than my hand, and it's shivering, despite the balmy night.

"Hi there, little guy. Where'd you come from?" He must have gotten separated from his mama. Tomorrow, I'll drive around the neighborhood and look for her, but for tonight…

I bring him to my bathroom, keeping him cradled to my belly as I fill the sink with warm water. A drop of my shampoo to make suds, and I wet a soft cloth. Gently, I wash the dirt from his emerald eyes and pointy ears. Then I bathe his frail body as he shakes, mewing pathetic little sounds that squeeze my bleeding heart. When he's clean, I rinse him off, wrap him in my softest towel, and carry him back to bed. It doesn't take long for his thin fur to dry into a dark fluff, like lint from a fuzzy sweater. He finally stops shaking, and I realize he might be hungry or thirsty.

Shit, I'm out of milk.

Since I eat most of my meals upstairs with the guys, I'm terrible at keeping my fridge stocked. His mews accompany me up the stairs, down the hall, and into the kitchen. Someone left the light on above the sink, lighting our way. Pouring some milk into a bowl, I set him down and place it in front of him. The little guy laps it up like he's never drunk liquids before, his little pink tongue working overtime to catch it all.

"Poor little thing, you were thirsty."

I might as well peek in on Nash while I'm up here. Tiptoeing silently down the hall, I push his door open a crack to see him in bed, lying flat on his face. His legs are twisted in the sheets, and he's restless, mumbling words I can't make out. He never reached out to me tonight, and I'm both disappointed and relieved. Before I slip out, an idea hits me. Looking down at the kitten in my arms, and then at the lonely, tortured man in the bed, I realize they seem like kindred souls, both alone, and lonely.

I place the little ball of fluff under Nash's arm, and he burrows into Nash's pit, mewling softly and licking his lips. Before I sneak out, the kitten is sound asleep, and Nash isn't moving a muscle.

———

I can hear their voices before I reach the kitchen, echoing down the hall.

"Did someone lose a rat?"

That sounds like Nash. *A rat? Figures.*

"Where'd he come from? We don't have a cat," Nacho adds.

"We do now," I say, popping into the kitchen. "Found him last night outside my door."

Nash still hasn't let him go or set him down. "What are you gonna do with him?"

"Figured I'd drive around the neighborhood after breakfast and see if I can find his mama."

"I'll go with you," Nash volunteers. *Big surprise.* He's clutching the kitten like he hopes we never find its mom.

"Food first."

I start on coffee while Nacho cracks eggs into a frying pan.

"You cook?" Nash asks.

"Shit." He laughs, drawing out the word in his Spanish accent. "I was a Navy cook for four years. Assigned to one carrier after another."

"I believe they call it a Culinary Specialist," Tex teases, flitting in wearing a satin peacock robe and black satin pants with a bare chest.

Nacho swats his ass with a spatula. "Check out the kitty."

Tex sighs dramatically. "How many times do I have to correct you? It's a bussy, not a pussy."

"No, *perra*, I meant the actual kitten."

"Ohhhhhh, pretty boy!" Tex flutters all over the kitten while Nash clutches it to his broad chest like Tex is trying to poison it or something. He's not letting go.

His eyes find mine, and he looks guarded and slightly panicked. Fuck, I hope I didn't make a mistake by letting him bond with the cat, in case we find its mom today.

He doesn't look like he's giving it up. Ever.

Nash doesn't usually have a strong appetite, but I've never seen him eat slower. He's dragging out breakfast, his fingers scratching constantly through the kitten's fur. Fuck me, if he didn't already have a hold on my heart, he definitely would now. I'm a total sucker for a vulnerable yet possessive man, and that description fits Nash to a T.

Wounded. Vulnerable. Possessive. Brave. Loyal. Badass. Capable…

Okay, fucking quit, Brewer. Get a hold of yourself, jeez. One hot AF man cuddling a kitten and you're jizzing your fucking pants.

"You finished?" Nash looks at his plate and then at the kitten, and nods slowly, almost reluctantly. I pop a handful of pills down by his glass and collect his plate. "Let's roll."

As we circle the neighborhood, I try my best to distract him by preparing him for his recovery plan.

"In addition to working the twelve steps together, you also need to continue with therapy, both mental and physical." Nash just nods, stroking the kitten between the ears. "There are some techniques I want to try to improve your PTS. We'll do those in my office, so we can control the environment. As for the stepwork and the counseling, I think we should find a different approach, outside the office. Something more natural."

"I like that idea."

I *don't* like the idea of being his therapist. Already, I feel compromised. Biased, even. But I also don't relish the idea of giving up control to someone else. There're only two people I trust most with Nash's mental health—me and him.

On my second trip around the block, I pull the car to a stop, biting my bottom lip. A dark lump lay in the street, clearly lifeless. It's the spitting image of the little fluff ball in Nash's arms, same black hair.

Was this going to trigger him somehow?

I feel like sometimes I walk on eggshells, trying to avoid setting him off, but that's no way to live, either. Slipping my hand in his, I concede, "We're keeping the cat. Might as well think of a name."

"Just drive, please," Nash rasps, sounding close to tears.

This huge man, with balls of brass, who has seen unimaginable horrors, endured literal hell on earth, was close to tears over a dead cat in the road.

Hell, so am I now.

Is he upset that the cat is an orphan or that his mom died a horrible death?

"Let me take you both home."

He's silent, stroking the kitten who licks his thick fingers like he's a tasty snack—*which he undoubtedly is*—until he blurts, "Carbine."

I assume he's choosing a name for the cat, but Carbine? As in the machine gun? *Mental face palm.*

"Do you think he looks like a Carbine? He's a little small for such a badass name, isn't he?"

Nash chuffs, almost like he's laughing at himself. "How about... Valor?"

"I think Valor sounds perfect." Fuck, those damn tears again. Blinking them back, I take a deep breath. "Nash's Valor."

"Your tongue feels like warm, wet velvet."

"Do you two need to get a room?" I tease, arching my brow.

He never puts the cat down, not for a second, like it's become an extension of his hand. Valor seems obsessed with licking Nash's fingers. Not that I can blame him. If I had a taste of Nash, I wouldn't stop, either. I would devour him whole.

Nash smirks. His sarcastic little smile does things to my stomach. Unsettling things. It's the way he pairs it with the look in his bright blue eyes, how he stares at me, so intimately, like he's challenging me, or maybe he's amused, I don't really care which, as long as he continues to look at me like that.

"So what were you saying about the first step?" He sounds about as interested as a vegan being presented with a cheeseburger.

"You have to admit that you're powerless over your addiction, and that your life became unmanageable due to your drug use."

"Well, of-fucking-course it did," he sputters. "Why else would I be here?"

"You have to state the obvious, Nash. You have to own it."

With an exasperated sigh, he recites, "I'm powerless over my addiction, and my life is unmanageable."

"Was that so hard?"

"Don't push me, Brewer," he warns.

"Moving on. What's the most regrettable outcome of your addiction?"

"This is fucking dumb. What do these questions solve? I don't understand how any of this is supposed to help me not want to choke on a handful of pills. In fact, I think it's having the opposite effect."

Smartass. "By all means, choke on them. If that's what you want to do, no one can stop you. You're responsible for your own choices, and the consequences of those choices. But if you want to recover, you'll answer the damn question."

His glare feels hotter than the sun beating down on us. The serenity of the backyard feels like the perfect place to get him to relax and open up to me, but even the tranquility of the sunny afternoon, with the birds chirping, and the sound of trickling water from the tiny electric waterfall, aren't enough to put Nash in an agreeable mood.

"The most regrettable outcome," he drones on with a sigh. "I don't know, that I pissed people off?"

"What people?"

"I don't know, *people*. Mandy, Liza, you," he adds, continuing to stroke Valor's soft fur instead of meeting my gaze.

"Do you actually care about letting those people down? That would mean you'd have to care about those people. Do you?"

"I don't know, maybe? A little bit."

"Dig a little deeper, Nash. Tell me the things you don't really want to say out loud."

His throat slides, like he's finding his courage. "I hate that I was high the day of the barbecue. That I was so close to Violet Gutierrez, and I was high. I feel like I tainted her son's memory. It was the first time I actually felt ashamed of myself."

Wow, I wasn't expecting that. His candor always takes me by surprise. "I'm not sure that she noticed you were there if that helps. The next time you have a chance to meet with her, face-to-face, I'm sure you'll present yourself in a way that makes you proud."

"Do you really think she wants to meet with me?" he asks, finally meeting my eyes.

"I do. The time will come. In the meantime, you have a lot of work to do on yourself."

"Fine. What's the next question?"

"Did you ever truly betray another person because of your addiction? How did you rationalize that?"

Minutes tick by without a word. Just when I think he's not going to answer me, he finally breaks his silence.

"I betrayed my best friend. Every time I tried to numb his memory and my pain, I betrayed him, I dishonored his memory, and his struggle to live. To *survive*. I took his dream of getting free so he could live again and trampled all over it with my muddy boots. I got out, I was given the chance to live, and look what I fucking did with it. Nothing. Not a fucking thing. I've done nothing but cower in the dark and gorge myself on pills and alcohol, just so I could forget how bad he suffered. I guess going back to the last question, that's my most regrettable action as well. I kind of hate myself."

"What matters is what you do going forward. Dwelling on the past doesn't get you anywhere."

"Maybe, but it doesn't make me hate myself any less."

NASH

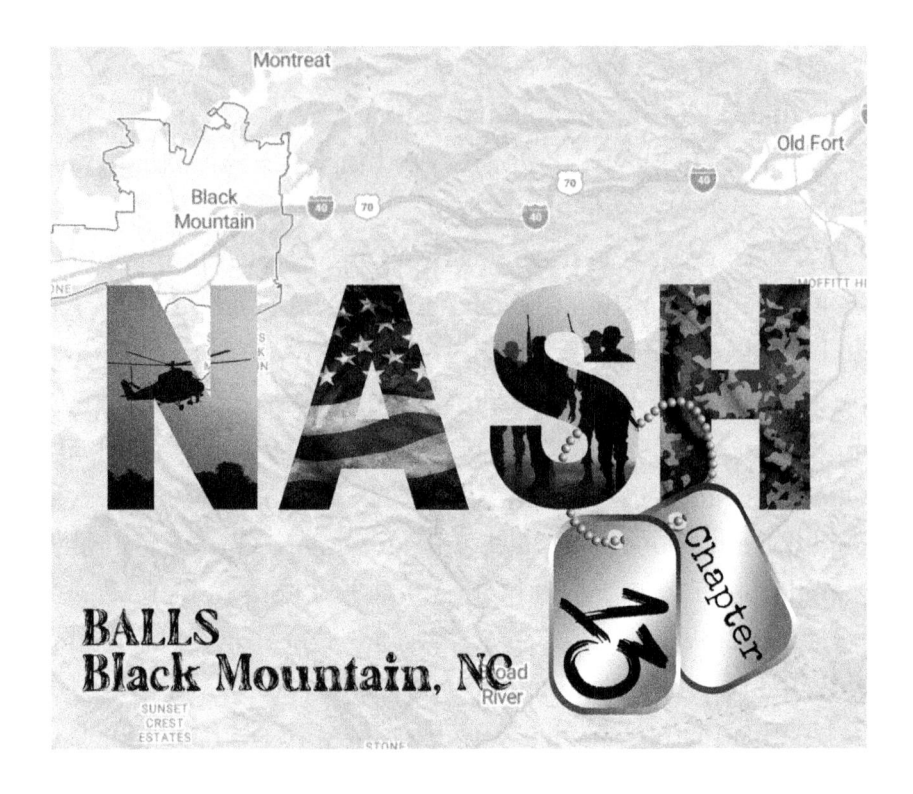

BALLS
Black Mountain, NC

Chapter 13

FUCK THESE BITCHES. I'M NOT READY TO SHARE.

Riggs gives me a pointed look. "Well, if that's all, we'll wrap it up."

The second it's over, Stiles descends like a nagging mother. "Hey, Sommers, how's retirement?"

"All I do is run from one group or meeting to the next."

He frowns. "You haven't had any fun yet?"

"Define fun."

"Shit, Defcon Five, Bitches! Give me a hand."

What the hell does that mean?

McCormick asks, "What's your idea of a good time?"

Blacking out and sleeping for three days straight. "My best friend and I used to hit up that place in Fayetteville, the one that does kids' parties, with the go karts and mini golf. We used to try and run each other off the track, play arcade games, and they have these loaded fries that are to die for."

"Sounds like a fucking plan, brother," McCormick exclaims.

"I'm in," seconds Stiles. "Jax?"

"Hard pass," he grumbles, shuffling out the door.

"Pussy." McCormick calls out, "Wardell? Aguilar?"

West Wardell turns to his partner. "You feel like getting your ass kicked on the track?"

"We're in," Brandt Aguilar declares.

Yay. I guess I'm going on a field trip with the Big Brother Bitches. I can think of worse ways to spend my day. But...

"What? What's that look for?" Stiles asks, probably thinking I'm backing out. *I am.*

"What if I have a..."

"A flashback?"

"Brewer calls them setbacks."

"Brewer can suck my—" Stiles chokes when McCormick jabs him in the ribs. "So the fuck what? I could have one, too, or McCormick, Aguilar, or Wardell. Shit, have you seen his? A real doozy. It's no big deal. We'll just talk you through it until it passes."

"That's it?"

"That's it, man. It's as simple as that. I wouldn't pass up loaded fries on the off chance I might have a '*setback*'."

Maybe it really is that simple.

"Let's ride. We're on bikes, so you're riding with the lovers."

They seem to take it in stride. I wonder if they ever get tired of being teased. Folding myself into the back seat of their Jeep, I tune out their banter, getting lost in my thoughts. A heaviness in my chest makes my next breath more difficult. The dark thoughts crowd my head, blocking out my rationality, erasing my earlier optimism.

"What's that look for?" Brandt's eyes find mine in the rearview mirror. I shake my head, but he won't let it go. "Say it out loud. Sometimes, we gotta snitch on ourselves."

Hell. "I feel like…I don't know, like I'm betraying my best friend."

"'Cause we're going to your old hangout? We can go somewhere else. Just say the word."

"No, 'cause I feel like I'm not allowed to—" *Just forget it.*

"You're not allowed to have fun?" West turns around in his seat to face me. "I get it. I feel like that every fucking day, man. I can't laugh or smile. I don't deserve to, as long as they're lying in the ground. If they can't enjoy life, why should I? It's fucking bullshit, Nash. They don't want me to be miserable. I'm only hurting myself when I do that shit. Don't punish yourself for something you couldn't control. You aren't responsible for his death, and you're allowed to live. He'd want that."

Swiping the tears pooling in my eyes, I swallow past the lump in my throat and nod. *He fucking gets it.*

"We're all just lost soldiers looking for our unit. You found it, brother. You're a Bitch. We've got you." *Fucking Bitches.* My damn nose is running. "Now listen up. When we're on the track, we're gonna sandwich those two fuckheads, Stiles and McCormick, between us, and squish the fucking daylights out of 'em. Got it?"

Now I'm sniffling and nodding. "Got it." It's exactly what G and I would have done. *My new unit, huh? I could have done worse, I guess.*

———

"I surrendered today. Didn't realize I was doing it until afterward, when I felt lighter. Hopeful, even. I thought of you. God, Brewer, all I could think of was telling you. I might not have even done it if not for you. The thoughts came back, and I wanted to run so bad, wanted to get high and lose myself, and instead, I opened my mouth and got honest. Is that what it means to surrender?"

His soft breaths are the only sound, a caress in my ear. I can almost feel his presence, even though he's a floor below me. Brewer's probably warm in his bed, maybe shirtless, maybe naked, and he's connected with me, through the phone, through our words. He's mine for these precious few minutes. *All mine.*

"I think you finally get it. Did you have a good time today?"

"Yeah, I was able to forget for a few hours. I felt guilty, but then I shed the burden of it and just...*lived*. I lived for a few hours."

"I'm so fucking proud of you, Nash." God, that tiny bit of praise makes me feel invincible. Like I'm capable of anything. "I wish you could feel like you're living every day."

"Maybe someday I will." *Only if you're gonna be there with me.*

"Are you going to be okay tonight?"

"No, you should come hold my hand."

He chuffs, and I can picture his sexy smile. "Goodnight, Nash."

"Night, Brewer."

No sooner do I close my eyes than the memories I evaded earlier come rushing back to claim me for the duration of the night, stealing my peace, tainting my dreams. They *always* find me in my dreams.

"I see you've got the hang of knitting." Riggs nods at the stitched accessory slung around my chest, a lime green body sling that goes over one shoulder and under the other arm. Inside, Valor is nestled against my chest, warm and safe.

"Shit, I can barely cast on my stitches. Mandy made this for me."

Riggs cracks a smile. "You're truly one of them now."

One of them. Even with all the fucked up shit in my head, I still belong somewhere. "Yeah, whatever. What torture are you putting me through today?"

"Today, I'm gonna make you sweat."

"I can handle sweat."

"Good, get your ass on that treadmill and start jogging."

"Jog? Hell, I can barely walk."

"And you never will if you don't get on the treadmill and push yourself."

"What about this thing?" I ask, motioning to my chest.

"Christ," Riggs complains with a sigh, setting down his clipboard. "I guess I'll hold your damn cat. Did you have to bring him?"

"He doesn't like to be alone."

"I swear to God, you piss me off, and I'll make you jog an extra mile just for fun."

As terrible as that sounds, I can't help but laugh. "Fun for me or fun for you?"

"Both maybe. Let's find out," he challenges with a wicked grin.

Turns out I cannot handle sweat. I can barely even breathe. With every step my foot slams down onto the conveyor belt, pain ricochets up my leg, threatening to shatter my femur all over again.

My face pinches with pain, and my hands grip the safety bar so tightly my knuckles turn white. Riggs tries to pace me.

"Half a mile left. Push through it, Nash."

My knee buckles, but I catch myself, crying out with a groan. "Don't...let me...quit," I pant, out of breath and sweating.

"Not a chance, Sergeant. You quit on me once, and you quit on yourself more times than either of us can count. I won't let you do it again. It's not gonna be easy. It's gonna hurt real bad, but I guarantee you that we won't quit until your pain level is below fifteen percent and so is your limp."

The timer beeps on the treadmill, letting me know I've reached the two mile mark, and I slow my pace. "You really think that's possible, Riggs?"

"I don't make false promises. I wouldn't ask you to bust your ass for me if I can't deliver my part. In fact, I have hope that we might even achieve a better result than fifteen percent, but I can't promise you that."

Stepping off the treadmill, I grab my water bottle and chug it, quenching my thirst. "That's good enough for me. I'm done running from my past. I'm ready to stand on both legs and fight for my future, no matter how hard it may seem, no matter how much it might hurt, I'm ready to fight."

"Hell yeah," he exclaims, clicking his pen. "There's the badass Sergeant I've heard so much about. The one that never quit, no matter how tough things got. The one who can handle anything life throws at him. He's back!"

That's not completely true. I can't handle anything life throws at me. I barely survived. But I'm too exhausted to run any longer, and I can't get stronger by hiding. Life has kicked me in the nuts over and over again, but it's still a life I'm willing to fight for.

―――

"I surrendered today."

Brewer startles, taken by surprise. He removes his headphones, pressing pause on whatever he was listening to on his phone.

"It's almost becoming second nature," he teases with a playful smile.

His smile is arresting, all even white teeth and crinkles around the corners of his mouth.

"Not quite yet. But I'm getting there."

He scoots aside on the lounge chair, making space for me. "Why don't you sit down and tell me about it?"

It's beautiful out here, with the sun shining dappled light through the leaves, casting just the right amount of shade over the lounger. Birds chirp, and his tiny electric waterfall gurgles soothingly.

"Riggs is kicking my ass. He's out for blood. Probably punishment for skipping out on rehab all those months."

"He is not," he laughs. "If he's pushing you, he's doing you a favor."

"Maybe. Maybe I'm not doing myself any favors. When I'm working out, the pain is so excruciating that I'm convinced the very next step is going to shatter my femur all over again. I'm scared of it. It makes me second-guess myself and want to quit before I reach my goal." I swallow, pausing to gather my courage before I admit this next part. "The sound of my bones cracking haunts me. When he shot me, before the pain set in, maybe because I was overwhelmed with fear and adrenaline, but the only thing I remember that first second or two was the sound of my bones cracking. It resonated inside my head, louder than the gunshot, louder than Gutierrez's screams. I'll never forget the sound of my femur shattering."

Brewer looks a little sick but completely sympathetic. "Nash, your fears are valid. Your feelings are real. But your leg is not going to break again. Not from working out. No matter how badly it hurts, you aren't hurting yourself by pushing harder."

I know he's right, but that's the thing about fear, it's never rational. "That's when I surrendered. Just like last time, I didn't realize I was doing it until after, and it made me think of you, again. I asked him not to let me quit, even though I wanted it more than anything. I asked him not to let me give up on myself, and for him not to give up on me, either. It would have been so easy to just stop running, to just give in and say that I can't do it, but I trusted in him when I couldn't trust in myself. I surrendered."

He scoots closer, close enough that I can feel the heat from his body. Close enough that I can smell his body wash. "Riggs isn't going to let you take on more than you can handle at once."

"Isn't that what they say about God?" I know I've heard that line recycled at NA meetings.

"Look," he chuckles, placing his hand over mine. Awareness dances along my nerves like a shot of adrenaline, making my heart race and my blood heat. "I only know so many clichés. Sometimes I have to serve them twice, like leftovers."

"So Riggs is God?"

"In this situation, it seems so, but if you tell him I said that, my punishment will make his look like a cakewalk."

Leaning closer, I confide, "You should have seen him. With his clipboard and his clickety pen and stopwatch, and that I'm-determined-to-make-you-sweat-till-you-bleed look on his face, wearing this lime green sling across his chest." Brewer laughs, and he's sitting close enough that I can feel his breath across my cheek.

"You didn't happen to get a picture, did you?"

"I wish."

"How unfortunate," he murmurs, dropping his voice to a whisper.

His warm brown eyes roam my face until they drop to my lips, and he swallows, his Adam's apple sliding deliciously. Every part of my body is aware of him, except my cock that refuses to harden. It would be so easy to take his lips right now, to lean in one more inch and claim him. But then what? I have nothing to give this man. All that he's given me, support, trust, empathy, and hope.

Most of all, hope.

But I've got nothing. When it comes to Brewer, I'm nothing but a parasite, a leech on his skin, sucking his resources dry. A black hole with no future. His tongue snakes out to lick his lips, making them shine in the sun, and despite my reservations and my common sense, I *need*. I *want*. I desire him like no other. It's like a fever, igniting every neuron in my body until my blood sings his name.

Brewer. Brewer. "Brewer," I whisper, allowing my lips to brush against his. And when he doesn't pull away, I allow myself to sin once more. Just for the memory, to take with me to bed tonight, and every night that I sleep alone.

He pulls back slightly, just out of reach. "I believe in you. Don't quit on yourself."

I wonder if he's really saying *don't quit on us*. No matter how hard it is to imagine I have any shot at a future, let alone a future with Brewer, I can't help but think it, especially after being teased with the taste of his mouth.

BREWER

BALLS
Black Mountain, NC

Chapter 4

"I can't stop thinking about him."

You and me both. "Can you tell me your concerns?"

"My son used to say Nash wasn't close with his parents like me and Victor were. Who does he have now? Who is looking after that poor man?"

I am. "I assure you Nash is surrounded by supportive people. He's learning how to ask for help."

"If I could just call—"

"Violet, he isn't ready. I promised you that when he is, I will arrange for you to meet with him, but not just yet. He still gets overwhelmed easily when he's confronted with his past, and I don't want to see him backslide when he's making such great progress."

Violet wrings her hands. I can see her worry. She wears it like a coat. "What if I make him some *pastelitos*? He can't be eating well enough. You could pass them on for me."

He has lost weight. Should I let her take on this burden? Would it benefit either of them, or just cause problems?

"Please, Brewer. He needs to eat. He needs food made with love, to reach not just his belly, but his *heart*."

Damn, she's good. I just hope this doesn't come back to bite me in the ass. "Okay, I'll pass them on."

Watching her face transform from burdened to pure joy takes ten years off her appearance. Even her shoulders have perked up.

Please don't fuck this recovery thing up, Nash. She needs this as badly as you do.

"Let's talk about you. Have you done any volunteering like we talked about? BALLS always has opportunities. You would be helping vets in need."

"I'm not ready yet, but I do agree it sounds like a great idea. Just...not yet."

"You'll get there. How are your headaches? Are you taking the medication for depression?"

"Yes, Brewer. You don't have to worry about me so much."

Of course not, it's only my job. "I don't know how not to worry. It's part of who I am. Everyone needs someone to look after them."

Violet tilts her dark head, her concerned eyes boring through me. "And who looks after you?"

The short answer to that is God. The longer answer, well, that's more complicated. I would love to have someone look after me. At least to have someone who cares. Someone who appreciates my fussing and caretaking ways. And the only name on that short list is just starting out on his long, long road to recovery. I'd be a fool to put my eggs in his basket.

"I won't say no to your pastelitos."

> Even sponsors need to surrender.

Nash:

It's 2 am. Is everything OK?

> Couldn't sleep. I had a dream about my buddy.

Three dots dance in the corner of the screen and then pause, and then dance again, and then pause, and then he knocks at my door. The soft light from the TV illuminates my path as I shuffle across the apartment to answer it.

"I figured if we're both awake..." His grin is lopsided, a lot like his rationalization. I can't say no to either one.

I step aside to let him in, and Nash makes a beeline for my bed. I didn't invite him into it, but does he really need an invitation? I didn't ask when I got into his bed. Either time. I just knew he needed me, probably the way he knows I need him right now.

When we're both tucked under the covers, our legs just

inches apart from each other, Nash turns on his side to face me. "Tell me about your dream."

"I'd rather not relive it again. I fell back to sleep for a little while but then I dreamt about getting high. It's been a hell of a night."

"How did you surrender?" His voice is a soft whisper in the darkness, making me feel as if we're the only two people on Earth.

Twisting my upper half, I reach for the blue book sitting on my nightstand. My Narcotics Anonymous book. "I read a couple of the stories, personal accounts from recovering addicts. You should read some. It's a lot like attending a meeting, but by yourself."

His face lights up. "Oohh, is that an option?"

"No, asshat, it's not a replacement for meetings, just something to help when you're alone. I read the first chapter again, about surrendering. It helps to let go of everything in my head, all the toxic thoughts and memories."

"And who did you surrender to?"

"My higher power. God. Have you worked that out yet for yourself?"

"Who my higher power is?" He thinks for a moment. "You?"

"I can't be your higher power." I laugh.

"It might as well be a chair or a coffee pot for all I care."

"You saying you don't believe in God? Did you ever?"

"Sure, before He proved to me He didn't exist."

"If He doesn't exist, how could He prove it?"

"Okay, asshat," he repeats. "I meant before the universe proved it."

"And how did the universe prove to you that God doesn't exist?"

"Because if He were real, He wouldn't have let my best friend die so terribly."

My heart sinks to the bottom of my stomach. I can't refute the unfairness of that. "God took my best friend as well. It doesn't mean He doesn't exist."

"Then why would He do that to me and to Violet and her now deceased husband? Why does He hurt innocent people? Good people? For what purpose?"

"I can't answer that for Him. But I do know that He has a purpose for everything. Then again, you don't have to believe in God as your higher power. Many recovering addicts don't. You just have to believe in something greater than yourself, some force or entity, or something spiritual, just so that you know you're not in control of your own destiny."

"Who says I'm not?" Even in the darkness, I can see his eyes twinkling. He's fucking with me.

"Let go and let God, that's my motto."

"How quaint. My motto is fuck the fucking fuckers before the fucking fuckers fuck you."

"How...quaint." I can't say it with a straight face.

His foot connects with my shin, but after he kicks me, he doesn't pull back, just leaves his foot resting against my skin.

"I'm working on it, okay?"

"I think the steps are designed to help you with your spiritual journey. But remember, nobody gets to tell you who your higher power should be. That's for you alone to figure out. Whatever works for you, keep working it."

He flips to his back, and I miss the warmth of his foot.

"Right now, my higher power is the people around me with more experience than me at staying clean. That's who I surrender to, who I ask for help. Their combined experience in recovery is a power greater than myself."

"I think that makes a lot of sense." If only my need to connect our feet again, to intertwine our legs, made sense.

"Can we get some sleep now?"

"Yes." I chuckle, turning to my side. He does the same, mirroring my position, and we're face-to-face.

Neither of us are in a rush to close our eyes. The intimacy sparking between us feels heavy, like a rope binding us together. Nash inches his hand closer to mine on the pillow, and then he's touching my fingers without actually holding them. My heart beats loud and heavy in my chest and ears, and I swallow nervously. It would be so easy to kiss him again. I've thought of little else since I tasted his lips yesterday, the smallest, briefest taste, my new favorite flavor.

He rubs his pinky against mine and hooks them together. The gesture seems innocent enough, yet it's loaded with possibility. He's asking for more, and every couple of seconds he takes another inch. Soon it will be a mile, and his lips will be on mine again.

"Nash, about that kiss."

"I don't want to hear it, Brewer, just stop talking. Go to bed."

Stubborn ass. "You have to hear it. I...shouldn't have let that happen."

"You didn't, I did."

"It doesn't work that way. I'm your sponsor. I know better."

"Better than what? To allow yourself something you wanted, that we both wanted? Why is that so terrible?"

"Because it breaks the rules."

"What rules?"

"You know the rules, Nash. It's strongly suggested that newcomers don't get into relationships for the first year of their recovery."

"A year?" He raises up on his elbow, peering down at me. "A year?" He repeats, sounding alarmed. "Ain't no fucking way, Brewer. Ain't. No. Way."

Again, I laugh, because it's so easy to do around him. For a man that feels no joy or light in his life, he sure brings so much laughter to others around him.

"It's just strongly suggested, not a hard and fast rule. If we can get your broken dick to work again," I tease, knowing it makes him blush, "it doesn't mean you actually have to wait twelve months to use it again. Addicts tend to use sex as a crutch. It can become an addiction. Anything can become an addiction. Making money, spending money, food, exercise, gambling, and sex. Anything to fill that void in our chest."

"And if it's not sex that I'm looking for? If I just want to be close with someone that makes me feel good? What about that? How can that be terrible for my recovery?"

"Because if that person inadvertently hurts you, if things don't work out between the two of you, you haven't developed the tools yet to cope with the rejection and hurt. It's easy to turn to drugs and alcohol to numb the pain."

"I guess I can see the logic behind that thinking, but that's what I have you for. And the meetings."

He's looking for loopholes, like any good addict would. "We don't always tell on ourselves when we should, when we're hurting the most. Sometimes, we crave the release of punishment and self-harm."

He exhales loudly. "Brewer, I can't do it. I can't wait an entire year. I need—"

Me. He needs *me.* I'm sure that's what he was going to say. If I'm being honest with myself, the idea of trying not to allow myself to touch him or kiss him again for twelve more months feels longer than a lifetime. I really don't believe it's possible.

"Brewer," he pleads, turning back on his side again to face me.

I see it in his aquamarine eyes—the vulnerability, the need, the longing and heat—everything he feels for me, it's all right there. My resolve crumbles to dust.

"I'll make you a deal. Six months. Stay clean for six months, work on your steps, build relationships with the people around you, and continue with your support group and your meetings. Get a plant."

"A plant? That's random," he laughs.

"It's what my sponsor suggested to me before I reached my first year of recovery. He told me to get a plant and keep it alive, and that if I didn't kill it, I just might be ready to be a nurturing, selfless, caring soul for another human being."

"The plant was your relationship indicator?"

"Basically." I laugh. "I know it sounds inane, but it makes sense. It takes discipline and sacrifice and selflessness to keep something alive, to take care of it every day. To cultivate it. If you can take care of a plant, just maybe, you can take care of yourself and possibly someone else."

He searches my face, silent for long minutes. I don't think I've ever felt this soul-deep connection with another person in my life. This all-consuming sudden importance of someone else's existence, like it's the most meaningful thing in my life.

It's absurd and yet makes total sense. *He* makes total sense.

There's a small corner of my dark heart that now belongs to Nashville Sommers, and I don't ever want it back.

"Okay, deal. Six months," he whispers in agreement.

His pinky finger hooks around mine again, and then he's squirming and laughing like he has ants in his pants. A small black lump crawls out from beneath his T-shirt, mewling and licking his face.

"Bedtime for you, little man," he insists, depositing Valor on the pillow between us. "Scoot over, Brewer. Don't squish my cat."

His chewing is louder than the grinding of my teeth. The crunching sound of the cookies he shoved in his mouth are making my jaw tick.

Cookies that *Dan* gave him.

Nash washes them down with a sip of his coffee.

Coffee that *Dan* made him.

I used to think Dan was a decent guy, now, not so much.

They laugh again, which they've done for most of the meeting, heads bent close together, making me feel like a third wheel. Like an *outsider*. Shooting Dan my best hall monitor glare over Nash's shoulder, I try to push them from my mind and focus on the woman sharing. Dan chuckles again, and I'm done. Absolutely finished. At the end of my fucking rope. Crushing my empty coffee cup in my grip, the coffee I made for *myself*, I set my jaw and laser-focus on the woman's story. She's talking about her anger issues. *Yeah, you and me both, sister.* Right now, I'd like to change the three letters of Dan's name to M.U.D.

I'm not usually an angry guy, or an irrationally jealous one, but Dan should know better! Nash isn't his. Dan has been clean for over five years. He knows Nash is a newcomer. Nash isn't available to him or anyone. And when he finally is? You can bet it won't be fucking *Dan* who's first in his line!

Fuck this meeting. Fuck Dan. Fuck Nash.

Smoothly but quickly, I make my way to the door and head outside for a breath of calming air. The night is still, quiet. No traffic or voices can be heard from the church parking lot. Breathing in deep, I feel my lungs expand, my heart rate slowing, my jaw relaxing, before blowing it out.

"Brewer?" Nash approaches. Thank fuck he's alone. "What are you doing out here?"

"Just needed a breath of fresh air."

His wary look says he isn't buying my bullshit.

"Are you okay? Dan said—"

Like a rubber band stretched too tight, my patience snaps. "He's thirteen-stepping you!"

"Thirteen? I thought you said there were only twelve."

Christ, he's so fucking brand new, so naïve. He's clueless. "The thirteenth step is a saying, a concept. It's when someone with considerable clean time hits on a newcomer and tries to take advantage of them."

Nash grins like I said something funny. "You worried about my virtue, Brewer?"

With a roll of my eyes, I insist, "He should know better. He's trying to prey on you. It's cringy."

Nash steps closer, dropping his voice to a whisper. "What are you so worried about? My dick is broken, remember? You said you could maybe fix it, so I'm holding out for you to make good on your promise. *Only you.*"

Great. My dick works perfectly, and it's working right fucking now. "You should be focusing on your recovery, not me fixing your broken dick." We both know that's next to impossible with the level of chemistry sparking between us.

His eyes drop to my lips. "I'm doing the best I can, Brewer. I'm not superhuman. I'm only a man."

Right then, the furious beating in my chest tattoos his name on my heart. It now belongs to him, completely. For the next six months, it will only beat for him. Until he can put us both out of our misery and make it whole again.

"Can we get out of here?" I ask, hoping to escape before the meeting lets out and we're swarmed by the crowd.

"You don't want to say goodbye to Dan?"

My glare has him marked for death. "Get in the car, Nash."

NASH

Black Mountain, NC — Chapter 15

I COULD WAKE UP NEXT TO THAT FACE EVERY MORNING AND die a happy man. He looks so warm and sleepy and just…damn, if I could just crawl between his legs and push myself against his perfect ass, just maybe I could get hard. My brain can't deny that it wants him, if only my dick would get the memo.

I showed up at his door last night, just after midnight, without asking. I knew he would be awake, same as me. Without a word, he let me into his bed, and we fell asleep just like most nights, lying face to face, staring at each other, memorizing the other's features, trying to see inside the other's soul.

Brewer may have different nightmares than I do, but his past is the same as mine. We've both lost someone we loved, someone that meant more to us than anyone else. Not only did we lose that person tragically, their lives cut unfairly short, but we lost them in a way that stayed with us, in a way that altered us forever. I watched as my best friend suffered unimaginable pain and fear until his fear became my own.

I know it's the same for Brewer. Although he lost his buddy in the blink of an eye, he regrets not being able to say goodbye, not being given a chance to try to save his life. Every time he closes his eyes, I know exactly what he sees. His best friend's face exploding in bloody fragments. He can taste it in his mouth, feel it coating his skin. That's the kind of shit you can't ever unsee. The kind of shit that haunts your dreams at night and keeps you awake until darkness morphs into daylight.

Sleeping beside Brewer helps. It doesn't take away the nightmares completely. I still dream, I know this because I wake up several times a night in a cold sweat, with my fight or flight reflex triggered. I just can't remember my dreams, and that's everything. When I wake up and look over to see him and Valor lying beside me, I'm able to fall back asleep almost immediately. They're like my security blankets. I hope I can be the same for him.

"Mind if I grab the first shower?" he asks, his voice full of gravel.

He sounds so sexy in the morning, and with his face covered in stubble, God, he's delicious. "Not at all. I've got to get back upstairs before the rest of the house wakes up."

"Yes, please do." He chuckles, climbing out of bed.

"I heard you talking in your sleep last night, but I have no idea what you were saying. More like mumbling. So mysterious.

What secrets are you hiding?" He disappears into the bathroom, waving me off with a laugh.

But really, what secrets is he hiding? I've always been curious by nature, but when it comes to Brewer, I'm a downright nosy motherfucker. I want to know *everything*. I would never look at his phone or mail or anything like that, but I sure as shit checked his medicine cabinet in his bathroom, and I'd love to know what he keeps in his nightstand drawer. Fuck it. I inch it open and peek inside. A flash of silver catches my eye.

What's that? Carefully lifting it from the drawer, I realize it's a bullet, but not one I've ever seen before.

Holy shit, is that... It is! Brewer, you dirty motherfucker. A prostate massager shaped like a bullet? Why is that the hottest thing I've ever seen?

Because you're imagining him using it, imagining the sleek tip sliding between his perfect cheeks, disappearing inside his tight, warm hole.

My cock kicks, the first sign of life from it in weeks. *You like that?* There's plenty more where that fantasy came from.

Lying back on the pillow, I get comfortable and spread my legs wide. Clicking the top of the cartridge, the bullet comes to life, vibrating in my hand. The thin cotton of my sleep pants doesn't provide much of a barrier from the toy. Lightly tracing the bullet over my soft cock, I soak up the vibrations, enjoying the tickle.

Imagine it's Brewer's mouth. He sucked you to the back of his throat, enveloped your cock in warm wet heat, and he's humming something to cause those vibrations. Without realizing it, I begin to hum the words to my song, the one that's always on my mind as I get lost in the intense sensations running through my shaft. The bullet is trying its damnedest to revive my limp dick, but it refuses to budge. Just kicks here and there, like a fish out of water. I wonder what kind of reaction I'd get from my dick if I were to slide the toy inside my ass. I've only ever bottomed maybe twice before, but the size and girth of the bullet doesn't seem intimidating and knowing it was inside Brewer's ass makes it even more appealing.

Tugging at my waistband, I pull my pants down to my hips but freeze when the little furball climbs up my chest. His tiny razor-sharp claws scratch at my T-shirt, piercing the thin fabric enough to make me wince.

"Good morning," I sigh, pulling my pants back up.

Jeez, it's like having a kid or something. I'm never alone. Great timing, though. Brewer opens the bathroom door, sending a cloud of steam billowing out. He's standing at the sink, brushing his teeth and shaving his face, and I use the opportunity to slip the bullet back inside the drawer where it belongs.

"You're a buzzkill, little man. A real cockblocker," I tease, scratching between his soft ears. Valor just stares up at me with his huge, innocent green eyes and licks his tiny pink button nose. He may be a buzzkill and a cockblocker, but I'm grateful for him.

"Do you have plans today?" Brewer calls out.

Why, does he want to hang out with me? That makes an abundance of serotonin rush through my veins. "I've got a lot of important shit to do, like shop for a plant."

The sound of his laughter floats across the empty space, bringing a smile to my lips.

"I thought we could meet for lunch," he suggests.

"Can I bring my cat and my plant?"

"You can bring anything you want."

"Then it sounds like a plan."

"Good, we can discuss starting your second step."

Yay, just what I want to talk about when I have him sitting across the table from me.

On the other hand, it's a step in the right direction. Forward.

"Hey, Brewer?" He pops his head out of the bathroom. "What's your favorite kind of ammunition?" Brewer looks puzzled, completely lost and thrown by the question, and I can't help but laugh, thinking of the bullet tucked away in his drawer.

Mandy answers my call immediately. "Hey, are you busy?"

"Just finishing up. I'm here at the hospital with Liza and West. We're doing the pre-surgery appointment for my micro dermabrasion."

"Liza? No wonder she didn't answer."

"What do you mean, you called her first?" He sounds slighted.

"That's besides the point. I need a favor."

"Anything, just name it."

"I've got an errand to run, and I need a wingman."

Mandy clears his throat. "Sure, sounds serious. Text me the location and I'll meet up with you when I'm finished here."

Before he can hang up, I ask, "Hey, do they have to put you to sleep for the procedure?"

"Yeah," he says, sounding deflated.

"Well, I'd like to be there. What is that thing you call West?"

"My ball buddy?"

"Yeah that, I want to be your ball buddy." The phone sounds like it's being jostled or passed around and then West's deep voice comes across the line.

"Listen, Sommers, he's already got one nutter buddy, and there's only room for two nuts in our ball sack, so find your own buddy."

My lips twist into a grin as I laugh. "You should get your head checked out again while you're there. It sounds like your TBI is progressing. Put Mandy back on the phone."

Jostling again, and then from Mandy, "See you soon."

Nothing but rows and rows of plants and flowers in every color. I'm completely surrounded and lost. Maybe even overwhelmed.

Mandy shakes his head. "Are you kidding me? This was your super secret errand? You had to buy plants?"

"I never said it was super secret."

"You said you needed a wingman," he accuses.

"I do. I know fuck-all about plants."

"What makes you think I do?"

Shrugging, I remind him, "Hey, that's why I called Liza first."

"What are we doing here?" Mandy asks, sounding genuinely confused.

"Picking out a plant," I say, pointing out the obvious.

"You don't own anything but clothes, and the first thing you want to buy for yourself is a plant? What am I missing?"

Exhaling loudly, my shoulders sag, and I roll my neck back-and-forth. "Brewer and I made a deal. He's willing to waive the one-year ban on relationships and reduce it to six months *if* I can keep a plant alive."

"That's it?"

"And go to meetings, therapy, take my meds, do my step work, go to group, and stay clean."

"Damn, that's a lot. But what's the plant got to do with it?"

"I don't know. He has some half-baked idea about if I can keep it alive, I'm not a total lost cause."

"So then what? What happens in six months if you're still clean and your plant is still alive?"

"I guess I can start dating."

"Is that important to you? Or is it just the idea of dating a certain therapist with wavy brown hair, dark, brooding eyes, and some fancy degrees hanging on his office walls?"

"What makes you think I'm doing this for Brewer?"

"Because I was there when you met him and I saw the way you looked at each other. Oh, and the way you tripped all over yourself and forgot your name."

"I didn't forget my name," I protest, trying not to sound embarrassed.

"Let me see if I can remember how you put it. Oh yeah, I'm

N-Nash. Nashville. Nashville Sommers. Aiden. Nashville Aiden Sommers, Sergeant, but you can call me Nash."

He's a fucking dick, but when he blinks his eyelashes coquettishly, I can't help but laugh. "I definitely didn't sound like that. Help me pick out a plant."

"So, what are we looking for?"

"Something I can't kill. Something low maintenance and hearty."

Mandy snorts. "That's a ringing endorsement for your capabilities."

"I never said I had a green thumb. I just need something I can't kill in six months. Nothing delicate."

"What about this guy?" Mandy points to a snake plant, rubbing his fingers down the long variegated spiky leaves.

"No, it looks weird. This one?" I point to a bushy plant with colorful leaves.

"I like the red."

"Forget it. Looks too tropical, too exotic. What about this guy?" I ask.

"Looks a little Charlie Brownish. I count seven pine needles."

Frustration and anxiety begins to cripple my head, making me feel rushed and unfocused. "Ugh, why is this so difficult?"

"I don't think it is. I think you're making it harder than you need to."

My heart rate spikes, causing a stabbing pain in my chest that feels like I'm having a damn heart attack. "I gotta get out of here."

"You okay?" Mandy looks concerned, setting down the

plant in his hands and coming closer. He takes my wrist and places two fingers over my pulse.

"It's the smell of all this dirt, it makes me think of... Yeah, no I can't." The saliva in my mouth thickens to a bitter paste.

"Point to something and then go wait in the car while I check out."

As my panic starts to rise and the smell in my nose becomes stronger, more potent, my eyes settle on a plant. The perfect plant. A thick, woodsy, braided trunk, dark, green leaves, not too fancy or too plain.

"That one," I point out.

"All right, go. I'll take care of it."

When he emerges from the nursery carrying my plant, I'm sitting on the metal bench outside the store, bent over with my head between my knees, rocking my body to stave off the rising nausea.

Mandy takes a seat beside me. "You good?"

"I think so."

In through my nose, hold it for the count of three, out through my mouth. In through my nose, hold for the count of three, out through my mouth. Rinse and repeat, until my heart rate slows, and my mouth isn't filled with saliva, which is usually what happens right before I empty my stomach.

"I think I would have lost it if you weren't with me."

"No problem. I'm glad I was here."

"What the fuck am I even doing?" I ask, sitting up. I scrub my hand over my face. Take another deep breath. "I'm worried about keeping a plant alive and dating? I can't even make it through a store without falling apart."

"It's not a big deal. I have setbacks all the time."

"You do?"

"Oh yeah. I think the worst is when I make kids cry because they're scared of my face." My gaze runs over the thick red scar tissue covering the left side of Mandy's face, a souvenir from the war. "I don't mind when they ask questions or ask their moms questions about my face, like I'm not even standing there, they're just kids. But when they look genuinely scared of me?" His face tightens, and Mandy just looks...sad. "Yeah, that fucks me up. Compared to that, the flashbacks are nothing. Just a few moments lost from my life that I didn't want back anyways."

His cavalier attitude about the flashbacks rewrites a lot of my internal bias against myself and PTS. He's right, it's just a few moments of my life lost. In the grand scheme of things, it's a drop in the bucket. Remembering those awful memories is going to happen either way, whether I lose time or not.

"How do you deal with that?"

His scars twist the left side of his smile into a grimace. "I remind myself that I'm a good man, I'm a good friend, and that I have a good heart that isn't scarred and burned like my face. I deserve to be happy. I deserve to be loved. I deserve good things, and so do you. Come on, Nash," he emphasizes, clapping me on the back, "we paid the ultimate price. We deposited all of our coins in the karma bank. It's time for some good shit to come our way."

How in the fuck does he stay so positive after everything he's suffered? "You really think I can do this?"

"Hell yeah, you're a fucking soldier. A warrior. This is nothing. You got this."

"I meant what I said. On the phone. I want to be there when you have your surgery. Even if I'm just sitting in the waiting room with West. I can't count how many times you've shown up for me, and it's time I deposit a few coins in my karma bank and give back."

"I'd like that. Just don't call yourself my nutter buddy. He takes that shit real serious." Mandy laughs.

"I didn't think you were serious when you asked to bring the cat and the plant," Brewer confesses, staring at the leafy potted plant taking up most of the available table space.

Scooting my chair closer to the table, I'm careful not to bump Valor, slung across my chest and sleeping. "What else would I have done with them?"

"Maybe leave the plant in the car?"

"It's too hot in there. It could wilt."

Brewer eyes me cautiously. "You're really taking this seriously, aren't you?"

Wanting to make my point without also making an obvious declaration, I stare right into his eyes. "You have no idea how serious I'm taking this."

You have no idea how serious I am about you.

"Well, that's good, I guess. When we get home, we'll find a good spot on the back deck."

"Hell no!" Brewer looks startled at my outburst. "I mean, it's too risky. Anything could happen to Leif outside."

"Leif?" he asks, sounding equal parts amused and horrified.

"Yeah, like leaf, but Leif. Sounds more like a proper name. I couldn't just keep calling him 'the plant'."

Brewer rubs his face, and I know he's hiding his smile behind his hand. "So, not outside?"

"Not a chance."

While I'm staring at Leif, Brewer is studying me. "What are some of these risk factors of the outdoors I'm not aware of? You know, just in case I should move my other potted plants inside."

"Uh, acid rain, a tornado, hail storm, lightning strike, a swarm of locusts? The list of possibilities is endless."

"Uh huh. I see." He goes silent, and I assume he's looking over his menu. "Nash?"

I look up to meet his gaze, and his face is soft, a warm smile teases his lips. His expression is full of affection. *For me.*

"I'm rooting for you, and the plant."

Fuck me sideways, he might as well tell me he wants to date me and my limp dick and my messed up head. "Leif."

"I'm rooting for you and Leif. And Valor, of course. You've taken on a lot of responsibility in a short amount of time, but it doesn't surprise me in the least. It's who you are. A soldier, a Sergeant, a leader. A hero. I think you'll do fine."

I'm definitely no hero, but Brewer can think what he wants. He'll never be wrong in my book.

"So, let's talk about the second step," he says, looking over his menu. "This step is all about handing over the reins. In step one, we admitted we were powerless and that our lives had become unmanageable. That can leave a lot of people searching for answers or feel like floundering fish. If we aren't in control, who is? The second step is about restoring hope. Someone is looking out for us and has brought us this far, and we have to believe they won't fail us now. You need to determine who that is for you. There are no wrong answers, but I want you to dig deep and keep an open mind."

He chuckles when I sigh dramatically, like I'm already exhausted from just hearing his talk about finding God, let alone actually having to do it.

"Can't we skip this step for now and circle back to it later?" *Or never?*

"No, nice try." Our waiter approaches, and Brewer places his order. "I'll have the turkey club, side of fries, and a glass of water, please. And he'll have the vegetable soup and the tuna fish salad. Thanks."

The longer I stare, the wider my smile grows, until it stretches from cheek to cheek. Brewer catches my grin, and his eyes grow wide. "Oh, jeez, I didn't mean to order for you, it just slipped out...because I know with your stomach, and the meds... I'm so sorry! Did you want something else?"

I'd eat liver pâté if he ordered it for me, just because I like his caretaking and ownership of me. But, "Tuna fish salad?" I ask, wondering where that came from?

Brewer looks chagrined. "In case Valor wakes up."

My heart. My motherfucking heart. It's melting. "Good call."

NASH

BALLS
Black Mountain, NC

Chapter 16

M*y head is a loud and foreign place.*

Like standing in a crowded auditorium, surrounded by hundreds of people all talking at once. Their voices blend together in a deafening cacophony of sound, drowning out my own thoughts, until I can't hear or even think. That's what I hear most of the time, but when things get dark for me, the voices become angrier. Louder. The staccato ricochet of a gun firing. Men yelling. The earth-shattering blast of a bomb exploding. Soldiers shouting in Pashto, shoving the barrels of their guns in my face, in my back. Roaring helicopter blades whirring like a million buzzing bees swarming.

Among the recent memories, pieces of my past sneak through, until I can't separate past from present, or reality from delusion. Fragments of conversation with other soldiers. A movie I watched years ago. Celebrating Christmas with my family when I was a child. I just want to escape for a few moments. Precious minutes of silence where nothing exists but the sound of my heart beating, the easy in and out of my breathing, feeling my chest and lungs expand with breath and with life.

Solitude. I want solitude. Nothing inside my head or outside my body. I want to disappear.

As I cower in the corner of my darkened bedroom, with Valor licking my bare toes, I try to block it all out, the nightmare that woke me, the memories that bombard me, the noise in my head. I try to let go of all of it, surrendering to the chaos, surrendering to the broken mess in my head.

I don't want to feel anymore. I don't want to fight anymore. I'm tired. Tired and empty. If only I could lose myself in the bottom of a bottle tonight or pop a couple of pills to put me back to sleep. Unfortunately, none of those options are available to me anymore. If I want to forget, I'll have to do it the hard way. *The healthier way.*

I can hear Brewer's voice in my head. *"Hand over the reins. Admit you're powerless."* I'm a floundering fish searching for answers. Who is in control if not me? Who do I pray to to restore me to sanity?

Right now, I'll pray to anyone to find sanity. *Donald Duck,* the neighbor's dog, the fucking washing machine. I just want to feel sane.

Sometimes, I forget what that used to feel like.

When I feel myself beginning to spiral, sometimes I'm

afraid that if I give in, I'll never find my way back. I'll get lost in the memory and never wake up. It may be an irrational fear, but it's a very real fear.

"Maybe it's you," I whisper to Valor. "Maybe you're my higher power. I see how hard you're trying to save me." I scoop him up and cuddle him against my chest, rubbing my cheek against his soft fur. He purrs loudly, his entire little body vibrating like a tuning fork. "But you're just a little man, and I'm a big guy with too much for you to carry. My burden weighs more than your entire body."

The movie continues to play in my head, a kaleidoscope of haunting images that have become the soundtrack of my life. I almost don't even hear the soft knock at my door before Brewer slips quietly inside my room.

"Nash?" He searches the empty bed for me. "Nash?"

"Over here," I croak.

"You didn't answer my texts. I came to check on you." Brewer crouches down in front of me, placing his reassuring hands on my weighted shoulders.

"I'm drowning. I'm doing everything I can to stay clean, but it's not getting better. I'm drowning, Brewer. And I don't even know if I want to be saved anymore. I'm tired."

"You don't need water to feel like you're drowning, Nash. You're clean, but you're not recovering. There's a difference. You can't begin to recover until you give up control and ask for help. Surrender."

He sits down fully beside me and tugs me until I scoot between his legs. His big strong arms wrap around my chest, and Brewer holds me tight, holds on to me as he rocks me and Valor, whispering soothing sounds in my ear.

"Shh. I'm here. You're not alone anymore. You'll never be alone again. I know you're angry with God. You feel like he stole something precious from you, that he cheated you somehow, cheated Victor Gutierrez, but you're only hurting yourself if you don't ask Him for help. Hasn't He forgiven you every time you fucked up? Why can't you forgive Him?"

His words resonate within me, but it's not that simple. "It's not supposed to work that way. He's supposed to be better than me. God doesn't make mistakes. That's what I was taught in Sunday school."

"I was taught a lot of things that don't make sense to me now, and nobody is going to tell me what is right and wrong for *me*. Your relationship with Him can be whatever you want it to be, whatever makes you feel comfortable. Don't let anyone dictate what you believe."

"I want to," I cry, rocking harder. "I want to believe. I want to forgive. But I'm so fucking angry, and if I let go of this anger, what do I have left? Some days I feel like it's the only thing fueling my body." Hot tears roll down my cheeks and drip onto my bare chest, bathing me in their frustration and desperation.

"You let go of the anger and you replace it with hope. Grab on to hope. Let it lift you up above the anger, above the guilt and the sadness."

The weight in my chest eases slightly, and I swallow hard past the constriction in my dry throat. "I'm afraid to hope. I'm afraid, Brewer. I hate saying that, but I am. If I hope and I fail, it's over. I can't come back from that."

"I won't let you fail. I'll never let you fail," he whispers fiercely.

For long minutes, he holds me, rocks me gently, his fingers scratching through my hair, his soft voice caresses my ear. And then he sings to me, and I can barely hear the words over my broken sobbing. It wracks my body with tremors, and I feel as if I'm breaking apart into thousands of tiny shards and being remade into a stronger man. A man who has hope. A man who isn't so afraid to trust.

A man looking for a miracle.

"The sun will come out tomorrow, Nash. You can bet that tomorrow there will be sun."

The kitchen is already crowded to maximum capacity by the time I shuffle in, searching for coffee. The smell lured me from bed more effectively than any bucket of ice water or bugle. In the desert, the *big voice* used to wake me. The overhead speaker could be heard from anywhere on the FOB, no matter where you tried to hide from the intrusive sound. But the smell of brewing coffee is a thousand times more potent.

"There he is," Nacho greets in his usual cheery voice. He's standing at the stove making breakfast, just like every morning. "I watered your plant."

He did not! "Tell me you didn't. You didn't use tap water, did you?"

"Is there a reason I shouldn't have?" Nacho asks, sounding confused. *I do not need to wake up to this shit.* "Just kidding, man, relax. I saw the jug of distilled water sitting next to the sink."

I'm instantly relieved until Brewer asks, "Really, Nash? Don't you think you're taking this too far?"

He's nursing a cup of coffee at the kitchen table. He's got to be as exhausted as I am. We stayed awake for hours, with him just holding me, singing to me, soothing my fears. Eventually, I fell asleep against his chest with his arms around me. Somehow, I woke up in my bed. I'll have to thank him for that later.

"I'm not taking it too far. There's chlorine in that tap water. Probably aluminum and lead, too. You're poisoning your plants," I inform him.

He just laughs. "Your meds are on the counter."

"I think it's sexy the way you take care of your plant and your kitty," Tex purrs, coming up behind me. "Maybe I'll call you Daddy, because you like to be responsible for everyone and everything."

"Don't you dare," I warn him. I can't even take him seriously with his fuzzy pink *Hello Kitty* robe over brown and red plaid pajama pants.

Where does this man shop? Forever 21?

"There's all kinds of stuff in that tap water," Miles confirms. "I think it makes you sound perfectly sane."

"I was never sane." I laugh, tipping my mug to him in salute.

"Okay, enough," Brewer concludes. "You have to get to work," he says to Tex. "You have a morning meeting you're going to be late for," he reminds Nacho. "And you," he says, looking at Miles, "I don't know what it is you do all day, but go do it. Nash, you're with me. I'm heading into BALLS early, and you have an appointment with Riggs in the gym. Bring a change of shorts or a bathing suit. Something you can get wet."

Hell yeah, he wants to go for a swim with me after my workout? I'm down. Studying Brewer over the rim of my mug, I ask teasingly, "Do you ever feel embarrassed when you have to tell people you work at a place called BALLS?"

"No, never," he deadpans. "I love BALLS."

"We all love BALLS, Brewer," Nacho jokes, slapping his dish rag down on the counter.

———

We pass Margaret Anne with a wave and continue on down the hall.

"I thought when I retired from the military that sweating before the morning sunrise was a thing of the past," I bitch.

"Well, you thought wrong," Brewer informs me with a smirk. As I'm about to head into the gym, he says, "Come see me when you finish. I'd like to start your EMDR today."

"EMDR?"

"Eye Movement Desensitization and Reprocessing Therapy. It helps with PTSD. It's still a controversial and experimental treatment, but I don't believe it's harmful, and I think you're the perfect candidate."

"I'll come find you when I'm done."

When I enter the gym, I see Riggs heading toward me.

"Did you bring a change of clothes?"

"I did."

"Go change in the locker room and meet me in the pool."

Meet *him* in the pool? Not Brewer?

After changing into navy swim trunks, I find Riggs in the pool area, except he's not dressed for swimming. Still wearing his track pants and BALLS T-shirt, his ever-present clipboard and stopwatch in hand, Riggs stands poolside like he's not getting in.

Am I putting on a show for him? Water ballet?

"Here, hold this for me," I say, depositing a little black ball of fur in his lap before he can object.

Riggs's eyes roll. "Come on, not again."

The echo of voices filter through the door leading in from the locker room.

"Sommers! You're joining us, man?"

West Wardell? And McCormick? *Whiskey Tango Foxtrot—what the fuck?*

"Joining you for what? A leisurely dip in the pool?"

McCormick laughs. "Is that what we're calling it now?"

No, no, no, this is not what I signed up for today. "Brewer made it sound as if we were going for a swim together."

"I bet he did," West jokes. "Hey, Riggs, do you think we have enough members now to form a synchronized swimming team?"

Riggs smirks. "We're getting there. Get in the pool."

"Don't start without me," Brandt calls out, jogging out of the locker room. He executes a beautiful dive, and when he breaks the surface of the water, he shakes his head, sending droplets flying into West's face.

"Damn man," he complains, wiping his face, "give me a

hand." West and McCormick are seated on the side of the pool, removing their prosthetics.

Like he either didn't hear him or is ignoring him, Brandt submerges under the water again, swimming to the other side of the pool and back while holding one breath. When he comes up for air, he shakes his head again, spraying West, and sticks his finger in his ear.

Maybe he's got water in it?

"Brandt!" West sends a volley of water flying his way. "Brandt," he calls out louder.

Finally, he turns toward West. "What's up?"

I slip into the pool and join them in the deep end. Instead of pointing out what happened or acting annoyed, West smiles affectionately. "Can you give us a hand?"

"Sorry," Brandt apologizes, making his way toward them.

I recall him sharing in the group about losing his hearing. I'm glad for him that he has a partner who understands his challenges. A partner who looks at him like that and loves him like crazy, in spite of his body failing him. It gives the rest of us hope.

"Don't you have to be short one leg to join this synchronized swim team?"

Maybe because he's looking at me, Brandt hears me, and he laughs. "I guess you could say I've got a 'leg up'."

McCormick takes him down, dunking his head under the water, and when he lets him up, Brandt spits a mouthful of water into McCormick's face. "Not cool, man," McCormick barks. "Only people with one leg can make leg jokes."

"Yeah, well, between the two of us, West and I have three

legs total, so really each of us has one and a half, so that qualifies me."

"He's right," Riggs calls out, "he's on the team."

These guys are nuts. Maybe this isn't as bad as spending an hour pounding the treadmill. Just because we're in the water doesn't mean Riggs gives us a break, though. By the time we're done swimming laps and dragging weights attached to our legs as we walk across the shallow end—just me and Brandt on that one—my legs feel as weak and wiggly as jelly.

In the locker room, I switch back to my jeans and West asks, "Are you gonna join us for group after this?"

"I can't. I've got to meet up with Brewer for therapy. He's gonna work some kind of magic mojo on my head."

"All right, I'll knit you a swim cap. So you don't get your hair wet next time," he teases.

Asshole. Yeah, he made me smile. "Hey, can you guys do me a favor?"

"Sure, name it."

"Can you babysit for me?"

From the second I enter Brewer's office, I'm pissed. At least, highly annoyed. Dropping a notepad on the table, he pushes to his feet, greeting me with a huge, silly grin.

"How was your workout?"

Glaring at him, I take a seat on the couch, since my legs aren't strong enough to continue standing, and I continue to glare, grilling him with my piercing gaze.

"What?" He laughs, pretending like he has no clue.

"You know what!"

"I have no idea what you're talking about," he says, taking a seat across from me.

"You led me to believe we were going for a swim. Together. *Alone.*"

"Did I? How...regretful. I can't imagine how we got our wires crossed. But as long as you had a good workout, that's all that matters."

"I did," I gripe.

"Where's your little shadow?"

"He's knitting swim caps with West and McCormick."

He's wearing that stupid grin again. The infuriatingly charming one that makes him look kissable. The one that means I said something amusing, and that he's falling for me.

"What?" I may sound annoyed, but inside, I'm hiding a grin just as huge and silly.

"Nothing, I just love how you're becoming a part of their community. Where's Leif?"

"With Brandt. Right about now, Leif is recounting the horrors of his short life. How he started as an orphan seed, and then went to live in the orphanage with all the other orphan seeds until he was sold to the highest bidder. He's had a very traumatic start."

Now he's full-on laughing at me. The overhead lights twinkle in his eyes, and they crinkle at the corners. Brewer Marx is a beautiful man, inside and out. What I wouldn't give to make him mine, not that I have much to give. But if I did...

His laughter dies off, but his smile remains. "You ready to get started?"

Why am I so fucking nervous? "Do you really think this is gonna work?"

"I do. Seventy to ninety-five percent of patients who undergo this therapy achieve reduced recurring episodes, and many have reported zero episodes."

"I can't imagine what that would feel like, complete and total freedom. But I'll take anything. Have you undergone this therapy?"

"I have. Several times. That's why I know it's safe for you."

"Did it work for you?" *Please say no. Please say no. I'm afraid to hope.*

Brewer sighs. "I can't help my subconscious thoughts, like when I'm dreaming and I have nightmares. But I often don't remember them when I wake up. After completing the last therapy, which was my fourth treatment, I have not experienced any conscious episodes, where I lose time, with one foot in the present and one in the past, nor have I completely regressed. Sometimes, I'm still triggered, but it's mostly just thoughts and memories. I can deal with those using the coping tools I've learned."

"Then I'm ready," I say with conviction.

"The good news is that you've already completed three of the eight steps. Mostly just assessments and intake questions since I already know so many details about your traumatic experience, like locations, time and date, names, and the sequence of events. I still have a couple of questions, though, like your main triggers."

Scrubbing my face, I breathe out tiredly. "I don't know, seems like everything triggers me. More so when I'm tired or already on edge with anxiety. The smell of dirt and earth. Anything musty and stale or dank. Small, dark, confined spaces. The smell of anything rotting, like garbage and food, especially meat." Just thinking about it makes a wave of nausea roll through my stomach. "Barking dogs. That's a huge one for me. Probably gunfire, but I haven't heard any since I've been home. Anything that tastes cold and metallic." Brewer picks up his notepad and pen and begins to write down my triggers. "I don't like being tied up or having my hands bound. I fucking hate rats, and the smell of piss."

He looks up from his notes. "That's a great start. You display fifteen of the seventeen classic symptoms of complex PTSD, everything but the hyperarousal and the autoimmune conditions."

"Hyperarousal," I scoff, "I wish."

Brewer smiles knowingly. "I think the autoimmune stuff is caused by prolonged heightened anxiety, which thanks to your prolific drug use, numbed most of it."

"You mean it was good for something?"

His sardonic expression tells me he's not amused. "I'm going to begin by running through deeper, more elaborate descriptions of your triggers." He grabs a pen from the small table beside his chair and clicks the tip. A small, focused laser light shines from the tip. "Follow this penlight with your eyes, keeping your concentration on the light." Brewer stands and crosses to the switch on the wall, dimming the lights low, but not off completely. "I know you don't like the dark, but this isn't an enclosed space and I'm here with you. It will help you to focus on the light instead of your surroundings or me."

"Are you trying to hypnotize me?" I ask jokingly.

"This is not hypnotherapy. I just want you to feel relaxed and open, but you are in complete control of your mind. I'm going to suggest replacement words for some of the ones that trigger you to try to retrain your thinking. Just follow my lead.

"Let's start with some breathing exercises. In through your nose, out through your mouth, hold it for the count of three."

After two minutes of breathing, Brewer raises the penlight, moving it left to right, and I follow it with my eyes for another minute before we begin.

"Dirt. Earth. Underground. Tunnels." He pauses for a moment, and I continue to follow the light. "Enriched soil. Seedlings. Healthy plants. Flowers and trees." Then he moves onto the next trigger word. "Musty. Stale. Dank. Cell. Dark. Confined." Brewer pauses again. "Fresh. Clean. Bright. Spacious. Alive. Life. Lemon-fresh."

He never stops moving the light from left to right. "Are you seeing and feeling these words?"

"Yes. I can smell them."

"Good. Let's continue."

He follows through the long list of my triggers, describing each one in depth, listing every possible variation that I could associate with them, and then replacing them with opposite words, healing words. The stark contrast is like night and day, and I can *feel* the words, I can smell them, like a sensory experience, both the good and the bad ones.

It's very possible the next time I'm caught in a memory with one of these descriptions, my brain might switch over to some of the positive reinforcement words, instead of latching on to all the negative ones. Not guaranteed, but very possible. Like Brewer said, it's a repetitive therapy, and I have to retrain my brain.

"Tell me about Victor Gutierrez. Tell me about a time when you and Victor were in the dark, maybe even in a confined space, and it had a positive outcome."

My eyes never stop tracking the light. "That's easy. It was the day the electricity went out in the barracks. G and I were caught in the elevator on the third floor. We were stuck in there for four hours, no light, no AC, no water, and he had to pee something terrible. I kept talking about the beach, describing the ocean and the sound of the waves, waterfalls, anything that might make him piss his pants. And the guys outside the elevator doors were constantly banging on them, shouting ridiculous things about what we might be up to inside the elevator. You know how they are. This was way before I came out as gay, so they thought it was real funny. Eventually, the electric came back on, but not before G pissed himself. They teased him about that for years, leaving diapers in his locker."

So fucking clever, Brewer, making me think of a time that I laughed with my buddy in the dark, in a confined space, with stale air and the smell of piss.

This goes on and on as I roll through old memories with G, reinforcing the belief that dark, confined spaces aren't always bad. That barking dogs and the smell of trash aren't always doom and gloom.

Before he ends the session, Brewer asks me to visualize my time in the desert through mental snapshots, like looking through a photo album of pictures.

"In your mind, I want you to create distance between then and now. Not just distance of time, but space. Those memories, those pictures, belong to another life, a long time ago, in a place miles and miles away on the other side of the world. That place can't touch you now. Then and now, two different times, two different places, two different worlds. Those pictures belong to a different Nash. An entirely different man. That life can't haunt you now, it can't hurt you now. Remove yourself from that life and create distance. Every time you think about it, move yourself further away."

He clicks the light off, and we go through the breathing exercises again.

"How do you feel?"

"A little disassociated. I'm definitely still back there in my head."

"Back where? In the barracks? In the good times? Or are you back in the desert?"

"Both. Everything is sort of mixing together in the same bowl. My head is everywhere at once."

"That's good, though. Get the memories mixed together. Dilute the bad ones with the good. Do you feel tired?"

I take a deep breath and blow it out with a sigh. "Yeah, I guess so."

"We're going to head home now, and I'm going to keep an eye on you the rest of the day. It's common to suffer headaches, or maybe even a setback after this, and I want to be there for you."

Suddenly, tears rush to my eyes, pooling and blurring my vision before they track down my cheeks. I don't even know where they came from, but I suddenly feel like bawling. In the blink of an eye, I feel overwhelmed and exhausted.

"Why am I crying?" I ask, sniffling as I wipe away the tears.

"Because like you said, we just stirred everything up into a big bowl and mixed it all together. The good and the bad. It's like opening the tops of ten different cans at once and combining all the ingredients. Those cans held your memories and your feelings. Everything is raw and fresh right now."

Brewer sits beside me on the couch, taking me into his arms. He turns his body sideways so that I'm lying against his chest, and he rocks me, like he did the other night in my bedroom, in the corner on the floor. The way he smells, like laundry detergent and deodorant, with a hint of musky cologne, is the most enticing scent I've ever smelled. Being held tightly in his arms, rocked against his solid chest, is the safest feeling in the world.

With the lights dimmed, and the soothing sounds he whispers in my ear, I close my eyes and drift away. When I open them again, I realize an hour has passed. A warm, soft lump of fur sits on my chest, sleeping soundly.

"Let me take you home," Brewer murmurs.

BREWER

Chapter 17

Serenity House
Black Mountain, NC

Hot breath caresses my skin.

The brush of soft lips.

My thighs are alive with sensation and the pleasure centers in my balls, lighting me up with need and heat and want. Silky hair tickles my skin, and the coarse scratch of his scruffy chin sets my nerve endings on fire. I throw back the covers to get a look because I *have* to watch. The sight of his blond head between my thighs makes my balls draw up tight. They're swollen with seed, the skin thickening, and I'm burning to release in his mouth.

I want to see Nash swallow my load. I want to see him lick his lips and ask for more.

His ocean blue eyes are trained on me, full of heat and need.

He looks filthy and wicked with my cock stretching his lips, and I buck my hips, feeding him another inch or two.

"Take it. Suck my cock." I barely recognize the sound of my own voice, so raspy and deep. Guttural. I'll die if I don't come soon. "I need you. Need your mouth." He sucks hard on the tip, making me shiver. "Please, Nash. Finish me."

I'm so beyond horny I don't care that I'm begging.

Just put me out of my misery.

He slides down to the root and back up again, circling the head with his talented tongue, dipping into my slit to draw out drops of pearly liquid. He shows me his tongue, the pale drop glistens before he swallows it with a wolfish smile.

Fuck, he's such a tease, the best kind of tease. I'm desperate to come but don't want it to end. I could go on and on all night, enduring the sweet torture of his wicked mouth. It's like being in both heaven and hell at once.

Palming the back of his head, I guide him down to the base of my cock, until his nose is buried in the nest of dark curls, and he breathes in my musky scent and rubs his nose in it before sliding back down my shaft.

He fucking loves it, he loves to suck my cock, and that thought gets me hotter than the warm, wet suction of his mouth. The combination brings me to the edge of sanity, and I clutch his short hair between my knuckles and pull as I bury my cock in the back of his throat and unleash my load.

The sound of his gagging brings on a fresh round of thick pulses, coating his tongue and cheeks. I want my flavor *everywhere*—in his mouth, in his nose, in his throat. I want him to memorize the taste of my cum, the weight of my cock on his tongue, and the feel of it stretching his lips until his jaw aches.

I want him to be sore tomorrow and remember how he gagged on my release.

Because *I'll* be remembering it, all day and all night.

"Come up here and let me hold you," I plead, tugging at his shoulders.

Nash crawls up my body, his skin warm and soft against mine, and he lays his head on my chest. Can he hear my heart beating for him? I can feel how fast it is from my orgasm. *He* did that to me.

"I love your mouth."

He doesn't answer because he's already asleep. The soft warm puff of his breath skates over the fine hairs on my chest, causing ripples of sensation that make my nipples tighten.

These unguarded moments, where I just get to hold him and treasure him and thank God for bringing him into my life, are few and far between. I'm not in any rush. I just want to lie here all night and stroke his soft skin, trace over his spine and count the vertebrae with my fingers, and drag them through his soft silky hair.

I want to savor him all night long.

Eventually, I drift off to sleep, and when I open my eyes again, Nash is gone. I'm disappointed but not surprised. He was never really here, was he? It was all just my head playing tricks on me, my desire ruling my subconscious. I dreamed him like a siren dragged from the darkest shadows into my hottest fantasy.

A fantasy I can't make real for another five months.

"Oh my God," Tex moans around a mouthful of meat, "this tastes better than sex."

"You outdid yourself, Nacho," I second, shoving another taco in my mouth.

The seasoned carnitas taste better than any restaurant I've ever eaten at. Garlic, cilantro, chipotle, lime juice. It's got it all. The flavors burst in my mouth like a party. *Like a fiesta.* A smile tugs at my lips. *Why was I born with the corniest sense of humor?*

"It's not terrible," Miles grudgingly compliments. That's high praise coming from him.

"Keep cooking like this, and I'm never moving out," Nash threatens.

Moving out? A spike of panic grips my heart. *Where the fuck is he going? When?*

"It's good practice for the food truck I'm going to open someday. I should have enough saved up in about ten years," Nacho jokes.

Nash takes a bite of his Mexican street corn and groans, sounding completely inappropriate and making my dick hard in seconds. He sounds just like he did in my dream, except that was a whole different kind of cob in his mouth.

"You know, you don't have to wait ten years," Nash points out. "I could invest in your food truck, and we could get it up and running in no time. I don't know anything about starting a business or about food, but I know this is the best taco I've ever eaten, and I'm willing to throw money at it to prove my point."

Nacho stills, his corn forgotten in his hand. "You mean it? You would invest in my business?"

"Yeah, I'm dead serious. I'm not just investing in your business, I'm investing in *you*. I see how passionate you are about cooking. It's a shame to waste your talent in somebody else's kitchen. They don't pay you nearly enough at that restaurant for you to squander your dream. You want the money, it's yours. I'm not doing a fucking thing with it. It's just sitting around collecting interest."

"I can't touch that money," Nacho says regretfully. "That's your money from the…"

"You're right, it is, and I earned it. Every fucking penny. Hazard pay, months of sitting around in the desert choking on that moon dust with nothing to spend my money on, collecting paychecks, retirement pay, and a settlement for what I went through. But what good does it do me going to waste? If I invest in your business, we'll both have a future. We'll both make plenty of money. I'll be a silent partner. I don't want to tell you what to do and what to change, I just want to eat your food," he says with a laugh.

"Can I think about it?" Nacho asks, sounding suspiciously like he's on the verge of tears.

"Of course, the offer stands. Let me know what you decide."

I didn't know it was possible for my heart to grow any bigger or hold any more affection for this man than it already does, but he just proved me wrong. He's so incredibly selfless, the best kind of friend you could ask for.

The kind of man I hope to someday have by my side.

"Ooh, maybe I'll change your name from Daddy to Daddy Warbucks," Tex gushes.

Nash picks a chunk of tomato from the salad bowl and chucks it at him.

Silence descends as we stuff our faces and our bellies until Nash remarks, "This is nice."

He's not talking to anyone in particular, just more of a comment or observation. How lonely has he been? So in need of a family dinner and friends.

He feeds Valor a nibble of pork, and I find myself envious of a damn kitten, getting to lick his fingers clean. What the hell is wrong with me lately? I'm acting as if I've never been laid before. Thoughts of him invade almost every waking hour of my day, sometimes several times an hour. I can't stop thinking about him. About his mouth, about his smooth hard chest, fantasizing about what his lower half looks like. I don't want to dream of it, I want to know from memory.

I want to experience him in the flesh.

"Brewer?"

"I'm sorry, what?"

"I said the toilet upstairs is running."

"Thanks for letting me know. I'll take care of it after dinner."

"I've always liked a man who is capable with his hands," Tex admits, doing some slinky thing with his body like a cat in heat.

"Shocker. You like all men for one reason or another," Miles points out.

"Hold off on seconds. I've got a tray of pastelitos for

dessert." I glance at Nash, and he looks back, raising his eyebrows in question. I've definitely got his attention.

When he finally takes his first bite, there's no longer any question. "These are from...Violet. G's mom made these."

"She did. She wanted to make sure you were eating well."

"Every time he went home to visit, he'd come back with containers of these things, and we'd sit in front of the TV and polish them off in one sitting," he recalls fondly.

"Maybe don't tell her that," I say wisely, laughing. "But I'm positive there's more where these came from."

Nash stares at the tray of pastries, looking conflicted, and I wish I knew what he was thinking. But then he grabs another and shoves it in his mouth, licking his fingers clean. Thank God I made the right call. He needs a bit of her love in his belly.

They clear the platter within minutes and then kitchen cleanup begins. We all take turns washing and clearing, and in under fifteen minutes, I'm alone with Nash, nursing the last pastelito and a cup of coffee at the kitchen table.

My phone chimes with a message.

Speak of the devil.

Violet:

Did he like them?

> Loved them. The platter is already empty.

Violet:

> I'll make more! I have a favor to ask. I don't know who else to turn to.

> Ask me anything

> Violet:
>
> I have a growing honey-do list since my husband passed. Do you know anyone I could hire to fix things around here?

> I'll see what I can do.

Compassion and sympathy tug at my heart. She lost her son and her husband in the same month. Now she's faced with maintaining a house all by herself, something she's never had to do before. She's lost. A lot like Nash. Speaking of, I look up to find him staring at me, a curious but amused smile teasing his lips.

"Are you planning a hot date?"

"Hardly," I scoff. "It's...Violet. She wants to know if you enjoyed her gift."

"Please tell her how much it meant to me."

"I've got to find a handyman to take care of some things at her house," I mention, glancing at my screen to see if she's responded.

"I can do it," he blurts.

Fuck. He's getting in deeper and deeper. But is he in over his head?

"You don't even know what *it* is."

"Doesn't matter. I can figure it out. Let me help her."

"Nash, we've talked about this. I'm not sure you're ready."

His hand curls into a white-knuckled fist. "Brewer, I need this. My life can't just be about meetings and meds. I *need* this," he implores, begging with his eyes.

Like I can say no to anything he asks. Especially when he looks at me like this. "Let me think about it."

"Why don't you ask Violet how she feels about it?"

Manipulative bastard. Always searching for a loophole.

There's a joke about addicts and how they're all qualified to chair the Ways and Means Committee because every addict excels at finding ways and means to get what they want.

"I said I'll think about it," I insist in my most stern sponsor voice.

I'm not just his sponsor, though, I'm his therapist, and his friend. I'm concerned for him on every level, afraid of making one wrong step that will set him back in his recovery. It's a huge responsibility to carry on my shoulders, but there's no one else I would trust with it. He's in good hands with me.

Oh God, don't think about your hand on the back of his head last night. Don't go there while he's sitting across from you.

"I'm going to go take a shower, and then I'm going to turn in for the night," I say, hoping to escape before I say or do something I'll regret.

Two hours later, I'm wide awake, staring at the shadows that dance across my ceiling. Have I become so dependent on Nash sleeping beside me that I can't rest without him? Or is it just pure, unadulterated longing that keeps me awake?

Leave him alone, Brewer. Let the man rest, let him recover.

Fuck it. I grab my phone off the nightstand.

> You awake?

No answer. Fifteen minutes later, and there's still no answer, yet I know he's awake. He's always awake. I didn't add a sedative to his cocktail tonight. He's slowly weaning off them, and without them, there's no way he can just knock out.

Damn it, what if he's having an episode? What if he's scared and suffering, stuck in the past and can't find his way back? What if he needs me?

I can't waste another minute on what if. Not if Nash needs help.

Climbing out of bed, I make my way upstairs, down the hall, to his room. When he doesn't answer the third knock, I quietly slip inside.

Jesus Christ.

"Jesus Christ! Knock first," Nash shrieks.

"I did, three times." Nash, shirtless and definitely wide awake, has his hand down his pants, and I don't need a degree in psychology to know what he's doing. "I'll just go..." *Does that mean it's working?*

"Wait." He blows out a frustrated sigh, removing his hand. "Why aren't the pills working? I'm starting to feel a little better, and I thought, I hoped..."

Fuck me silly. Fuck me silly. Fuck me silly. Don't do it, Brewer. *Do not* offer... "Do you want some help?" *Fucking Brewer! You idiot.*

"I mean, yeah? Yeah! Definitely." The longer we maintain eye contact, the more awkward this becomes. "Are you fucking with me?"

I wish. "No, I promised you that I would give you a hand." His eyes go wide, and I realize my blunder. "I mean, not *my* hand, but *a* hand, as in, I can help." *I'm not helping. Not at all.*

"Are you sure it can't be your hand?"

Fucking Nash. "I'm sure." I laugh. As if I haven't already fucked up colossally, I take a seat at the end of his bed.

"So how do you want to do this?" he asks, looking way too hopeful and eager.

"You should lie back and close your eyes."

"Definitely!" he exclaims, complying immediately. "Do you do this for all your patients?"

"More or less." *Definitely less. Much less.*

"Now what?"

Just lay still, so I can stare at you. "Keep your eyes closed, and do that breathing thing we've practiced."

As I try to calm my racing heart, he slows his, breathing in through his nose, holding it for the count of three, and blowing out through his mouth.

"This isn't something you're going to cure with touch. You can jack off until you rub it raw and the skin peels from your shaft and you're still not going to come. This is a psychological problem, and it can only be solved in your head."

"Are you sure? Maybe we should go back to the part where you said you would give me a hand."

"Hilarious. But no, no furious jerking. The more frustrated you become, the faster and harder you jerk it, and the further away from orgasm or even erection you get."

"So what do I do?"

"If you have to touch it, do it softly, slowly," I emphasize. "But the focus isn't on the action, it's on your thoughts. Your imagination. If you could be anywhere right now, where would you be?"

"Right here, with you, hands down."

Me, too. "What are you wearing?"

"This."

That tells me a lot. That one word speaks volumes. He wants the intimacy, so he has no shirt, but he feels too vulnerable and embarrassed or ashamed to remove his pants. I bet if he were easily able to achieve an erection, that wouldn't be the case.

"Okay, and what am I wearing?"

For a brief moment, he opens his eyes, giving me a sardonic look. "Really? Take a wild guess."

"No guessing. This is a visual exercise. Tell me what I'm wearing."

"Not a fucking thing. Wait, actually, you're wearing everything you've got on."

"Really?" I wasn't expecting that.

"Yeah." He chuckles. "I want to savor the moment when I take it off you."

And I'm hard. Just like that. "Tell me what we're doing."

"Jesus, Brewer, you want me to spell it out for you?" Nash peeks at me with one eye open.

"That's exactly what I want you to do."

"Fuck," he moans, giving his soft shaft a long slow rub. "You're sitting there, just like that, watching me. You've got your reading glasses on, and you're taking notes."

Oh, he's going for the full fantasy. A smile twists my lips. "What am I taking notes on?"

"How many times I touch it, how slow or fast. The size, the color. You keep asking me that classic therapist question. 'How does that make you feel?'"

This time, I laugh out loud. How did he manage to make that sound sexy? "Go on."

His left hand slides across his chest, teasing his nipples into hard, tight peaks. "I'm imagining your mouth on me."

"Where?" I ask.

"Everywhere. First you taste my skin, nipping at my belly. Then your lips part as they brush over my nipples, and you suck them into your mouth."

It's a good thing his eyes are closed so he doesn't see me adjust myself. My cock throbs, desperate to be touched, but I can't, which is the sweetest torture.

"Then you lick them and blow on them, cool air that makes them tighten so hard they burn."

Sensitive nipples, duly noted.

"And you suck a wet trail up my neck, nipping at my jaw, tasting the salt of my skin. And when you get to my mouth—" His eyes pop open. His bright blue eyes fix on me. "You're going to have to use your imagination on this one, 'cause I'm not going to spoil our first kiss."

Damn. He's got me. Completely fucking owns me. Technically, my lips have touched his once before already, but it was so brief that I wouldn't classify it as our first kiss. Squeezing my thighs together to relieve some of the ache, I ask, "What next?" in a voice that's barely coherent.

"Your knee presses softly against my nuts, kneading them as you slide your fingers into my hair. Every time you rub my scalp, it takes me away from the present, like I'm floating on clouds."

Mental note. Get my fingers into his hair as often as possible.

"Then you touch all the parts of me that are just parts of me. Nothing sexual. My shoulders, my arms, my hands."

Oh, Nash, every part of your body is sexy. Don't you know that?

"My stomach," he continues. "My face. Like you've lost your sight, your fingers just map the features of my face, learning it, memorizing it."

I could draw you with my eyes closed, that's how many hours I've spent staring at you as you sleep.

"Then you move on to my legs, my feet and my calves, my thighs."

The image of his head between my thighs comes back to me with crystal clarity, and my dick kicks like it has a mind of its own, which I'm sure it does.

I can't tell if it's his hand or his shaft, but I definitely see...something.

His strokes continue, soft and slow, a light touch, just like I suggested. His hips shift, and I realize he's definitely becoming aroused. Like he's feeling it throughout his entire body, not just between his legs.

"I can smell you, feel the warmth from your body, and I just want to get closer to you. I want more. But you pull away, licking down my sternum, down the center of my abs. I want you to touch me there so badly it almost hurts. And then you do. Your mouth parts and your lips mold to the shape of my cock. Through the cotton of my pants, you trace my shaft with your lips, your warm breath caresses it like—*fuck, Brewer*," he moans as he gives it a hard tug. "I want to feel your mouth so bad."

Nash bucks his hips off the mattress and then lies flat again, bending his knees. He's definitely *feeling* now.

"My pants are growing wet, from your mouth, and because I'm dripping, and then you taste the spot, you lick the saltiness from the cotton, and... *Fuck*...I need...touch me, Brewer."

His eyes are open, and I realize he's not continuing the story. He's not fantasizing. Nash is talking to me, begging me for relief. I can't breathe. I can't think. If I don't leave right now, I'll do it. I'll touch him.

"Congratulations," I breathe in a rough whisper, swallowing past the constriction in my throat. My mouth is as dry as the desert I once served in. "Your dick works."

"Brewer," he pleads, sitting up.

"I've got to go. I'm sorry."

"Don't go."

Why does he have to look so wounded and disappointed?

"Goodnight, Nash."

NASH

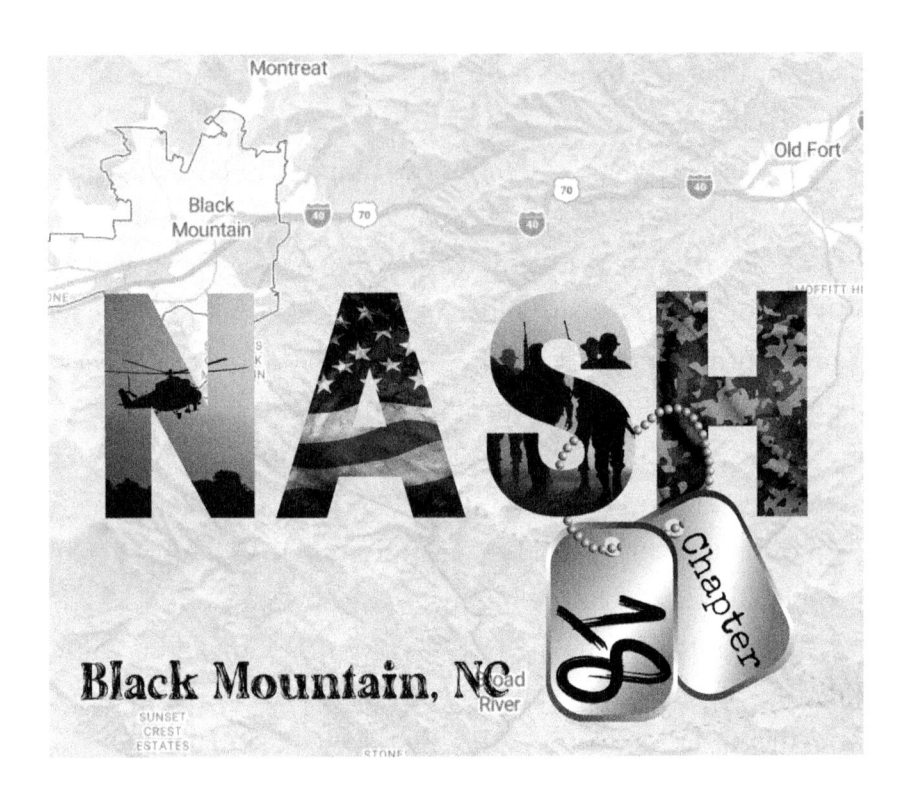

Black Mountain, NC — Chapter 28

If anyone could fix my dick, my money was on Brewer. But when he left, the moment died, along with my erection. It's been two weeks, and I haven't been hard again since. Not that I've tried, because really, what's the point if he's not watching or participating?

What was I expecting? For him to actually touch me? To put his mouth on me? He's made it clear time and again about his intentions and our boundaries, and the reasons for them. He doesn't do it to deny me or tease me, he's doing it for my own good. Brewer is denying his own desires in order to put me first, something that I respect him for. But every chance I get, I try to cross the line.

How rude of me.

I would kill to be his lover, pay any price, jump through any hoop, but the reality is, I may never be his lover. I may never be able to offer that to him, or anyone. Maybe he's right, maybe it's not my dick that's broken, maybe it's my head, something I've known for months now.

I'm not the same guy I used to be. Being over there, it rewired my brain. I don't want the same things anymore. My priorities have shifted. Hell, they didn't shift, they packed up and moved to another ZIP Code. My romantic life used to consist of one-night stands and one-hour hook ups. What more could I have asked for being gay in the Army in a position of leadership? But now? I'm not interested in casual sex. If that's all they have to offer, I don't want it.

The only thing that matters to me now is finding that one person. That one person I can connect with, that one person I can trust, that one person I would fight to stay alive for if I were ever trapped beneath the ground again.

For me, that one person is Brewer.

I trust him like I've never trusted anyone else before. I can let my guard down with him and be myself. I can show him all the broken ugly pieces. Brewer makes me want to be a better man and live a better life.

I'm not saying I would stay clean just for him, because that would piss him off, but he motivates me to keep working on myself, and on my bad days, I can find refuge in his arms and know that I'm safe with him. That he wouldn't do anything to hurt me or add to my trauma. Brewer understands the horror movie that's playing in my head, he's seen it himself, bought the ticket, and still has the stub.

That's why I trust him, and because every time I've ever needed him, he's shown up for me, usually without being asked.

Slipping out of bed, I'm careful not to wake a sleeping Valor as I pull on my sweats and head to the kitchen in search of coffee. But what I see sitting next to the coffee machine wakes me up more effectively than a straight shot of caffeine.

Yellow and brown leaves litter the counter around the base of Leif's pot. I left him in front of the window to catch the early morning sunlight but he's...he's dying!

"Leif! No!" In a panic, I rush to him, prepared to perform some sort of plant-based CPR. I check his soil, but it's moist, and I don't see any bugs or fungus affecting the leaves. "Help!" I shout, and when I turn, I see three men standing in the doorway, casually leaning with their arms either in their pockets or folded across their chests, but not one of them looks to be in a rush to play hero.

"Don't just stand there, do something! He's molting."

"Plants don't molt, birds do," Miles points out.

"Did you take its temperature?" Nacho asks.

Is that a thing? "How do I do that?" I bark, desperate to try anything to save Leif.

Without turning, I hear them snicker, and I know they're full of shit.

"There's nothing wrong with your dick-meter plant," Miles informs me in a calm and rational voice. "They're pranking you."

"What? How? Who?"

"We used the leaves from the tree out back," Tex says, before he doubles over laughing.

"Dick-meter?" Why am I stuck on that instead of kicking someone's ass?

"That plant's health is directly related to your dick. If it doesn't survive, you can't ever get laid again. It's your dick-meter," he surmises with a shrug.

"You're all in on this?" Fucking traitors. I thought they were my friends. Just goes to show you can only trust yourself and your cat.

"It's just a joke, lighten up, Daddy Warbucks."

"If you're all finished, I need to talk to Nash. Alone." Brewer's stern tone has the same effect as a bucket of ice water. Everyone scatters.

Still pouting over my plant's near death experience, I fill my mug with coffee and slump into a seat at the table. But the first words out of Brewer's mouth perk me right up.

"Violet would like to have you over to fix some things. I spoke with her at length, and I made her agree not to coddle you. She is to let you work. Then, if she wants to feed you and fuss over you, that's up to her, but you have a job to do."

"Good, I want to help her. But I'm not taking a dime from her in payment. You have to understand that I could never accept money from her."

"I do understand that, and I explained that to her. Hopefully she won't even offer. Are you prepared to talk about Victor? I can't promise she'll ask, but if she does, will you be okay?"

"I think I need to. We've undergone three EMDR sessions and my flashbacks have become less severe and less frequent.

I'm never going to find closure if I keep running from it. I think Violet is the closure that I need."

"Do you think you're ever going to accept that it's over? Is there such a thing as closure when it continues to haunt you every day?"

"Probably not, but there are things I need to tell her. Maybe they can help her find closure, or at least some measure of peace."

"Do you need me to go with you?"

Yes. "I think I need to do this on my own, even though having you there would make it easier. Sometimes, I need to do the hard thing, not the easy thing."

I just had to pick the hard thing, didn't I? Since when do I know what's best for me? Why would *anybody* listen to me?

Violet and I dance around each other in awkward steps as she runs through her list of things that need fixing. It's a long fucking list. My guilt multiplies with every item she ticks off. She needs help and whether she knows it or not, she needs *my* help.

After fixing the latch on the gate in the backyard, I move on to the back patio. It's screened in, and the screen is torn and needs replacing. Then I move inside to change the batteries in her smoke detectors.

Violet wrings her hands in the kitchen, trying not to hover, but I can feel her presence as if she's holding the step stool steady for me.

"Let me help, Sergeant." Then she's actually behind me, holding the damn thing steady. Probably because of my bum leg.

"Please don't call me Sergeant, Mrs. G. Just Nash."

"Could I convince you to call me Violet?"

"Not a chance," I chuckle, "and thank you for sending the pastries. They were delicious."

"I have more for you to take home today."

Of course she does. "They tasted just like..." *Old times.*

"I know. I remember how you boys devoured them."

The word boys makes my heart squeeze painfully. Before we deployed, that's what we were, just boys, green and dumb. But the desert changed us, changed *me*, and I came home a man. A broken, fucked in the head, haunted man.

What I wouldn't give to go back to being naïve boys again, playing video games and drinking beer with my buddy. *If only.*

"I wish you would let me pay you, but Brewer said not to ask."

"Then don't ask," I tease with a laugh.

"Can I pay you with food?"

"I won't ever say no to your cooking, Mrs. G."

When I'm finished with the last detector, I climb down and fold up the stool. "Anything else?"

"Now you sit with me and let me feed you."

As good as that sounds, I know she wants to talk, and as much as I know we need to, I also know it's gonna hurt.

Taking a seat at her kitchen table, I try to imagine the family dinners that took place here with G and his mom and dad. Laughter, conversation, love—so different from the kitchen I grew up in. Violet sets about making me a sandwich, not just any sandwich, though. One of those monsters like G used to make. He called them *Medianoche,* a midnight sandwich. A thick sweet, doughy roll, roasted pork and sweet ham, spicy mustard, sweet pickles, and cheese, toasted and squished flat so the melted cheese and mustard ooze together into an epicurean dream.

"Did you retire yet?"

"Working on it. Any day now I should get the papers in the mail." My last official day on the United States Army payroll is in six days. After that, I trade a paycheck for a settlement. A fat one. "Did you get everything squared away with your survivor benefits?"

"I did. Although it's no substitute for my boy."

Of course not. Not even close.

"Brewer tells me you're staying with him? Do you like it there?"

"I do. I live with several roommates, but I have plenty of privacy and they're good company." Does she have good company? Or is she lonely?

Violet slides the sandwich in front of me and takes a seat. My first bite makes me moan with sheer pleasure, and she giggles, but then the only sound is my chewing. The silence grows heavy and awkward.

"I miss him so much," she confesses, her voice breaking on the last word.

Fuck. "So do I."

"They returned his dog tags and his gold cross to me. He

died wearing it. That brings me some small comfort. God was with him when he died."

She swipes tears from her eyes, and I hold my tongue, biting back the acidic words I want to hurl at her. Victor Gutierrez did not die a comfortable death. God was not with him or with me. God fucking quit on us the moment we entered that building! It was the sound of my voice singing to him, *my* touch, that brought him solace and comfort in his last hours, not a gold fucking cross hanging around his damn neck. Certainly not God!

Fuck these tears! I wipe them with the back of my hand and drag a deep ragged breath into my lungs.

"He talked about you. He was thinking of you at the end. He missed your paella," I admit with a teary sniffly chuckle.

"He loved my paella, just like his Daddy, God rest his soul."

Violet makes the sign of the cross, and I hastily copy her, although I'm pretty sure I got it backwards. I grew up Protestant and went to church maybe a total of three times in my life. What the fuck do I know about religious etiquette?

She looks so much like G when she does that. Whereas I would knock on wood or something, G used to make the sign of the cross and kiss his gold cross before tucking it back into his shirt. I'm glad she has it now.

"I never buried him like they wanted. The Army wanted to put him at Arlington, but I couldn't part with him. I wanted to keep him close, so I had his body cremated. His ashes are in the living room." Her gaze falls to her lap. "I know that sounds silly, wanting to keep him safe even though he's gone."

The heaviness between us punches me squarely in my

chest, landing there like a crushing weight that makes it hard to breathe, hard to swallow, hard to...Christ, I'm losing it. *Deep breaths, count to three. Touch something solid.* All the tricks Brewer taught me. I reach for the only solid real thing nearest to me, Violet's hand.

She clutches me back with a strong grip. A rope to tether me to the present as the past tries to tear my mind to shreds.

"He's exactly where he wanted to be. At home with you. You did the right thing." My voice sounds incoherent, warbled and broken with grief. "He'd want to be here, where you can talk to him, and he can smell your cooking. Where he can look after you." At least my mind isn't slipping, it just hurts. It hurts so bad. Wrenching sobs break free of my constricted throat, and Violet grabs me in her strong, reassuring arms. Her motherly hug holds all my broken pieces together like duct tape. "All he wanted was to come home."

I can't tell her more than that. Most of it is classified, and even if it wasn't, those aren't the sort of details I would ever burden her with. There's no peace or solace in those torturous details. Only pain and heartbreak. That kind of pain only belongs to me. It's between me and G, and I'm trying like hell to bury it with him, in the past.

"You come visit with him anytime you want."

I'm not so sure about that. Talking to a jar of ashes doesn't hold much appeal for me.

"Can I..." I have to swallow twice before I can get the words out. "Can I come visit you?"

"You'd better." She warns. When she pulls back, I can see tears in her eyes. "Anytime you want, just drop in."

"Can I take care of things around here for you?" Jeez, I sound like a kid, asking his mom for chores.

"I'd like that very much."

Struggling to pull air into my constricted lungs, I take a deep breath and feel a bit calmer, more settled. My time with Violet isn't coming to an end, just a brief pause. What I won't say out loud is that I need her memories of him. I need her to lean on me and let me look after her in order to honor my unpaid debt to my best friend, a debt that will forever remain unpaid, no matter how many hours I spend with Violet, fixing things and keeping her company.

My phone beeps with a message.

Brewer:

Valor and Leif are doing fine. Take your time.

Always there for me. Checking in without making me feel rushed. Reassuring me. Brewer is an unexpected gift I can never repay. A Godsend, which, granted, He fucking owes me, so it only makes sense that He sent me the best of the best. That's what Brewer is, the best of the best.

So what the fuck does he want with me?

———

"So, I heard you met with your buddy's mom. How'd that go?" West asks, his prosthetic leg propped up on the coffee table, his big body half-sprawled over the vinyl-covered couch in the waiting room, a Mad Libs in his hand.

"It was heavy. But I'm glad that I went."

We've already killed two hours in this lobby, waiting for Mandy's procedure to wrap up. Most patients who undergo microdermabrasion are in and out of their dermatologist's office the same day, but with Mandy's extensive scarring and delicate skin, it's a much more involved procedure, and his recovery time is almost triple. I feel guilty that I fucked up so badly that I had to move out. He needs a next-door neighbor right now to look after him, like he looked after me when I needed help.

"You gonna see her again?"

"Yeah. I'd like to check up on her often, fix stuff around the house, wash her car, get the oil changed. What if she's lonely? I mean, she's got to be, right?"

West stares at me, like he's staring *through* me, and a smile spreads slowly across his face. "About as lonely as you are."

"I don't have time to be lonely, you Bitches won't leave me alone. Then I've got the guys that I live with, Brewer and Riggs, hell, loneliness sounds really good right about now."

West laughs. "You wish. People would kill to have friends like us. We're fucking awesome."

Shaking my head, I pick up my needles again, trying for the hundredth time to get the stitches right. I suck so bad at knitting it's not even funny. How does anyone find this therapeutic?

West looks confused. "What the hell is that supposed to be anyways?"

"A plant cozy." I deserve points for saying that with a straight face.

"What the fuck does a plant cozy do?"

"The fuck if I know, West. It's decorative. It goes around the pot. It's all I can manage, a simple circle. I can barely even manage this." West chuffs, half of a laugh, eyeing all the holes and pulled stitches in my knitting. It's a fucking mess. "Keeps people's fingerprints off it," I mumble under my breath.

I guess he hears me because he's laughing loudly now, and it's growing more intense by the second.

"Do you Windex it?"

"Fuck off."

His laughter dies down to a chuckle, and he returns his attention to his Mad Libs. "Give me a vehicle and a word that rhymes with aloe."

I have to think for a minute. "Van and woe?"

"I can work with that." He scratches in his pad, and a moment later, he says, "It's a poem, you want to hear it?"

"Sure. Entertain me."

> *"There once was a man who lived in a van.*
> *He lost his way, but was saved with Narcan.*
> *His best friend was a plant and a kitten the size*
>   *of an ant,*
> *And a rowdy, but handsome bunch of*
>   *sycophants.*
> *The man was full of woe because he didn't plant*
>   *aloe,*

A natural lubricant to prevent blisters whenever he thought of his mister."

His dark eyes are lit with a wicked glint, his lips twisted in a smirk, and his arm making an obscene gesture like he's jacking his cock.

"I don't know how Brandt puts up with you."

West slumps on the sofa, howling with laughter. *Fucking numb nut.*

"Wardell?"

"Yeah, that's me." A nurse approaches us. "Mr. Cahill is waking up. He'll be ready to go home soon."

"Perfect, thank you," he says, sitting up straight. "I'm going to take Mandy home with me for a day or two until he feels a little better. But you're welcome to come by and check up on him."

"You don't mind if I stop by your house?"

"Not at all. It's good for him to know people care."

"I do. I don't know how or why, but I do. He cared about me when I was at my worst, and he didn't have to do that. I want to be there for him now."

"Yeah, that's just Mandy. He's got a heart bigger than the size of North Carolina."

"How did we all find each other?" I marvel, shaking my head. "I mean, I was convinced I'd lost the only person who ever cared about me, who ever would. And now I've got all of you. How in the hell did that happen?"

"I ask myself the same thing every day." His cocky grin reaches his eyes, lighting them with wicked humor. "It's the power of BALLS. Ball power. It works like a magic genie. If you rub them, good things happen."

I want to laugh, I really do, but I won't give him the satisfaction. "Oh my God, can we just get the fuck out of here now? I can't take another minute of your bullshit."

NASH

Serenity House, Black Mountain, NC

Chapter 19

Does it make me a bad person if I lie and say I'm having flashbacks at night just to get Brewer to sleep with me again? Because at this point, I'm desperate and willing to try anything, even something as low down and dirty as that. It's not the nightmares keeping me awake anymore, for the most part, it's the longing, the wanting. Pining for Brewer is driving me out of my mind.

It must be early because I'm alone in the kitchen, for once. I set up the coffee machine and reach for a mug in the cabinet above me just as Brewer comes up behind me, reaching for the same cabinet. I can feel the heat from his body at my back, I can smell his body wash from his morning shower. His soft, warm breath tickles the shell of my ear.

"Excuse me," he murmurs, electrifying my senses with awareness.

If I could just lean back, press into him, if he would just wrap his arms around me and hold me tight to his chest, for just a stolen moment, I could have something good to carry with me throughout the day.

Brewer inhales, like he's breathing in my scent, and then grabs a mug, and he's gone, making the longing and wanting I feel for him multiply tenfold. Filling my cup with coffee, I take a seat at the table and watch as he fills his mug. He didn't have to do that. There's a clean mug in the dish rack next to the sink. Maybe he didn't see it?

Maybe he just needed a stolen moment to carry with him through the day as well.

My phone chimes, a reminder from my calendar that I have exactly one hundred and two days left of Purgatory before I put us both out of our misery and make Brewer mine. It's the same reminder I get every morning, giving me hope to focus on as I countdown the days.

With his cup full, and a granola bar in hand, Brewer steps out onto the patio, and I follow, taking a seat on the wooden bench. He joins me.

"I want to talk about the progress you've made on your second and third steps before we move on."

Blowing out a tired breath, I take a sip of my steaming coffee. "I feel like I failed the second step."

"That's not possible. You can't fail at stepwork, you just do the best you can, answer truthfully, and the next time around when you work this step, you'll—"

"Next time around?" *Is he fucking kidding me?* "You said there were twelve steps."

"There are," he chuckles. "But when you finish, you start over from the beginning. Every time you work the steps and celebrate another year clean, you become a different person, and your answers will change. Maybe you dig a little deeper, get more honest with yourself each time, and discover new things about yourself. New insights that help you define yourself."

"That sounds like a fucking scam, Brewer. What the hell?" *It never ends! I'll be doing these goddamn steps for the rest of my life.*

Brewer's chuckle turns into a full laugh. "It's not a scam. It works, honest to God."

"Right, it works if I work it, so I should work it because I'm worth it." I repeat the mantra with an eye roll and a huff. *Sounds like I'll be working it the rest of my life.*

"I think you're starting to get the hang of this," he jokes, clapping me on the back. "So tell me why you think you failed."

"Look, I'm willing to admit that I believe there's a God up there, somewhere, in charge of it all, even though sometimes I think He turns a blind eye. But I'm not saying I'm ready to hand over the reins and let Him have full control of my life and my decisions. I'm not handing Him my will just yet. He broke his trust with me and He's got to earn it back. In the meantime, I do believe G is up there and he's watching over me. He's got my six, just like he always did. Maybe reaching out to him is a little easier for me."

"You didn't fail, Nash. The way you feel is perfectly natural. Establishing a relationship with your higher power takes time and trust, and, like you pointed out, you're not ready to trust him yet with good reason. So have you reached out to Victor?"

"A few times. I mean, I don't know how you do it, but I don't get on my knees and pray, or make some big ritual out of it. I just... Talk to him, you know? When I'm driving in the car, or when I'm in the shower."

"That's fine. Everyone does what works for them, and that's what you should do. I talk to my buddy Eric all the time. I'm not in favor of the formal approach either. But this next step, the fourth step, is a doozy, and I just want to make sure you've established a connection with someone you can reach out to because you're gonna need it."

"Fuck, Brewer. What do you have in store for me now?"

He laughs again, easy and open, and the sound is like music to my ears. I could listen to him laugh again and again. It soothes my soul.

"So, the fourth step is to make a searching and fearless moral inventory of ourselves and our shortcomings."

"What the hell does that mean? Do you want to know that I'm a bad dancer, and that I forget to floss my teeth?"

"No, I already knew those things. You should make a list of the people you've wronged, and how you wronged them, because the next step is to make it right with them. It's never easy to take a hard, honest look at yourself and see the ugly truth of your actions."

"I gotta tell you, Brewer, all this stepwork is having the opposite effect on me. It just makes me want to get high."

Again, he laughs. The sun catches his eyes and the auburn highlights in his hair. He's fucking gorgeous.

"Some people have a longer list than others, but what matters is that you tell the truth."

"I didn't use for years, and I don't have a family that I lied to and neglected. I'm not really sure what you want me to say."

"I just want you to be honest with yourself. Trust me, the more you think about it, the more answers you'll come up with. Don't rush it."

Brewer gets to his feet and heads back into the kitchen, and my phone chimes with an incoming message.

> Mandy:
>
> You coming over to West and Brandt's for movie night?

Mandy. Fuck, there's one amends I definitely need to make. Make that two, 'cause I'm going to have to apologize for lying about being busy tonight. They're going to watch *Top Gun* again, I just know it. They played it last month, and I'd rather swallow glass than watch it again.

> Can't, I'm busy.

> Mandy:

Liar 🤥

A searching and fearless moral inventory? I might as well add Liza, Riggs, and most importantly, Gutierrez to the list.

The door opens again, and Tex pokes his head out. "Can you give me a ride to a meeting? My car won't start."

"Sure," I grumble, not really wanting to. If I drive him, I'll have to stay for the whole thing. Not really how I wanted to start my day.

"Sweet, we've got to leave in fifteen minutes. I'll go grab my bag and meet you at the car."

"Did you want me to take a look at it for you?"

"Sure. It's held together with duct tape and prayers. I'm surprised it's lasted this long. But if you can figure out how to get a few more miles out of it, I'd be so grateful."

I feel kind of bad for the kid. He washed out of the Army after his fourth year, wisely deciding not to renew his contract, but never learned a valuable skill. He doesn't have much money but says that he's not the academic type either, so he has no plans to put his G.I. Bill to use. Tex skips around from job-to-job, a lot like he lives the rest of his life, bed-to-bed, day-to-day. He makes decisions on a whim and thinks responsibility, career, and future, are cuss words.

Then again, he has a heart made of pure sunshine and a smile to match. He's an easy-going guy who always makes time to help others. His Sergeant must have had a field day with him when he was enlisted. I couldn't lead a man like that, he'd be washing toilets every day until his contract ran out. But he's a valuable asset to have as a friend.

He hands me the keys to his car and climbs into mine.

"So, I overheard." He shoots me a coy look, trying for innocence, but I'm not buying it. Not for a second.

"Of course you did."

"Purely accidental," he says, holding his hands up. "You're working the fourth step? I remember when I did mine. It was a long list." He laughs.

"I bet."

"Have you started yet?"

"Yeah, and I'm done. I've got like four names."

Tex shoots me a what the fuck glance. "You have to have more than four names."

"I don't have a lot of friends, so I didn't piss off a lot of people."

"It doesn't work that way, soldier. It's not just about people you pissed off. You have to take a full accounting of your actions. List all the dirty deeds you're ashamed of that you wish you could take back. You can't tell me you don't have regrets."

"I mean, I guess?"

"Of course you do," he insists, turning the radio station to something he favors. "We all have regrets. You don't have to make amends to every one of them, you just have to own it. If there's three things addicts can do best, it's lie, cheat, and steal. Now, we have to be held accountable for our actions, and that means getting completely honest about all the dirty shit we did."

"Wow, I bet your sponsor's ears are burning."

Tex laughs, a beautiful feminine sound that matches his pretty face. "Brewer is my sponsor."

"Get the fuck out."

His smile grows wider. "Don't you feel better now? Knowing that anything you say can't possibly be as bad as my list? Takes some of the pressure off, doesn't it?"

"You're a fucking mess," I tease.

Throughout the meeting, his words weigh heavily on my mind. I've done plenty of shit I'm not proud of, even before I started using. But I spend most of my day running from the past, trying not to collide with it again for fear of the explosion in the aftermath. Recounting my past deeds is the last thing I want to do. Can I ever just find any fucking peace? From the man I used to be, or from the life I used to live? Can't I just wipe the slate clean and move on?

My stomach feels torn up, and I don't know if it's the bitter coffee or my thoughts. Most likely my guilt. Brewer's words come back to me, acting like my conscience, like *Jiminy Cricket*. If we don't remember the past, we're destined to repeat the same mistakes.

I hope all of this soul-searching bullshit makes me a better man in the end, one deserving of a man like Brewer, so that it's not all for nothing.

Two weeks later and I've got a complete, somewhat complete, list of my unfortunate transgressions. I scoop up Valor, depositing him in the sling, and head to the kitchen to make lunch. Valor's purring and vibrating against my chest is a familiar comfort. When he's not doing his motorboat routine, I feel almost naked.

Slowly but surely, my appetite is returning, and I've added a third meal to my day. Sometimes snacks, too. It has a lot to do with my mood. With my list burning a hole in my pocket, I throw together a peanut butter and jelly sandwich and take a seat at the table.

It's Sunday, so most of the guys are home. Brewer joins me, taking a seat at the table with his ham and cheese sandwich, and I slide the folded piece of paper across the table.

"What's this?" He unfolds it and scans the list. "You did a good job. But you're forgetting one thing, the most important name on this list."

Leaning forward, I take a look but I can't find what's missing. The most important name on the list is G, and I wrote his name first.

"I don't think so, I've got everyone I can think of."

Victor
Liza
Riggs
Mandy
Past physical therapists
Warrant Officer Burgess

He grabs a pen from the counter, rejoining me at the table, and scrawls a name at the top of my list.

Nashville Sommers

Cute, Brewer.

"Don't ever forget to put yourself first. You owe yourself a huge apology for everything you put yourself through. You should never be last."

Point taken. My gaze collides with his, and suddenly, the minutes stop ticking by, the air between us thickens with unspoken thoughts and words, with feelings we're both trying to keep a lid on, but they're boiling over. My stomach churns with heat. My skin prickles with awareness. One minute we're filling out a list, and the next, I'm ready to pin him to the table and climb on top of him.

His throat slides as he swallows. "We should—"

Fuck that. I'm tired of what we *should* do. All I know is what I *want* to do, what I *need* to do.

"Brewer, I can't keep fighting it. Every machine needs fuel, and you're mine. Your touch is what fuels me, gives me the energy and the strength and the determination to get through each day. I want to keep going, but just give me *something*. Just a little taste."

He groans, like he's suffering physically, and drifts closer, inch-by-inch, closing the distance that separates us. I can taste his breath. Toothpaste and coffee. I want his taste in my mouth.

I want to carry it with me the rest of the day, to think of him every time I swallow.

"Eighty-seven days, Brewer," I whisper over his lips, like a caress. Like a kiss.

"Just a taste," he agrees. "To keep you focused," he murmurs, sounding almost hypnotized.

The only thing I'm focused on right now is seeing if he can make my dick hard again. It's throbbing like it has a pulse of its own, like it's trying to fill with blood. And if it does? I'm not wasting this opportunity.

Nothing could prepare me for the taste of his kiss. Not the three months I've already dreamed of it. Not even if I waited another three months. It's not just the brush of his lips against mine, the way they tingle, or how my mouth waters. It's more than that. My heartbeat trips over itself, trying to sync with the whooshing of blood in my ears, the way it's pumping too fast through my body, thinned by adrenaline and endorphins. The buzz of dopamine in my brain, tricking me into believing I'm high. High on lust. Yeah, my dick is definitely growing thicker, thanks to Brewer.

The first slide of his velvety tongue against mine steals my breath. But when his lips seal against mine, I'm convinced we fit together perfectly in every way, not just our mouths. Nothing has ever felt this good. Nothing ever will again. Everything I endured, everything I survived, was for this moment. This is my reward. His kiss is my salvation. Everything that comes after this only gets better from here on out.

He gasps into my mouth, and I swallow the sound, growing fully hard. It's actually throbbing now, possibly even dripping.

Weeks, no, months of unspent seed collected in my balls, aching and full, begs to be released.

My tongue dances with his, transferring to his mouth, my fingers tangle in his hair, just above his collar, and I'm practically climbing over the table to get closer to him.

"God, yes, Nash. Finally," he breathes into the kiss, his words vibrating against my lips.

He fists my shirt like he's reaching for a lifeline. *Me. I'm* his lifeline.

The way he feels in my arms, his scent, the way he tastes, there's nothing else but Brewer. He blocks out everything. There's no anxiety, no memories or PTSD, no acid reflux or ED. No migraines. There's nothing but his kiss. It's the best healing therapy I've found. If only it could last forever.

Except I'm about to blow, so it's only going to last another ten seconds. Fifteen at most.

Brewer rises from his seat, like he's coming across the table, and the kiss turns frantic, wild and desperate. I'm breathless, and his harsh panting grows louder. He claws at me, and I fist his hair.

I need...more. If I could just get him under—

"Who's hungry?" Nacho's deep voice echoes down the empty hallway, and Brewer and I jump apart like we each received an electric shock. I struggle to catch my breath, trying to play it cool as he enters the kitchen. "Oh, you've already got food. I guess I'll just have a sandwich, then."

"My settlement cleared my bank. Let me know when you find a good truck and we'll go purchase it."

"You really wanna do this with me?"

"We're not going over this again. I offered the money. It's yours."

"I've got my eye on a truck. Maybe we can go take a look at it tomorrow."

"Sounds perfect. Let me know when."

He brings his sandwich to the table, and Tex strolls in. More like struts in, which is his usual style when he's in a good mood. My head snaps up, and the look on my face catches everyone else's attention.

Nacho whistles. "It's a little early to dress up for Halloween, isn't it?"

"It sure is, which is why this isn't a costume. It's my new work uniform."

"You're a...a..." Brewer stutters.

"*Hooters* girl?" I finish for him.

"Hooters *boy*," Tex corrects me.

"They actually hired you?" Nacho sounds as stunned as I feel.

"Of course they did. Diversity and equal opportunity and all that."

Maybe for most businesses, but I've never heard of a *Hooters* boy. "Do you make enough in tips to even bother? I would think most of the guys are there to see the girls."

Tex points a slender finger at me. "You would be wrong. I cleaned up last night. Made more than most of the waitresses combined. Catty bitches," he mumbles under his breath. "I mean, look at me. How good do I look in this? Be honest."

He poses like a showgirl, hands in the air with one foot turned out. The cropped t-shirt shows off his slender, toned stomach and belly button. His skin is smooth and hairless. The skimpy orange nylon shorts barely cover the cheeks of his ass, and are stretched tight across his groin. There's no mistaking his dick print, even when it's soft. His long, thin legs taper down inside thick slouchy, white socks, and chunky white sneakers. Tex's longish blond hair and pretty face make him look like a California boy more than a Texan. I don't see a trace of the soldier he used to be. He turns toward the window and the sun highlights the pale glitter eyeshadow on his lids.

Twinks aren't really my type, but damn, he looks good. I bet a lot of closeted and repressed guys who frequent *Hooters* are saving their money to tip him big.

Suppressing my laughter, I lift my bottled water in a mock toast. "Congratulations on the new job."

Brewer still hasn't said a word, and by the look on his face, it's easy to tell what he's thinking. He's not happy. "Good thing I'm not busy tonight," he mumbles.

"What, are you gonna go tie up one of his booths all night spying on him?"

His glare speaks louder than words. *How cute, an overprotective Brewer.*

Chapter 20

I'm obsessed with his kiss. With *HIM*.

I can still recall the flavor on his tongue.

The scent of dryer sheets that clung to his T-shirt.

His spicy clean body wash.

Is it obsession? Lust? Or the beginning of something else, something deeper?

The joys of being an addict, always having to second-guess your motives, to be sure you're making healthy choices.

This morning, I've sat through three sessions with patients and the entire time, my mind was on Nash.

What is he doing?

Is he thinking about the kiss? *Of course he is.*

Is he going to try to kiss me again? *God, I hope so.*

Maybe a handful of stolen moments will be enough to get us through the next two and a half months.

Who am I kidding? My heart almost stopped when we were nearly caught.

People look up to me to be an example of the right way to recover, thinking I work a good program. My patients, the guys at Serenity House, my sponsees and friends, other recovering addicts—they look to me to show them the way. My clean time and experience deceives them into thinking I'm beyond mortal, that I'm infallible.

Nothing could be further from the truth.

I'm just a man. A seriously flawed man who sometimes lets his desires rule his reasoning. I'm not naïve enough to believe that Nash isn't going to obsess over that kiss, whether it never happens again or if it happens a dozen more times. I know the way his mind works. He's exactly like me. A kiss isn't going to corrupt his recovery and send him back out the door. But with so many eyes on us constantly, there's nowhere to hide.

At home, we're never alone. At meetings, I watch him constantly, check out his profile, long to slide my hand in his as we sit side-by-side. Every night, I stare at my phone as I lie in bed, waiting...hoping...he'll call, that he'll need me. What a terrific therapist I am! Hoping my patient backslides so I can crawl into his bed.

This is why there are rules. These are the consequences of breaking them.

Guilt, obsessive thoughts, worry, sleepless nights, heartburn, and headaches. And yet, none of them is enough of a deterrent to make me stop. If I could just get him alone for a few hours, long enough to put my hands on him, my lips…

"Brewer?"

"Sorry, what?"

Nash tries again. "I said, I'd like to plant a garden for Violet. Maybe transform her backyard into something beautiful like ours. But my aversion to dirt, the smell of it, makes me wary to even try."

"Have you tried since completing your EMDR therapy?"

"No. Do you think I should? I'd need you to be there, in case I…you know."

He thumbs through the pages of a gardening magazine, looking all googly-eyed at the lush, colorful pictures. Despite his struggles, his heart is always in the right place. That tells me everything I need to know about him.

With my mind made up, I suggest, "You want to get out of here this weekend?"

His head snaps up fast enough to give him whiplash. "Where to?"

"We could check out some gardens, get your hands in the dirt, and see what happens." His smile grows and my fear that I've made the wrong decision fades. Am I thinking with my dick instead of my head?

Probably—well, my dick *and* my heart.

"Can we leave right now?"

His eagerness is cute, and I laugh. "Go pack a bag. We'll be gone overnight."

Like a blur, he disappears faster than my eyes can track him. Fifteen minutes later, he climbs into my car with his duffel bag, his plant, and his kitten. It's a package deal. Nash comes with baggage, and not only the mental kind. Where he goes, the plant and cat follow, without fail.

"I don't know where we're going, but I'm ready."

A little chuckle. A big smile. That's me when I'm with him. Happy. At ease. *Right where I belong.*

Turning off the A/C, I roll down the windows, turn the radio up and back out of the driveway.

An hour later, we pull into the parking lot of DuPont State Recreational Forest, just one of the many gorgeous parks in the Pisgah National Forest preserve surrounding Asheville.

Nash breathes out in awe as he takes in the majestic mountains surrounding us. "What are we doing here?"

"Reprogramming your brain."

I grab my backpack, packed with water bottles, my phone and keys, and granola bars, and head down the trailhead with Nash by my side.

I feel free like I haven't felt in...ever? Wide open spaces, fresh air and unforgettable scenery, no obligations or appointments, and the man I feel the most comfortable with walking ahead of me, his tight ass swaying deliciously with each step.

Yeah, this is living.

Nash stops every so often to check out the ground cover and plants, taking mental notes of what he likes. We point out birds and a hawk. Squirrels with fat, bushy tails scamper across the trail. The sound of rushing water draws us off the path, and I catch a glimpse of a waterfall that empties into a wide but shallow stream.

"Come on," I say, an idea forming in my head. Leaning against a boulder, I kick off my shoes and socks and step into the icy water. It licks at my calves, the cold temperature turning my skin pale white. Nash wears a boyish smile as he splashes after me.

"What are we doing?"

"Just walk with me."

He stops to pick up a river rock, smooth as glass from years of being washed in the current, and puts it in his pocket. Then he scoops up a handful of the pure mountain water and offers it to Valor, who laps it up. When he catches up to me, his hand bumps mine, and he hooks his pinky finger with mine. I slide my whole hand in his, and he grips me back, smiling brightly.

He's so fucking beautiful. Brave, strong, yet fragile. Nash's fragility is unique, like him. He isn't fragile like a flower. He's fragile like a bomb, waiting to detonate at any moment. His memories are like shards of shrapnel, slicing into your soul like damaging cuts, capable of leaving permanent scars that won't ever heal.

I'm trying my best to heal his scars. For his sake, and for mine.

"Stop. Bend down." He looks at me curiously. "Put your hands in the water." I do the same, grabbing handfuls of the dark silky silt from the riverbed, and let it sift through my fingers. Nash copies me. "Feel that? It's dirt, but it's so different from the dirt you fear." Understanding dawns in his sky blue eyes. "We're not in the desert anymore. We're home, in North Carolina. The dirt here is different. It's clean and pure, it's healing. Things grow and thrive here in this dirt. The desert sand imprisoned you. It took Victor's life. But this sand is beautiful. It's a world away from the past, and it has nothing to do with your captivity. This dirt can set you free."

He scoops up another handful as tears gather in his eyes, making them shine like glass. Nash watches the wet sand fall through his fingers and comes to some sort of epiphany. I can see it in his face as it relaxes, in his shoulders going slack. He raises his eyes to mine, and I see...freedom. He's finally free. However free he possibly *can* be.

He's never looked more tempting.

I only mean to hug him, to just feel him in my arms, to feel his body release the fear and tension it's been holding onto for months and take a deep breath, but when I get close, Nash's lips find mine, as natural as breathing. His wet hands wrap around my back, and he releases that freeing breath into my mouth. I soak it up, sealing my lips with his, sliding my tongue along his, careful not to crush the tiny kitten between us, slung across his chest. The sun beats down on my head and shoulders, the cool water swirls around my ankles, burying my toes in the soft sand, and the man in my arms melts into me, fusing his mouth and his body with mine. That's when I let go, when I give him my heart.

My whole heart, not just pieces of it.

It's not a conscious decision, it's not a choice. It just happens.

As natural as breathing.

This kiss isn't hurried and desperate like the last one.

This kiss is slow and sensual. He explores my mouth, and I take my time memorizing his taste. The feel of his warm skin beneath my fingers. The kiss comes to an end but Nash doesn't pull away. He buries his face in my neck and breathes me in, and then I feel his body quake with silent sobs. His hands dig into my shoulders. I squeeze him back, keeping him safe as he falls apart. When he's finished, I'll pick up the pieces and put him back together again.

I'll make him whole.

———

I've stayed in much nicer hotels, but when you make a reservation in the middle of summer in the Blue Ridge at the last minute, you can't expect much. The Motor Court Inn, with its cracked sink and one bed, will have to do. I only pray the sheets are clean.

"Sorry about the bed."

Nash scoffs. "Yeah, I'm real broken up about it. You might have to go sleep in the car, to protect my virtue, and my recovery."

Cute. Real cute. "I'll definitely consider that at bedtime."

"You're not going anywhere," he growls, sounding all playful and possessive and sexy. Nash grips my hips and pulls me into his body. It's just a hug, but it feels so good.

"You fixed something inside of me today. Something I thought would forever be broken." My chest tightens, like a heavy weight is crushing me, making it difficult to breathe. *Fuck, he's going to make me cry.* "With the loss of my sex drive, I'm starting to realize that intimacy isn't about sex, it's about truth. When you find someone you can tell your truth to, when you can bare your soul and know you're safe with them, that's intimacy. That's the kind of shit I held onto when I was down there. When I thought I had nothing left to live for, somewhere in the back of my mind, I'd hoped that if I made it out, I would find that someday with someone. Someone like you. I would find what we have."

"I..." If I keep going, give into the exchange of feelings, allow him to keep touching me, it's a forgone conclusion where we'll end up. "Let's get unpacked and figure out dinner."

I try to take a step back, but Nash doesn't let go. Disappointment is written all over his face. I hate that I put it there, but that's not what I brought him here for this weekend. Yes, I wanted to be close to him, sneak a few unguarded moments, maybe even steal a couple of kisses, but no more than that. This weekend was about healing Nash from the inside out, or the outside in.

It wasn't about declarations of feelings and love and sex and intimacy.

Before he lets me go, Nash pulls me in for another hug. He buries his scruffy cheek in my neck. I get it. I don't ever want to let go either, but every time he touches me, it escalates quickly, from zero to sixty in less than a second. Just enough time for me to lose my head.

How am I going to get through the entire night sleeping beside him? Without touching him? Without kissing him?

Nash disappears into the bathroom with his toiletry kit and

his plant, because he swears it loves the steam, and I hear the shower come on. He leaves the door cracked a couple of inches, and a cloud of thick steam billows out. It conjures images of his hard body, wet and soapy, getting pounded by the hot spray.

What I wouldn't give to join him.

"I think I figured out where we can go for dinner," he calls out.

Grateful for the distraction, I ask, "What do you have in mind?" I'll take him anywhere he wants to go. A steakhouse, seafood, Italian. He hasn't indulged in good food in almost two years.

"*McDonald's*. I hear they have the fanciest *McDonald's* right outside of the Biltmore estate, and I've always wanted to check it out."

In a million years, I never would have guessed that would be his choice. Of all the places he could have chosen, *McDonald's*? Speaking of the Biltmore estate, he has no idea what I have planned for him tomorrow. But if all he wants is a greasy burger and some overly salty fries, who am I to say no?

"Anyone ever tell you you're a cheap date?"

"As long as I'm *your* date, I don't care what else you call me," he responds.

My lips twist into a silly grin. I love his answer. He's just so easy to please, and the things he says, about wanting to be mine, stroke my ego in the best ways.

"Wow, I can't believe how fancy this place is."

"I know, right? I feel like I should be dressed nicer," Nash jokes, as if he doesn't look mouthwatering in his fitted, dark wash jeans and the dark heather gray T-shirt stretched tight across his chest. It worked out great that he decided on *McDonald's*, since we have Valor in tow. I don't think he would be appreciated at a fancy steakhouse.

Unfortunately, I've eaten a lot of *McDonald's*, but this place is like nothing I've ever seen. A stone-covered fireplace with rocking chairs, live violin music accompanied by a pianist. A raised roof with chandeliers and columns! It's nice enough that I don't feel so bad about it being our first official date.

"You know I would have taken you anywhere, don't you?"

"I would have been happy with gas station hotdogs. As long as we're together."

Gas station hotdogs?! "You've been hanging around McCormick too much," I tease, drawing a laugh from him.

When we're seated with our burgers, fries and shakes, Nash picks up his burger, but pauses halfway to his mouth. "I don't know what you have in store for us tomorrow, but I'm already feeling inspired. I want to give Violet the most beautiful garden, filled with all the things she uses in her cooking. Tomatoes and peppers, herbs, and some root vegetables. But I also want to make it serene and pretty with flowers. Maybe some edible flowers? I have to research that. Maybe some flowers that attract butterflies? She could sit under her covered porch and watch them."

"I hope you're going to keep her company on the porch. What Violet needs more than a garden is someone to share it with."

"You're right. And I've already committed to visiting on a

regular basis." He takes a sip of his shake, and my eyes are drawn to his throat, watching it slide as he swallows. "It was hard to talk about G, but I felt so much lighter when I left. I need her memories of him. I need her to share them with me. All the bad shit that comes to mind when I think of him feels like I'm dishonoring his memory. I don't like remembering him that way. He was so much more than that. I need her to remind me of that, to remind me of the man he was beyond his captivity. I've reduced his life to the twenty-two days we spent together in hell, but that wasn't who Victor Gutierrez was. Not to me, he wasn't. He was funny as hell, always laughing and cracking jokes. He cooked the best burgers."

Nash looks down at the burger in his hand and then lays it back on the wrapper untouched. When he continues, his voice sounds shaky. "He sucked at keeping our place clean, and he sucked at paperwork and inventory. But damn, that boy could shoot. He could hit critical mass on every target, no matter how far away it was placed. He loved *Star Wars* movies. He loved grocery shopping at the PX, even though he hated to cook. He ran the fastest mile in our unit, but he always slowed down so he could talk to me."

He's getting choked up as he talks. I can see the moisture gathering in his eyes. "You know, you can talk to me about him anytime you miss him."

Nash pulls a fortifying breath into his lungs, trying to study his emotions. "You can talk to me about Eric, your buddy you lost. I think…" He plucks a fry from the packet and chews it quickly. "I think I want to see about creating a position at BALLS to do what I'm doing for Violet. She can't be the only widow or widower in need of help around the house. I could build handicap accessible ramps for their houses. I could fix things, or coordinate contractors and handymen to come and fix things. Maybe even just pay them a visit, sit with them and share a meal. Maybe they need someone to share their memories with like Violet does."

How can my heart continue to grow bigger and bigger to fit all of my feelings for this man? At some point, it's surely going to burst.

"I'll look into it. We don't have anything like that, but I can talk to the board about creating it and even see about making sure it's a paid position."

Nash hesitates before speaking, like he's choosing his words carefully. "Does it bother you that I don't have a job? You've accomplished so much since your contract ended. You have fancy degrees and shit." His quick summary of the years it took me to finish my schooling makes me laugh. "You have a real job, a proper job. I have a few dollars invested in a food truck with a guy who can burp the entire alphabet."

"Yeah, Nacho has many hidden talents besides just cooking," I agree with a chuff. "And no, it doesn't bother me at all. Let's be realistic about your limitations. After what you've been through, there are only so many types of jobs you could be productive at. I think you're doing an amazing job figuring out what those are, and I think it's important for you to keep busy and find an outlet for the creative ideas you have, for your knowledge and experience, and for your skills. But you don't have to push yourself and you don't have anything to prove, not to me or anyone else."

He picks up his burger again, finally taking a bite. When he swallows, he says, "You're wrong, Brewer. I have everything to prove to you. And I swear to Christ I won't let you down."

Spending time with Nash is so easy that it passes in a blur, and it's not until we're walking back to my car that I realize we have no plans but to head back to the hotel. Every time I think about going back there and getting into bed with him, images of the night he touched himself in front of me come back to me. My head is filled with memories from that night. Watching his hand disappear inside his sweats, the way it moved up and down, pulling the fabric tight over the outline of his erection. I imagine how warm and hard his cock must have felt in his hand. I can still see the look in his eyes, the heat, the need, the way his tongue snaked out to lick across his bottom lip, tempting me to suck on it.

Yeah, I can't go back to the room just yet.

"We should go for ice cream, walk around the town."

"We just had chocolate shakes," he points out, sounding confused.

"Coffee then. Come on, we're here. We might as well check it out."

From the expression on his face, I can tell he doesn't give two fucks about coffee or checking out the town, but thankfully, he's willing to go along with my diversion. But I can only drag him to so many places before his suspicion turns to irritation.

"I don't want to sound like I'm not enjoying myself, but my

leg hurts. Between the hike earlier, and now this urban crawl, I've got to rest it."

Damn, how irresponsible of me. Of course he's hurting.

"Brewer? You wouldn't be avoiding going back to the hotel with me, would you?" His eyebrows are raised in question, and a playful grin twists his lips.

Busted.

"Of course not. Don't be ridiculous."

Nash chuckles, like he can see right through me. "I didn't think so. Because the Brewer I know doesn't avoid uncomfortable situations. He confronts them head-on."

He steps closer to me, gripping my hips like he did in our room earlier, and pulls my body into his, until our hips are fused and his soft bulge presses against mine. His scent always makes me want to bury my face in his chest and just breathe him in.

His breath is a warm caress over the shell of my ear. "Nothing is going to happen unless you want it to. I probably can't do anything anyways, even if I want to."

I definitely want to. And I know he wants to. But what about what we *should* do?

Being alone together, without a house full of roommates with their listening ears and prying eyes, feels like we're playing outside the rules, like we're on a hall pass for the weekend. All bets are off, no consequences. Whether that's true or not, I don't know, but my manipulative mind loves to find the morally gray area of any situation and twist it to suit me.

The rational part of my mind, the part that has been recovering for the past twelve years, is screaming at me that of course there are consequences to my actions. That I'm being selfish and irresponsible. But if we're both willing to pay the price, isn't it worth it?

Damn, right it is. No matter how high the price, just a second of his hands on me or my mouth on him would be worthwhile.

"Let's go."

This is a bad idea. A *terrible* idea.

When we've done this in the past, at home, we're usually wearing sweatpants, and sometimes T-shirts. Nash chose to come to bed in only his boxer briefs. He gave a pointed, amused glance at my sweatpants before climbing under the covers. I felt like a prude virgin, so I ditched the sweats, and now we're both in our underwear. His leg creeps over the invisible safety line and rubs against mine. The short hairs on his leg tickle my skin. His bare foot feels slightly cool, but not cold enough that I want to pull away.

"Brewer?"

"Yeah?" No matter what he's going to confess, the darkness makes it feel safe, a false sense of security for sharing secrets.

"You know how I feel about you, right?"

My heart rate triples, and it's beating so hard I'm sure he can hear it. He can also hear how loud I swallow. "Yeah, I know." I scoot closer so that our thighs are fused. "I feel the same way about you."

My connection with him feels so easy, so right, it's everything else that makes it so difficult. There's no denying the derisive judgmental looks I'll receive from my fellow addicts.

With over twelve years clean, I'm supposed to know better. I *do* know better. But I also know that I've found the man I want to spend the rest of my life with. I've found the one man I'm capable of having a soul deep connection with, that I can trust without question. A man I can tell all of my secrets to, bare my tarnished soul, and still feel worthy of. Is all of that worth shouldering the stigma of a forbidden relationship? Fuck yeah, it is.

No matter what Nash learns about me, I know he'll still look at me like I'm priceless, like I'm a precious treasure. Like a gift he doesn't deserve to receive. Which is total bullshit, but I know because it's the same way I feel about him.

Why should we have to keep waiting? What difference will two more months make?

I know they'll talk about me behind my back, maybe some even to my face, and that my rationale will sound like defensive excuses and selfish justifications, but I don't live my life to please them, and I'm not going to deny myself and Nash to appease them. You would think a bunch of hardened addicts wouldn't clutch their pearls so tightly over who I choose to date, but you would be wrong.

Apparently, recovery makes the immoral very, very moral.

Fuck them. Fuck all of them.

"My plant is still alive. And I've got the cat. I haven't killed either one yet," he murmurs. His hand finds mine in the warm space between our bodies.

I make a chuffing sound. "That sounds a lot like commitment."

His index finger traces back-and-forth over the center of my palm in a tender, yet suggestive move. "Like a fuck ton of commitment."

"Nash," I whisper, swallowing hard. Damn, I'm nervous.

"Don't deny me, Brewer. Touch me," he pleads, sounding as desperate as I feel. His other hand, the one I'm not holding, strokes his cock beneath the covers, and I don't have to see it to know that it's getting hard.

The sounds my body is making—my heartbeat, my breathing, the sound of my swallowing, the blood pumping through my veins and my ears—is so loud they can probably hear it in the next room over.

"If I touch you, I'll never stop."

"I hope you *never* stop," he whispers thickly, turning his body toward mine.

Mirroring his position, so that we're both lying on our sides facing each other, my fingers curl around his jaw, and I pressed my lips to his, sliding my tongue inside of his mouth. Nash moans, a sound ripped from his throat that I can't define. Is it agony or relief? He grips my biceps, his fingers digging into my flesh, and holds onto me as if he's in danger of slipping away.

"You have no idea how long I've dreamed of this."

Yes, I do. One hundred and forty-three days, same as me.

His lips taste my skin, lightly nipping and pecking at my jaw, my neck, igniting every one of my senses. He trails his hand lower, down my stomach, to tease the top of my briefs.

"Touch me," Nash begs, and my heart and my conscience split in different directions, rendered in half so permanently they might never work in sync again. I've got to stop this, before it goes any further, but I just want to feel his hand cup me before I stop him. I want to know how well I fit in his palm.

"I'm so fucking hard for you, Brewer. Please," he begs, destroying what little resistance I have left. "I'll die if I have to wait another day for you, let alone forty-five of them." My fingers skate over his hip, teasing the elastic band of his briefs. His skin is soft and warm. "Even God can't keep me alive that long," he whines, making me smile. "I know he doesn't want me to suffer like this. You said so yourself."

I can't even kiss him because I'm laughing so hard. My shoulders shake with silent laughter, enough to interrupt the kiss. "Always trying to find a loophole, aren't you?"

"I'm not manipulating, I'd really die. A month and a half is a long time. Forty-five mornings where I'd have to wake up hard and alone. Six weeks where I'd have to stare at your lips across the breakfast table and fight the urge to kiss you. Forty-five nights I'd have to fall asleep without you by my side. Forty-five—"

"Okay, I get the picture. It's a long time."

Nash kisses away my smile. "It only feels that way when you want something so much."

My fingers slip inside his briefs, slowly walking down to the thatch of soft, short curls. He bucks his hips like an invitation, or a command, for me to touch him.

"Nash, how can you love someone else when you don't even love yourself?"

Why are we even discussing this while my hands are in his pants? The chemistry between us works like a drug on me, driving me out of my mind with lust.

Between sweet nips and pecks on my lips, he says, "I may not love myself completely, but I love the things you love about me." Then a longer kiss, the glide of his velvet tongue along mine, a kiss so deep it robs me of breath. Nash lifts his head and grips my chin, staring into my eyes, into my soul. "You've painted a picture of me through your praise that I don't see when I look in the mirror, but I believe you see it, and I believe it's there, somewhere, buried under all the layers of shit I've been through. Eventually, I'll find that man. He'll rise to the surface because you called him."

Manipulative bastard. But I can't deny his reasoning. Loving yourself is a journey that takes time. It's a process that never ends. And it's not just lust that's driving me out of my mind. I wouldn't jeopardize his recovery for lust. Nothing is worth getting my rocks off when it comes to gambling with his life. What I feel for Nash isn't going away anytime soon, but I also don't know if I can wait forty-five more days to express how I feel, to show him what he means to me.

Sometimes, a thought pops into my head, when I'm just going about my day, and my first thought is that I want to share it with him, and when I realize that I can't, I feel an ache and a loneliness so deep it actually hurts. Sometimes, I catch his eyes across the room, whether it's in our crowded kitchen or in a meeting with fifty other recovering addicts, and I feel a connection so strong it's as if he's standing by my side, holding my hand or in my arms.

I'm tired of waiting.

I'm frustrated with waiting.

I want his hand in mine.

I want him in my arms.

Flesh and bone, not imagination and fantasy.

I want the real deal.

I want to *live* the dream.

"I have condoms," he suggests. "Do we need them?"

"No. All I need is you."

Chapter 12

"Did you bring it with you?"

"Did I bring what with me?" I can't think straight with the heat from his palm searing through my cotton briefs. He's touching me, through a layer of fabric, but he's touching me, *finally*.

"The bullet. From your nightstand drawer."

His words penetrate the fog of lust blanketing my brain, the heat I felt a moment ago gathering in my gut and in my groin now rushes to my cheeks. "You know about that?"

His eyes are twinkling, like his wicked grin. "I almost tried it out, but I was cockblocked by my kitten." He looks back over his shoulder, checking on Valor to make sure he's still asleep, curled up in Nash's T-shirt on the floor, and not about to cockblock him again.

"When—how?"

"How often do you use it?"

His giant palm rubs over my cock, and I can't think, or breathe, or— "Huh?"

"The bullet. How often do you play with it?"

"I-I don't know. Sometimes. When I'm—" Nash squeezes the head of my cock, now engorged with blood and sensitive, and I gasp. "Lonely."

"Lonely? What about when you're not alone?"

"I'm—" My head is going to explode. *Both heads.* "Why would I use it when I'm with someone?" I buck my hips, driving my cockhead through his fist. A drop of precum drips out, staining the cotton. "I mean…I'm never with someone."

"That's the right answer," he purrs, nipping at my neck, at my jaw. "What if you were with me? Would you use it with me?"

My eyes pop open, and he frames my chin in between his thumb and index fingers, turning my head to face him.

"You want to watch?"

"I want to watch," he confirms, dropping a kiss on my lips. "I want to help," he adds, nipping my bottom lip. "I've fantasized about it since I found it weeks ago. I've got to see it in person."

"You're…fuck, Nash, that's…nasty." The idea is already growing on me, exciting me, taking root in my imagination with fantasies of my own taking shape. "We could definitely make that happen."

He grins down at me. "Yeah?"

I kiss away the smile from his mouth, replacing it with my lips. My tongue delves into his mouth, sliding along his, tasting him. He pops the head of my dick free of my briefs, leaving a sticky mess on my stomach that he swipes with his thumb. Nash pops it into his mouth and sucks my flavor, his grin growing more wicked.

"I want more of that."

He dips his head and sucks the tip of my dick between his lips, making me shiver because it's so sensitive. He laughs, loving my reaction, and does it again, exposing more of my shaft with each pass. I'm caught in his snare, lost to the magic of his mouth, and yet dying to get my hands on him. Nash runs his tongue underneath my foreskin, swirling it around my cockhead. It's too sensitive, too good. I can't take much more, not when I've waited so long.

"Let me touch you," I rasp, eyeing the hard peaks of his nipples. I want to tease and torture every one of his senses, to draw this out and make it so good for him.

"Better not. I'm lucky to even be hard, let's not tempt fate. You touch me and it's all over."

"Look at me," I demand, holding his gaze. "No matter what happens, we're in this together. Remember what you said about intimacy? How it's not about sex, it's about feeling comfortable with another person and baring your darkest secrets to them? If you lose your erection in the middle of this, that doesn't mean it's over. We'll just improvise."

"Deal," he grins before taking me into his mouth again.

The incredible heat and suction of his mouth ramps up my

arousal quickly. Seeing his big body curled in half over my lap, pleasuring me, finishes me off. I'm reaching my limit, my balls drawing up tight against my body. His tongue traces along the vein on the underside of my shaft, making my damn toes curl. I don't even care how loud I am, groaning and gasping, my breath coming hard and fast, like I'm about to.

"Okay, enough," I pant, pushing at his head.

He sits up on his knees and strokes his cock as his eyes roam my body. "I like this," he says, bending to nip at the tattoo covering my hip. The NA symbol with sticks marked off to demarcate my clean time in months.

Rolling onto my side, I show him the ones on my back. Beneath a rainbow is the date I came out. Below that, covering my ribs, is the Army crest and me and my buddy Eric's ID numbers. Nash kisses each one, as if learning them with his tongue.

He urges me to my back again and positions himself between my legs. Nash runs his hands up and down my thighs before hooking them behind my knees and scooting me forward, so that my ass kisses his cock. It's not my favorite position, mostly because it leaves me feeling vulnerable and I don't usually fuck guys I feel a soul-deep connection with. But with Nash, I don't mind feeling exposed. I'm at his mercy in more ways than one that have nothing to do with the position I'm lying in.

"I want you just like this, so I can watch your face, and kiss you, and hold you in my arms."

Yeah, this position works fine for me.

He has a small bottle of lube ready in his hand and smears

it over his shaft with one hand while his other hand rubs over my stomach. I love that he wants to touch me, that he loves what he sees. I'm nowhere near as cut and toned as he is, even with the muscle tone he lost recently. My chest and stomach are furred with a scatter of dark hair, whereas Nash is smooth. Our differences are numerous, and yet we're perfectly matched.

"Feels like I've waited a lifetime for this. It's a shame it's gonna be over so soon."

Swallowing nervously, I look into his eyes, pulling his gaze from my body, and venture, "Hopefully, we have the rest of our lives to do it again and again."

Nash's eyes soften, and he leans down to take my lips in a soft, yet searing kiss that turns my bones liquid.

"I hope you mean that," he breathes over my lips, "because I'm not going anywhere."

Then he straightens up, leaning back on his haunches to peer between my thighs. He slides his slippery fingers between my cheeks, tracing up and down the dark crease, and with each pass over my tight pucker, I clench, hungry to be penetrated. He taps my hole before pushing his finger inside in a twisting motion that rubs against my inner walls in a way that sends thousands of tiny electric sparks shooting through my system. My body feels awake, alive with need and heat.

"This is what I'm gonna do to you with the bullet. Watch it sink in and out of your body. Listen to you beg for more as I slowly drive you insane."

His words, as much as his actions, have me close to the edge again, like I was when his mouth enveloped my cock. He turns me into a needy mess, lust-drunk and senseless, with just one word, one touch, just the smell of him.

"Give me more. Give me your cock."

"It's a lot thicker than my finger or the bullet. Are you sure you're ready?"

"I'm ready." What I leave unsaid is that I hope it burns because I get off on the sting of pain before pleasure. That feeling of being stretched to the point of agony, the lingering soreness—it's addicting.

He slips his fingers free of my body, wipes them on his shaft, and lines his tip with my entrance. His head is swollen and thick like a mushroom. There's no way it's not going to sting as he pushes through my rim. It's been so long, and even though I play with my toy, it has nothing on his girth.

Slowly, he applies pressure, pushing until he pops through the tight ring of muscle. My body welcomes him as he glides deep inside, burying all seven inches in one thrust.

"Fuck, you should see how amazing this looks. Like your ass is swallowing my dick."

I want to laugh, but he's serious. He's truly mesmerized by the sight and the intense feeling. "Please, move." I feel so full, stretched beyond reason, and if he doesn't move, it feels like my body will burst apart in burning pieces.

He moans, sitting back to watch the first few strokes in and out of my body, his finger tracing around my stretched rim, before he plants his fists into the mattress on either side of my shoulders and hovers above my face. He brushes his lips over mine with each stroke, and when he bottoms out with a hard thrust, I cry out into his mouth, and he bites my bottom lip before sucking it between his lips to soothe it. I feel the suckling pull of my abused lip in my balls. With each draw of his mouth, each swipe of his tongue, my dick twitches and my sac begs to release.

"You feel like heaven. Your body…your arms…you're my heaven."

He can't see the moisture gathering in my eyes from his words.

I'm his home?

It's all I've ever wanted to be for him. A safe place to land. A permanent place of belonging. *Home.*

His lips blaze a heated trail over my jaw, down my neck, across my collarbone, and down my chest where he latches onto my nipple, sucking hard enough to make me cry out. His hips drill into me relentlessly, pegging that sensitive spot inside my ass until I scream his name.

"Nash!" The single word sounds like a tortured plea ripped from my chest. "I'm…" *Coming.* I can't complete the sentence because there's no more breath left in my lungs. I'm spent. Every muscle in my body tightens, as if I'm on the verge of paralysis, and I can't move, can't speak, can't breathe until the tremors quaking through my nervous system subside.

"Me…too…," he pants just before his hips sink deep and go still. I can feel it inside of me, his pulsing shaft, the heat of his seed filling me.

Nash collapses on my chest, hot and sweaty and breathless. When I can move again, I wrap my arms around his back, running my fingers over his damp skin as I trace his shoulder blades and his spine. I plant kisses on his sweaty hair and breathe in his scent.

Yeah, we definitely have the rest of our lives to do this again and again. I'll never get my fill of him.

———

"Daddy had a good night, and Valor had a nap, and now everybody's happy," he croons to the kitten. Valor stares up into his eyes like he understands every word, and then his little pink tongue sneaks out to swipe Nash's nose.

"I'd like to take you to a nice lunch, no fast food this time, and Valor isn't exactly welcome at a place like that. He also isn't going to fit into our plans for the day."

"What are we going to do with him?"

He's serious, like he can't figure out another option. *Adorable.*

"We're going to leave him here. He's a cat, not a baby. He has food and water, his litter box, and his cat bed. He'll be fine for a few hours alone."

Nash looks torn. "I don't like to leave him alone. I don't think he likes it either."

"I know. It's one of the things I love about you. The way you love him. But I promise he'll be fine. We'll be back before you know it."

"I'm sorry, buddy. Daddy will bring you back a treat. And I'll miss you the entire time." He places the kitten and his balled up shirt on the floor, his makeshift cat bed for the weekend, and places a toy beside him.

"Come on, let's get some food in you." He follows me out to the car with one last longing glance at the door to our motel room.

When I pull into the parking lot of the steakhouse, he whistles low, clearly impressed. "It might be almost two years since I've had a good steak. Right before we were deployed, a bunch of the guys from my unit went out for steak one night. Man, we got rip-roaring drunk," he recalls fondly.

We're seated at a small table covered in white linen, and we bypass the wine menu in favor of ordering iced teas. "This is definitely a step up from *McDonald's*," he jokes.

The waiter serves a basket of rolls while we look over the menu.

"I think I'm going with the prime rib, medium rare, and maybe a loaded baked potato and a Caesar salad. What about you?"

"A well done filet for me, with a sweet potato and French onion soup." I look up to find him smiling at me. "What?"

"Nothing, I just like seeing you do your thing."

"My thing? What am I doing?"

"Ordering. Like, you're just a normal guy, a soldier, you work with your hands, like to get dirty, but then there's this whole other side of you, this uptight, fancy side, the therapist side. You're an educated bookworm who likes French onion soup and true crime novels."

"And?" I fail to see his point.

"And I love both sides. And all the angles in between. You're multifaceted," he reveals with a grin, "and I love it. *I love you*," he adds in a whisper.

Now I'm grinning as well. "I love you, too," I whisper back.

The waiter slides our salad and soup bowls in front of us. "You're really not going to tell me where we're going today?"

"You really don't like surprises, do you?"

"I've had enough surprises to last a lifetime," he says without humor.

"This is a good surprise, I promise."

We're served our main courses, and when I cut into my steak, I close my eyes and savor the taste. Nash emits a little moan, like he's in rapture.

"Here, try a bite of mine," he suggests, offering his fork to me.

I pop the prime rib into my mouth and chew. It feels as soft as butter on my tongue, but the flavor and the smell of the rare meat, way too rare for my liking, kicks my gag reflex into overdrive. Discreetly, I spit it back into my napkin and wash my mouth out with tea. I have to take several studying breaths before my stomach feels solid again.

Nash is doing that smiling thing again, like he finds me funny. "What?"

"I love to see evidence that you're normal. Well, far from normal, actually, like me. What was that just now?"

"The taste, and the smell, it triggered a memory."

"You almost threw up, in this fancy restaurant," he says, looking around at the other diners. "That's something I would do." Then he shrugs, focusing on his plate again. "Makes me feel normal, more at ease."

This is one of those moments where I feel both horrified and enamored at once. Horrified because the meat triggered my worst memory, the taste of my buddy Eric's blood in my mouth. And enamored because he's right. I get him, he gets me, and it's a bit horrifying that we bond over our darkest memories. With a sigh, I take another sip of my tea and skip my steak, moving on to my potato.

With lunch finished, and our bellies full, we head to our next destination, the luxuriously exclusive *Omni Grove Park Inn Spa*.

"Are you fucking kidding me?" Nash looks like he could be knocked over with a feather as he stands in front of the stone façade with his mouth agape.

"Time for a little pampering and R&R."

First, we take our time looking around, exploring the hotel and grounds, taking in the magnificent views of the mountains, and there's even a waterfall. Then we head inside, where beneath the hotel they have an underground mineral pool, decked out like a rock cave. The dim lighting makes the place feel private and intimate, and I would love nothing more than to fuck him in this pool and to swim naked, but this isn't that kind of hotel, and I'd hate to get kicked out before couples massage.

We do a lot of cuddling. The PG kind, where he swims into my arms and just lets me hold on to him. Then he glides through the water effortlessly with me on his back, my arms around his neck. Wet kisses, beads of water dripping down his chest and torso, the water reflecting in his beautiful blue eyes, and the way his swim trunks cling to the outline of his cock as he climbs from the water—the whole thing is an extended and torturous form of foreplay for me.

Next, we hit the eucalyptus steam room, where the invigorating scent cleans out my sinuses and opens my head and chest.

"You know," I point out, reclining with my eyes closed, "this is supposed to do wonders for migraines. The next time you get one, we should try a DIY version in our bathroom."

Nash just grunts in response, probably too relaxed to even speak. When we're finished steaming, we shower off and wrap ourselves in the plushest robes I've ever laid against my skin. It really feels like being hugged by a cloud. As we wait our turn in the massage room, we sit in the lounge and drink a cup of hot herbal tea.

"I'm never leaving. I don't care what it costs to live here, I'm moving in," Nash swears. I chuckle because I'm in complete agreement with him. Whatever this place costs is worth every penny.

"I've never felt more relaxed in my life," I add, taking a long slurping sip of my tea.

"Thank you," Nash murmurs.

"Thank me after the massage. It's going to get even better."

And it does. Laid out on tables, side-by-side, with the lights dimmed low and scented candles burning, I close my eyes to the sound of rainfall and ocean waves playing softly in the background.

Nash's steady breathing becomes quicker and harsher when our masseuses join us. I don't want to ask him what's wrong and make him voice his fears and insecurities in front of two strangers, so I try to put myself in his shoes and replay his experiences, looking for the trigger.

A dark small room, strange men touching him. He probably

feels vulnerable and at their mercy. He doesn't like to be touched by strangers.

Fuck, I fucked up. This is not relaxing for him at all. But then he reaches out for me, and I take his hand, squeezing back reassuringly, and his breath steadies again.

"I'm here," I murmur, "right here with you."

Despite our little hiccup, by the time we leave the spa, we're feeling relaxed. At this point, Nash is excited about the next item on our agenda. His enthusiasm is contagious. I haven't seen him smile this much or heard him laugh so often as I have today. He wears happiness well. It makes him look breathtaking.

"Oh my God," he breathes in awe when we pull up to the Biltmore Estate. "Brewer, quit."

"What?"

"What is this weekend costing you?"

"Don't worry about what it's costing me. Just enjoy yourself. Nobody deserves it more than you."

The ticket line is long, and as we stand there, patiently waiting, Nash recalls a story I've never heard.

"I don't know if you remember, but we had these programs like BOSS and MWR. Basically, it's a morale support group for single soldiers. Every month, they plan these outings, and it's all completely paid for by the Army. We've gone deep-sea fishing, parasailing, skydiving, ridden ATVs through the mountains, and a bunch of other fun shit. Oh God, one time we played paintball, and G nailed me right in the—" He pauses and looks around at the people eavesdropping in line with us. "Anyway," he continues, skipping over the NSFW parts of the story, "they organized a trip to the Biltmore Estate once, but on the way here, we all decided no one was really interested in seeing it, so we ditched it and just bummed around Asheville for the weekend. There were maybe twenty of us, and God, we had the best time."

I love hearing his stories, seeing his face light up with happiness as he remembers the good times. "Touring old castles may not be your thing, but this place is amazing at Christmas time. But that's not why we're here."

"It's not?" He looks around at the imposing mansion, the largest in the country. "Then what are we doing here?"

"You'll see," I tease with a secret smile.

We bypass the tour of the house and head around back to the gardens.

"Holy shit," Nash breathes.

"This is why we're here."

"This is incredible!"

"It is. If you're looking for inspiration for Violet's garden, you won't find any better than this. They have every kind of ornamental garden there is. Look at how beautiful it is," I say, pointing to a grouping of hibiscus in every bold color of the rainbow.

"I am," he insists, and when I look back at him, I find him staring at me. His eyes are as soft as his smile. "I'm crazy about you, Brewer Marx."

"Well, fuck. I'm kind of crazy about you, too." I smile against his lips as he tries to kiss me, which makes him laugh.

We spend the afternoon touring the gardens until the sun begins to set over the ridge, casting the mountains in shadow. We've taken a hundred pictures with our phones, and Nash even took voice notes about certain species of flowers he wants to add to Violet's garden.

"I feel so inspired," he muses as we drive back to the hotel. "I can't wait to get started."

I just love to see the fire in his eyes, the motivation, his brain firing on all cylinders. It's the first time I've ever seen him excited about something. This is a glimpse of the old Nash, the man I've never met, the man he used to be.

"We all have wings, some of us just don't know why. Figure out why God gave you wings. Find out what makes you fly. If it's gardening, or if it's just helping others find their passion, and being of service to others in need. It doesn't matter what it is, how big or small, if it makes you feel alive, chase it with both hands and grab onto it and don't let go."

Nash gives me a tiny smile and laces his fingers with mine over the console. "You make me fly. Loving you, that's what gives me wings."

Of course, Valor is fine and still alive and healthy when we return to the Motor Court Inn. Nash is beyond relieved, as if he actually doubted it. He scoops the tiny kitten up in his big hands and cradles him against his chest. I start the shower, letting the bathroom fill with steam as I listen to Nash recount our adventures to Valor in his kitten voice. That's what I call his high-pitched tone he reserves just for the kitten. It's adorable as fuck and quite hilarious coming from such a big, hardened guy.

Stripping down to nothing, I kick my clothes aside in a heap and step into the shower stall. It's barely big enough for one let alone two grown men, but that doesn't stop Nash from joining me. He takes the bar of soap from my hand and his big arms come around me to suds my chest and stomach. His hands glide over my nipples, sending shivers dancing down my spine, and then he soaps my hips before moving down to my dick. The slippery glide of his hand makes my shaft thicken quickly, and he sets the bar of soap aside so he can double fist me, gently pulling back my foreskin. The constant, squeezing pressure of both his big hands is the sweetest torture. Drops of pearly liquid gather at the tip, mixing with the soap on his next pass.

"Ugh, don't stop."

His chin rests on my shoulder so he can watch. I can feel the hard shape of his dick slide through my cheeks. He thrusts in sync with the pumping of his hands, rubbing over my hole with the slightest pressure. The combination drives me insane. The head of his cock slides down my crease, over my taint, and bumps against my balls, making them ache to release. Nash sinks his teeth into my shoulder, and I can't hold back another second. The bite of pain pushes me over the edge of ecstasy, and thick white ropes erupt from my slit, painting the tiled wall.

As soon as I finish, his hips stop moving, and he nuzzles my neck with wet kisses. "That was sexy as fuck."

"It felt incredible. Did you finish?"

"I, uh..." I turn when he hesitates to finish his sentence. He's soft, so he must have finished. "I lost it," he says sheepishly, and I can see that he feels embarrassed.

Fuck that. "We talked about this, Nash."

"I know."

"What did we say?"

"We said that it doesn't matter, that we're partners and we're in this together."

"Exactly. What else?"

"I don't know, Brewer, I'm frustrated as fuck. What did we say?"

"We said that we would find alternatives. There's not just one way to love each other and be intimate."

"Yeah, we did say that," he agrees halfheartedly.

"Let's get washed off before we run out of hot water, and then we can crawl into bed and cuddle."

"Cuddle?" He snorts. "We're two grown men. Battle-scarred veterans. Recovering addicts. We don't *cuddle*." He says it like it's a derogatory word.

"Oh no? Then, what do you call it when two men lie beside each other in bed and hold each other close, steal each other's heat, with roaming hands and kisses?" I step aside so he can stand under the spray. "And let's not forget about the kitten, who will undoubtedly be joining us."

"Marinating, macerating, steeping…"

"What's with all the cooking terms? Are you hungry?" He glares when I laugh.

"Fine, it's cuddling," he grumbles under his breath.

Chapter 23

Black Mountain, NC

I haven't been home for five whole minutes before my roommates start with their bullshit.

"Hey, look who it is! The honeymooners are home," Nacho teases.

"Did you come back married? Pregnant?" Tex jokes.

"Welcome home," Miles grunts, surprising me, because really, that's a lot of words for him.

The entire drive home, I feared this. I don't like to be the center of anyone's attention. Makes me twitchy, as if ants are crawling beneath my skin.

Tex rushes forward and relieves me of my plant and my cat. "Leif, Valor, I missed you so much."

He scoops them up and presents me with his back,

completely ignoring me, as if he never spared me a single thought the entire weekend. As if he prefers the company of my plant over me. *He's so full of shit.* It's not like I would say he's my best friend or anything because I don't do best friends anymore. Not after Victor. But I can admit the tiny Texan is beginning to grow on me.

"Do whatever you have to do to settle in and unpack because the guy I bought the truck from is dropping it off in an hour, and you volunteered to help me clean it out."

Nacho tosses me a rag and a bottle of some sort of all-purpose cleaner, and I have to drop my duffel bag to catch it.

"I volunteered? I wasn't even here," I point out.

"I volunteered you," Tex admits, disappearing up the stairs with two of the three loves of my life.

"This is bullshit," I complain to Brewer, who just laughs.

"No, this is home." He drops a kiss on my cheek and heads downstairs to unpack.

"Fuck, it's hot out, too hot to be sitting around doing nothing." I tip the can of ice cold *Fanta* to my lips and take a long swig. It burns icy cold and fizzy down my dry throat.

"You're supposed to be helping," Nacho grumbles, sounding irritated. Must be the heat.

"I am helping. I'm providing moral support."

"How many people do you think can fit in that death trap at once?" Tex adds, backing me up. He holds up his *Fanta* and I toast him, laughing with him.

Nacho fires a spatula out the door of the truck, narrowly missing me.

"Hey, watch it," I warn, dodging to the left. "Throwing random objects at me triggers me."

"It does not," Nacho yells, his voice echoing inside the truck.

"How would you know?"

"It wasn't on the list," Tex informs me.

"What list?"

"The list of things that trigger you. We all got a copy before you moved in."

What the fuck?

"We get one for every newbie that moves in. So we don't set them off."

These guys knew about me from the get-go and they still embraced me with open arms? Damn, I knew they were good guys, but... *Damn*. Feeling guilty for being lazy, I exhale with a tired sigh and offer, "Do you need a hand?"

"I wouldn't want you to break a sweat, Ken," Nacho calls out.

"Who's Ken?"

"I'm Barbie, and you're Ken," Tex explains.

"Since when?" How can he look so pleased to be called Barbie?

"Well, I'm wearing a pink crop top, and...you know," he waves in my general direction.

"No, I don't know." I'm starting to feel like there's a movie playing in his head that no one else can see.

"Your face, you look like Malibu Ken."

I just stare, wordless and slightly open-mouthed. "I think the sun baked your brain," I snort.

"I think you're both fucking half-baked," Nacho insists, peeking his head out of the serving window. "The equipment looks like it's in good shape, it just needs to be deep-cleaned. The truck has brand new tires, and the refrigeration unit was replaced about six months ago, so everything looks pretty good."

"We're in business," I shout, slapping my leg.

"He's the cook, you're the investor, so what am I?" Tex asks.

Nacho laughs. "You really want me to answer that, Barbie?"

"Fuck all y'all," he pouts, finishing off his *Fanta*. He burps, long and loud, a sound completely at odds with a man wearing a pink crop top and red plaid shorts.

How does that match?

"You gonna spill the beans, Ken, or what?" Nacho asks.

"What beans?"

"About your honeymoon," Tex clarifies.

"It wasn't a honeymoon," I say, but I'll be damned if I don't feel heat rise to my cheeks, and it's not from the sun. I shift my weight, making the cheap lawn chair creak.

"Whatever you wanna call it, you still gotta tell us about it."

"I don't have to tell you shit, Tex."

"Trust me, it's worse if you let me fill in the details with my own imagination."

He's probably right. "What do you think happened?"

"What I think, what I *know*," he stresses, "is that the two of you were pining for each other's dicks when you left and you don't look like you're pining anymore, which means you either got over it or you got *on* it. Do you want to guess which one I'm going with?"

Fucker. I refuse to let him think he has the upper hand here. "Well, I guess you got it all figured out then, Barbie."

"Not you, too," he whines.

"Are you happy?" Nacho asks. "That's really all that matters."

My smile is genuine. I feel it all the way down in my soul. "Yeah, I'm happy."

"I'll drink to that," Nacho cheers, popping open a fresh can of *Fanta*.

"You got soft on me while you were gone," Riggs taunts. "Pick up the pace, Sommers!"

"Soft? I hiked miles! Christ, we walked all over Asheville. My leg's killing me."

"Not as much as it's gonna be if you don't catch up to McCormick and Wardell," he warns. "They've each got one leg, for fuck's sake. If you can't beat them, you'll be swimming extra laps until the sun sets."

Wonderful. I hold my breath and push off from the wall, slicing my arms through the water. When I surface on the other end of the pool, the guys are already deep in conversation about me. *Did I say conversation?* More like *speculation.*

"Wonder what made him lose his edge?"

"Yeah, it really shoots Riggs's theory about your sex drive being a great motivator, doesn't it?"

"Unless...his appetite has been sated, in which case..." McCormick bends his finger down slowly, to emulate an erection going soft. He makes a dying whistling sound and then... "Poof," he says, mimicking an explosion.

Asshole. I thwack him hard on his back. *Too* hard. "What's the matter, Hot Dog, did you swallow too much chlorinated pool water?"

"No, I wasn't choking," he plays along, knowing damn well I didn't think he was choking. "I was showing West an example of your dick, I mean your sex-drive," he hastily corrects, "going soft."

McCormick has no idea I suffer from limp-dick, so I can't be offended. He's just joking, trying to be clever about my weekend getaway with Brewer. Was there anyone who didn't know? *Fuck.*

"Oh, I get it. No wonder you're the fastest swimmer," I tease with a wink. "How long's it been, four months? Five?" He splashes me in the face and takes off for the other end of the pool.

"Nice," West laughs. "It's been almost six," he clarifies before taking off.

The Bitches' bullshit continues in the locker room, and then down the hall as we head towards group.

"Where's Brewer?" Jax asks, making a show of looking all around me and behind me.

"In his office, I guess. Why?"

"Figured since he has such a tight leash on you now, he'd be right behind you." He smirks, and my hands itch to wipe it off his face.

"Come here, fucker. I'll show you what a tight leash feels like." I'm supposed to be joking—my smile says I'm joking—but am I?

Of course, Brewer chooses the worst possible moment to stop by and poke his head into the classroom.

"There you are," he exclaims brightly. "How'd your workout go?"

Fuck me. All the Bitches start making kissy face sounds, like a bunch of two-year-olds. Are they serious? Is this a support group for battle-scarred veterans or a fucking daycare?

Closing the distance between us in the hopes that not every juvenile delinquent in this classroom can hear our conversation, I answer in a low voice, "It went great. I feel really good. I'll catch up with you after the meeting. Can I take you to lunch?"

Brewer's sexy little smile melts me. "Sure can. Come find me." He gives me a quick peck on the lips, not nearly long enough, and my stomach swirls with butterflies. It happens every time he touches me, kisses me, or looks at me like I'm something special.

My cheeks are flaming red when I turn back to the class. No one says a word, but Brandt slaps a twenty-dollar bill in West's palm.

West smirks. "Pay up, Reaper."

"Dammit," Brandt snipes.

"That's what you get for doubting me."

They fucking bet on me? Jesus Christ.

Thankfully, I'm not the only side show in this classroom.

Stiles stomps in, his heavy motorcycle boots echoing loudly with each step, with McCormick hot on his heels.

"That's the last fucking time! Never again!"

"What? What'd I do?" McCormick asks, sounding confused.

"You know what you did. Same bullshit, different day." Stiles takes a seat, pulling a ball of black yarn from his canvas tote bag. It's the same one we all have, with the Bitches with Stitches logo that says, 'healing hearts one stitch at a time'.

McCormick sits next to him, as if they're not arguing and everything is peachy. "You're out of your mind. I think you inhaled my exhaust."

"You'd have to be going faster than me for that to happen. Fat fucking chance." He shakes his head. "I can't believe you did that."

McCormick throws up his hands. "What?!"

"Fucking got off your bike at the red light. You pulled a pack of baby wipes out of your saddlebags and started polishing your fucking bike. At the red light!"

"And? There's a lot of pollen out right now. She was dirty."

"I can't," Stiles insists, palming his face. "Never again. You're a fucking embarrassment to the ALR. Maybe you should look into getting a membership with the TWT instead."

"What's the TWT?" McCormick asks.

"Tykes with trikes."

That's too fucking funny, even to me. I join the other Bitches in laughing.

Jax wheezes. "Oh my God, can you imagine McCormick riding a tricycle with a bunch of toddlers? Dude, you did that shit with me last summer on that road trip to Maggie Valley. It was embarrassing as fuck."

"Right?" Stiles says, gaining support. "I'm revoking your American Legion of Riders membership card. You're out."

"*You're* out," McCormick insists, "out of your fucking mind."

I pull a ball of blue yarn out of my bag and try to sort out the hot mess I've made on my needles. It's supposed to be a scarf for Brewer, the same color as my eyes, but with all the dropped stitches and gaping holes, it looks more like... Blue Swiss cheese? I don't fucking know. I'm trying my best. Clearly, my talents lie in other areas.

According to Brewer, I'm talented at—

"Pharo, you're back!" McCormick exclaims, interrupting my thoughts.

"Good to see you, man," Stiles adds, clapping the newcomer on the back.

"You, too. You been good?"

"Can't complain. We're all hanging in there. Are you still in one piece?"

"They haven't taken me down yet, brother."

The dark giant takes a seat next to me. Christ, he smells fantastic. Who is this guy? I'd remember seeing someone like him, and I've never been high enough in my life to forget a face like his. Shoulder length, dark, wavy hair, beard scruff covering his high cheekbones and square chin. Golden almond-shaped eyes, and a body built like a linebacker. I may not remember him, but it seems Jax is dying to forget him.

"I'm out," he calls out, grabbing his tote bag, and pushing to his feet in a hurry.

"Why don't you sit the fuck down and stop whining like a bitch?" Pharo sneers, his lip curling.

"Why don't you mind your own fucking business," Jax returns, getting in his face.

Jesus Christ, I definitely missed something. What's going on between these two?

Stiles jumps to his feet, stepping between them and putting a hand on both their chests. "Everybody sit the fuck down and shut the fuck up. Right fucking now."

With one last look of contempt for each other, both men take their seats.

"I don't care what happens outside this classroom. That's your business. You do what you want. But when we step into this room, we leave that shit at the door. This circle is sacred, and within the circle, we're all brothers and we're all friends. For sixty minutes twice a week, we have each other's backs, and if you can't fucking commit to that, get the fuck up right now and leave, because you're not a Bitch."

I know he means to sound inspiring, and also intimidating, laying down the law like that, but does he realize that he ruined it by calling us Bitches? I mean, technically, I guess we are, *Bitches with Stitches*, but does he realize how it sounds? I guess not because his face still looks deadly serious. Yet I can't help the fit of laughter I can't seem to shake off. It starts as a snort, almost a hiccup, but then it becomes repetitive. The harder I try, the harder I laugh.

Brandt and West must have picked up on it as well because

now they're laughing. Fuck, it's contagious because now Mandy is giggling like a bitch. Thinking the word just makes me laugh harder. I can't hide it. I give up. Doubled over with my head between my knees, I laugh until tears blur my vision. Someone, I think West, snorts like a pig while laughing.

"I'm a bitch," McCormick confirms, sounding really happy about it.

Fuck it, I can't take it. My laughter turns loud, and I sit up because I can't breathe. Tears stream down my cheeks as I struggle and wheeze to take a deep breath. West's head falls into Brandt's lap as he combusts with laughter, and Brandt whacks him on the back.

Stiles clears his throat, glaring at each of us in turn. "You're not helping. None of you are helping."

"Don't mind me," Jax snides. "I'll just be over here knitting a bunch of ball gags."

I fall apart all over again. My stomach and my cheeks ache from laughing so hard. I haven't laughed like this since before I was deployed. It's been way too long.

"Gentlemen, let's get a hold of ourselves and bring this meeting to order," Riggs says with all seriousness, taking a seat next to Jax.

An hour later, we were on our way to lunch.

"These wings taste like shit," West bitches. "They've got nothing on the Black Mountain Tavern."

"Agreed." Brandt makes a face as he swallows and chases the unsavory chicken with a swig of his soda. "Why are we even here?"

"I can't figure that out either," Mandy agrees, sucking the

grease from his fingers. "These *Hooters* girls don't do a thing for any of us."

"Speak for yourself, nutter buddy. I wasn't always gay," West smirks, glancing at Brandt for confirmation. Brandt chuffs.

"Wait for it," I warn, spotting my target from across the restaurant. He was incoming like a missile—scratch that, like a MOAB—in about three seconds. Two. One.

Impact.

"Hiiiii, welcome to Hooters. I'm Tex, your server. I was just on break, but I'll be taking over for Charlotte now that I'm back. I see you already got your food, but I figured a bunch of big rowdy boys like yourselves must have big appetites to fill, so I brought some onion rings." He slides them on the table amidst the used napkins and plates of food.

The effect he has on the rest of the table is better than I could have predicted. Every one of them has their mouth hanging open, slack-jawed with unchewed food. Not that I can blame them. Tex is a showstopper, especially in that skimpy cocktease of a uniform.

"You were saying about being attracted to girls, West?" How can I not throw that dig in there when he's gaping like a fool?

"What about you, big man?" Tex wraps his fingers around Mandy's thick biceps. "You must have a huge appetite. What can I bring you to satisfy it?" Mandy is speechless. "I bet you have a sweet tooth," Tex continues, unfazed by Mandy's silence. "I'll bring you a slice of chocolate cake. And if you can't find your tongue, maybe I can help you find it," he flirts slyly, whispering in Mandy's ear.

Tex sashays off to the kitchen, and suddenly the table comes back to life.

"What in the fuck was that?" West asks, his french fry suspended in midair, halfway to his mouth.

"*That* was the Tex effect. He's like a tornado."

Brandt reaches for an onion ring. "No shit. Since when do they hire guys?"

"Since now, I guess."

"I don't go for that type of man, but I'm oddly turned on," West admits, his hand disappearing beneath the table. I'd bet ten dollars he's adjusting his junk. Brandt just laughs at him.

The only person who has yet to say a word is Mandy. He seems to be having trouble swallowing his burger. He's completely checked out of our conversation, his eyes constantly darting around the restaurant, following Tex from table to table as he checks on his customers. When Tex finally returns with his chocolate cake and the bill, he places it in front of Mandy and then dips his finger into the frosting, making a show of sucking the icing from his finger.

Rolling my eyes, I grab the bill and reach for my wallet. "My treat." I don't mind paying since I insisted we all come here. Mostly, I just wanted to support Tex in his new position and ensure that he received at least one good tip today. In addition to the bill, I drop two twenties in cash on the table. "Are you all ready?"

West and Brandt slide out of the booth. Mandy remains. "You coming?" I ask.

"You all go on without me. I think I'm gonna hang back for a minute and finish my cake."

He's so full of shit. I know he's full of shit because not only are his eyes brown, but they're laser-focused on the cute waiter wearing sheer glitter tights over his long legs.

"Enjoy, buddy." I clap Mandy on the back and follow the lovers out the door.

"Looking good, Nacho," I call out on my way inside. He's hosing down the outside of the truck, giving it a good scrub.

I drop my keys on the kitchen counter next to a stack of mail. On top is a letter with my name on it. The return address catches my eye. Department of Defense. *What the fuck do they want?*

Carefully, I peel open the envelope and pull out the letter inside. I can feel my anxiety mounting as I scan the first couple of introductory paragraphs. That sick swirly feeling is sloshing around my gut, and the residue is crawling up my throat, giving me heartburn.

Have I not given enough? Must they always ask for more?

"...want to honor your service and sacrifice with the Prisoner of War Medal. Other medals being awarded include the Purple Heart, for service members who have been wounded or killed as a result of enemy action while serving in the US military."

Please, no. I don't... I don't want this. I can't...

Panic grips my heart and squeezes painfully. My breath comes short and fast.

A solemn distinction for those who have greatly sacrificed themselves or paid the ultimate price? What the fuck did I do?

All I managed to do was to stay alive. How fucking meritorious and heroic is that? It was just luck, or sheer stubbornness.

"No!" I shout, grabbing my head. The pictures, they're coming back, mental snapshots flipping through my head like a film strip. I shake my head, harder and harder, but I can't clear them from my mind. Blood pumps loudly in my ears, and a cold sweat breaks out across my skin, making me feel clammy. I shiver, a full body shiver, and pressure begins together in the base of my skull. It moves behind my eyes like a pulsing heartbeat.

I grab onto the edge of the counter, feeling the cold granite beneath my fingertips. Five... Four... Three... Two... One... I take a deep breath through my nose and hold it for the count of three before releasing it.

The sour stench of urine invades my nose. The screeching gets louder, the sound of the rats, searching for their next meal. I pull a ragged breath into my lungs, willing myself not to disappear. I don't want to time travel back to the past. I want to stay here in the present. I don't want to lose myself again. Not ever again. I bite down on my bottom lip hard—hard enough to draw blood. The pain keeps me grounded in the present.

Don't slip...don't slip...don't slip away...

Pain spikes in my head, and I crumble the letter in my fist and stumble to my room. Drawing the black out curtains, I lock the door and crawl under the covers.

Sergeant Nashville Aidan Sommers. United States Army. 89-6717-4613. Sergeant Nashville Aidan Sommers. United States Army. 89-6717-4613. Sergeant Nashville Aidan Sommers. United States Army. 89-6717-4613.

There's a knock at the door. It starts out softly but gets louder the longer I ignore it. I don't want to hear the knock. I don't want to know who's standing on the other side of the door. The chanting in my head becomes louder until I speak the words out loud, over and over again.

"Sergeant Nashville Aidan Sommers. United States Army. 89-6717-4613. Sergeant Nashville Aidan Sommers. United States Army. 89-6717-4613. Sergeant Nashville Aidan Sommers. United States Army. 89-6717-4613."

Repeating them lulls me into a trance, a false feeling of safety and security, and I cling to the words, facts I know about myself to be true and correct, until it all fades away to black.

Until *I* fade away.

"Sergeant Nashville Aidan Sommers. United States Army."

"Sergeant Nashville Aidan Sommers."

"Sergeant Nashville."

"Ser—"

NASH

Serenity House
Black Mountain, NC

Chapter 2

"Hey, Brewer." Riggs creeps into my office, shutting the door behind him for privacy.

"Hey, Riggs."

"Anything yet?"

I stare out the window of my office, but my mind is on *him*, not the scenery outside. "No, nothing yet. It's been twenty-four hours, and I haven't heard a word."

"Do you have any idea what set him off?" Riggs takes a seat across from me, on the couch reserved for my patients.

"I found a torn envelope from the DOD on the counter in the kitchen. There was a letter in his bed, crumbled into a ball." I transfer my gaze to Riggs. "They want to honor him with a

POW medal and a Purple Heart." I breathe out a tired, heavy sigh. "Violet Gutierrez got the same letter."

He whistles long and low. "That'll do it. I remember when Wardell and Aguilar got their letters. They struggled for a while before the banquet. I remember they shared about it in the group a few times. But they had each other to lean on, Nash..."

Leaning forward, I brace my elbows on my knees. "I thought he would lean on me, that he would come to me when he was hurting, but I guess I was wrong."

"I don't think you're wrong, Brewer. I think some things are just too much to process at once. Think about all he's been through, and now they want to make some sort of fucking spectacle out of it for the press. Do you think he would hurt himself?"

"No," I answer honestly, leaning back again. My gaze returns to the tree outside my window. "He's never tried to in the past, and I don't think that's what he wants. I think he just wants to escape. God, I hope he's not using. He's come so far, worked so hard. I know how bad he wants this." When I look at Riggs again, he's leaning forward, giving me his full attention, his throat working as he swallows.

"What does your gut tell you?"

"My gut tells me to give him space. That if I keep rescuing him, he'll never learn to stand on his own and trust himself. But my heart," I scoff, "my heart tells me to get in the car and go find him, to save him, to baby his ass. I can't make him do this my way. He's got to find his own way or he never will."

"I think you're right. Nobody knows him better than you do, Brewer. You know what he needs, however hard it might be to give it to him. The guys are dying to go look for him, but I feared it might just make things worse."

I shake my head. "I think it would definitely do more harm than good. He doesn't need an intervention, he needs some tough love, some compassion and empathy, and he needs space. We just need to trust in him right now, trust that he's learned everything I've tried to teach him, and the tools to take care of himself."

"And if he hasn't?"

I take a deep breath to calm my racing heart. "Then we start over again, from the beginning." Another deep breath, and then another. I check my watch and swallow. Why is it so hard to swallow? "I think I'm gonna step outside and clear my head. Get some fresh air."

Riggs smiles, a small, knowing smile. "Sounds like a good idea. Do you need a ride along?"

I should have known he would see right through me. "No, but if I do, I'll call you."

I push to my feet, and Riggs stands and wraps his arms around me. It's the strong, reassuring hug I need to keep me solidly on my feet. The kind of hug that only a caring and concerned friend can offer when you need it most.

I've circled this town twice without a trace of him. I've checked every park, every meeting and church, and every back alley and café. I even called Violet. Defeated and worried sick, I pull the car over to the side of the road and put it in park. I'd love to give in to the irrational impulse to bang my head against the steering wheel over-and-over until he magically appears beside me, but I know that's not going to happen.

Should I give up and go home or keep searching? Does he even want to be found? What if he's waiting for me to find him because he can't get out of his own way and reach out?

Fuck! Fuck...fuck...fuck...

Maybe I should check the house again. I feel like I'm chasing my tail in circles, but I put the car in drive and step on the gas. Three blocks down I pass the Black Mountain Tavern, and something, maybe it's my higher power, maybe it's my gut, hell, maybe it's Victor Gutierrez talking to me from beyond the grave, but *something* draws me in. I pull into the parking lot and park the car, but I don't get out yet.

Resting my head against the steering wheel, I surrender.

God, grant me serenity to accept the things I cannot change, courage to change the things I can, and the wisdom to know the difference. Amen.

When I raise my head again, I take a deep breath, feeling calmer and stronger. I recite the prayer two more times before reaching for the door handle.

When I walk into the bar, I sigh with relief.

My search is over.

This is the downside of being in love. The pain you feel from caring too much. Sometimes, love is a bandage that heals the deepest wounds. But sometimes, it can be a double edged sword that cuts you in half and leaves your heart bleeding out.

Nash sits alone at a high-top table, with his head in his hands. The full glass of bourbon sitting beside him feels like a stab in my gut. I pull out the chair, and he doesn't even flinch at the sound of the legs scraping across the wooden floor.

There're so many things I want to say. So many things I *should* say. But mostly, I just want to wrap him in my arms and breathe him in.

"Are you avoiding me? Or are you avoiding yourself?"

"Neither." Slowly, he lifts his head. "Both." He looks like shit, with red-rimmed eyes lined with dark shadows under them. "What are you doing here, Brewer?"

"I could ask you the same thing." My eyes drop to the untouched glass beside him.

"I haven't touched it. I swear." He pushes it toward me and then reaches into his pocket and pulls out an orange prescription bottle. I don't know whose name is on the label, but I can bet it's not his. "I haven't touched these either. Please," he shoves them at me, "take them."

"How much longer are you planning on running?"

"I'm too tired to keep running," he says, slumping in his chair.

My heart breaks for him, but I can't show that sympathy right now. I can't give in. Feeling sorry for him isn't going to help him out of this hole he's dug for himself.

"So you finished your fourth and your fifth steps. You made a list of everyone you wronged, all the actions you regretted, and you made amends for each of them." A waitress passes by carrying an empty tray, and I motion for her to clear our table. "Sounds like you've forgiven everyone but yourself."

"I can't understand why you haven't given up on me yet," he says accusingly, like I've wronged him in some way by supporting him and believing in him. "Can't you see how broken I am? I'm a lost fucking cause, Brewer."

Does he have no faith in himself whatsoever? "I don't think you're broken, just a little bent, maybe, but it's nothing we can't straighten out."

"I'm done trying. It's not working. Can't you see that? It's not working, Brewer. I thought I was doing better, but here I am again, one breath away from making a bad choice."

He's feeling frustrated and hopeless. I can see it in his eyes, pooling with tears.

"No." My voice sounds fierce.

"No, what?"

"No, you're not allowed to give up. You're not allowed to just quit!" My fist pounds the table, finally garnering a reaction from him. "You made promises to a lot of people. You asked them for forgiveness. You made promises to *me*," I hiss. "And your plant and your cat. But most of all, you made a promise to yourself! Does that not mean anything to you, Nash? You may not have forgiven yourself yet, but everyone who loves you has forgiven you, and I refuse to let you quit on them." I struggle to take a deep breath. "You're not going to let them down, and you're not going to let yourself down either. This is the part where you step back and take a deep breath and look at how far you've come. Try to remember everything you've learned. What is the next right step, Nash?"

I hold my next breath in my lungs, anticipating his answer. *Come on, Nash. Say the right thing.*

The light fades from his eyes. He just looks...defeated. "I

have to surrender." His shoulder sag even more under the weight of his decision.

I'm so overcome with relief that I can't hide the tears that rush to my eyes and run down my cheeks. They match the wet streaks on his face. "You know what you need to do. Don't step foot inside of our home until you've surrendered and you've forgiven yourself."

Swiping my tears away, I lean in close, holding his gaze. There's so many emotions in his haunted sapphire eyes. Guilt and shame, defeat, exhaustion, anger. I'm trying so hard to find some hope, just a trace of it, but I can't seem to find any.

"Don't look too closely. It's dark inside there."

"Nah, you just need someone to shine a bright light so you can find your way through the darkness within."

"I thought you were my light," he sobs brokenly, drowning my heart in his tears.

"I *am* your light. It's still inside you. I'll hold that fucking flashlight for you every single day and night for the rest of your life. But you can't see the light if you don't open your eyes, Nash. You've got to open your eyes and trust that the light will be there."

He lets his tears fall, heedless of the other patrons in the bar. For a grown man not to care who sees him fall apart, he's got to be in an incredible amount of pain.

"Will you bring me home?"

His voice sounds so small, so afraid, and I stand up and swallow past the lump in my throat, and somehow, I find the courage to voice the second hardest thing I've ever had to say. The first was when I admitted I was an addict for the first time.

"You found your way here, you can find your own way home. When you're ready."

"Brewer, wait!"

Just keep walking. Don't look back. Do not turn back, Brewer!

Chapter 25
Ft. Bragg Fayetteville, NC

THAT MOTHERFUCKER ACTUALLY WALKED OUT ON ME! I can't blame him. I deserve far worse. For months, I've begged him to take a chance on me, to trust in me, and at the first sign of trouble, I let him down.

Fuck it, I have to admit that I let myself down.

He's absolutely right. I don't get to take the easy way out and bail on the people I made promises to. That's not who I am or who I've become. Brewer taught me the tools I need to face down my demons. I'm done running, I'm fucking *exhausted*, and as scary as it is to confront the people I've hurt, I'm ready.

Fishing my phone from my back pocket, I pull up my email and fire off a letter of apology to my warrant officer, Burgess. I prefer to do it face-to-face, but I have no intention of ever seeing him again, so this will have to do.

Next, I shoot Mandy a text.

> Is it too late for me to drop by?

Mandy:

It's never too late for you.

Shit, that right there is why this man deserves an apology. He's been nothing but good to me. Better than good. How the hell am I going to get there? I left my car parked in the driveway at home. I just started walking and never looked back. I'll have to take an Uber.

Twenty minutes later, the driver drops me off at his door.

"Where's your car?" Mandy is waiting for me before I even knock.

"Long story. Can I come in?"

"Sure," he says, stepping aside. "You don't look so good. Can I get you something? Water? Soda? A week in rehab?"

With a snort, I shake my head and plop down on his couch. "I'm not using, though I came close. But an angel saved me."

"You look like you need to talk, so talk. I'm listening."

I guess I caught him off guard, stopping by at the last minute. Mandy is dressed in navy blue sweats and no shirt. The scars that cover half of his face continue down his neck and over his shoulder, ending part way down his back. It's a reminder that I'm not the only one facing demons. I just seem to be running away faster than anyone else.

He catches me looking at his body. "I'll just go grab a T-shirt."

"No." I hate that I made him feel self-conscious, even for a second. "I've just never seen them before. I didn't know how bad it was, not that it's bad, but—"

"Relax, I know what you mean. Are you sure you don't need me to put a shirt on?"

"I don't ever want you to be anything but yourself with me. I guess that's why I'm here. You've seen me at my worst and, I don't know why, maybe you're just really fucking lonely and desperate for friends," Mandy snorts, "or you've got some sort of savior complex, but you didn't turn away from me. You welcomed me with open arms. Maybe you're a total fucking narcissist."

This time, he laughs out loud. "Yeah, you've got me all figured out, Sommers."

"I didn't know that I needed you, but you're exactly what I needed. I was just so lost and afraid. You were there for me at my lowest. You were still there when I hit rock bottom. Maybe you saved me that day, I don't know, but I'm always gonna be grateful to you. I need friends like you in my life, Mandy. I don't wanna be alone. I'm just sorry that I wasn't good to you from the start."

Instead of placating me, Mandy opens his arms and hugs me

so tight he threatens to squeeze the breath from my lungs. "As long as we don't ever talk about why I couldn't go into your bedroom."

My shoulders shake with silent laughter as I recall how I freaked him the fuck out that day he came over to fix my wall. I bet if he knew I had a Gutierrez lump buddy in my bed, he wouldn't be hugging me right now.

"Some things are better left unsaid."

He laughs and claps me on the back twice before letting me go. "We're good, brother. I appreciate your apology, but I didn't really need it. All that is water under the bridge. It's just the kind of bullshit friends do for each other."

"I'm grateful for you. I wish I could stay and hang out, but it's getting late, and I've had a shit-tastic day."

"Can I take you home?"

"Yeah." I'm not too proud to beg, not after I've walked all over Black Mountain today on a bum leg.

"Let me just grab that T-shirt and a pair of shoes and I'll meet you downstairs."

As we're cruising down the highway, Mandy turns down the radio and asks, "Do you want to talk about today?"

"No. Not at all. I guess I just needed a reminder to do the next right thing." The scenery passes by in a blur, and with each mile, I feel more exhausted, down to my bones. "When you're going through your medical shit, and you're afraid, you always reach out and ask for help, no matter how it makes you feel to humble yourself. I guess," I let out a tired sigh and shift my gaze to his profile, "I guess I need to take a page from your book and humble myself." All of my fear and humiliation is gathered in a knot, in the middle of my throat, making it hard to swallow. "I need your help. I'm scared. When they give me that fucking medal, will you be there with me?"

"Like your ball sack buddy?" He grins, making the scars around his mouth stretch in a way that pulls his lips down, like he's frowning.

Fucker. "Exactly like that. Will you share a sack with me?"

"Of course, I'd love to be your other nut. Just don't tell West."

I'm reminded of that old saying, when God closes a window, He opens a door. I lost my best friend, but now I have more friends than I can count. The Bitches, the guys at Serenity House, the other addicts I've met at the meetings. I didn't ask for any of this, but I wouldn't trade it for anything. I guess that's the thing about friends, they always do the exact thing that's gonna piss you off. Like loving you when you don't think you deserve it, forgiving you before you can even ask, driving your sorry ass home in the middle of the night, or forcing their friendship on you when your life is falling apart.

Mandy parks along the curb. "Damn, that's a big ass taco truck." He laughs to himself. "Call me if you need me."

"I'm always going to need you, brother." Sliding my arm around his neck, I give him a one-armed hug before climbing out of the car.

I can feel his eyes on me as I shuffle up the front walk and can feel the weight of his curiosity as I slump into a rocking chair on the front porch instead of going inside.

"Did you forget your key?" he calls out the window.

"Nah, I think I'll just sit here for a moment. I've got to take care of something before I go inside."

"Do you want me to wait?"

"No, I'm good."

Mandy doesn't look convinced. "Do you want me to park down the street and idle the car for fifteen minutes?"

That makes me laugh. "Nah, I'll call you tomorrow."

I wait until his taillights disappear down the road. I'm tired, fucking exhausted, and the remnants of my earlier headache are threatening to make a comeback. I pinch the bridge of my nose and rub.

"Don't look at me like that, G. Neither of us is perfect. Fuck, since you've..." I pause, searching for the right word, "ascended, you've really gotten holier than thou. In fact, I remember when you used to...you know what? Never mind." Sighing loudly, I scrub my face.

"You're right, I fucked up. I bailed when the going got tough. It's just..." The damn holding back my tears and my pain bursts, and all of my messy emotions rush forth. "I can't, G! Fuck, I don't want the goddamn medal. You and I both know I didn't do a fucking thing to earn it. All I did was stay alive, mostly because I wasn't gonna give those fuckheads the satisfaction of seeing me die." Using the hem of my shirt, I wipe the tears and snot from my face. "Can I tell you something? Mostly, I was afraid of what they would do with our bodies if we both died. Feed us to the dogs? Leave us there to rot so the rats could have us? Drag our bodies through the streets as they cheered? Fuck no! I stayed alive to make sure they wouldn't do that to you. I made a promise to you, G." A fresh round of tears fall, blurring my vision. "I promised to get you home, and the only way I could keep that promise was if I stayed alive. I just wish I hadn't failed you! You deserved to come home alive, too." It hurts to swallow because my throat is so swollen. "Your mom needs you. *I* need you." Dragging a shaky breath into my lungs, I wipe my face again.

"I need to tell you how sorry I am. I don't know what I could have done differently to change the outcome, but I hate that I didn't try. If I had fought back, they'd have killed me for sure. Then, after they shot me, there really wasn't much I could do, anyway. Fuck!" Leaning forward, I drop my head between my knees and press my fingers to my temples. "I did the best I could, G. You know that, don't you? Did I make it any easier for you? The little that I could do, did it help at all?" Raising my head, I look up at the night sky, at the dozens of stars shining down on me, and wonder if one of them is my best friend.

"I need you to forgive me. I need you to tell me that what I did was enough. I love you, G, I always will. Don't disappear on me, okay? I need you to keep looking out for me." Pushing to my feet, I wince at the sharp stab of pain that shoots up my leg into my hip. All that walking earlier, I definitely overdid it. "I'm sorry, G. So fucking sorry, but mostly, I'm sorry that I tried to forget you."

I can barely keep my eyes open any longer, and all I want to do is go lay down, but I made Brewer a promise that I wouldn't step foot inside our house until I forgave myself. I lean my back against the front door and take a deep breath.

I have a good heart.

I'm a loyal friend.

I have good intentions, even if I don't execute them well.

I'm a good soldier and leader.

I tried my hardest to keep my buddy alive.

I know that if I had tried to fight back, it would have been in vain.

I kept my promise to bring my buddy home to his mom.

I'm not responsible for the death of Victor Gutierrez.

I'm *not* responsible for the death of Victor Gutierrez.

I'm not responsible for the death of Victor Gutierrez.

I'm ashamed of myself for the way I handled my grief.

I forgive myself, and I promise to do better, *be* better.

I don't know what I expected after I forgave myself. A meteor shower? A shooting star? A damn ticker tape parade? None of those things happen. But I feel a little lighter, like I checked a huge important box off my to-do list. What I said is the truth, and I can stop blaming myself for shit that had nothing to do with me. My feelings stemmed from guilt, but not truth. I know deep down in my heart, underneath the anger and the grief and the survivor's guilt, that my best friend forgives me, and that's good enough for me to forgive myself.

Sliding the key into the lock, I let myself inside and head straight for my bedroom, hoping to find my cat because fuck, I really miss him. But my room is empty. More than anything, I want to crawl into bed with Brewer, but I'm worried he doesn't want me there.

How badly did I fuck things up between us?

Just the possibility of being rejected by him makes me feel panicked. I wouldn't be able to survive that.

I creep downstairs on silent feet, avoiding all the soft spots in the floor that creak, and breathe a huge sigh of relief when I find his door unlocked.

Does that mean I'm welcome?

Pale moonlight filters in through the window facing the back of the house, illuminating my path to the bed. I can hear his soft snores, drawing me closer like a beacon in the darkness. Quietly, I strip down to my boxers and slip under the covers. The sheets feel cool in contrast with his warm body. Inch by inch, I scoot closer, as close as I can, until I'm snug against his back. A dark furry head pops up over his shoulder, and Valor's bright green eyes glow like a neon sign welcoming me home. He purrs like a motorboat, and I scratch between his ears.

"Hi, little man, did you miss me?"

"Welcome home," Brewer murmurs, his voice soft and warm.

I could cry, because it sounds so good, because he didn't kick me out of bed, because he's taking care of my cat in my absence, because he's the answer to every problem I've ever had, and because he's my future. The only future I dream of.

I slide my arm around his stomach, teasing my fingers through the soft hair on his belly. For the first time today, I take a deep breath, and I feel everything inside of me shift and release.

This man is my antidepressant. He is my anti-anxiety med. He is my mild sedative and my sleep aid. He is my *Viagra*.

Brewer is the only drug I need in my system, the only cure for what ails me. A healthy addiction.

I owe this man *everything*, beginning with an apology.

"Brewer," I have to swallow twice before I can finish. "I'm so fucking sorry." He slides his hand over mine. I crave the connection and comfort of his touch. Just that one small gesture is my absolution.

"It's so hard for me to come to you with my shame, and my guilt and my anger. I should have humbled myself and asked you to stand by me, to lend me your strength, but I felt so inferior, so *unworthy* of you, and I felt like... I don't know, I felt like, maybe if I pointed out those flaws, that you would see them, actually *see* them and not sweep them under the rug or look at me with rose-colored glasses because you love me. And that maybe, if you saw my flaws, if you saw all the ugly corrosive shit in my head and in my heart, the shit that taints my soul, you would see me differently, and that maybe—" I can't, I can't even say it without feeling sick. With a deep, shaky breath, I spit out the words that are so hard to admit. "That maybe you wouldn't love me anymore. That you *couldn't* because, if you saw me the way I see myself, how could you possibly love me?"

Jesus Christ with the fucking tears again!

Brewer gently places Valor to the side and turns in my arms, so that we're chest-to-chest, face-to-face. He slides his hand along my jaw like a caress.

"The only thing I see when I look at you is my heart. You are the embodiment of my heart walking around outside of my body, and I trust you to keep it safe for me. When you screw up —when you say or do the wrong thing—I still trust that you're going to make it right. I see your flaws, Nash. I see what's in your head and in your soul. It's not corrosive. It's pain and grief and anger and guilt, it's fear and insecurity and anxiety, it's all the things that convince me you have the most beautiful heart and soul of any man I've ever known. That you can feel so many of those feelings, and keep going, keep living, keep loving, is a testament to how fucking strong you are, and resilient and brave. I love you, Nash. I love everything about you, even the stuff I don't like too much. Your flaws make you who you are, just like your assets shape you into the man you are. It's all part of the greater whole." He brushes his lips over mine, softly, like a whisper of a kiss. "And I'm head over heels, irrevocably and forever in love with the greater whole."

My lips part for his kiss, for his tongue, and he slips inside my mouth. The way his tongue moves against mine makes his declaration feel very convincing.

In the morning, he's the first thing I see when I open my eyes, his arms still wrapped around me, our bodies so close together we're practically squishing the kitten between us. With his eyes still closed, a playful grin teases his lips, and his warm hands cup my balls, sliding up my shaft as he purrs louder than Valor.

"Damn, look how hard you are. I don't know where it came from, but it would be a shame to waste it."

I place kisses on his eyelids, and he laughs before opening them, staring at me with the warmest brown eyes richer than the finest chocolate. "It's amazing what forgiving yourself and being forgiven can do to your body."

"Maybe don't tell that to people. You'll put me out of business," he teases, stealing a kiss from my lips. We've woken Valor, and he begins to lick Brewer's chin. "Nash, move your damn cat," he orders, laughing, "so I can suck your impressively hard cock."

Fuck, "Move, cat!" Scooping him up, I plop him gently on the floor and turn on my back, peeling my boxers off and spreading my legs. Morning blowjobs? That's all the motivation I need to try to overcome my struggle with ED. I want to wake up like this every day.

The first thing I feel is his warm breath ghost over the sensitive, swollen tip of my cock that's peeking out of its hood. A shiver runs through my body, and I groan, dropping my head back on the pillow. His teeth lightly graze my cockhead before his lips close over the crown, gently sucking it from its sheath into his mouth.

"Oh, shit." I'm going to enjoy the fuck out of this. "Do that again."

I can feel his tongue sliding over the underside of my shaft. The slurping and sucking noises he makes are so loud and filthy, I have to raise my head again to watch. His mouth is full of saliva that coats my dick with each pass, making it shiny with spit. He pops off my cock, stretching the string of saliva connecting my tip with his lips before licking it back up again.

"Fuck, Brewer."

The sight of my dick disappearing into his mouth, his swollen, wet lips moving down my shaft, over each vein and ridge, has my balls drawing up tight in no time. They grow warm against my body, and the muscles in my thighs quiver and twitch.

"I'm close. Real close." My neck strains, but there's no way I'm not watching him swallow my load. "I'm gonna fill your mouth and watch you swallow every drop."

"Mmmm," he moans, increasing his pace. He's really going to town on my dick now, making a mess of it, making a mess of himself, too. Spit drips down his chin and lands on my balls, and when it slides down my taint, over my hole, I bust open in his mouth, squirting thick ropes down the back of his throat.

"Now swallow," I demand, bucking my hips to feed him another inch.

He takes it all and swallows the entire load, and then goes back for seconds, sucking lightly on my over-sensitized cock to make sure he didn't miss a drop.

My head flops onto the pillow, and I sigh with contentment. "Can we do that again?"

"Nope, we're gonna get dressed and go to a meeting now."

"A meeting?! This early?"

"They've got coffee and donuts," he promises with a grin, winking at me.

I don't care if they have a personal chef and a breakfast buffet, it's a disappointment after Brewer's mouth. But an hour later, I've got my cat slung across my chest, a paper cup of shitty-tasting bitter coffee in one hand, and a stale donut in the other. But I've got Brewer beside me, and that counts for everything.

"Hi, I'm Nash, and I'm an addict. It's been a long week, and it's about to get longer, but I keep surrendering, and I keep getting humble and asking for help, and knowing that I'm not alone makes it a little easier. I have faith, just for today, that I'm gonna get through this."

"Thanks for sharing, Nash," the meeting moderator says. "Keep coming back."

NASH
Epilogue
Chapter 26

"Here, let me help you."

Brewer takes the towel from me and turns me toward the mirror as he dries my body. When I stepped out of the shower, my hands shook so badly I could barely towel myself dry. The blue eyes that stare back at me from the mirror look scared shitless, not the eyes of a brave warrior about to receive a medal for heroism.

What the mirror doesn't show is the heartburn clawing at my chest, the anxiety churning in my gut, and the tremor in my hand that's now spreading up my arm, making my shoulder ache with tension. It doesn't show the giant oak tree that's taken root in my mind. I remember clearly where the roots lead, how they spear down deep into the earth, loosening the dirt so that it makes an easy grave. Each leaf on the tree represents a memory, a moment in time in the twenty-two days I spent in captivity with my best friend.

I can't shake that tree or the memories today. I feel as if I'm standing directly underneath the limbs, and the leaves are falling on my shoulders, big, thick leaves, burying me under a pile of rotting foliage.

"We could stay here, crawl back in bed and watch a movie. Or we could go to that Thai place for lunch that you love and then go for a walk in the park."

Brewer laughs. "Wow, you hate walking in the park. You're pulling out the big guns, aren't you?"

"Brewer, please." His eyes find mine in the mirror, and his reflection stares back, pinning me with compassion and empathy.

"It's going to be fine, Nash. I know how much you don't want to do this, but you're going to do it. You're going to hold your head up high and walk in there, and accept that award. It's the very least they can do to reward your sacrifice." His hands rub over my shoulders, squeezing. "And if you still want to walk through the park when we're finished, I'll be more than happy to escort you."

Snorting, I shake my head. Fuck the park. Fuck the Thai food and the movie. I just want to crawl back into bed and bury my head under the covers.

"You'll be there with me, right?"

"Every step of the way."

When I step out of the bathroom, my dress blues are hanging in a garment bag on the closet door. Every fiber of my being resists donning the uniform. I don't want to play soldier anymore. When I was a kid, it was all I dreamed of, all I talked about. Playing war with the kids in the neighborhood, watching war movies, reading all the books I could get my hands on about D-Day and Vietnam—it was an abstract idea, a child's dream. I was lured in by the promise of action, the excitement of danger, the camaraderie and brotherhood, of being a part of something greater than myself, but when I got to the desert, I realized war isn't anything like that. It's hell on earth, a living, waking nightmare. The things I saw will stay with me for the rest of my life.

I'm done. I want to be a man of peace. I want to garden and help people and make things grow with my hands. I want to look after the ones left behind, like a shepherd of the casualties of war.

The casualties are not just the soldiers we lost. The casualties are the survivors and the families of those we lost. They are the ones that have to suffer through each day with their grief. The ones who can never forget what they lost.

I am a casualty of war. Violet Gutierrez is a casualty of war. Brewer is a casualty of war, and so are Navarro Riggs, Mandy Cahill, Brandt Aguilar, West Wardell, and the rest of the men from Serenity House and the Bitches with Stitches. We're all casualties, carrying with us every day our grief and the memories of those we lost.

The definition of a prisoner of war is a person held captive by a belligerent power, during or immediately after an armed conflict. Yes, they had possession of my body for twenty-two days. But what about my friends and their families? Are their hearts and minds not held captive by a belligerent power? Are grief and anger not belligerent powers? They certainly feel all-consuming and devastating.

When I receive this award today, I'm accepting it on behalf of each of them, for the captivity that still grips them because they've lost far longer than twenty-two days of their lives.

Brewer helps me dress, fastening the buttons of my coat, straightening the stripes on my breast. He looks at me fondly, proudly, and maybe... Is he getting turned on by the way I look in uniform?

"Brewer," I laugh, "do I even want to know what you're thinking?"

He grins, looking guilty but not sorry. "Probably not. I don't want to dishonor your uniform, so I'll just keep it to myself." Brewer straightens my collar and plants a kiss to my chin. "But later, I'd like to help you undress," he adds, eyes twinkling.

How did I not know this man has a uniform kink?

"Come on, Sergeant. It's time."

Nacho, Tex, and Miles are waiting in the living room. Their heads snap up when they see me, phones in hand forgotten, and they whistle low.

"Looking good, soldier," Tex purrs.

He holds the door open for me, and when I walk outside into the bright sun, it's like walking into a parallel universe.

What the fuck is going on?

My once peaceful street is lined with motorcycles, with men and women dressed in black leather, motorcycle boots, and with American flags and POW flags affixed to their cycles.

McCormick, Stiles, and Jax step forward. "Sergeant Sommers, it would be our honor to provide you with a motorcade of veterans from the American Legion of Riders Association."

A fucking motorcade? Are they kidding me?

"Come on, Sergeant, you have a medal to accept. You can't keep everyone waiting."

"I kind of can. They can't really start without me."

McCormick laughs and claps me on the back. "Damn right!"

I slide into the passenger seat of Brewer's car, and he pulls out of the driveway, followed by my housemates in the car behind ours. But in front of us, and behind the guys of Serenity House, is a long line of distinguished riders who think I did something special or that I deserve something special. The honor they're paying me and silently, Gutierrez, makes me feel choked up inside. Not because I deserve a medal and fanfare, but because of the feeling of brotherhood, of feeling like I belong to something greater than myself. It's a feeling I haven't felt in a long time.

It's the reason I joined the army so many years ago, and it's the driving principle behind the twelve steps of Narcotics Anonymous. The feeling of fellowship. So many nights since I lost him, I've felt so alone, abandoned and broken, and like I would never fit in anywhere again. I was a fucking mess, who would have me? Since then, I've realized the answer to that is *everyone*. Everyone would have me—my housemates, the Bitches, the guys in my unit, my buddy's mother, my fellow addicts in NA. They would all have me and accept me with open arms.

Just because I'm an addict doesn't alienate me. Being a

POW doesn't either. I don't have to run, I just have to surrender.

There are way too many people in this fucking room. Too many for my peace of mind. Again, I tug at my collar, although it's not the reason I can't breathe. Colonel Bullwater drones on and on about sacrifice and service and duty, but all I can hear is the beating of my own heart echoing inside of my head. I have to remind myself to take a deep breath, to keep taking them, to keep my heart rate under control so I don't sweat through my uniform or spiral out of control. I search out Brewer, who's sitting in the second row. In front of him is Violet Gutierrez, in a seat of honor in the front row. Brewer keeps his hand on her shoulder, and her hand is clasped over his, making sure he stays close.

My cheering squad fills up the last two rows in the back. The Bitches and the men of Serenity House.

"...medal for service members held captive 'while engaged in an action against an enemy of the United States; while engaged in military operations involving conflict with an opposing foreign force; or while serving with friendly forces engaged in an armed conflict against an opposing armed force in which the United States is not a belligerent party.'"

The Colonel clears his throat, then presents me with the black velvet box that contains my medal. I open it, and he pins it to my breast. He says a few more ceremonial words, more bullshit, and then he hands me another box. Again, I open it, revealing a Purple Heart. The Colonel pins it to my chest. Instinctively, I reach up to cover it with my hand, feeling the cold metal against my palm.

How can something so tiny feel so heavy?

Then it's Victor's turn. Violet comes up on the dais to stand beside me, and I take her small hand in mine. The Colonel repeats all the same words, and then presents her with the same two boxes. She leans over to press a kiss to my cheek.

"Say something nice about my Victor," she whispers in my ear.

This isn't the time or the place to spill my secrets. To tell the entire room about my shortcomings, about how I failed to keep my best friend alive, how I failed in my mission as Sergeant to lead my team to safety. This is about survival. This is about pomp and ceremony, yes, but also about what we got right that day. Not the day I fell through the hole in the floor, but the day I left through the mouth of the cave. The day the United States Army came and dragged my ass out. The day they brought me home.

After thanking the special forces for their assist, I thank my unit and my command. And then, with a deep, steadying breath, I thank my best friend.

"He's the real hero. Victor is the only reason I'm still alive. He kept me going, he kept me sane, and if I was ever brave, it was because he needed me to be. When my mission failed, he became my mission. I vowed to him every single day and night that I would get us home. No matter what I suffered, or what they did to me, I couldn't let him down, and I couldn't let his mother down. That's why I'm still here. Victor Gutierrez saved my life."

Everything after that is a blur. The handshakes, backslaps, and the pictures. Reporters and journalists shove mics in my face. I just block it all out and focus on Brewer, waiting patiently in the wings. Then there's Tex, wearing a leather messenger bag strapped across his chest. He grabs my hand and shoves it inside the bag.

"Jesus, Tex, what the hell?" I have no idea what he's doing. Is he setting me up? Am I about to grab a handful of slime or a dildo?

Something warm and soft and furry touches my skin. A sandpaper-rough tongue licks my palm.

"You brought Valor?"

"He didn't want to miss your big day," Tex grins. "He's really proud of you."

Fucking perfect. How can something so small as a tiny kitten make me feel so strong?

"Nashville? Nashville, honey—" *That voice.* I'd know that voice anywhere. It's my fucking— "Congratulations on your award. Is that what you say, congratulations? Anyways, it's not an award I'd hoped you'd receive after so many years in the military, throwing your life away, but—"

I haven't seen my mother in years, and I can count on one hand the amount of times I've talked to her in that time, and the first thing she says to me is another of her famous backhanded compliments. *Fucking figures.*

My father holds his hand out, and I shake it. The kind of overly strong shake he expects from his son, a decorated soldier.

"Good job, son. It's a shame about your leg, but at least you're still alive, unlike your friend."

Overwhelming fury boils over inside of me, like an unwatched pot, and I lunge forward, ready to tear his throat open with my bare hands, until someone pulls me back. *Brewer. And Stiles.*

"These are the kinds of dangers your father and I warned you about when you joined the Army," my mother adds, completely unaware that I'm about to commit murder. "At least now that you're finished with all that business, you can go back to school and get a real job. Your father's accounting firm is hiring."

"Nash, don't do it, man," Stiles hisses in my ear.

"I have a job, Mother. But thank you for your concern."

She hasn't even hugged me yet. She came all the way from Arizona, and she won't even put her arms around her son.

"Well, that's good news. Doing what?"

"Looking after the surviving family members of fallen soldiers. Taking care of things that need repair around their houses."

She shares an incredulous look with my father. "You're a glorified handyman? Oh, come on, Nashville. You can do better than that."

Nostrils flaring, I ball my hands into fists and take a deep breath. "I'm not a—"

"Mr. and Mrs. Sommers, it's a pleasure to meet you. I'm Brewer Marx, Nash's therapist."

"Therapist? Are you ill, son?"

"Ill? No, why would I be ill? Fucked in the head, yeah. I

spent twenty-two days in captivity being tortured while I watched my best friend die slowly. I guess I just needed someone to talk to," I finish lamely, lacing my voice with sarcasm. "And Brewer isn't just my therapist, he's more than that. He's the man that I'm in love with and plan to spend the rest of my life with."

My mother makes a sour face, like my choosing to sleep with my therapist is in bad taste. Then she fixes him with a less than polite look, and that's when I've had enough. Absolutely fucking enough. If she wanted a reunion, she could have chosen any day besides today. This day isn't about her, it's about me, and Brewer, and Violet Gutierrez, and my friends. It is not about my parents.

Brewer slides his hand in mine, reminding me that I would rather be anywhere other than here. "Thank you for coming to see me accept my *award*." *Award*, fucking bullshit. It's a goddamn medal of distinction, two of some of the highest honors you can receive in the military, and she acts like it's a second place ribbon at the science fair. "Don't let me hold up the rest of your afternoon."

Brewer still has my hand, all the way to the parking lot. Touching Valor made me feel strong for a moment, but my real source of strength is Brewer. He wraps his arms around me, and I take a deep breath for the first time today. All of my anxiety settles. All of my broken pieces come together.

"Can I take you home now?"

"Fuck, yes."

A man who was just awarded a Purple Heart and a POW medal for bravery should not be curled up in the fetal position in another man's arms. It isn't dignified.

Fuck dignity. I need my man.

Brewer strokes my bare back, his body cradling mine protectively—comfortingly. He runs his fingers down my spine, causing tiny goosebumps to surface over my skin. Softly, he hums the song guaranteed to make me feel better. *Tomorrow. The sun will come out tomorrow.* It always does.

"Feel better?"

"How can they award a medal to an addict? Not even five months ago, I was chasing my next high."

"And now you're facing your fears and learning to cope with them instead of running away. You are worthy of the medals you received. Both you and Victor."

"I can't believe I tried to forget him. I don't ever want to forget him." Fuck, my voice breaks, and the tears rush forth like a broken dam. My throat feels thick, and my mouth feels dry. "The fucked up part of it is, the drugs didn't make me forget, not really. They just gave me a reason to validate my self-hatred. Motherfucking hero," I hiss, swiping my tears with the backs of my hands. "I acted like a loser, like a coward! I never tried to fight back. I never did a fucking thing but endure the torture and the pain. I sat and watched as he died day-by-day. And I did nothing!" My entire body shakes with sobs, and I can feel the pressure building in my head, behind my eyes, signaling that a migraine is on its way.

"You're not," Brewer insists vehemently. "You're not either of those things! What were you supposed to do, break through your shackles and face down twenty men armed with guns? You were weak and starved and beaten, and you were outnumbered. They would have killed you before you even reached them. There was no way you could have saved him."

I know what he's saying is true, but it doesn't erase my guilt and my anger, and it never will. It's always going to be there, staining the edges of my conscience. My tears continue to fall, no matter how fast I wipe them away. My head feels like a throbbing, snotty mess, pulsing with pressure and emotions that I'm trying like hell to hold back. It's too much. I'm swamped with emotion. After today, my nerves are raw. My heart feels like it's been filleted with a thousand cuts.

He drags his fingers through my hair, the anger gone from his voice, now replaced with a soothing whisper. "It's not self-hatred you feel, it's survivors' guilt. It's worse than hatred. It crawls beneath your skin and suffocates you. Suffocates your soul. It chokes all the goodness and the pride out of you until you have nothing left to live for and nothing left to like about yourself. Until you can't even look in the mirror."

"I don't even recognize that guy anymore," I cry. "Sometimes, when I look in the mirror, the guy staring back at me is a complete stranger."

"I do. I recognize that guy. I didn't know you back then, but I know what kind of man you are, Nash. It's easy to see. It's written all over you. You're a good man, a brave man."

He kisses the soft spot behind my ear, and I close my eyes and savor the contact. When I feel my ugliest, he makes me feel beautiful.

"You don't want to be called a hero? Fine, I won't call you

one, but it doesn't change who you are on the inside." His hand covers my heart, a heart that only beats for him. "You're someone I can be proud of. Someone *you* should be proud of as well. At the end of the day, there's not much difference between the kind of man you are and a hero."

"Is it always going to hurt this bad?"

"No," he whispers fiercely. "I promise it won't. But when it does, I'll be here to hold you together when you fall apart. Every. Single. Time."

I love you. I love you with all of my heart. The heart that you saved, the heart that you pieced back together with duct tape and superglue, it belongs to you.

"My mother is a fucking bitch."

I can feel him quietly laugh behind me. I can feel his body shake with it. "She's not a fucking bitch. She just... I don't know, as your boyfriend—"

"My boyfriend?" Funny, how one word can dry up the tears in a heartbeat. "I like the way that sounds."

"Yes," he's still laughing, "your boyfriend, I would say that your mother can't get past her own bitter disappointment in your career choice because her own expectations are more important than your dreams. But as your therapist, I would say... she might have an undiagnosed personality disorder," he whispers, and now my body is shaking with laughter, just like his.

Sniffling, I wipe the last of my snot and take a deep, ragged breath. "I spent so many years writing letters home, sending her certificates and awards I earned along the way, all in a desperate attempt to get her to accept my choice and just, I don't know, just be proud of me. I've always just wanted her to tell me she was proud. Even today, she just couldn't do it. It fucking hurts," I admit, bringing on a fresh round of tears.

"*I'm* proud of you," he swears. His lips trace the shell of my ear, making me shiver. "She wouldn't have shown up if she wasn't proud of you. I don't know why she can't say it, but I can bet she feels it."

Snorting, I point out, "She called me a glorified handyman."

"Mmm, does that job title come with one of those sexy tool belts?" His lips close over my earlobe, and he sucks gently, making my dick twitch.

Grinning through my tears, I tease, "I'll make you a sexy calendar for our first anniversary."

Epilogue

SEVEN MONTHS LATER

"Oh, my God, there's a party in my mouth," I manage to say around a mouthful of rice. "Nothing beats your paella, Violet."

She laughs, accepting the compliment with a smile. "It's your special day, so you deserved a special meal."

"Thank you," I say sincerely.

Every time I come over, she cooks for me. We sit in this beautiful garden we've created together, and spend time talking, laughing, and just connecting with each other. She's the mother I always wanted. Violet Gutierrez is the very definition of unconditional love and support. She's one of my favorite people, hands-down.

"The potting shed is finished, and I've stocked it with that organic compost you love."

"Thank you, *mijo*."

Mijo, my son. It's more than a word, more than a label, or a term of endearment. It's a sense of belonging, a sense of family, of rightness and completeness. I've found a place in her heart, and she's earned one in mine. It's a connection, a bond forged under the toughest conditions, and now it's unbreakable.

"You come back again tomorrow and show me that special medallion you've earned. I'll have some pastelitos ready for you to celebrate."

"I will, I promise." I clear the plates from the little wrought iron café table on her patio and bring them to the kitchen, depositing them in the sink.

Last week, she had me and Brewer over for dinner. The week before that, I brought Mandy with me, and he helped me begin construction on her potting shed. Violet immediately adopted him and fed us until we were too stuffed to work. It's just her way, food is her love language. She opens her arms and her home to everyone she meets. This place has become a second home to me, after Serenity House.

Yes, I still live there. Will I ever move out? Not as long as Brewer wants to remain on site to look after the guys. His little flock of recovering ducklings. Miles and Nacho have moved out, and now have their own places to live. Tex still remains, for now, and doesn't seem to ever want to leave. There will always be a turnover of vets coming and going from Serenity House.

That's the point of it, to help as many recovering addicts as possible, but just because they move out doesn't mean they move on. Nacho and Miles come over for dinner a couple times a month. I still meet up with them all the time, and we often go to meetings together. My circle just keeps growing larger and larger.

I still have bad days among the good, but definitely more good than bad. It's been a while though, since I've had the kind of flashback that takes me out of the present, the kind where I lose time. My anxiety and blood pressure have lowered significantly, which has reduced a lot of my symptoms like acid reflux and indigestion, and I was able to stop taking my blood pressure medicine, which has made a huge impact on my ED. I still have nightmares almost every night, where I wake up in a cold sweat, or I flail and yell out, but Brewer is always beside me when I open my eyes, pulling me back to the present.

Leif is huge. I swear he's growing like a weed, not a plant. I had to replant him in a much larger pot that now sits by the window in the living room. Tex threatens almost weekly that one day when I come home, Leif will be planted in a shady spot in the backyard, but I know he's just bluffing. I could never plant him outside because, you know… The acid rain, and the hailstorms, and God only knows what else. I just can't risk it.

My ever-present shadow, Valor, is no longer a kitten. He's a full grown cat, he just doesn't know it. He still expects to be carted along everywhere I go, strapped to my chest. If he's not in the sling, he sits there anyway, like a chest warmer, purring away like a motorboat and licking my face. He's become a master at cock blocking. If he wants attention while I'm getting it from Brewer, he'll do something ridiculous, like knock over a glass of water or a picture frame from my dresser. He refuses to be ignored or come in second place.

I still meet with the Bitches twice a week, and we always go for wings afterward and catch up. I also see them throughout the week, because I've never met a bigger bunch of stalkers in my life. Nosey-ass meddling man-babies is what they are. I can't fart without them commenting on it in our group chat message thread. They have an opinion about *everything*.

Brewer and I are taking life one day at a time. I know without a doubt I'm going to spend the rest of my life with him, but we're not in any rush to make it official. There's really no need because when you know you know, and when it comes to Brewer, *I know*.

―――――

"Get your legs up on my shoulders."

Brewer hooks his ankles over my shoulders, and I wrap my arms around his thighs and pound deeper into his ass. I love this position because I can see everything, the ecstasy on his face, his balls bouncing every time I bottom out, and my cock sliding in and out of his stretched hole. He loves when I go hard, when I nail his prostate with each thrust. The sounds he makes are pure filth and nonsense, and it turns me on that I can reduce him to such an incoherent mess.

His head bangs against the wooden headboard.

"Push against it so you don't keep hitting your head, 'cause I'm not slowing down and I'm not going softer."

He clenches around my cock, squeezing the blood from it, enveloping my shaft in the tightest heat, and the pleasure pushes me over the edge. My balls draw up tight against my body. A wave of adrenaline spikes, making my heart beat faster, giving me a surge of strength, and I push hard into his body, burying myself balls deep as the spasms start in my stomach and radiate down through my thighs. Every muscle in my body tightens, and I freeze up as my orgasm rolls through me. Brewer clenches again when I start to fill his ass. It sets off his own orgasm, and I watch, mesmerized as thick white ropes pulse from his cock, painting his stomach and chest with seed.

Out of breath and sweating, I collapse between his parted thighs, landing right on top of the sticky mess. Brushing my lips over his, I slide my tongue inside and kiss him until I steal the breath from his lungs and he's panting like me.

He laughs into the kiss, and I finally pull away.

"That was an amazing anniversary present. You know how hot watching you use that bullet gets me."

Just watching him fuck himself with that rifle cartridge dildo drives me insane. The way he teases his hole and then pulls it out, making his ass clench like it's hungry for more. Watching his body writhe in pleasure and listening to the filthy sounds he makes. Yeah, walking in on him and finding him playing with that toy sent me over the edge. I tore his ass up.

"Happy one-year anniversary, my love. Are you going to let me up so we can shower? Otherwise, we're gonna be late."

"I guess, if I have to. But I'm not promising I won't take you again when we get home."

One whole year clean and sober. Three hundred and sixty-five fucking days without a pill or a drop of alcohol. No one ever could have convinced me this was possible twelve months ago, when I was lying in a hospital bed with Liza on my ass, wondering if I was going to live or die. I didn't even care at that point, I was feeling so low. And now, just a year later, my life is drastically different and I *definitely* want to live. It's totally fucking crazy. I'm the last person who would have believed it was possible to recover.

My cheering squad takes up an entire row in the back of the meeting. Miles, Nacho and Tex, Riggs, Stiles and McCormick, Brandt and West, Mandy, Jax, and Pharo sitting at the opposite end—they're all here to support me, to celebrate with me. It's a Saturday night meeting, so it's packed full with recovering addicts, and when the last addict finishes sharing, they go straight to the celebration of clean time. After handing out the plastic poker chips that denote the months leading up to the first year, it's Brewer's turn. He squeezes my hand and then makes his way to the front of the room.

"Hi, I'm Brewer and I'm a recovering addict. One year ago today, I met a man that changed my life. Even though I didn't know him, I knew within minutes of meeting him that he would become someone special to me. He was a disaster at first, much like we all are in the beginning." He pauses while everyone laughs with him. "He used to sit in the back of the room, where he's sitting right now," his eyes find me, and he smiles, "with his arms folded across his chest and a pissed off look on his face, completely in denial, and bitch about the coffee."

Again, everyone laughs. The shitty coffee is a well-known fact, not an opinion.

"The man that's sitting in his seat today is not the same man I met twelve months ago. Not even close. This man is no longer in denial, although he still thinks the coffee tastes like shit. He's learned how to surrender and ask for help. He's had a spiritual awakening that changed him. He has friends and commitments and responsibilities, and most importantly, he likes the man he sees in the mirror. I couldn't be more proud of my Sponsee. Everyone told me not to do it, that I should know better than to fall in love with him, but how could I not? How could I not fall in love with him when everything about him convinced me that he was the other half of my soul. That God put him here, in my way, just for me. For me, and for him." Brewer chokes up, and tears gather in his eyes, just like they're gathering in mine.

"I knew you had it in you to become the man that you are today. I saw all that potential inside of you when I met you, and you didn't disappoint. You'll never disappoint me. Come on up here, Nash, and tell us how you did it."

Fuck, how can I speak with my throat closed up, and now I'm crying. *Son of a bitch.*

Everyone claps and slaps me on the back as I make my way down the row, and down the aisle, to the front of the room. The hug that Brewer gives me feels so good that I don't want to let go. He squeezes me for all he's worth. I guess he's pouring all of his love into it. When I pull back, he places a gold medallion in my palm. In the center is the Narcotics Anonymous symbol, a diamond, with the Roman numeral one etched inside. Around the perimeter of the diamond are the core principles of the program.

Self

God

Society

Service

Freedom

Goodwill

These are the cornerstones that have helped shape me into the man that I've become this year.

Wrapping my fingers around the medallion, I slip it into my pocket, beside the original white chip that Brewer gave me when I first surrendered. A token I carry with me every day.

Brewer takes his seat, and it's my turn. It takes me a couple of tries before I can speak. I swallow twice more, take a deep breath, and dry my eyes again. Then I clear my throat.

"My name is Nash, and I'm an addict. I can't believe it's been a whole year. Life has a funny way of blindsiding you, and you never know what's coming around the corner. When I was shipped back stateside, my life became a series of events I never could have planned for or imagined. And each one set in motion the next, and the next, and they brought me to where I am today. I was given the most belligerent and caring nurse in the hospital who hooked me up with a place to stay. That place came with an undercover Angel as my next-door neighbor, who saved my ass when I threw a shovel in the wall. Then he dragged me to a place that became my salvation, a support group of men who always have my back, and that's when I met

Brewer. He showed me how to recover, how to surrender, and he showed me how to love myself again."

My voice cracks on the last word, and tears roll down my cheeks. I don't even try to wipe them away this time, fuck it, let them fall. There will be more. Clearing my throat, I drag another deep breath into my lungs and continue.

"I never would have thought I could recover. I was in a dark, dark place, and as miserable as I was, I was fine staying there. I guess I thought I deserved it. But Brewer showed me another way. If you're sitting here tonight, wondering if this program really works and if it could work for you, believe me when I tell you that I am the last person who thought he could recover. Never in a million years would I have guessed that I would be standing here tonight telling my story. I promise you, if you just keep coming back, this program works. You *can* recover."

Another deep breath. *You can do this, Nash.*

"Brewer said I was in denial when I first came in. He's right, I was pissed off at the world and pissed off at myself even more, and you can't believe how pissed off I was at God. I sat in the back and didn't want to hear a fucking thing. And yeah, the coffee tastes like shit. The only reason I kept coming back was because he dragged me with him, and I would follow that man anywhere. This place is a lot like gardening, a passion of mine that I've discovered since being clean. Little-by-little, the things said here were like tiny seeds being planted in my mind. All the serenity prayers, and the clichés, and people sharing their stories, all the coffee and the hugs and the reading of the literature, they stuck underneath my skin like porcupine quills, and they began to take root. Slowly but surely, I began to listen with an open mind, and as I started to work the twelve steps, I began to listen with an open heart. Each step, each meeting, each friend I made, changed me little by little. Every hug I received repaired a little broken piece of my soul."

I have to stop and get myself under control so I can continue. Each breath feels like a struggle because my chest feels so heavy.

"Now, twelve months later, my soul is mostly intact, held together with superglue and duct tape, but at least it resembles a soul. Most importantly, I've found peace, and I've forgiven God and myself. I've learned to love myself again. Forgiving myself was the hardest thing I've ever had to do, but it changed my life. If you're sitting here tonight, feeling miserable and lost and alone, I want you to raise your hand so that I know who you are, and I can find you after the meeting and give you a hug. Each hug is a tiny seed that I want to share with you. It's like they say, it works if you work it, so work it, you're worth it. I used to laugh at that and think it sounded like fucking nonsense, but I swear to God, you are worth it, and it does work. Again, my name is Nash and I'm an addict in recovery. Thanks for letting me share. Keep coming back."

As I make my way down the aisle, I'm bombarded with people giving me hugs and shaking my hand. And when I get to my row, they come to their feet and tackle me in a dog pile of love and hugs and praise. That's when I fucking lose my shit completely, letting the tears flow unchecked.

I did it. I fucking did it. And I have to keep doing it every day for the rest of my life if I want to keep what I have, and I do, more than anything.

The meeting wraps up, and we make plans to go out to eat and celebrate. It takes another twenty minutes to walk to our car because I have to pass through a throng of well-meaning addicts who want to recall every one of my worst moments, teasing me good-naturedly.

"How are you feeling?" Brewer asks, checking in.

Fastening my seatbelt, I let out a deep breath. "That was a lot. I can't believe I did that. Twelve fucking months, Brewer." Slipping the medallion from my pocket, I clutch it in my palm, reading the words etched into the shiny surface. Each one resonates deep within me. "You know, you're as responsible for this as I am. I couldn't have done it without you."

Brewer places his hand over mine, squeezing. The way he looks at me, with all that love, is enough to melt my heart into a puddle in my chest.

"I can't do the rest of my life without you," he vows, kissing my knuckles.

THE END

———

Before your book hangover sets in, let me reassure you there's more Nash and Brewer and the Bitches in the third *Scars And Stripes book,* **Warrior's Walk.**

Grab Riggs and Rhett's book today!

DEAR READER_

Thank you so much for reading **The Darkness Within,** the second novel in the *Scars And Stripes* series.

If you enjoyed Brewer and Nash's romance, **please leave a review** to tell other readers how much you loved them. Telling your friends and spreading the word on social media helps people find their new favorite book.

With love,
   Raquel Riley

NEXT IN SERIES_

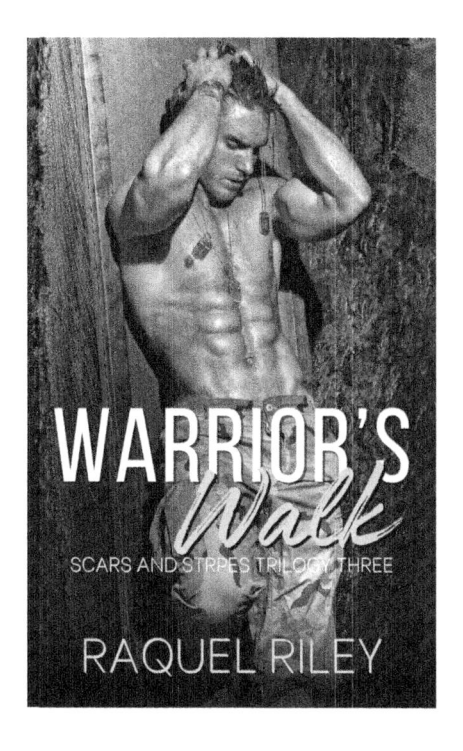

Warrior's Walk is available on Amazon and Kindle Unlimited!

Fate only takes an instant to play her hand.

Rhett Marsh

When my leg shattered, I thought my whole world was shattered.

Riggs pieced both back together again, and then he disappeared.

I never expected to see him again on the other side of the world.

Navarro Riggs is a lot of things…

Devastatingly hot.

My savior.

A brave warrior.

But, my physical therapist? Yeah, I didn't see that coming.

I'd consider it a gift from the universe, if only he wasn't trying his damndest to stay far away from me.

Navarro Riggs

We met on the battlefield under a hail of bullets and blood.

Our bond was instant, forged in trauma. Unbreakable. Everlasting.

He wasn't just my patient, he was *mine*.

I trust Rhett with my life, but can I trust him with my heart?

Warrior's Walk is the third book in the *Scars And Stripes Trilogy*. This MM romance tells the story of trauma bonding, disability and mental health struggles, starting over after you've lost everything, and finding your inner warrior. Other tropes include age gap, found family, and possessiveness.

ABOUT THE AUTHOR_

Raquel Riley

ROMANCE AUTHOR

Raquel Riley is a native of South Florida but now calls North Carolina home. She is an avid reader and loves to travel. Most often, she writes gay romance stories with an HEA but characters of all types can be found in her books. She weaves pieces of herself, her family, and her travels into every story she writes.

For a complete list of Raquel Riley's releases, please visit her website at **www.raquelriley.com**. You can also follow her on the social media platforms listed below. You can also find all of Raquel's important links in one convenient place at **https://linktr.ee/raquelriley**

ACKNOWLEDGMENTS_

Tracy Ann, your feedback is so appreciated! You help me shape these books and characters and give them life. Thank you for your continued praise and support of my stories and for keeping me organized.

Dianna Roman, your sense of humor breathed life into this book. Thank you for the Bitches and the BALLS, and for the inside look at life in the Army.

Also, thank you to my **ARC/street team** for your insightful input and reviews and outstanding promotion.

A huge thank you to the **86'ers!** Dianna Roman, Tracy, Jenn, and Emma. You crazy bunch are guaranteed to make me laugh at least fourteen times a day.

I can't forget the **Secret Circle!** You four keep me accountable and sane and cheer for every one of my accomplishments, both big and small.

Marsha Adams Salmans I'm so grateful you came into my life. Your dedication to my reader group and promotion of my books is invaluable. Thank you for being irreplaceable and amazing!

Emerson Beckett Thank you for spitballing ideas with me. Your creative storytelling instincts are priceless.

Last, but never least, thanks to my family for being so understanding while I ignore you so I can write.

Printed in Great Britain
by Amazon